Entering Normal

Entering Normal

ANNE D. LECLAIRE

BALLANTINE BOOKS • *New York*

A Ballantine Book
Published by The Ballantine Publishing Group
Copyright © 2001 by Anne D. LeClaire

www.ballantinebooks.com

Library of Congress Cataloging-in-Publication Data is available upon request.

ISBN 0-345-44572-4

Manufactured in the United States of America

First Edition: June 2001

10 9 8 7 6 5 4 3 2 1

in memory of sandra lee

Just give me one thing that
I can hold on to
To believe in
This living is a hard way to go

JOHN PRINE
"Angels from Montgomery"

Acknowledgments

Many people helped me write this book, and I am indebted to them for their encouragement and guidance.

I owe a special thank-you to:

The Virginia Center for Creative Arts for multiple residencies that provided me with the time and space to write major portions of this book.

My agent Deborah Schneider, who, besides being wonderfully supportive and a person of great integrity, wields a magic wand.

At Ballantine, Maureen O'Neal and Gina Centrello and Kim Hovey. No author ever found herself in better hands. Their enthusiasm and commitment made all the difference.

Jacquelyn Mitchard, who insisted on the title, supported me when I was discouraged, and never once wavered in her belief. Marilyn Kallet for her kind words and skillful eyes. Margaret Moore for asking the right questions and holding me steady. Jebba Handley, Ginny Reiser, Ann Stevens, and Lorraine Brown for listening to excerpts early on and never waning in their enthusiasm. Mauny Plum, for opening her heart so that I would "get it right." Diane Bliss of Luscious Louie's for keeping me in cookies.

The following gave generously of their time and expertise: Judge Robert A. Scandurra; Kathleen Snow, Esq.; Pamela B. Marsh, Esq.; Dr. James Kawalski; Gretchen Kolb at the Rocking Unicorn; Captain Billy Flynn and Firefighter Joel Goucher at

ACKNOWLEDGMENTS

the Harwich Fire Department; Dave Coomber; Kyle Shiver; Rob Zapple; Pat Vreeland at Chatham High School; and Mimi Gulacsi, R.N. at the Cape Cod Hospital.

And—as always—love and thanks to Hillary, Hope, and Chris. For everything.

Entering Normal

THE SUN HAS BEEN IN AND OUT ALL DAY. NOW IT FINDS cracks in the clouds and threads through in ribbons, what Gram Gates used to call fingers of God.

Opal welcomes the fingers. They constitute a celestial hand beckoning her forward, and even though she will be the first to tell you she does not believe in any god and most certainly not the Presbyterian god of her grandma, she will gratefully take them as a sign of astral endorsement.

Opal lives by signs. She counts on them the way other people put their faith in heaven or weathermen or the possibility of everlasting love. She believes in them absolutely and holds tight to her conviction despite the number of people who offer the opinion that there is no sign by which one can foretell the future, no omen to warn of the disasters entire lives are hell-spent avoiding—or pursuing.

In two days she has covered stretches of six states and is now on the central section of the Massachusetts turnpike, nerves high-wired from too many Hershey bars and too much drive-thru coffee in thin paper cups. Her eyelids sting from lack of sleep.

She hopes she is heading directly north, but she can't shake the feeling that she took a wrong turn somewhere back in New York. If Billy were along, sure thing he'd have picked up a road map somewhere along the line, but Opal can't be bothered. This is one way they differ along gender lines. He's a man but willing to be dependent; she's a girl and scorns it. If she has misjudged direction, it won't be the first time in her life. By twenty she has made more than her share of wrong turns, and yet, for a fact, she does not regret a one. Certainly she doesn't regret the misstep that brought her Zack. Billy, now there was a big mistake. But not Zack. Never Zack. And so, perhaps in some sense, not even Billy.

She glances in the rearview mirror, checks the backseat, lets her eyes rest too long for caution on her five-year-old son. Tucked in between the cartons that hold her doll makings and as many of their belongings as she'd dared pack, he's out cold, his pomegranate mouth slightly open, chocolate smudges on his chin. Even in sleep, he keeps a tight hold on his stuffed tiger. Watching him she feels a familiar jolt in her stomach, the sharp, sweet terror of motherhood.

She returns her attention to the road, catches sight in the mirror of a car bearing down from the rear. She eases up on the accelerator, eyes the speedometer. She's below the legal limit; still her breath doesn't come right until the vehicle is close enough to see it's neither a cop nor Billy's black Ram pickup. While she slows for the car to pass, she thinks again that there will be hell to pay when her parents hear what she's done.

"You've told them you're going?" Billy asked the night before she left.

"Yes."

"And they know where you're heading?"

Again she lied, said yes. Of course she hadn't said a word to them about her plans. Particularly to her mama. Melva's projected response comes to her with depressing predictability: the sniffy self-righteous rant about how once again they are *so* disappointed in her, how once more Opal has been reckless, acted irresponsibly, let them down. The echo of Melva's voice presses against her, cold and hollow as fog. She opens the window an inch or two to bring in fresh air, to breathe.

The story she came up with for Billy is that she needs some time away to think. She's just taking Zack to Ohio to visit an aunt on her daddy's side.

Actually, she hasn't a clue as to her destination.

If she were alone, without the responsibility of Zack, she would have just taken off and driven until she had a sign that said plain, *This here is the place.* But with Zack along, she knew she would need a concrete plan. And so the night before they left, she rolled one of the dice from Billy's Monopoly game. It came up a three. A good sign. Six would be too many for Zack; one was nowhere near enough for her. So the plan is to head out and keep going until she has used up three tanks of gas—exactly three tanks, no cheating, not even if she comes upon a place that looks promising after she has gone through two and a half. She brought the die along for good luck, and now it sits on the dash, keeping company with a half dozen Happy Meal figures, an empty coffee cup, a yellow plastic rose she plucked from her grandma's hall arrangement, and an amethyst crystal in the shape of a pyramid that the lady said contained a chip of real opal.

She checks the fuel gauge. The needle edges toward empty, the final gallon of her third tank. She tries to collect her mind to see an exit or some other sign that will reveal to her what her next step should be. If her faith is to be repaid, she will catch sight of one soon.

Opal's belief in signs riles Billy. He thinks it's stupid and is fixed on conveying that opinion to her. "Raylee," he said to her just before Zack was born, back before she changed her name. "Raylee, you can't go living your life looking for signs. It's just about the dumbest thing I ever heard."

"It's not dumb at all," she said. "You hear me, Billy Steele. Not dumb at all. You'll come to my way of thinking. You just wait and see."

"How am I going to see if I don't believe in what I'm seeing?"

"Well, that's exactly what I mean. You won't be *prepared*."

In the past six years they have had that conversation more often than she can bear to remember. While she has given up trying to convince him that there are signs everywhere if you'll just open your eyes and look, signs holding important information, her own belief remains resolute. When you come right down to it, what else is there?

The clouds have lifted now, and the sun beats on the Buick's hood. She cranks the window down another notch, checks the backseat again. She needs music, something upbeat yet mellow. Taj Mahal would go a long way toward steadying her caffeine-stoked nerves, but she hesitates, worried the tape will wake Zack. Then, just as the needle on the gas gauge trembles into the red, just when she is praying she'll reach the next exit before she runs dry, just at that moment she sees the sign: ENTERING NORMAL. She laughs right out loud and the tiny nugget that has been caught in her chest ever since she buckled the seat belt around Zack and left New Zion, that hard little pea just melts away. As she flicks the right turn signal and veers into the exit lane, she feels the gambler's high, the wallop that comes when you've bet your stake against house odds and won. For two and a half days she's been thinking about the consequences of her actions, and now, as the old Buick rolls down the ramp toward a new life in a town named Normal, she doesn't care what Billy or her parents will say.

"Well now, haven't I just done it," Opal says aloud. "I've done it and screw all consequences."

She is going toward something, and even though she doesn't know exactly what it is, she trusts it. The weight of the past six years shifts, then lifts, and although she can't recall the last time she experienced the pure and simple sensation, she feels beneath her breastbone a combination of happiness and heartburn that might very well be hope.

❧ F A L L ❧

CHAPTER 1

❧ R O S E

NED IS SNORING, A THICK THUNDER THAT ROLLS UP from his chest. His arm is flung over Rose's ribs, and she takes a breath against the heft of it, the pressure that recently seems to have increased.

Back in the middle of summer, she mentioned getting twin beds, but his response was sharp. Typical Ned. "Whadda you crazy?" She explained how his arm made it hard for her to breathe, how she felt pinned down by it. "We've slept in the same bed for thirty-five years, Rosie," he said, his gaze level. "Exactly when did my arm get so heavy?" Not willing to go where that subject might lead, she dropped it flat.

He snores again, a long, rippling snort with a catch in the middle, like he is swallowing his breath. It's a wonder more women don't kill their husbands. Half asleep, she imagines herself picking up the pillow, holding it over his open mouth.

What on earth is the matter with her, thinking something crazy like that? Ned is a good man. Where she would be without him she hates to think. She gives him a slight nudge, just enough to make him stop snoring, but not enough to wake him. The last thing in the world she needs right now is for him to wake and ask her what's wrong.

What's wrong?

This is a question she doesn't want him to ask, not when all that is wrong swirls through the room, hangs above her face like smoke. The digital clock on the nightstand glows 1:40, red numerals that remind her of eyes, the alert eyes of some nocturnal animal. The time changes to 1:41. She wishes they still had their old dial-face clock, the one that didn't need resetting every time there was a power failure. Very carefully she lifts Ned's arm from its hold across her ribs and scratches her stomach, hard.

It's still there. It's bigger. Maybe.

The itchy spot first appeared toward the end of September, the same week Opal Gates and her boy moved into the house next door. At first Rose figured it was an insect bite of some kind, or dry skin, what with the furnace coming on in the evening now. Yesterday she finally took a reluctant look at it—she doesn't much like looking at her stomach—and even without her reading glasses she was able to see the small, raised welt right over the mole on her stomach. Red circled out from the brown center. Definitely a bite she decided, pushing away darker possibilities conjured up by the Cancer Society leaflets she's read in Doc Blessing's waiting room, their bold letters enumerating the Seven Deadly Signs.

She doesn't think it is anything significant. If something important was going on in your body, you'd know it. No, she's sure it's just an insect bite. They are into October now, late for mosquitoes, but it's been a particularly mild fall, the first frost not coming until the last of September.

She lies in the dark, reminded suddenly of the mosquito bites she used to get summers at Crystal Lake when she was a girl, great welts that rose on her arms and legs and ankles until she looked like she had a tropical disease. "Don't scratch," her mother would say as she swabbed them with calamine lotion. "It makes it worse." Rose scratched the bites until they bled. Then, the summer she was sixteen, she fell in love with her best friend's cousin, and just like that she stopped scratching mosquito bites. Instead she dug her thumbnail directly across the swollen spot and then again in the opposite direction, forming the shape of a cross, her magic remedy, better than calamine.

Lord, she hasn't thought about those things in years. Rachel's cousin. The thin, dark boy from out of town who made all their mothers edgy. What was his name? Randy? Roy? She struggles futilely to reclaim it from the chasm of memory. His name she can't dredge up, but the image of him surfaces as if she had seen him only last week. This was the summer of Elvis—someone else who made their mothers nervous—and he wore his hair in a DA just like the singer. He drove a motorcycle and—even in summer—dressed all in black. Rose remembers his leather jacket, the zippers at the wrists. The risks she had taken for him. She remembers the night she lied to her mother, the first falsehood she can recall telling, how she said she was going to Rachel's and had pedaled her blue Raleigh over to the lake where he waited. When he kissed her, his tongue pushed insistently between her lips, filling her with a confusion of fear and desire—startling, hot desire—until she opened her mouth to him. As if, even in sleep, he can read her mind, Ned's arm drops back across her ribs, tightens its hold.

It was on the same spot at Crystal Lake, enfolded by the scent of pine and her cologne, that Ned asked her to marry him. Two years after she kissed the boy with the Elvis hair, she lay in Ned's arms, let him caress her, heard him promise to love her forever, eagerly returned the vow.

Forever. What is forever? How long has it been since she believed it possible to hold on to someone or something for eternity? How could she have known then that love is not as resilient as one might think? That loss and pain and life take a toll beyond what she could have imagined? That Ned's sinewy arms, which held her so tenderly that summer night by the lake, would grow cumbersome over the years?

Crystal Lake. When she was a child, long before she lay in Ned's young arms or before she kissed a dangerous dark-haired boy whose name she has forgotten, years before she taught Todd how to swim in its water, she and Rachel would go ice-skating there. Once, while tightening her skates, she lost a glove, a red mitten knitted by her grandmother that one of the older boys swooped up and skated away with. By the time she went home, her fingers were deadened with the cold. At first it didn't hurt, just a tingling numbness as if they had gone to sleep; but later, when her mother took her fingers between her palms and rubbed the heat back into chilled flesh, chafed the numbness away, then the pain began.

The itching is worse now. She raises Ned's arm carefully, edges out of bed, almost makes it.

"S'matter?"

"Bathroom. Go back to sleep." She freezes, willing his breathing to return to its heavy, half-snoring rhythm, then, using the illumination from the night-light at the top of the stairs, makes her way to the hall. The shadowy outline of Todd's door beckons in the dim light, and she almost allows herself to give in, to sit in his room and wait.

It has been a long time.

Months have passed since she sat there and hoped for a sign from Todd. Hoped, not prayed. She has long since lost her belief in the power of prayers or God; the most she can hold on to is hope, and even that has dimmed lately. Five years. If she is going to get some sign from him, feel some connection, wouldn't it have come by now? But even the dimming of active hope does not bring the resolution or the peace she might have expected, only more pain. She fears this deficiency of hope is bringing her one more step closer to really losing him. Memory and grief are all she has left, and after a while even memory dims. In spite of her attempts to hold on in her mind, the whole of him is beginning to fade.

In the bathroom she catches sight of herself in the mirror and, without glasses, sees a younger version of herself, her face firmer, without lines. She is trying to learn to look at herself with corrected vision, trying to see the truth of her aging face, which looks more and more like her mother's. She opens the cabinet and removes the bottle of Jergens, slathers it across her belly, easing, for the moment, the itch of the mole that woke her earlier. She returns the lotion to the cabinet, automatically brushes her hand over the counter. The green Formica is specked with tiny black dots, the pattern a mistake. The dark grains remind her of the flecks that rim the sink after Ned shaves.

ON HER WAY BACK TO HER ROOM, SHE CHECKS THE STREET. Next door, at the Montgomery place, light spills from the dining room. *At this hour.* It is nearly 2:00 A.M. If Louise Montgomery still lived there, Rose would be tempted to ring over, see if everything was all right, but she has no intention of getting involved with that girl. And yet, what in the name of heaven is she doing up in the middle of the night? When does she sleep? Rose supposes she should find comfort in the fact that Opal Gates is awake, that she is not the only one unable to sleep this night, but she feels no nocturnal bond with her new neighbor. In the few weeks since Opal moved in, it has become clear that there is nothing but tribulation in store for that one. All you need do is take one quick look and you can see the whole story. Plain as day. Girls like Opal *suck* trouble to them.

She leaves the window and returns to their bed. Ned snores on peacefully. The relief the lotion gave is short-lived, and she gives her stomach another quick scratch. Perhaps it's an allergy. Or shingles. *Shingles.* Such an odd name for a disease. Who decides what to call an illness, anyway? She had a second cousin over in Athol who had shingles. The woman was married to a farmer, a nervous little man who worried about everything. Notice it was the wife who got the itching. She tries to remember what she has heard about shingles, something about if the inflamed skin encircles your waist, girdling it like a belt, you will die. Can this be true, or is it only an old wives' tale? It seems to her that her cousin died of a heart attack, but she can't recall for sure. She hitches her nightgown up slowly and risks two or three real gouges. Ned doesn't move a muscle, and she is grateful for that. She doesn't need his questions about what she is scratching. No doubt if he knew he'd take right over, have her at Doc's before she could stop to tie her shoes. She doesn't know. Maybe she should go. But the itch is worse at night. If it were really serious, wouldn't it bother her during the day? She only has to get through the night, hold tight to the thought of dawn, and she will be all right. She certainly doesn't want to go see Doc.

For a while, after the accident, when she couldn't cook or do much of anything around the house and heaven knows she didn't want Ned touching her, Doc gave her some little yellow pills to take. She didn't want them, but under Ned's insistence she caved in. They were tiny, octagonal-shaped pills potent beyond what their size suggested, making everything in sight seem sallow, jaundiced. Wavy and dull. After a while this was worse than anything, so she quit taking them. Plus all those drugs are chemicals, and Rose doesn't trust chemicals. Who knows what they are really doing to a person? No, she thinks, better to wait and not let on to Ned about the red-edged mole that itches.

She twists her head on the pillow and looks at her husband, studies his face in the slippery light of the moon. Even in sleep he looks tired. She doesn't need her glasses to see the deep lines that etch the skin between his eyes and make gutters from his nose to his chin. He is fifty-seven. We're getting old, she thinks. Her heart almost softens.

Sometimes she wonders why it is so easy for Ned. Isn't he angry about all the things that have been taken from them, simple things they have every right to expect would come to them, like Todd growing up, marrying, having a child of his own? For five years she has tracked all the things that will never happen, bitter anniversaries that keep grief alive and sharp but that she cannot stop her mind from recording: Todd's senior prom. His high school graduation. The fall he would have entered college. Doesn't Ned ever think about these things?

Once, three years ago, they were staring at some program on television and she blurted, "He would be in college now."

"For Christ's sake!" Ned shouted. The green recliner snapped to an upright position, and he stalked from the room. As far as he is concerned, Todd is over, closed subject.

Men are different, she thinks. But no, look at Claire Covington. The summer after their son drowned, she was back swimming at the lake, in the very water that still held the molecules of Brian Covington's last breath. But maybe, Rose thinks in sudden inspiration, maybe submerging herself in the water was Claire's way of getting close to her son. Lord knows, Rose can understand that. Then she pictures Claire laughing, splashing in the water, dressed in a bathing suit a good yard shy of the amount of material appropriate to a woman of her age. No, when Claire Covington went to the lake, it wasn't to merge with whatever remained there of her son.

ALTHOUGH SHE CANNOT REMEMBER FALLING ASLEEP, SHE must have dozed off, for the next time she looks the clock reads 6:00. Beside her, she feels Ned move. Soon he will get up, releasing her. She'll take a shower, let cold water flow over her stomach, cooling it down.

Ned moans softly; then he's awake. This is how he does it every morning. One minute he's asleep, the next he's talking.

"Time to get up," he says.

"Yes," she says.

She lifts the weight of his arm from her ribs and takes a little breath, inhaling dawn. In the morning light, for one brief moment, she can almost believe she has only imagined the itch, can almost believe that she has already experienced her lifetime's allotment of pain and grief.

CHAPTER 2

❧ R O S E

THEY GET THROUGH BREAKFAST COURTESY OF THE
Today Show. Four years ago, Ned installed a thirteen-inch Sony
on the counter beside the refrigerator. The TV and his newspaper have erased much of the need for a whole lot of conversation,
and what is spoken tends to be one-sided. This morning he switches
on the set the second he walks in the kitchen, then folds the Springfield paper open to the Sports section. Dependable as daylight. Rose
waits for him to tell her who won what game the night before. Every
morning, he fills the air with news of scores and draft choices, the hir-
ing of million-dollar players and the firing of losing managers, and
depending on the season, all the other daily matters of the Patriots, or
the Bruins, or the Sox. After all this time, she can't for the life of her
see why he imagines these things are of any concern to her. Still, if he
didn't give her the scores or his opinion on matters like the designated
hitter or the new baseball commissioner, would they talk at all?

This morning, Ned is quiet. The Sox must have had the day off
yesterday. Or is the season over? Rose doesn't always listen and gets
easily confused about these things.

She starts the eggs, gritting her teeth against the blare of the television. Some days the noise of it seems to drill into her brain and settle there, buzzing on and on. It is surprising that someone in
Washington, D.C., has never investigated what television waves do to
peoples' brains. Or maybe they have and are keeping it quiet since it

would be bad for the economy. They have certainly kept other upsetting things to themselves for years and years. Like the results of research on cigarette smoking, or all the horrid side effects from the stuff women have injected in their breasts to make them bigger. Silicone. That's right. Rose remembers the term suddenly as she is cooking Ned's eggs in a fry pan that is silicone coated. How could any woman actually want to have that put inside her body?

Some days she wants to snatch the set right off the counter, cart it out behind the garage, and take an ax to it. She would just hit it and hit it until there was nothing left, until someone coming upon the remains would not have the least idea that just hours before Bryant Gumball had been smiling out from it.

Calling the anchorman Bryant Gumball instead of Bryant Gumbel is Ned's morning joke. He says it every morning and then laughs as if this is the first time in his life he's ever said it. If he says it today, she thinks, I swear I'll hit him in the head with the skillet. She stays at the stove until the urge passes.

A voice chirps from the Sony, brightly offering dependable relief from incontinence. *At breakfast.* Why would advertising people think anyone would want to hear about that sort of thing with their morning coffee? She is continually astonished at the things the TV people come right out with, bold as brass—things like sanitary tampons, which weren't even whispered about when she was a girl.

"What's on your agenda?" Ned asks when she serves his eggs.

As long as she can remember, he's asked this exact same question over breakfast. Years ago she made up the answers. *Oh, lunch with Rock Hudson and dancing with Fred Astaire. Just a quick trip to Bali, but I'll be back in time for dinner.* "Rose, you're a card," he would say, as if she were the funniest person on the planet.

"Nothing special," she answers, serving up his eggs.

"Can't imagine how you keep yourself busy all day," he says between a mouthful of eggs and a swig of coffee. He still has hopes that she will return to her job at Fosters.

"I manage," she says.

He pours himself another cup of coffee, one he will take with him. That makes his third cup so far, and he has only been up a little more than an hour. He should cut down. But he's a grown-up. It's up to him.

AFTER HE LEAVES, SHE FLICKS OFF THE TV, THEN DOES THE dishes. She wipes down the counters and replaces the quilted rooster over the toaster. As she does every morning, she empties the trash although the two of them barely generate enough to warrant the task, then goes upstairs to strip their bed and put on new sheets. For weeks now, she has been changing the sheets every day, hoping that will help her get rid of the itchy spot on her stomach. So far it hasn't made a difference. But she likes the feeling of getting in bed each night and sliding between clean linen, linen slightly rough and smelling like the sun. It's like having a fresh start every night.

A woman would notice something like this right away, but of course Ned hasn't mentioned one word.

He has been gone about an hour and she is coming up the stairs from the basement, walking sideways so the basket holding the laundry won't get stuck, when the phone rings. She lets it ring about five times while she decides whether or not to answer. She recognizes the ring. People think that a phone sounds the same no matter who is calling, but it isn't true. It has a specific sound depending on who's on the other end and what they're calling to say. A call from a friend has a markedly different ring to it than the call from one of those telemarketing people who always phone when you're eating dinner. Or a call announcing bad news. After Todd died, she began paying real attention to matters like this.

It makes people nervous when she says things like "after Todd died." As a rule, most people, Ned's sister Ethel for example, prefer words like "gone" and "departed" when they mention him, as if he has just run off on a short trip and any minute now will come walking through the door wearing his red high-top sneakers and asking what's for dinner. Of course, the real truth is Ethel would be happiest never having to hear his name again at all, like there is some kind of contamination to it and she doesn't want it to rub off on her boys, though you notice she was happy enough to have them wearing his clothes. Well, he is not off taking a trip. He's dead. "Dead" is a good word. It sounds just like it is.

Now, by the pitch of the phone's bell, she knows it is Anderson Jeffrey. He has been calling on and off all month—he's more persistent than you might give him credit for—and it makes her physically ill to think that he might call sometime when Ned is home. How could she explain a call from a teacher when she has told Ned this exact same teacher has canceled the writing class because he had to leave town on an emergency?

The class was Ned's idea. When he found the college catalog on her dresser, he latched on to it, hung on to it the way he insisted on cleaving to hope. Dorothy Barnes, the regular checkout clerk at the Stop and Shop, had given her the pamphlet, shoving it into her shopping bag along with the weekly sales circular. If Ned had handed it to her, or Doc Blessing, she would have thrown it away without taking a second look, but since it came to her by accident, she kept it, even gave it a quick glance, scanning the listing for the fall semester Adult Education courses at the local community college. As soon as Ned saw it, that awful expression of hope spread over his face, as shiny and conspicuous as if it'd been drawn on with engine grease. *She's finally going to return to normal.* That is his phrase: "Return to normal." As if a state of mind is easy to find, as if all you need is a road map. But things aren't as simple as men like to think.

"Well, now, Rosie," he said when he picked it up. "Aren't you just full of surprises." He stood in their bedroom, leaning against the bureau, looking over the brochure. There were about a dozen classes listed: small engine repair, upholstering, personal computers, creative writing, conversational French, emergency first aid, and quilt making. She could see what he was thinking—what he was hoping—see it as clear as day.

"It's nothing," she said. "Just junk." Still, she has to admit the quilt-making class caught her attention. All the sewing she has done and she's never made a quilt. She could almost see herself taking the class, cutting up pieces of everything she'd ever worn, shaping them into little triangles and squares. She'd use some of Todd's things too, items she had managed to store in a box before Ned gave most of the things to Ethel for her kids. It hurt Rose something fierce to see Todd's shirts on another boy's body, but Ned said she was being foolish and there was no sense in good clothes going to waste. "They're just clothes, for God's sake," he said.

She thought if she made a quilt with bits of her son's clothes, maybe it would be a little like having something of Todd just for her, something that no one knew about and no one could take away. She'd piece it all together in little tiny stitches, so even and small it would look like she'd done it on the Singer, and maybe, sewing and piecing and putting it together in a pattern, everything would come to make sense to her.

She was getting ready to tell Ned that perhaps she'd like to take that quilt-making class at the college when he came home wearing what he could have called a shit-eating grin and made his announcement. He'd enrolled her for creative writing, had even paid the tuition. Right then she could just see that quilt she never made fading away, disappearing just like the clothes that Ned had given to Ethel. It made her dizzy it slipped away so fast.

But what was Ned thinking of? She had absolutely no intention of writing. She planned it in her mind so she'd go once or twice and then she would tell Ned that she'd tried, really, she'd tried, but writing just wasn't for her. The professor—a man named Anderson Jeffrey, like somewhere along the line he'd gotten his first and last names switched—well, he never even gave her a chance to put this scheme into action.

AT LAST THE PHONE STOPS RINGING. SHE WISHES SHE COULD put the whole business of Anderson Jeffrey out of her mind, or at least revise the details of it. She has listened to people alter the past, heard them reshape their memories to fit the way they wished things had been, but this is a skill she herself has never acquired. Her past is crystal clear, without one fact shifted out of order.

She takes the sheets out to the line. In a month, the first snow will fall, early this year according to the *Old Farmer's Almanac*, harbinger of a long, cold winter, but today is warm and sunny, and the sky stretches out in endless blue without a cloud, like this day the ocean has reversed itself and flooded the heavens. It is the kind of Indian summer day that always fills Rose with sorrow.

Yesterday Ned mowed the grass when he came home from the station, and now the cut blades stick to her feet, staining her shoes green. Years ago, when they first moved into this house, Ned always raked the lawn when he finished up with the mowing. Later, when Todd got old enough to help, raking was his job. She can't remember the last time Ned troubled with it. Still, he keeps the property up. The evening before, standing at the kitchen window, she watched while he crisscrossed the lawn, making grim patterns with the mower, his shoulders slumped in an old man's posture, and she wondered why he bothered.

Except for the clothesline, their lawn is absolutely empty of decoration. There is not a single lounge chair, barbecue, or picnic bench anywhere in sight. No skateboards or bikes lying in the drive in danger of being run over. Ned took the basketball hoop down years ago. If it weren't for the narrow perennial bed behind the garage, and the laundry on the days she hangs, and the fact that Ned keeps the lawn mowed, the shrubs trimmed, you could mistake this house for a place where no one lives.

A blast of noise from the Montgomery place startles her out of her reverie. She glances over and sees that Opal Gates person come out to the back porch carting a sleek black box that Rose immediately identifies as the source of the noise—that loud, horrid stuff young people mistake for music. Then the door opens again and the child comes tumbling out of the house—back door slamming behind him—and skips down the steps.

Throughout the past weeks, from a second-floor vantage point, Rose has watched their comings and goings. Initially, before Ned brought home the facts, she took the girl to be the boy's older sister. She certainly doesn't look a day over sixteen. She is scrawny, thin as a playing card. Not exactly what you'd call pretty. With red hair like nothing Rose has ever seen in captivity.

"She's the kid's mother," Ned reported one night, sharing the information he has picked up over coffee at Trudy's: Her name is Opal Gates; she is from the South—North Carolina according to the plates on the Buick—and has rented the Montgomery place for a year; hers is the only name on the lease; the husband has not been sighted.

Right then Rose understood the whole story. The girl has gone and gotten herself pregnant and had a shotgun wedding. Probably a high school dropout. Well, at least she didn't have an abortion. Give her credit for that. The husband has either abandoned her or enlisted. Rose can't make up her mind which.

The most interesting thing is that Opal Gates makes dolls. According to Maida Learned over at the Yellow Balloon, the girl can take a photo of a child and produce a doll that's nearly a twin. Maida has already ordered several for the store, although Rose can't imagine this is the kind of thing you can make a living at.

Other bits of gossip have surfaced. The general opinion is that the girl is far too casual with her care of the boy. Gloria at the Cutting Edge said when the pair turned up for the boy to get a haircut, he was allowed to run wild. "Nearly tore the shop apart while she just sat there and didn't say a word." And Gloria's daughter Marcia had seen them at the playground. When she tried to warn her about the jungle gym, the one the Levitt child broke her collarbone on just last month, Opal Gates laughed and then went right ahead and allowed her son to climb the bars. "Now don't you go worrying about that," she said to Marcia. "Boys bounce." *Boys bounce.* The audacity of it. The carelessness of it.

Boys *don't* bounce. They break.

Rose herself had been a devoted mother, insisting on breast-feeding Todd, even though Doc didn't want her to, although now, don't you know, the experts say breast-feeding is good, that it protects and enhances an infant's immune system. Of course, Rose knows that nothing can really make people immune, that nothing on God's green earth can keep people safe, that no amount of money or goodness, fame or love can protect. Still. *Boys bounce.* The unfairness of it.

In the yard next door, the girl continues to fiddle with the radio with no improvement in the music, while the boy runs around in circles, arms extended like wings, screeching like a little banshee. Rose hopes she isn't going to be expected to put up with this kind of racket. If it keeps up, Ned will have to go over and have a talk with her. And here it is October and neither of them wearing shoes. You can't blame the boy, he's too young to know better, but the mother should use her head. Barefoot in October. A flea would have more sense. Rose isn't prejudiced and doesn't like to form judgments about people, but it looks to her that the girl is what you'd call Southern trash.

Rose is pinning up the last pair of Ned's socks when she hears the girl's shouted "hello." Naturally, she ignores this. She has no intention of mixing in. Nothing but trouble there.

It galls her that someone has probably already told the girl about Todd. "That's poor Rose Nelson," they tell newcomers, as if that is her full name. *Poor Rose Nelson. The woman who lost her only son in that dreadful accident a few years back.* Spreading her business to anyone who will listen. People here couldn't keep quiet if they were paid to. Then she wonders, as she has all month, what brought the girl and her boy to Normal.

NORMAL REALLY IS THE NAME OF THEIR TOWN AND THERE ARE plenty of jokes about it. Back when she used to care about things like that, Rose liked living in a place called Normal, thought it sounded like the name of a Southern town. People in the South do have a sense of poetry about the naming of things that doesn't seem to exist in other parts of the country. The time she and Ned and Todd took the trip to Virginia to visit Ned's first cousin Ben, they passed grocery stores with names like Piggly Wiggly and Harris Teeter and Winn Dixie, names that just moved with poetry. Rose shops at the Stop and Shop and thinks that you'd have to feel different shopping in a place called Piggly Wiggly. She thinks Normal would be the perfect name for a Southern town.

Their town is named after a Civil War hero who was born here, Colonel Percival Winfield Normal. Even though he was a lesser figure in the War between the States, a statue of him stands in the square in front of their town hall and every year on his birthday, the school-children have a little parade in his honor. Percival Winfield Normal, now there is a Southern name if ever there was one. When she walks by his statue, Rose often looks up at the colonel and wonders how he ended up in western Massachusetts.

But then, nobody really ends up where they think they are heading, do they? Look at her. Look at Ned.

Look at Todd.

CHAPTER 3

❧ O P A L

"**F**UCK," OPAL SAYS WHEN THE PHONE RINGS.

The line has only been hooked up for two weeks and already Melva has called eight times. Eight calls, eight arguments. Conversations Opal would rather not rehash this morning. Try as she might, she can't make her mama understand why she had to leave New Zion.

Four rings. Five. For a fact, sooner or later she will have to give in and answer; Melva is nothing if not determined. Also, Opal believes her mama has some kind of telepathy regarding her and that Melva knows that she is standing here in the kitchen not two feet away from the phone. *Don't you bite; don't you grab the bait,* she counsels herself as she picks up the receiver. *No matter how much she provokes you, stay cool.* Staying cool is not one of Opal's strong points. Her fuse was born short.

"Raylee?"

"Raylee's not here." She's proud as can be to hear her voice is perfectly calm.

Twice in the two full years since she changed her name, Opal has sent Melva copies of the court order and the printed legal ad that appeared in the local newspaper, but her mama continues to proceed as if these things have never arrived at her door. Melva believes the whole name-change episode is just another difficult phase Opal is going through and that eventually she'll return to her senses and reclaim her given name.

"Raylee? Is that you?"

No winning this game. "Yes."

"Well, thank the Lord. I thought I misdialed. I was just going to hang up. Are you all right?"

"I'm *fine*."

"How's Zack? Does he miss his Melvama?" Melvama is the name Melva has coined for Zack to call her. She's much too young to be a grandmother.

"Zack's fine, Mama. We're both doing just fine."

Melva barely pauses for this response. "Billy drove on over and joined us for dinner last night," she says. "I swear, that boy looks just dreadful. He misses you both terribly."

Just when did her mama turn so soft on Billy? And why on earth would she invite him to dinner? Opal can't imagine what they'd found to talk about. Talking is definitely not Billy's strong suit. If you take away basketball and Zack, conversation is pretty much *extinguished*. Well, guess now they talk about Opal.

"He loves you, Raylee. I hope you know that."

Opal should know this since she heard precisely these words during yesterday's call.

"Naturally, he's worried about Zackery, and he's just sick with missing you both. It about breaks my heart to look at him."

If he really is that flat-out concerned wouldn't he be at her door, telling her face-to-face instead of using her mama to relay this information? Three tankfuls of gas is not that great a distance.

"It just breaks my heart," Melva repeats. "Breaks my heart in two to see the way he misses his boy."

The same boy, Opal wants to tell her, the same boy he wanted me to abort the instant he heard a rumor about his existence, the same boy he can't even be bothered to call and check on. She holds her tongue. With her mama, every conversation is a minefield, every word uttered something that will later be used against her.

"You know, Raylee, there are plenty of girls in New Zion who would jump at the chance to get a taste of Billy. Just jump. You can't expect him to sit around forever, just waiting on you. You hear me, girl?"

Opal can't even sort out all the emotions this statement provokes.

"Raylee, why are you doing this to him? To your daddy and me? Where is your head, girl? Your heart made of stone? When are you coming home? When are you going to get all this foolishness out of your head and bring our grandbaby back here where he belongs?"

Opal considers all the answers she can give but takes the coward's way out. "I don't know," she says.

"If it's a question of—"

"Listen," Opal breaks in. "I've got to get going." She says the one thing she knows will get her off the hook. "Zack needs me."

ZACK DOES NEED HER. BUT HE CERTAINLY DOESN'T NEED Billy, a for-shit daddy whose idea of fatherhood is to teach his son how to pop the flip top on a can of Bud. She can't imagine why Billy is hang-dogging around her parents. He doesn't really want Zack. Or her. He just wants what he can't have. Nothing new about that.

She zaps her coffee to boiling, then goes to check on Zack. Three days ago, he created a makeshift tent by draping a blanket between two ladder-back chairs. Since then he regularly disappears inside for great lengths of time. A teepee? Cave? Space station? Opal doesn't dream of taking it down, although Melva would not have allowed something like this to remain in her living room for the better part of one day.

Items vanish inside. Pillows. A set of toy trucks. A flashlight. Plastic bowls. Food. "Provisions," he tells her. *Provisions.* She truly can't imagine where in the world a five-year-old came up with a word like that. He's so bright it frightens her. She can't begin to figure out how she'll manage to raise him. There should be a class in that. She loves him. She knows that for certain. She hopes it's enough.

Sometimes she likes to think she just strayed into motherhood, like a character in a movie who drifts on screen and sort of hangs around but doesn't have many lines to say and no responsibility for the way the story turns out. This altered version is easy to live with, but eventually she has to look at a more complicated picture.

When she is looking real straight and trying to be honest, she has to ask herself if deep inside she wanted to get pregnant.

It's pure fact that that is one of the questions Emily asked her during their first counseling session. Therapy was part of the deal her mama made. Opal could keep the baby, but she had to see a psychologist. Of course this compromise about killed Melva, who still hasn't forgiven Opal for ruining the family's reputation. Her mother has an inflated opinion of their standing in town. First thing she did after she married Opal's daddy was upgrade herself from Methodist to Episcopal. As far as Opal can see, her pregnancy hasn't yet caused any fatalities for the New Zion rescue squad to contend with.

Melva got Emily Jackman's name from Madeline Horsley, the New Zion High guidance counselor who promised she'd be the soul of discretion about the entire situation, a lie so barefaced Opal doesn't know why her tongue didn't fall out.

The first thing Opal noticed about Emily was that she was a good listener. Her own family isn't tops in the listening department, and she never realized how good it could make you feel to be heard, to be listened to as if what you said really mattered.

Opal thought Emily would try to convince her to give the baby up, but she never did. What she did do was make Opal talk about her family.

She learned from Emily that the "majority of unwed, pregnant teenagers" came from homes with at least one dominating parent, usually the mother. According to Emily, becoming pregnant was often used as a way of escaping, of establishing independence. Opal hated being a teenage statistic, being lumped with the other unwed mothers.

She insisted her pregnancy was an accident. She certainly hadn't tricked Billy the way Suzanne Jennings trapped Jitter Walton.

"Perhaps not deliberately," Emily said. "Unconsciously."

"No," she replied, remembering how relieved she was those months when her period came right on schedule.

"Why didn't you use contraceptives?" Emily pushed.

"We did. Sometimes."

" 'Sometimes' is the Russian roulette method of birth control. You know that."

But even when she was directly confronting her, Emily never judged her or made her feel ashamed. And one day, after she had again asked her about whether or not she had wanted to become pregnant, she said something so true that Opal wrote it down on paper the moment she got home.

Emily said that it wasn't sex that had gotten her in trouble, it was loneliness. "Never underestimate the power of a hungry heart," she said.

When she is honest, Opal has to admit she always liked the idea of having a baby. Even the Modern Living class hadn't dimmed this desire.

Modern Living—an idiotic name that sounded more like a magazine than a high school class—was a requirement for New Zion juniors. Miss Grady, the Home Ec teacher, lectured them about things like relationships and money management and budgeting. Mid-semester, for one week, the juniors had to experience make-believe parenthood.

The year before, the class had been given eggs that they had to pretend were babies and cart everywhere—even football practice. If an egg got broken, the student flunked. Of course, everyone in town heard how the football players hard-boiled their eggs, although Miss Grady professed not to know. Opal's class got dolls instead of eggs, computer dolls named Baby Think It Over that the school received a state grant for. They each weighed nine pounds and had a computer that was set to go off at certain times—day and night—so the doll would cry and the only way to make it stop was to pick it up and insert a key and hold it and find out if it needed changing or feeding or just to be rocked. And you had to keep a log of how you cared for it, when you fed it, how long it slept.

Most of the New Zion faculty complained that the dolls disrupted their classes, and by the end of two days half the kids in the class hated their dolls, but Opal, who'd never had a younger brother or sister or even a pet, really took to hers. She didn't even mind waking in the night to hold the doll. Of course after she had Zack, she found out there was a world of difference between a doll, even a computer doll, and a for-real baby.

But had liking Baby Think It Over made her want to get pregnant? She doesn't think so. If she were going to set about getting pregnant, she would have chosen someone better suited to fatherhood than Billy Steele.

When Emily asked her if she had fallen for Billy because he was a star basketball player, she had to laugh. Opal and Sujette were just about the only ones in school who didn't think the jocks were gods. They used to make fun of them, imitating the way they would walk through the cafeteria with total attitude like they were special messengers from heaven, though you couldn't really blame them for that because most everyone in the school was of the opinion that the athletes danced on water and conversed with God. Opal didn't see how anyone could be seriously interested in someone whose entire life ambition was to play guard for the Tar Heels.

She believes Billy first noticed her because she was just about the only girl in the school who didn't faint when he walked by. He began sitting at her table at lunch and letting everyone know he was after her. Then, with all this attention focused on her, she began to taste what it was like to feel special. She liked the power his wanting gave her.

Of course, after they had sex, the power switched. Sex unhinged her. It was all she thought about. Kissing. Touching. Tasting. God, the tasting. Who knew you could acquire a liking—an appetite—for the taste of another person? She can totally understand how sex causes so much trouble in the world. With Billy she felt like she had finally found what she was born for. Although at first he liked her enthusiasm, it soon made him nervous. Like it wasn't quite natural for her to like it *that* much.

For now she has sworn off sex. Who needs it? She has absolutely no intention of getting caught again. Plus she is responsible for Zack. Having a child makes you old that way, which is another thing Baby Think It Over hadn't prepared her for.

"MAMA?" ZACK REAPPEARS FROM THE BLANKET TENT. HE runs to her, gives her a damp hug. She wants to smother him, kiss him, taste the sweetness in the crease of his neck, nibble at the tender skin, actually bite him, but she holds back, deliberately striking a casual note so he will not be frightened by the ferocity of her feelings.

She knows there will be a day in the not-too-distant future when he won't let her ruffle his hair, the inevitable moment when he will barely tolerate her touch. She dreads the day he grows up, becomes a man, becomes one of the enemy. She can't think of him that way.

The first time she held Zack, she finally realized what love was, understood it in a way she never had with Billy. With Billy it was lust, sex, infatuation, nothing compared to the protective, tender, intense love she feels for Zack. If anything ever happened to him she would die. She would seek and welcome death.

"I'm hungry," he announces. "But our cupboard is bare."

Where does he come up with these statements?

"Sounds like we need to take a safari to the store."

"Exactly," he says.

For a fact she and Zack will be just fine. They don't need a man. Or anyone else.

AT THE CHECKOUT COUNTER OF THE STOP AND SHOP, SHE stacks groceries on the conveyor while trying to keep Zack away from the candy display rack. Without Melva at her shoulder criticizing her every choice, she is free to put whatever she wants in her grocery cart. As she sets each item on the counter—Fruit Loops, two packages of Twinkies, a six-pack of small plastic bottles filled with sweet colored water, a loaf of white bread, hot dogs, corn chips, a jar of bright yellow mustard, another of grape jelly, a third of marshmallow fluff, two boxes of macaroni and cheese—it occurs to her that it looks as if Zack has done the shopping. She has to get serious about nutrition soon.

"Coupons?" The cashier's eyes catch hers then slide away to take in her bare legs, her chipped and broken nails, her too-long hair—hair Opal hasn't cut since fifth grade.

Opal recognizes disapproval on—her gaze falls to the green plastic badge—Dorothy B.'s face. What is it about her that elicits this tight-lipped disapproval from older women? She notes the woman's sallow complexion, her badly dyed hair that screams home perm. No chance *she* ever appeared on a Homecoming float.

"No, ma'am," she says. "No coupons."

"No, ma'am," Zack parrots, making a little tune of it.

Dorothy B. rings up the Twinkies and corn chips, then lifts the hot dogs, flips them over, sighs. "You know the price?"

Opal shakes her head, first at Dorothy B. and then at Zack who is trying to reach the Twinkies.

"I want one," he whines.

Pager in hand, Dorothy intones, "Price check from Deli." Her monotone echoes through the store.

"Not now, sugah-bun," Opal says to Zack.

The stock boy, a teenager with serious acne, takes the package from Dorothy. Opal can't imagine why the management would hire him. A face like that can't be good for business.

"New in town?" Dorothy asks.

"Yes."

"Didn't think I'd seen you before. Visiting?"

"No. We moved here."

"From the South, right?"

Opal nods.

"I knew it. The accent gave you away."

No shit, Sherlock, Opal thinks. Maybe she'll forget about the hot dogs, just get out of there, go home, convince Zack to take a nap so she can grab one herself. The last weeks have left her sleep deprived. There was the trip from New Zion, the day traipsing around with the real estate agent looking for a rental, then the unpacking and settling in, finding a nursery school for Zack, all the while amusing him, feeding him, tending to his needs, spending the enormous amount of emotional energy mothering takes, fielding all Melva's calls. It has been a rough spell, made more difficult by the nagging apprehension that she is making a huge mistake.

How could something that seemed so right—so *fated*—back in New Zion now feel like a mistake?

The last Sunday in August, the day of the picnic, the one her mama had held every year as long as she could remember, was the day she decided to leave. Sitting on the porch while her daddy, his face all shut down, was grilling his special chicken and Zack was wading in the kiddy pool and Billy—Billy who didn't even *like* her mama—was flirting like Melva was his girlfriend or something, Opal felt a heaviness settle hard on her ribs. Then he called out for her to fetch him a beer. His old lady, he called her. She was *twenty*.

Her heart actually stopped beating—she felt her pulse cease—and in that icy moment she saw the rest of her life playing out in front of her, playing out in picnic after picnic after picnic.

That was when the extraordinary idea took hold. She could leave—just take Zack, pack up, and go. She hugged the thought close. If Melva looked over at her, for sure her mama would read this plan plain on her face. But her mama was busy with Billy.

Later, driving back to her apartment, she swung down County Road, the long way home, by the intersection at Jefferson. She stared straight ahead, fixing on the signal swaying overhead. Green light, go, she whispered. Red light, stay. Green light, go. Red light, stay.

She sailed right through that go light. Sailed, eventually, all the way to Massachusetts.

"THIS IS YOUR SON?" THE CASHIER'S QUESTION PULLS HER back.

Opal nods.

"I thought so," Dorothy says. "The red hair and all."

Rocket scientist, this one. Opal holds her tongue since statements like that just alienate people and are exactly the kind of thing that caused Billy to tell her she has the tongue of a Gillette Super Blue. "Gosh darn, Raylee, do you have to be so sarcastic?" he asked whenever she thought she was only observing a truth. That is exactly the problem. Most people don't want to hear the truth.

"You don't look old enough to drive let alone have a child," the cashier says.

"I'm twenty-two." She automatically tacks two years on to the age. She hates the way people look at her when they tally up the numbers and figure out she was pregnant at fifteen, like her teeth are broke and her eyes are too close together.

"I want a Twinkie," Zack says.

"Okay, sugah," she says. "You can have one when we get home."

The stock boy returns, hands a priced package of dogs to Dorothy.

The cashier rings them up. "Where are you living?"

"Chestnut Street." She mentally pushes the woman to finish ringing up the groceries so she can escape before Zack really starts pushing.

"Big white house at the end of the block? Green shutters?"

"Mmmmmmm-hmmmm."

"You're in the Montgomery place. Right next to poor Rose Nelson."

Well, isn't this the first interesting thing to come out of the woman's mouth? Opal tears a wrapper off a Twinkie and hands the cake to Zack. "Poor Rose Nelson?"

"Tragic thing." The woman leans in toward Opal, lowers her voice. "Tragic. The way she lost her boy. Only child, too. Rose and Ned only had the one."

Opal puts her hand on Zack's shoulder.

"He was sixteen. Let's see. It must have been five years ago now." Dorothy pauses to calculate. "That's right. Exactly five years ago this month. Poor Rose. Course, after that she's never been quite right."

Well, duh. Fuck. God help her. How could you ever be "all right" again after you lost a child? How could you go on breathing in and breathing out?

BACK HOME, AS SHE UNLOADS THE GROCERIES FROM THE trunk of the Buick, she casts a quick glance over at the neighboring house. Although the grass is kept up, the house has a vacant look about it. The shades are drawn; there is no car in the drive. She pictures her neighbor inside the house, surrounded by silence. After the accident, she should have moved away. Opal knows she would have. There is a lot to be said for geographic cures.

She totes the grocery bags up the back steps and into the kitchen. The room spans the back half of the house and is a study in avocado and gold, a decorating scheme Opal figures had its triumph before she was born.

The entire house is decorated out of a *Family Circle* of an earlier era, but it's roomy, certainly bigger than she expected to find on her budget. Even with the luxury of Aunt May's check, she has to be careful.

"It's a great deal," the realtor pushed as he showed her the property, a two-story Dutch colonial with a narrow front porch. The owners, recently retired to Florida, had agreed to rent until there is a sale. It is situated at the end of a cul-de-sac, and it is this more than the realtor's sales pitch that convinced Opal to take it. Here Zack will be protected from speeding cars, reckless drivers. She is still innocent enough to believe vigilance is all that is needed to keep her son safe.

She is unbagging the groceries when, through the window above the sink, she catches sight of someone in the yard next door.

She moves over to the larger window by the Formica dinette set, taking care to stand to the side, out of line of vision should her neighbor happen to glance over. Although she has seen the husband several times—late yesterday she watched him mow his lawn in conscientious, methodical stripes that reminded her of her daddy—this is the first time in a week she has had a real good look at the woman.

The cashier's words echo as she peers through the window and watches her neighbor make her way across freshly mown grass to the clothesline: *Poor Rose Nelson.*

She is surprised to see how ordinary the woman looks, how solid, standing there in a housecoat and sweater, her head wrapped in a floral scarf, babushka style. Opal has envisioned Rose as someone thin, someone who looks like there is something broken about her, inside her, maybe needing a cane to prop her up against the weight of her terrible loss, but in the flesh, Rose seems solid, close to plump. She moves slowly at her work, carefully pinning up each sheet, as if this chore requires thought. The words "pioneer stock" jump into Opal's head. Watching Rose clip a sail of white linen to the line, she is reminded of square-shouldered prairie women and Conestogas they learned about in eighth-grade history, and then—although she has never seen one—she envisions a figurehead carved on the bow of a ship, cutting through waves, splitting fog, leading the way through storms. To Opal, Rose doesn't look "poor" at all. She imagines at that moment there is something Rose knows that she needs to know, although she cannot for the world imagine what it might be.

CHAPTER 4

⤙ ROSE

"Mama?" THE BOY CRIES OUT IN THE NEIGHBORING yard.

Before Rose can steel herself against it, the memory comes full up, taking her hard, striking her breath away.

There is no guarding against memory. That's the devil of it. It slips in before you can catch yourself, closing your throat, startling your heart. Lord, if she knows about anything at all, it is the treacherous power of memory.

Anything can trigger it—the unexpected convergence of a particular sight and sound, a specific smell, a song. Anything. And there is absolutely no way to protect against it.

Now, the sun on her back, the clean smell of the laundry mingling with the crisp air of fall, the sound of the child next door shouting for his mother just as a transport from Westover flies over—all converge to flip her back five years. She was hanging the wash that day too, doing chores without one clue that her real life was about to end, that she was about to see her son and touch his warm body for the last time, to feel his arms squeeze her and hold her in far too casual and quick a way to last forever.

THE BACK DOOR SLAMS AND TODD COMES OUT. HE BLINKS against the sudden sun. His eyes are still fogged by sleep, and he wears the

*bewildered look he always has when he first wakes up, a childlike vulnera-
bility that wrenches her heart. He takes the steps two at a time. His shoelaces
are undone, dangling loose, ready at any moment to trip him, cause him to
stumble down the steps, cause him to scrape something, break something.* Tie
your shoes before you trip. Have you eaten breakfast? More than
toast? *She forces the words back and carefully pins one of Ned's undershirts
on the line. Slow down, she wants to shout.*

*Since he turned sixteen, everything he does is too fast, too loud. He lives in
extremes. Sleeps twelve, thirteen hours. Or only three. Skips a meal or eats
enough for a family of seven. It seems to her he courts disaster. At the lake, he
dives too near the shallow end, close to hidden rocks, and none of her warnings can stop him.*

*Ned doesn't worry. Never has. She's the one who since Todd's birth has
carried this vast helplessness inside. No one ever warns you about that. No one
ever says that having a child is like having your heart walk around outside
your body, bumping into things.*

*The eclipse of a C-130 heading back to Westover briefly shadows the yard,
then slides on.*

"Mom?"

*She watches as he lopes across the yard. All angles and joints. Gangly. Yet
even in a body so suddenly large there is an awkward grace. He will be a
graceful man, she thinks, and feels a rush of pride.*

"Jimmy and I are going out to the Quabbin. There's been a sighting of
new eagles."

"What about work?" *She hates for him to go to the reservoir. There have
been at least two drownings there in the past few years.*

"I already checked with Dad. He said as long as I'm back by noon."

That Ned has already given his okay irritates her. "I don't know—" *she
begins.*

"We'll only be gone a couple of hours."

*She shakes out another undershirt, clips it to the line. She wishes he
wouldn't hang around with Jimmy.*

"And I was wondering. Can I borrow the car? Dad said ask you."

*So he's asked Ned first. Just this once why couldn't Ned say no? She looks
over to the drive where the Pontiac is parked. As a surprise, Ned registered it
in her name. Her pride in this is foolish, she knows, but it is the first new car
she has ever owned.*

"Can I?"

She hesitates. Although he has been driving since he was fourteen—

outings that she wasn't supposed to know anything about when he and Ned would head off to practice on old unpaved country roads—he has only been driving legally for three months. If she had her way the driving age would be eighteen. Twenty. Safely in the future. "Why don't you take the pickup?"

"Dad might need it at the station. I'll be careful. Promise."

If he were going alone, on a short trip to the store to pick up something for her, or down to the station . . . If she could go along with him, watching from the passenger's seat to warn him about other drivers . . . But to think of him driving out to the reservoir, almost an hour away, the twisting roads, with Jimmy, in her new car, a car with not one single scratch or dent. No.

"Not today," she says. "I have some errands I need to do." She turns her face so he can't see the lie sitting on her lips. Not today. Two words. Quickly *said. Two words that change the universe.*

"Okay," he says. "We'll take Jimmy's truck. Catch you later." He gives her a hug. Quick and casual. Busy with laundry and still irritated that he is going to the reservoir, she doesn't return the embrace. "Be careful," she says.

THE THIN VOICE OF THE CHILD IN THE NEXT YARD BRINGS Rose back. Her heart is fluttering, the pulse erratic, beating with the familiar flutter of guilt and grief, heavy with a secret too shameful to bear. Boys *bounce.*

The pain of memory comes in spasms, cutting across her stomach like monthly cramps. Then the boy next door laughs, and Rose feels a contraction of longing as involuntary as a hiccup. She picks up the empty basket and flees to the house.

CHAPTER 5

✦ N E D

AFTER LUNCH, NED SERVICES THE TRANSMISSION ON the Dowlings' '89 Olds. He drops the pan and lets the fluid out, then replaces the filter. As he slips the new gasket on, he feels the familiar band stretching across his temples. The headaches have been coming on more and more lately.

He replaces the pan, scrapes a knuckle, swears. He's already had a bitch of a morning. Tyrone Miller, his part-time mechanic, hasn't shown, and now Ned is so far behind he's going to have to carry at least two jobs over to tomorrow, screwing up another day.

He's still looking at oil changes on two Renaults. The green '91 that belongs to Dick Carrington and Bill Grauski's gray '87. If he could afford to turn away the business, he would refuse to service them. He hates Renaults. The way they make those things you have to have the hands of a six-year-old girl to work under the hood. People should have to buy American. That's the problem with the country. Whole balance-of-trade thing would be settled if Americans would support their own industries instead of the Japs and Germans.

Now Fords. There is a car a man can work on. Ned loves to see a Ford pull up, especially the '70s models. You can raise the hood on one of those honeys and find room to lie down inside, not like those damn Renaults. But then what can you expect from a car made by Frogs?

He drops a wrench, swears again. When he bends over to retrieve it, his head pounds, a pulsing red beat that tells him this one is going to be a real bastard. It's digging in behind his eyes, across his temple, up over his skull. The coffee he's consumed doesn't help. He should cut down. He has probably had at least ten cups already, and it's only 1:30. Plus, at lunch he grabbed a sub from Trudy's, and the hot peppers aren't sitting right.

He finishes up with the Olds and goes to the counter to recheck the day's sheet. The headache is in full swing now, and he would love to quit early.

He looks over at the second lift, where Bob Rivers' Dodge waits for a brake realignment. He'll let Ty finish it up tomorrow. If he shows up. Then there are two regulars who want their ACs recharged. He thought he was done with that this year, but there's been an unexpected hot spell and now he has four or five more scheduled. Five years ago, he could do the whole job in half the time, half the paperwork. Used to be, he could just add a can of Freon, but now, thanks to Uncle Sam, it takes at least an hour. He has to hook the damn system up to the recycling box; clean, filter, weigh, and return the gas to the system; and then add in what's needed. To top it off, the recycling box, a piece of equipment that set him back five thousand bucks, is already obsolete. All the current models require new equipment that he's already decided he won't buy. It is a big expense, and he'll be lucky if he recoups the initial investment in a year. Let people just open their windows. It isn't like this is Florida, for God's sake. Personally, he wouldn't take air if the factory threw it in for free.

He continues down the work sheet. After the ACs, there's a carburetor job on a Pontiac, and he has promised Stu Weston he'll take a look at a car his kid wants to buy, see if it's a lemon.

At 2:30, head pounding so ugly it's an effort to keep his eyes open, he gives up and heads home.

He hasn't gone more than three blocks when he remembers that this is the day he intended to drive out to the college, straighten out the mess over Rose's tuition. He has already put it off for two weeks. He hates doing things like this and the headache isn't helping, but he wants it cleared up.

It was his understanding that the class was to run a full semester and he paid a damn good bit of money for Rose to take it. It isn't about the money. He is glad to do it. Rose isn't like a lot of wives, Joey Doherty's for instance. Now there's a woman who goes through money like a dose of salts. No, he has no complaints on that score with

Rose. He hadn't minded paying for this writing class; he was happy to do it if that was what she wanted. But the thing is, the class was supposed to run for four months, and if they cut it short—whatever the reason—it doesn't seem right not to give some sort of refund.

Afternoon classes are in session, and he has to circle the lot three times before he can find a parking spot. Between that and the headache, he's in a sour mood by the time he reaches the registrar's office. There's only one person behind the desk, someone he instantly knows he doesn't want to deal with. A student, but he doesn't have a clue as to which sex. The crewcut hair and plaid work shirt say boy, but the fingernails—long, painted yellow—indicate girl. *Yellow!*

"Can I help you?" A female voice.

There is something in her nose—he averts his eyes discreetly—but a second glance shows him it's a gold stud. What are her parents thinking of? No daughter of his would leave the house in a getup like that. Pierced nose. A crewcut, for Christ's sakes. None of this is helping with the headache. He holds his hands over his eyes, presses his thumb and forefinger into his temples.

"Yes?" the girl prompts. "Do you need help?"

He drops his hand, doesn't even try not to stare at her hair. Girl gets a buzz like that, she should be used to people staring. "I'm here about a refund."

Her voice turns flat. "Which class?"

He gives her the information. "Of course, I don't expect the entire amount," he says. He wants to be quite clear about that.

While she punches the data into her computer, he stares at her shorn scalp. He shakes his head and thinks of Tyrone. The mechanic wears his hair in a ponytail, has a pierced ear. Somewhere along the line kids today have gotten confused, gotten the roles blurred.

The girl looks up from her screen. "That class is still on the schedule."

"What?"

"It's still on the schedule. It hasn't been canceled."

"It sure has," he informs her, thinking, God, these people don't know what's going on around here. How do they expect to teach anyone anything? With more patience than he feels, he repeats what Rose has told him. "My wife should know. She was taking the class." He stresses "wife" to show this girl that she's dealing with adults here.

The girl frowns and taps more keys. The long yellow nails make a clicking sound. "No," she says. "Professor Jeffrey is still teaching that course. In fact, it's in session right now. In room 306 Dalton. Dalton Hall. The humanities building. If you parked in Lot A, you walked right by it."

Ned stands his ground. There is a mistake, a mix-up. Maybe this girl doesn't know how to use a computer. Fingernails like that, she's probably struck the wrong keys. He'll have to ask for the person in charge.

"What's your wife's name?" she asks before he can act.

"Rose Nelson. *Mrs.* Rose Nelson."

She taps more keys on the board; they both wait while new information pops up. "Ah, here it is," she says in her flat voice. "Rose Nelson." She stops reading and casts a funny glance at him.

"We have Rose Nelson entered as a voluntary withdrawal. Of course, there's no refund after the first month of classes. If she'd withdrawn a week earlier, you'd be entitled to a partial refund. Sorry." She returns to her work, dismissing him.

He is pretty sure, would have bet the shop on it, that Rose has never in her life lied to him. Why would she tell him the professor had an emergency, had to leave town? If she doesn't want to take the damn writing class, she could have told him she quit. At that moment he could kill Rose. Not about the money, the hell with the money, but for embarrassing him in front of this ridiculous creature.

ON HIS WAY TO THE PARKING LOT, HE PASSES DALTON HALL, and it comes to him that something isn't right about this. He can just feel it. He looks about and, seeing no one in sight, crosses the walk. He pauses a moment, inhales a time or two, gets his bearings. He still wears his work clothes: green pants stained with oil, grease, and engine fluids that mark him as a trespasser. He doesn't have one clue what he'll say if anyone challenges him, asks him what he's doing here.

Room 306 is on the third floor. Out of breath by the time he's climbed three flights of stairs, he's glad to find the corridor empty. He passes by closed doors, checking numbers, peering into oblong windows of near-useless glass the size of a carton of milk. The room is midway down the hall.

All it takes is one quick look. The guy standing in front of the class is younger than he expects, and wears a shirt, no tie. And jeans, for

Christ's sake. Ned has his number immediately. A know-it-all kind of guy, the kind that talks about movies you've never seen, makes a pain in the ass of himself at town meetings. He'd bet a week's profits the guy drives something foreign. Probably a Volvo.

Immediately, looking at this guy, Ned knows what happened to Rose, realizes how she'd written something in his class and this son of a bitch had ripped it to shreds. Naturally Rose is too embarrassed to return. A spasm of fury takes Ned for what this bastard has done to his Rose, but it passes quickly. His stomach for confrontation, his capacity for sustained rage, has long ago been exhausted.

THE HOUSE HAS AN EMPTY FEEL.

"Rose?" he yells as he enters. "Rosie?"

He checks the kitchen and then upstairs. She isn't in their bedroom. Todd's door is closed, and as he approaches he hopes to hell she isn't in there. He hasn't found her in there in months, and he clings to this as a sign she is getting better. He opens the door, smells stale air. Years ago the last traces of Todd's sweat and shaving lotion evaporated, but everything else is the same. Over on the bureau, Rose has set up a little arrangement of some of his things, junk for the most part: A ceramic tiger he made in day camp, broken and repaired at least twice—even from the door Ned can see a thin line of glue at the tail. Two framed snapshots, one of him at six and one at fifteen. His watch, a cheap blood-encrusted Timex they stripped from his wrist in the emergency room. (Rose kept it set to the correct time for months until the battery ran down.). A scrap of wrinkled paper on which is scribbled a note telling them he will be late for dinner. A couple of years ago, Rose added a votive candle. It looks like some kind of shrine, for Christ's sake. Sick.

If Ned has his way, they would turn the room into a den, should have done it a long time ago. A place where he can do paperwork for the station instead of the cramped space he now uses where he can never find anything. Tax time is a nightmare. Naturally, Rose won't hear of it. Where is she anyway? "Rose?" he calls again.

He's nervous when he doesn't know where she is. He's already lost sight of too much of her. It's as if Rose is a balloon lost in clouds overhead, and if he doesn't keep her tethered, she'll float completely off, be gone. He believes if he can just keep hold of the string, the other part will come back.

He goes out to the hall. From the upstairs window, he takes in the reassuring sight of laundry blowing on the line. Over in the yard at the Montgomery place, he sees two figures, hears, then through the window, the thump of rock music. Bad enough he's got to put up with Ty's stuff at the station. Now it looks like he won't get peace in his own backyard.

The Gates girl moved in last month. No husband on the scene, just her and the kid, although in Ned's eyes, she isn't much more than a kid herself. Personally he thinks she's a fruitcake: not evil, just no good sense. She's as thin as oil slick—looks like one stiff breeze would knock her over—and she runs around in bare feet and flashy skirts that either swing around her ankles or cut high across her thighs. No middle ground with that one.

A couple of weeks ago she stopped by the station to use the pay phone and fuel that old Buick she drives, and it wasn't two minutes before she had Tyrone's tongue hanging near his knees. The mechanic wasn't much good for the next half hour. It makes Ned nervous her being next door, so close to Rose.

Before the Gates kid moved over there, Ned had high hopes for the Montgomery place. He fantasized that a couple about his and Rose's age would move in. A nice childless couple. The woman who would come over and get Rose talking about curtains and slipcovers and what was on sale at the grocery store. And maybe the two of them would start sewing, the way Rose used to. Ned can't remember the last time he's come home to the whirring of Rose's sewing machine. The noise used to annoy the hell out of him, but now he would welcome any indication that Rose is returning to her normal self.

Instead of this neighbor he envisioned, a woman who would show Rose the road back to herself, this crazy kid moved in, this wisp of a girl with a mouth on her that would put Ty to shame.

Again he remembers the day when she stopped by the station to use the pay phone. Her line was supposed to have been connected the day before, and she wanted to blast the phone company. "The fucking phone company," was what she said. Right then, as soon as those words flew out of her mouth—"the fucking phone company"—Ned saw his hopes for Rose fly right out the window.

The boy seems nice enough, though. No bouts of temper as far as Ned can see. He says "sorry" when his ball rolls over to their yard. Not his fault his mother has a mouth on her. When Ned was out mowing the lawn the previous night, he saw the kid playing all alone, tossing an old whiffle ball up in the air, awkward hands missing it on its arc down, tossing and missing, tossing and missing, over and over until it made him dizzy to watch. It reminded him of all the nights he'd spent with Todd, teaching him to catch—a boy needs a patient man for that—and then he remembered all the baseballs he'd bought for his son over the years.

There is a whole carton of that stuff in the garage. The balls and gloves and Frisbees in that cardboard box would be doing a lot more good if that boy had them. As it is, every time Ned goes out to get the mower, his eyes fall on the carton, a concrete reminder of the worst kind of pain a man could ever expect to have. He had wanted to give the lot of them to his sister Ethel for her boys. But Rose wouldn't hear of it, although he couldn't imagine what she had been saving them for. It hadn't made any sense. Still doesn't. As far as he can see, all this holding on to Todd's stuff doesn't help anything. If he had his way, he'd just get rid of it all. But there was hell to pay the one time he gave some of Todd's clothes to Ethel. Clothes, for Christ's sake.

He had wanted more than the one child, but it hadn't worked out that way. They just had the one. Rose was thirty-three when Todd was born and had almost lost hope. If you have more than one kid, at least there are others if something happens to one. Not that he's blaming Rose.

Sometimes, when he allows himself to think about Todd, he is hit with an actual pain, a physical ache he can feel in his muscles and sinew and organs.

He notices the bathroom door is closed. "Rose," he says. "Rosie, you in there?"

"Go away."

He tries the knob, finds it locked. He sighs, caught between anger and resignation. "Rosie," he says to the door. "Open up. I need a couple of aspirin. I've got a hell of a headache."

After a moment or two the door opens enough for her to extend an arm, hand him a bottle of Excedrin. He should push it open, take her by surprise, grab her and shake her and put an end to this nonsense.

He takes the bottle and waits—helplessly—while she withdraws her hand. He listens to the thick chink of the lock being turned.

Downstairs, he stands at the kitchen sink, turns on the faucet, runs the cold tap until it's icy, then cups his hands and ducks his face. Again and again he bathes his face, but this does not relieve the tightness across his temples, the pounding behind his eyes. He takes the Excedrin, then walks down the hall and opens the front door, stares across his driveway to the lot next door. The boy has gone inside.

The lawn over there needs mowing, and the old growth on the foundation shrubs hasn't been trimmed. A street like this, once you let one place get run down, the whole neighborhood goes to hell. He wonders which realtor handled the rental, who he should complain to. Looking over at the house where he now has for a neighbor a perfect nutcase, Ned again feels a heavy, familiar helplessness.

He would like to ask someone what do to about Rose. Doc Blessing hasn't been able to help. Oh, he gave her pills, but after a week, she refused to take them. Reverend Wills has talked to them both, but that hasn't changed a thing. It's as if Ned married one woman—a woman who was a kind and good wife, a good mother, too, who took an interest in things—and then one day, an accident, a stupid goddamned accident, and nothing was the same.

Rose closed. Just plain shut up. The first thing was she refused to drive. Just downright refused to drive. Initially, he supposed it was because she was afraid of something like getting in an accident herself. Patiently he pointed out how foolish this was, how lightning didn't strike twice, how after the Covington kid drowned in the lake, the rest of the family hadn't stopped swimming, for Christ's sake. "Sell the car," she told him. Sell the car? The Pontiac he bought her just the month before? The first new car they ever had? The car she was so crazy about she washed it nearly every day, like a teenager? He put it off, offering excuses, sure that she'd come around, until the day she told him if he didn't sell it, she would. He knew by the expression on her face that she meant it.

He keeps waiting for her to get over her grief. He tries to recall what it was like before. Nights, he sits in his recliner, staring at reruns of "M*A*S*H" and tries to remember Rose. His Rose. Before. He goes back to the beginning, when he and Rose were young, long before Todd. One night his brain slipped right back to a time before they were married, the picture so clear it could have been playing on the screen in front of him. A hot summer night. He and Rose in the car. A Chevy, the blue-and-cream '63. They were heading over to the lake, to the old pavilion where they used to hold Saturday night dances, the one the town still rents out to the Polish for their polka parties. Lying there next to Rosie on the army blanket he took from the Chevy trunk, lying so still he scarcely dared to breathe, resting his hand on the fullness of her breast, feeling her heart rise and fall under his palm, feeling the life there, feeling all the promise Rose held in that sweet and perfect breast . . . Lying there he felt his hand begin to tremble, shake beyond his control. Then she put her hand over his, steadying them both. He was so in love with her then, he would have given her anything, given her the sun had she asked, so in love with her it scared him.

Remembering never helps. It only makes the ache worse. In addition to losing a son, he's lost his wife, too.

Why can't she come back to him? Doesn't she think he misses Todd? Doesn't she know something breaks inside a man when he buries his son? Doesn't she know that when he put Todd in the ground, a lot of his dreams were buried there, too?

God knows, he loved his son. And he loves Rose; he really does. He loves Rose, but she is trying that love. Things happen to people: Accidents. Illness. But people get on with their lives. Christ, it isn't right, not normal to act like the funeral was yesterday, instead of five years ago.

Rose's grief, Ned thinks. Rose's grief will kill me, too.

CHAPTER 6

❧ R O S E

"Rose?"

She hears Ned calling her from the hall. "Rosie? You in there?" The bathroom is the only room in the house with a lock, but even this can't prevent his questions from sliding through wood panels. "Rosie?" His voice holds a mixture of concern and aggrievement. It seeps through the door like smoke.

She can't make herself answer. She sits on the toilet and rocks back and forth, her arms wrapped around her midsection. She hasn't had a spell like this for a while. Weeks. Months.

After a while, the sound of laughter pulls her to the window, and she looks down on the neighbor's yard. That boy is still outside. Now he is kicking a ball around the grass. She yanks the shade to the sill, as if it were possible to shut out the unfairness of it. How is it possible that Opal Gates be given a child, *blessed* with a child when she is little more than a child herself, when she doesn't know enough—or care enough—to put shoes on her boy's feet?

She moans, and the sound curls inside her chest like smoke, too deep to escape.

Ned knocks again.

"Rose, let me in. I need some aspirin. I've got a hell of a headache."

There's aspirin in the kitchen, on the shelf by the sink, but she goes to the medicine cabinet, takes out the Excedrin, unlocks the bathroom door.

She catches a quick glimpse of him, his face pale, slack with pain, and feels a spasm of guilt. Recently he's been getting these headaches. She is truly sorry that she can't help him, can't come out of the bathroom. She can almost picture what she should do, what in fact she has done in the distant past, what he wants now. She should lead him to the living room, to his green recliner. You just relax, she should say. Just sit here and rest while I go heat some milk. He'd close his eyes, and she'd run a hand over the furrow between his brows, her fingers cool on his skin. When she came back with the cup of warm milk, she'd bring a washcloth, one she'd wrung in ice water. Rosie, he'd say, you're an angel. What would I do without you? He'd reach an arm out, his eyes still closed, and his hand would rest on the curve of her hip, the touch comforting to them both, more soothing than words. She allows herself to hold this picture for a moment, but the woman offering the cup of warm milk, the woman who would welcome the weight of a heavy hand on her hip, this woman is someone else—not her. She lets this scene slip from her grasp, from possibility. She hands the bottle to him, relocks the door, shuts out the sight of his tired face. There is room in her heart for only so much pain.

She listens to his footsteps on the stairs; then the house falls quiet. Has he gone to the living room? Is he in the recliner? She hears the muted sound of voices from the television.

The medicine cabinet is still open. She straightens out the contents, the minutiae of their lives. Q-Tips, toothpaste, dental floss, an old half-used tube of hemorrhoid ointment, Ben-Gay, tweezers, a hand mirror, a box of Band-Aids. A vial of oil of cloves, nearly empty. Ned's Tums and his bottle of Pepto-Bismol. Jergens lotion.

Downstairs, the phone rings, a shrill sound that cuts into the air. For a moment, she fears it is Anderson Jeffrey, although in the past he has called only in the morning.

THE FIRST NIGHT OF THE WRITING CLASS—THE ROOM smelled of chalk and dry books, of anxious hope and dusty disappointment, like every childhood classroom she'd ever been in. That first night, he came in looking all neat and newly shaved with the cleanest fingernails she'd ever seen on a man outside of Doc Blessing and Reverend Wills—cause enough for suspicion right there—and before they had time to catch their breaths or decide whether or not they liked him, Mr. Anderson Jeffrey had them writing.

"Make a list of things that are important to you," he said. "Things you care about." All around her, Rose heard the scratchings of pens and pencils on paper, as if forty years had vanished in one instant. She felt sweaty. Sick. It had been a mistake to come, but leaving would be worse.

She risked a glance at the other students. Middle-aged women mostly, although there were two older men—both bearded—and one young woman with a layer of makeup you wouldn't wear at night let alone in broad daylight. Rose couldn't imagine what any of them were writing down. What was so important to them, and how did they know it so fast, without even taking the time you'd think you'd need to consider something like that? She dropped her hands to her lap, smudged her palms across her skirt. Here she was past fifty, and she might as well be twelve with the scratchy, busy sound of the other students writing still holding the power to paralyze her. She wondered if it was too late to transfer to the quilt-making class.

At least she could be doing something productive. *Milk*, she printed carefully. *Eggs. Coffee. Bisquick. Tums.* For Ned. The bottle by the kitchen sink was nearly empty. *Tuna fish.* Starkist was on sale this week. *Margarine. Ajax cleanser.* She was almost finished when she heard Anderson Jeffrey say, "Okay. That was the warm-up. Now we're going to write." Hot writing, he called it.

"Just choose a word from your list," he said. "Pick a word that speaks to you and write whatever comes to mind." As if it were that simple.

"What if nothing comes?" the painted woman asked. He smiled and said, "Put down anything; just keep your pencil moving. Or write, 'Nothing is coming; I can't write. Nothing is coming; I can't write.' And keep doing it over and over until something comes."

Rose couldn't imagine. What kind of teacher was he anyway?

There was a giggle from the back of the room.

Anderson Jeffrey smiled. "Trust the process," he said.

"How long?" one of the bearded men asked.

"Until you stop," he said.

Rose stared at her paper. *Milk. Eggs. Bisquick. Tuna fish.* If she'd dared, she would have left right then. She supposed she could write

Nothing is coming for a while and that was easier than the commotion of leaving. She took up her pen and put down the words *I can't write; Nothing is coming*, filling nearly half the page.

She was beginning another line when her eyes flashed up to the grocery list and landed on *Tuna fish*. She copied the words and then, without even planning it, she was writing about the sandwiches her mother used to make for picnics when she was a child, how she'd empty the contents of a can, mash it with a fork, then fold in celery she'd chopped fine, and then salad dressing—always salad dressing instead of mayonnaise so there would be just the right touch of sweetness—all the time humming gaily so that for years after Rose associated tuna fish with happiness and the promise of an outing at the lake.

And then the class was over.

She imagined Ned would be furious when he learned how he poured good money down the drain so she could write a grocery list, a half page filled with *I can't write*, and a paragraph about fifty-year-old tuna fish. Of course, as it turned out, he had a lot more to worry about than the money he had wasted on the class.

ROSE PUSHES ALL THOUGHTS OF ANDERSON JEFFREY AND THE writing class from her mind. Perhaps she will go downstairs, act as if this were an ordinary night, as if she has not spent hours locked in the bathroom. Before she can gather herself together, Ned returns.

"Are you going to be making dinner?" The aggrieved tone in his voice has gained ascendancy. He has traveled from concern to exhaustion to anger. She can't face any of this. He wants too much from her.

When she doesn't answer, he gives up, goes back downstairs. Kitchen sounds float up, reach her through the locked door. A cupboard door closing. A pan slapped down on the range with more force than required. Sharp noises, each a messenger of Ned's anger, telegrams of his resentment, his frustration. The sound of the television is louder now. The excited tones of a sports announcer rise up the stairs.

She can't stay here forever. Eventually, she'll have to unlock the door, return to life. She raises the window shade and watches the sky turn pink. *Red sky at night, sailor's delight*. It doesn't matter to her. Good day or bad. Rain or sun. In the house below, the ball game ends abruptly. She hears the distant sound of water running through the pipes as the toilet flushes in the downstairs bath. He is done trying to reach her. Through the door she hears the sounds of familiar ritual as he readies himself for bed. His footsteps on the stairs. The chink of coins as he takes them from his pockets and sets them on the dresser, the rustling of clothes as he undresses. The sound of a drawer opening as he takes out his pajamas. The click of the switch on the bedside lamp. The long sigh he always gives as he climbs into bed, as if letting out an extra breath he's held all day. She pictures him slipping between sheets he won't notice are fresh, being careful to stay on his side of the bed, even though she is not yet there. She can imagine the scent he brings to the bed, a smell that recently has altered. Body chemistry betrays us, she thinks. It reveals every change. Doctors should pay more attention to this.

She remembers smells: the clean milky smell of Todd as an infant, his firm little body perfumed with the intoxicating scent of baby sweat, the occasional acidity of spit-up; then later, when he turned from toddler to boy, the scent had sharpened to a childish sweat, a smell that held the fresh richness of wind and sun, like laundry just taken in from the line. And later still, the teenage years when he'd come home from the practice field wrapped in a serious, manly smell. Vibrant and salty and strong.

And Ned. How she once loved the scent of him. Coccooned in his arms, she would inhale the odor seeping from his pores, drinking it in as if she could never get enough. Lately there has been an acrid smell that reminds her of her father, a sourness that hangs in the air around his skin. Again it brings home to her that Ned is getting older.

She lifts a forearm to her nose, inhales. Her skin smells dry, like something stored in tissue.

SHE OPENS THE DOOR, GOES OUT TO THE HALL, TO TODD'S room. She stands for a moment at the threshold.

After the accident, she would come here every night. She believed the strength of her love, her connection to her son, couldn't be sheared, not even by death. She believed that somehow he would come to her. If you believe enough, it can happen. So she sat in his room waiting, holding on to something of his—a piece of his clothing, a favorite toy, once his toothbrush, another time a sweat-stiffened sock she could not bring herself to throw away or launder.

Now she continues down the hall, past their room. The sound of Ned's snoring drifts out to her. He has left a night-light on at the top of the stairs, and she uses its faint glow to navigate her way down the steps. In the kitchen, she flips on the overhead light. It takes a moment for her eyes to adjust to the harsh brightness. Her empty laundry basket sits by the back door, a reminder that the wash is still on the line. Ned has left his dishes in the sink, and she reconstructs his meal from the traces. Toast, a can of Campbell's Hearty Man Vegetable Beef Soup, a wedge of leftover tart cherry pie.

There is one slice left, and she warms it in the microwave—another appliance she distrusts, all those invisible, powerful waves doing who knows what. She eats standing at the counter, letting the cherry filling sit in her mouth with agreeable sourness. When she is finished, she fills the sink with water, squirts in detergent, submerges her hands to their chore.

After she has rinsed the last plate, she checks the back door. Ned has already locked it. Thirty-five years ago, when they first moved into this house, neither of them locked a door, but Normal has changed a lot in three decades. Now, in addition to the Yale, they have a dead bolt on both their front and back doors.

She listens to the familiar creaking of the house as it settles into sleep. The droning of the refrigerator, the deeper hum of the furnace, the scratching of a rose briar against the kitchen window. They should be cut back, before the deep frost. Another chore for Ned.

"Foolish of us to keep this place," he told her over dinner last night. "It's too big for the two of us. Too much upkeep." They were eating roast pork, and when he said that about the house being too big for them, the piece of meat she was swallowing stuck in her chest. For the rest of the night it stayed there, lodged and burning beneath her breastbone. Finally, sometime after midnight, she had to get out of bed and take two of his Tums.

More and more he has been talking about a time in the near future—three to five years is his plan—when they will sell the house and the station, take the profits, and head south. Buy a place in Florida. He painted the picture for her. No more winter blizzards, or state taxes, or days spent repairing busted transmissions. When he talks this way, Rose's heart congeals with something close to hatred. Like the time three years ago when they repainted the kitchen and he wanted to brush right over the pencil marks on the framework of the doorway going into the hall, lines demarcating Todd's growth from toddler to teen. Rose wouldn't hear of it. These are the visual marks that their son existed, that he stood precisely two feet eight inches at two years and five feet three at twelve. Why would Ned want to forget?

"Let's make a move while we're still young enough to enjoy life," he said through a mouthful of pork, as if Rose could ever again enjoy life. "It makes a lot of sense," he said.

Not to Rose. Nothing on earth could make her move from this house. Just the thought of someone else moving in makes her physically ill. The first thing the new owners would do is paint over those lines on the kitchen doorjamb, erasing the yardstick of their son's growth. Doesn't Ned understand? This house is Todd's house. If Ned wants to get rid of the station, that is his business, but she isn't selling the house.

Lord knows, since Todd's death she has no illusion that she can control one single thing in this universe, but she can't help but cling to the nearly superstitious belief that if she can just freeze things, keep them the same, she and Ned will escape further harm and she will get a sign from Todd. In spite of all contrary evidence she clings to this last belief.

Lately, in spite of her efforts, things are changing. Her balance is precarious, as if deep inside she is undergoing a tectonic plate shift, like the one she heard about on a *Nova* show Ned watched. When the narrator explained that imperceptible and subtle movements occur within the earth's crust and that these alterations precede earthquakes, she felt a jolt of recognition. Since the accident this feeling has been growing, and she has especially felt it this fall, as if her interior world were oscillating in minute and dangerous movements. Danger hangs invisible in the air. Threatening.

She turns out the kitchen light and heads up the hall stairs, guided by the faint glow of the night-light Ned has left on for her. The world outside is silent save for the distant barking of the McDonalds' collie.

She undresses in the dark, slides into bed, careful not to disturb Ned. He is a good man. Honest and hard working. She is lucky to have him. She repeats these words like a prayer.

He moans slightly in his sleep. She wonders if he is sick—those worrisome headaches—and she feels the unpleasant sting of guilt for turning him away earlier. What if he has a tumor? An aneurysm?

Could she stand to lose him too? Could she stand to lose another member?

After Todd died, Reverend Wills gave them a book written for couples who experienced the loss of a child. "A lost member," the author wrote. Like a leg lopped off, Rose thought as she read the words. Or an arm. The book said that the death of a child could bring a couple closer or drive them apart, that couples either turned to each other for comfort, tried to make sense out of the tragedy and discover spiritual support, or they divorced, the assault of a child's death too much for their marriage to withstand.

Neither has happened to her and Ned. They just float, suspended in time, waiting for a life raft to find them.

CHAPTER 7

❧ O P A L

DURING HER FIRST TWO MONTHS IN NORMAL, OPAL had prepared herself for a call from Billy, but the weeks have passed without so much as a single word except for the messages he relays through her mama, messages Opal knows enough not to trust. Melva can carry on all she wants about Billy missing her and Zack, but if he misses them all so goddamned much, why doesn't he at least call? At first this lack of communication irritated Opal, but now she is reassured by it. It reinforces her belief that Billy is relieved to have them out of his life, that he won't make any fuss.

When he finally does call she is so totally unprepared that his voice sends a jolt straight to her stomach.

"HI, BILLY," SHE MANAGES — COOL AS YOU PLEASE — AND thinks, *Shit*. She slides down to the floor, her back against the cupboard, and cradles the phone base in her lap, unconsciously taking the same pose she held every night the fall of her junior year when, night after night, she would slouch down on the living room carpet and hold the phone tight against her ear. For hours, they would talk in whispers, tones varyingly cottony or tender, silky or hushed, as they progressed through the stages: attraction to flirtation, first date to dating, steady dating to phone sex. Phone sex led to the real thing—sex on the bench seat of his black Ram or behind one of the gravestones at the back of the Baptist cemetery, anywhere they could be alone for five minutes. Who would believe that what began with hot whispers and the thrilling tenor of one boy's voice could lead to such trouble, that it would end in tears of disbelief and crisis—unimaginable crisis?

"Shit, I miss you, Opal." He has lowered his voice. First time they've talked since she left New Zion, and he's acting like they spoke last week. He is *so* out of touch with reality. "How's Zack?" he is saying.

As if he anything like cares. "Well, he's just fine." She lets her eyes roam around the kitchen and finally fix on the small yellow-and-blue spot stuck straight in the middle of a cupboard door.

The sticker—peeled from a banana—was there when she moved in, a remnant left by the Montgomerys. It was so startlingly out of place in the sterile, avocado kitchen that Opal had immediately taken it as a sign. Stuck like that in the middle of the cupboard, what else can it be? She has not yet figured out the meaning. *Chiquita.* Wasn't there a singer from South America with that name? Or is she confusing her with the character in the banana ads?

"Opal? You still there?"

She pulls her attention from the decal. "I'm here."

"I miss you, Opal."

She pauses, knowing the prescribed response, the answer Billy waits for: *I miss you, too.* The wire hums with her silence.

"How're you doing? You okay?" he asks, as if Melva hasn't been feeding him regular reports.

"I'm great," she says in a baton twirler's chirp. "Just great."

"Yeah, well that's wonderful," he says in a voice suddenly gone flat.

"I've rented a house," she says, "two stories, three bedrooms, a backyard. It's on a dead-end street which is good—safe for Zack—and there's a nice older couple next door." She knows she is babbling but can't stop. "I've enrolled Zack in preschool and there's a toy store here that is interested in the dolls."

Instantly she regrets mentioning her work. Although it is the first thing she was ever good at—really and surprisingly good at—Billy hates that she makes dolls, though what it is about them that makes him so mad is beyond her.

"Well, I'm glad to hear everything's so terrific with you, Opal, because—not that you asked—but me, I'm not doing so great."

Crap. Not five minutes have passed in the first conversation they've had since she left New Zion and already it's heading straight downhill. It was mentioning the dolls. She stares at the yellow sticker, and just like that the singer's name comes to her. Not Chiquita. Carmen. Carmen Miranda. But that doesn't help her figure out the meaning of the sticker.

"That story you fed me," Billy says, "about going to visit a relative?"

Reluctantly she drags her attention back to the call. "Yes."

"Well, damn it all, Opal. You lied."

Whatever. "Lied?"

"About visiting a relative."

Ancient history, Opal thinks.

"Your daddy told me you don't even have relatives in Ohio," he says in an injured tone, as if this is the important part of her lie.

"I know," she says. Sometimes he can be so *thick* she has to wonder if someone has to zip his fly for him.

"Well, shit, Opal. I believed you."

"I'm sorry," she says. A bone tossed from the safe distance of six states.

"Sorry doesn't count for much right now," he says.

"Let's don't fight," she says. "There's no point."

"There is a point, and the point is I miss my boy, Opal."

Well, just how did he grow him a paternal streak? Here she's been away for more than two months, and he's just now getting around to calling her. Is she supposed to think he gives an honest damn? And it isn't like he ever paid all that much attention to Zack. He was a bum daddy when they were in New Zion, and Opal can't see why two months' absence would improve matters. Billy barely held Zack when he was an infant, wanted no part of feeding him or—God knows— changing him. And as Zack grew older he whined, "I'm no good with little kids. I don't know what to do with them." So now he's suddenly learned? Quick learner.

"Listen, Opal," he says with a voice so serious that an unexpected thrill of fear courses through her, "I want you back here. I want us to get married, be a family. I mean it, honey."

Fat to no chance of that, she thinks. Just because she made a mistake by getting pregnant, she isn't going to compound it by marrying him. Billy's last name should be He Always Wants What He Can't Have. The most popular kid in New Zion High and the only reason he chose Opal was because she kept him dangling for weeks. Gave him only a little at a time. Had ideas and interests beyond his pretty butt.

"I mean it, Opal. We could get married right away. Give Zack a proper home."

She hears Melva's voice in the "proper home for Zack" comment.

"We've got to talk about this, Opal. We've got to work something out. You can't just stay away like this."

"My being here has nothing to do with you, Billy."

"But Zack has something to do with me. He's my son, too. My blood."

"Like you really wanted him."

His reply is muffled. She hears in the background a voice that is definitely female. A flash of jealousy turns quickly to anger. Calling and acting like he wants to marry her when all the time he's with some slut. Someone like Caryl Jackson who for sure wears her Junior ROTC uniform while she's making out. Caryl Jackson who is as flat as a board without her padded, push-up bra. Well, let him have a battalion of women. It's none of her business.

He cups the receiver with his hand, murmurs something on his end, then says into the phone, "When we're done, your mama wants to talk to you."

"You're calling from my mama's?"

"Yeah."

"What are you doing there?" This news floors her. Is he living there now or what?

"I just stopped by for dinner."

Stopped by? It isn't like her parents' house is exactly on his way home.

"Opal, we got to talk. You can't shut me out like this." There is another muffled exchange on his end, and then the phone is handed to Melva.

"This isn't easy for any of us," her mama begins. "I'm ashamed to think a child of mine could behave in such an irresponsible way."

"This isn't about you, Mama," she cuts in—Lordy, hasn't she heard all this before—but Melva is off and running.

"If you can't think of my feelings, or your daddy's or Billy's, you could at least consider your son. He needs a daddy."

Opal is not as indifferent to this as her mama might think and has spent many nights brooding over this very point. From day one, she has been concerned about how the separation would affect Zack, and several times it has occurred to her that she should mention Billy to Zack, ask straight out if he misses him. But then she thinks, why disturb sleeping dogs? Of course she would die before giving her mama this much ammunition.

"For the life of me," Melva says, "I can't figure out what you're doing. Sometimes I think you deliberately set out to upset people's lives, to break people's hearts."

Shit. Doesn't her mama know she'd never deliberately set out to hurt people or break their hearts? How can she make Melva understand she is just trying the only way she knows to keep from drowning in the sea of other people's hopes and plans and expectations, from letting herself be talked into a marriage she knows in the deepest part of her heart would be a mistake?

"Are you listening to me, Raylee?"

"Mama," she says. "I can't do this with you."

"Do what?" Melva gets her hard tone on.

"This conversation. We've been over this all before."

"For all the good it did." Melva says. "Now you listen to me—"

Listen to her? Hasn't she been listening to her all her life? Lecturing at Opal is the sum and total of her mama's concept of mother-daughter relating.

"You can't expect people to accept this sort of thing lying down. You can't turn people's lives upside down and expect them to sit by and do nothing."

"What the hell is that supposed to mean?" Melva is working on her last nerve here. In spite of her best intentions, Opal is shouting.

"There's no need to raise your voice to me," her mama says. "I just want you to realize that your actions have consequences."

Actions have consequences. Hasn't she heard this original piece of philosophy from Melva about three trillion times in her life? "You gave me that lecture when I was a kid, Mama. I'm not fifteen."

Fifteen. Standing in the living room unable to meet her daddy's eyes. Melva ranting on about shame and disappointment and how she won't be able to hold her head up around town and how she, Raylee, had her whole life still ahead of her, then getting down to the business at hand. *We know a doctor . . . this early on . . . a safe procedure.* Her mama couldn't bring herself to say "abortion," yet the word hung in the air like a sour smell. Her own reaction, a swift plunge into lethargy—just let her mama take command—was followed by rationalization. She wouldn't be the first in her class; she could go on as if nothing had happened, an easy way out. She was as surprised as her mama and daddy when she heard herself say no.

That was fifteen.

"Well, stop acting as if you were," Melva continues. "You're so gosh darn wrapped up in yourself you can't see we're heartbroken here. Absolutely heartbroken with missing our darling boy."

Opal can't traverse this territory one more time. "I have to go, Mama. I just got Zack to bed, and I think I hear him crying."

"Of course he's crying. He misses his daddy. He misses all of us. What you are doing to him is beyond irresponsible. It's criminal. Actions have consequences," she repeats. "Don't you be coming back to me down the road and saying I didn't warn you."

After Opal hangs up, Melva's words echo. *Don't you be coming back to me and saying I didn't warn you.* She closes her eyes and concentrates on rubbing away this message. She won't let poisonous thoughts spark her own fears. This is just another of her mama's idle threats, more manipulation to gain control and talk her into returning to New Zion.

She stares at the Chiquita sticker as if it could provide her with the answer. She sure could use a sign about now.

The first time she had a date with Billy, she saw a sign. He pulled up in front of her house in the Dodge Ram pickup he was so proud of, a truck with a cab so high off the ground she knew she'd need his help to climb aboard. Immediately she caught sight of the windsurfer sticking up out of the truck bed, and even from a distance she could read the purple letters scrawled across the board's broad fiberglass body: *No Fear.* Much later she wondered how she could have misinterpreted a message that, on the surface of it, seemed so obvious.

Reading signs is like hearing music. They're always there; you've just got to tune into the right frequency. She stares at the sticker. She hasn't got the dial nailed on this one.

The phone call reverberates in her head. She's wounded to think her mama believes she goes through life setting out to shatter people's hearts. Is Billy's heart broken? She has no idea. But she won't marry Billy just so Zack has a daddy, just so it looks good for her mama, just so her mama can hold her head up. She doesn't love Billy enough, even if—she has to admit now—his voice still has power over her. Even if that night up in the old burial ground behind New Zion Baptist she had done things with Billy that even now could make her blush.

The power of sex. And where does that get you?

Jesus, he'd turned her on with his touch in ways she wouldn't have imagined possible. It got so if he just drew his fingernail down the inside of her arm, she would get wet. Now, remembering, she feels heat spread through her belly. Well, shit. It's this appetite for sex that got her into this fix in the first place.

She's heard about that big-league ballplayer who had a sexual addiction and thinks this is what she had with Billy. Out of bed, the honest truth is, he bored her. But give him five minutes alone with her in a bed and her brain disappeared, her body like a country invaded by a foreign power. One of the hardest things about splitting from Billy is missing sex. Well, forget sex. She has no intention of getting caught in that trap again.

So what does the banana sticker mean? Is she supposed to move to South America? Sometimes she thinks it would take a distance that far to escape from Billy—and Mama. That far to find out who she is and what she is meant to do with her life.

SHE CLIMBS THE STAIRS TO CHECK ON ZACK. IN THE DIM light she negotiates her way through the rope Zack has strung across his floor, a cat's cradle that interlaces the legs of his bureau and bed. This web is a new creation, one he relies on to trap the werewolf, a monster that has come into his imagination—and bedroom—since the Halloween party at school.

He is bathed in the glow of his Batman night-light, already lost in the hard, serious sleep of childhood. Even in sleep, he looks remarkably self-possessed, as if he has gone to a place she does not know. Sometimes the intensity of his sleep frightens her.

She pulls the blanket up over his stick arms, then reaches over and brushes a sweaty twist off his forehead, fingers the fine hair just behind his ears. A quick stirring moves in her breast, a nearly sexual twist in her belly. When he was an infant, her nipples dripped milk whenever she held him and, holding him, smelling him, she'd feel sweet, deep spasms grip her pelvis.

She is astonished that she can feel something so fiercely outside of herself. Yet Zack is a part of her, too, such a true part that if she were led blindfolded into a room of three hundred five-year-olds, she knows she would be able to locate him easily, instantly, like an animal finding its young. All this love by accident.

She tucks the blanket around him, reluctant to leave. She could spend hours watching him sleep. Often she gets lost in the meditation of watching him, her breathing unconsciously and automatically adjusting so that her chest rises and falls in concert with his.

He sleeps exactly like Billy—on his back, one arm flung out, palm up. But then there is a lot of his daddy in Zack. In his lanky body, his straight eyebrows, his stubborn jaw, the way his ears jut out a little. Sometimes it seems like the only thing she has given her son is his red hair. And his name.

During her pregnancy, Opal made lists and lists of names. Almost from the first she knew she was going to have a son, a boy her mama wanted to name after her own father, Opal's granddaddy, a choice utterly out of the question since, besides being ugly, Hackett meant "little hacker." No way her son was going to carry a name with a meaning like that.

It was not easy to find a name that, according to her copy of *1000 Names for Your New Baby*, matched up to a powerful meaning. Gunther, for instance, meant bold warrior. Great concept, but *Gunther*? By the second day of school the whole class would be calling him Grunter.

"Why can't we name him William?" Billy asked when she showed him the final list of prospects. She was more than seven months along by then and they had no sex life to speak of, which only made her nudgy as a mule.

"We just can't." She had done a lot of thinking about the subject and tried to convey some of these thoughts to him. "Names are important," she said. "It's the naming, the calling, that creates a thing."

"Raylee," he said, this being three years before her own name change. "Raylee, what the hell are you talking about?"

It was a difficult thing to explain, especially to Billy. It was one of those ideas she got—a perception that she latched on to as it floated by and that she understood at once the importance of, even knowing there was still more meaning to be got. How could she have explained it to Billy, who liked things concrete and laid out in front of him precise and unchanging, like the free throw line in the gym where he'd spent so many hours?

At times, when Opal is explaining something, words come out of her mouth that she doesn't even know she's been thinking. It was like that when she tried to explain to Billy. "It's the calling that creates a thing," she repeated. "It's by naming a child that we both possess him and give him away."

"Raylee," he said. "I hate it when you talk like that."

AS SHE TIPTOES OUT OF ZACK'S ROOM, SHE REPLAYS THE phone call, trying to pin down why she feels uneasy. Months later, remembering this night, she will wonder how she could have ignored her mama's warnings, how she could have forgotten about the strength of Billy's resolve once he made up his mind to something. How could there not have been a *sign*?

CHAPTER 8

❧ OPAL

THE CALL HAS LEFT OPAL TOO EDGY FOR SLEEP, AND SHE heads into the dining room, where her current project lies on the cutting table.

The Montgomerys' maple drop leaf works just fine for cutting and sewing, and Opal has set up a card table for painting. Squares of fabric—tulle, cotton in a variety of prints, satin, organza, and denim— are piled in one corner of the room. Bags of kapok are stored beneath the table. Several plastic tackle boxes are stacked against one wall, their individual compartments filled with buttons, rhinestones, aglets, sequins, snaps, and hooks and eyes.

She picks up the order form and studies the girl in the photo attached. Dutch-cut brown hair and serious eyes that peer out through round-framed glasses. "Leave out the glasses," the grandmother has noted on the form. She wants a ballerina, the number one choice for girl dolls. Why can't people use their imagination? It's clear as warts on a toad's back that this child—Ellen, she reads on the form—was not consulted about the decision. Opal sees intelligence in the girl's eyes, determination in her mouth. This child wants to walk on the moon, not pivot on knuckled-under toes. People can be so blind.

In the past few weeks, word has spread about her dolls. Opal has picked up a half dozen orders from some of the other mothers at Zack's preschool, and the local toy store has already reordered. The owner has promised to put her in next year's Christmas catalog—if Opal is still here next December.

The dolls were an unexpected side effect of her pregnancy, and she has the Horse to thank for that.

The minute news of her condition reached the school, Miss Horsley called her in for a conference. New Zion High policy prohibited pregnant girls from attending school, like they had some communicable disease, but Opal would be allowed to graduate with her class if she kept up with a tutor. Well, that suited Opal just fine. The last thing she needed was to have Caryl Jackson and the rest of the Junior ROTC corps gawking at her belly, whispering about her in the cafeteria, ragging on her in the girls' locker room when no teachers were in sight.

Hanging around the house didn't strike her as such a bad alternative, but nothing turned out like she expected. For one thing, her mama watched her every move, fixing her with an eagle's eye, as if five miles down the road there was more trouble Opal was fixing to get into.

No free ride here, young lady, so don't you be expecting one, Melva said, although the last thing on earth Opal knew she could expect from her mama was a free ride.

You're old enough to be having a child, you're old enough to be helping out around the house, her mama said, and then practically turned her into a slave.

For the life of her, Opal couldn't figure out why women liked to keep house. Cleaning the same rooms over and over. Washing the same clothes, doing the same dishes. Making the same bed, which when you think about it, is a colossal waste of time. She looked at her mama's friends and wondered how they stood it.

Except for Sujette, none of her own classmates wanted much to do with her, and the women she used to sit for no longer called, acting just like Miss Horsley, as if being pregnant made her unfit to watch their children, even though she had been sitting for them since she was twelve. One afternoon, well into the fourth month of spine-curling boredom, she was flipping though one of Melva's magazines when she saw a pattern for making a doll.

Right away she saw she had a knack for it. Her first time sewing and it turned out real good, the making of it satisfying something deep inside. She could understand then why her Grandma Gates could spend hours embroidering designs on pillow slips. There was something *pleasing* about creating. Inside of a month she had made four more dolls. And even using the same pattern, each one turned out with its own individual personality. Of course Melva thought the whole thing was foolishness, but it calmed Opal, and Lord knows by the sixth month, between Billy and Melva, her last nerve could use all the soothing it could get.

At her Aunt May's urging, Grandma Gates took several of the dolls to the Presbyterian Church fair, and before an hour went by, every single one of them sold.

After Zack was born, Opal continued to make the dolls, and by the time he was two she got the idea of painting their faces to look like children she knew and dressing them in costumes. Miniature sailors and pilots, doctors and artists, cowboys and football players, movie stars and dancers.

The toy store in New Zion carried her work, and before she knew it she had more orders than she could keep up with. Double your prices, Aunt May advised. Stupidity, said Mama. According to Melva, doll making was not an occupation fit for an adult. Her mama kept a running tally of Opal's classmates: which ones were married, which ones graduated college.

You're a disappointment that just keeps going on, her mama said. I don't know how you can let yourself settle for so much less. Well, shit, nothing Opal could see about Melva's life was anything you'd want to sit up nights waiting for.

SHE REACHES ACROSS THE TABLE AND PICKS UP ANOTHER order form. The child in this snapshot is pretty in a blank-faced way that reminds her of Suzanne Jennings before she latched on to Jitter Walton and began prancing all over town in his letter jacket. This one she is supposed to make into a Roaring Twenties flapper. Honestly, where did these people come up with their ideas? The most successful projects are those where the parents or grandparents leave the costume decisions to her. Usually she can look at the photo of a child and just know what to do. Sometimes a serious face can hide the temperament of a clown. And this one—this pretty child who looks like she is slow in the department of serious ambition—Opal can see that behind the blank stare this is a child who wants something more.

But then, everyone wants something more. Sometimes the longing is empty, a nameless yearning, but if you're lucky, you can put a name to it. Billy for instance, once wanted to play basketball for the Tar Heels. He wanted to be famous. Now, if she can believe him, he wants to marry her.

Opal's "something more" is a real family. Not a family that sticks together out of habit or because it looks good to outsiders, like her parents, or one where you stay there because you have to, out of duty, like Billy wants. She wants a family that stays together because every person knows that is absolutely where they *belong*, a family where people care for each other. This is exactly what she plans to have with Zack. She knows that she will be a better mama than Melva.

She sets the doll aside and heads for the kitchen. Her period's due in about four days, and she has a serious case of the munchies.

Plus she's horny.

In spite of her best intentions to once and for all be done with sex, hearing Billy's voice has set things moving. How can sex do that to you? Stir an ache so deep it's almost like something growing inside? Make your skin feel too tight?

She pours herself a glass of Coke and combs the cupboards for something sweet. She rejects a jar of applesauce, shakes out a handful of Fruit Loops. She would kill for a brownie about now—can almost feel the velvety weight on her tongue. Cereal just doesn't cut it. Her craving for chocolate reminds her of being pregnant. It had been lemon then. Cake, candy, sherbet, pudding, anything with citrus.

The kitchen clock reads 10:40. The Stop and Shop is open for another twenty minutes.

She climbs the stairs to Zack's door and listens to the sound of his steady, deep inhalations. The blanket is still tight up over his chest where she had tucked it earlier. She considers waking him, bundling him up for a quick trip to the store, then thinks of how it will be such a hassle later, trying to get him settled down and back to sleep. It seems like way too much work. Maybe she'll just forget the whole thing.

Or she could slip out by herself.

Not once in five years has she left Zack alone. Not even for five minutes.

She weighs the need for brief moments of freedom—for chocolate— against the risk of leaving him. The trip out to the store and back won't take more than fifteen minutes. Total. Round trip. What could go wrong?

She picks her way through the webbing of twine woven across the floor to his bed.

"Zack?" she whispers, then, a shade louder, "Zack?" He does not move. She recalculates the time it will take. Twenty minutes tops. What could happen to him asleep in a locked house?

She searches for a sign and finally decides she will say his name five times—one for each year of his life—and if he doesn't wake, that is the sign he'll be all right alone while she runs to the store.

"Zack?" she whispers. "Sugah? Zack?"

He doesn't even twitch.

"Zack." Louder this time. Then two more times before she picks her way back across the room.

Simple choices. A hunger for chocolate. Such an *ordinary* thing. How could she have foreseen that it is the beginning of all the hurt and sorrow that is to come?

AS SHE DRIVES ALONG MAIN STREET SHE CAN—EVEN IN THE shadows beyond the streetlights—pick out the library, the town hall, the bank. The realtor told her they are constructed of granite cut from quarries on the outskirts of the village, adding that early in the century the quarries had been a major industry in Normal. Opal thinks it gives a real solid touch to the town. This is a place that could give a person *roots*. She passes by the Catholic church, also forged of stone, and then the Methodist and Baptist churches, these of clapboard, with soaring steeples that pierce the sky. The Halloween decorations haven't been removed yet, and there are cornstalks at the base of every lamppost along the main street. A farmer's wagon with a scarecrow in the driver's seat sits in the center of the square adjacent to a statue of a uniformed man on horseback. The bed is heaped with pumpkins.

The single traffic light is set on blinking yellow, and she slows even though there isn't another car in sight. There is something she likes about being the only one on the street. It reminds her of being a child and the nights she would wake and creep downstairs, going from room to room in the dark, listening, as if the secrets of their house would be revealed at night.

She continues past a small row of shops that occupy two entire blocks of the village center, by large clapboard houses with brick walks that lead through boxwood hedges up to narrow porches. Several of these buildings have been converted to businesses. One is a funeral parlor, another an insurance firm, a third the day care where she has enrolled Zack.

She passes the police and fire stations—lights on inside—the Creamery, which is open, and a diner, which is not. There are a dozen cars in the parking lot of the ice cream shop—couples, she imagines, who have stopped after catching a movie. She is swept by the sudden yearning for the simple pleasure of a Friday night date, for the care-free feeling of being *young*. She drives on past the corner occupied by Ned Nelson's service station and swings into the supermarket parking lot.

At this time of night there is a small crew on, sweeping floors and stocking shelves. Dorothy Barnes is the only cashier.

Opal heads directly for the bakery aisle and is debating between the brownies and eclairs when a voice breaks into her deliberation.

"Got a sweet tooth?"

The first thing she notices is the scar on his cheek, so raised and wide it looks like no one bothered to stitch it up. The second thing is that—scar or not—he's about the best looking guy she's ever seen. She feels a little jolt and for a moment is alive to *possibilities*.

"Me," he says, "I'd go for the brownies. I bet you're Opal."

She manages a nod. Merciful God, he *is* good looking.

"Ty Miller," he says, holding out a hand. "I work for Ned over at the station."

The moment their hands touch, just like that, Opal can feel her heart swell in its cage of bone, can feel her pulse race. No mistaking the spiking of chemistry. She sees trouble coming, stretching ahead like ten miles of bad road.

"I've seen you when you've come by the garage," he says in a deep voice, a voice with the hint of song to it, the kind of voice that can thrill you later just by recalling it. She knows for sure she hasn't seen him before. Like she could forget.

She wants the brownies but because he has suggested them, she grabs the box of eclairs. "Gotta go," she says. "Nice to meet ya."

"You're out late," Dorothy says. "Where's that boy of yours?"

"Sleeping," Opal says. "With the sitter." Her hand still feels tingly from Ty Miller's touch.

"Count your blessings." Dorothy nods toward the rack of tabloids at the end of the counter. "I'll tell you, my heart goes out to her."

"Who?" Opal says. Her heart has still not returned to its regular beat. He must think she's an idiot, racing off like that. *Gotta go*. Jesus.

"Her. You haven't heard about it? It's been on the news for the last day and a half."

"Our television isn't hooked up yet." Opal looks back over her shoulder, but Ty is nowhere in sight.

"It's tragic. Makes you wonder what the world is coming to." Dorothy points to the headline above the photo of a young woman: *Distraught mother begs: Please return my sons*. "It's a crazy world. Something like this happening." She reaches over and grabs the paper off the rack, folds it open to the centerfold. "Those are her boys."

Opal wants to look away. The older of the two children is a sweet-faced boy with huge brown eyes. He looks the same age as Zack. There are other pictures: a child's birthday party, a full-color photo taken in front of a Christmas tree. Opal searches the four smiling faces—mother, father, boys—but can not detect the slightest omen in that photo of any trouble to come.

"Kidnapped," Dorothy announces, dragging the box of eclairs over the scanner. "In Texas. By a Mexican. He jumped right into her car when she was stopped at a red light."

"God." *Zack.* Had she locked the door when she left? She tries to visualize herself turning the key.

"He forced her out of the car at gunpoint," Dorothy continues. "Then he took off with those two poor children still sleeping in the backseat. The mother was on the news this morning, crying. Pleading with the man to bring back her boys." She holds up the paper. "You want this?"

"No." The last thing in the world Opal wants is anything to do with the paper or the tragedy it holds, as if the disaster could leak out, taint her.

Dorothy takes a ten from Opal, hands her change. "That's Texas for you. Course I'm not saying the same thing couldn't happen here. You just never know. The world's turned crazy. I blame it on drugs."

Would Zack even wake if someone broke in?

"We've started a collection." Dorothy indicates a coffee can by the register. Someone has cut a slot in the plastic lid.

"Collection?"

"For a reward. There's a fund. We're sending a check at the end of next week."

Opal stuffs her change through the slot.

FOR SURE SHE LOCKED THE DOOR. SHE *SEES* HERSELF DOING it. The light at the intersection of Main and Maple blinks yellow, and as she slows, she imagines Zack in the backseat, imagines a man approaching the car, wrenching open the door, pointing a pistol at her, sliding into the seat beside her, ordering her to drive. Could she stay calm? Would she panic? Would she dare try anything heroic? That sort of thing works in the movies, but in real life, would it be too dangerous? How could you be sure you wouldn't end up killing everyone in the car, including the child you were trying to save?

The newspaper image of the little boys and their frantic mother plays in her mind. Then Zack's face flashes in front of her. How far would she go to protect him? What would she risk? Everything, she knows. Certainly her own life. At least that.

Her hands are shaking by the time she pulls into the driveway. She has trouble with the house key, the door locked after all.

Inside the quiet is broken only by the hum of the refrigerator. She sets the pastries on the counter, checks the clock. It's 11:15. She hasn't been gone for more than half an hour. She heads for the stairs, and halfway up she hears him.

He is on the floor at the top of the landing, his face puffy from tears.

She takes the remaining stairs two at a time. Sweet Jesus. She'll never leave him again. Not for a minute. A second. Never.

"What happened? Zack. Sugah? What happened?"

"Where were you?" he accuses.

"Downstairs," she says, lying automatically, sinking to the floor by his side, wrapping an arm around his shoulders.

"I called and called." He gives a shuddering breath that collapses into little ragged hiccups.

"I'm sorry, sugah bun." She will never, ever leave him alone again. *Ever.*

"I fell," he announces. The twine from the cat's cradle entangles his feet.

"It's okay, Zack. I'm here now." She tightens her embrace and he yells. It's the pain yell, not the sad yell.

"What is it, Zack?"

"My arm," he says. Tears brim.

"Let me see," she says. In the glow from the downstairs light his arm looks fine, but when she runs her fingers over it, he cries out.

"Okay," she soothes. "Okay, sugah, I won't touch it."

She carries him to her room, careful not to touch the arm, and settles him in her bed, quiets him with two baby aspirin.

"I'm thirsty," he whimpers. "I want Tigger."

She finds the toy on the floor by his bed, brings it to her room, tucks it in beside him, gets him a glass of Coke.

Later, when she is sure he won't waken, she turns on the bedside lamp. His arm *looks* okay. There are no markings. But when she strokes her fingers over his forearm—really barely touching the skin— he whimpers in his sleep.

Months later, when everything begins to fall apart, she comes to believe it was not leaving New Zion that set the nightmare in motion. Not the string of lies she told, lies as tangled as the web of twine that tripped Zack that night. Not even Ty Miller. These things were just *complications*. The beginning was this night. It was the one grievous error of leaving Zack alone while she went to out to satisfy her hunger.

CHAPTER 9

↝ R O S E

AS SOON AS NED DRIVES OFF—EARLIER THAN USUAL since he has a backlog of jobs—Rose gets out the Hoover and starts vacuuming, an unnecessary chore since the house is spotless. All she does every day is housework, over and over, room after room, a mechanical occupation that produces a gleaming house. This past week, she has finished up the fall cleaning: screens taken down, hosed and stacked overhead in the garage; windows washed; curtains laundered and ironed; summer cottons washed and packed away; woodwork scrubbed; kitchen cabinets straightened. This ritual cleaning used to fill her with pleasure, but now she does it mindlessly, without even the dim satisfaction of accomplishment. With just the two of them, the place hardly requires it.

She scratches the spot on her belly. No question it's worse this morning. Earlier she checked in the hand mirror and saw a definite ring of red encircling the mole. No use pretending there isn't *something* going on there, but she is more determined than ever not to let Ned know. If he had a clue, he'd have her at Doc's before she could say Jack Robinson.

We've got the future to consider, Rosie, he'd say, thinking about that day in Florida when they wouldn't have to shovel snow or pay state taxes.

Rose doesn't care about the future. All the future she had died with

Todd. She knows that when a loved one dies, people say things like "a part of me died, too," but a real part of her died in that crash with Todd: The part that goes on to tomorrow. The invisible cord that stretches out like a stream through time, linking one generation to the next. In that one encapsulated moment when Jimmy Sommers spun his pickup into the old elm on the corner of High and Church her future was ripped away. And the hard and bitter truth is that there is no way on earth she can ever reclaim it. Of course, this is the last thing on earth that Ned wants to hear.

You're holding on to grief, he accused her last year. What else do I have, she asked him. You have me, Rosie, he said. You have us.

It isn't enough.

She carries the Hoover into the dining room and slides the floor attachment wand onto the end of the hose. She is bending over to plug in the cord when a loud banging at the back door makes her jump. She's pretty sure who it is. Who else could it be, banging like a wild person? She tightens her grip on the cord and closes her eyes, as if this could make the person outside disappear. Two days ago she saw the boy urinating out by the maple tree. *Urinating.* She can't be expected to put up with this. At the kitchen door, the urgent knocking persists.

She stands perfectly still, but beneath her feet she can feel the floor tremble. The shifting of a continental plate.

"Mrs. Nelson. Mrs. Nelson."

If Rose knew a sign for warding off affliction, she would have made it. Instead, she opens the door. Opal Gates stands there, her face so twisted it is nearly ugly. Her hair sparks out wild. She carries the boy in her arms. His face is pale as flour.

Rose wants to turn right around, shut the door and hide in the safety of her home.

"Zack's hurt," the girl says. "His arm. I'm afraid it might be broken."

The McDonalds' dog yaps in the distance. Crows pick at the turf by the front walk. Grubs, she thinks, although it is well past the season for them. On the street, a black sedan drives by, slows, circles the cul-de-sac, passes again.

"I need to get him to the emergency room. Will you drive us?"

"I—" It has been five years since she has so much as touched a steering wheel. "I don't have a car."

"We'll take mine."

Rose steps back.

"Please. There is no one else I can ask."

Ned, Rose thinks. I need Ned.

The morning of the accident, Ned was there faster than she would have thought possible. John Denton came to the house to inform her of the accident, and when he took one look at her, he phoned right over to the garage. Ned took over, shoring her up, driving them to Mercy, speeding the entire way although all she could think was that he should drive—must drive—faster. In the end all that reckless speed proved futile.

I can't. "I don't drive," she manages.

"I'll drive. You hold Zack and point the way." The girl doesn't wait for more argument. Still carrying the boy, she lopes across their yard to her car, sending the crows flying.

"Don't run," Rose says. "It will jar his arm."

The car floor is a mess, just *thick* with Coke cans and fast food wrappers and Lord knows what else. Rose uses her toe to nudge them aside. As Opal transfers the boy to her, she braces herself. Even so, the familiar weight of a small body against her stomach catches her off guard. Before she can steel herself, a knife blade of something distantly akin to pleasure catches her. She tightens her mouth, stiffens her arms.

The girl chatters nonstop, talking a blue streak, and Rose has to bite her lip to keep from shushing her.

"Hold on, sugah," Opal repeats over and over. "We're almost there." She pronounces it "thaya." Once or twice she takes a hand off the wheel, reaches over, squeezes his knee. "It's gonna be okay, Zack."

As soon as they get to Mercy, Rose plans on calling a taxi.

OUTSIDE THE DOUBLE DOORS OF THE EMERGENCY WING entrance, Opal rolls to a stop, switches off the engine, and runs ahead, calling for Rose to follow. There is nothing for it but to carry the boy inside.

The nurse on duty at the desk takes their name and directs them to the waiting room. *The waiting room.* The room for waiting. The room where she and Ned waited.

Everything is exactly the same, is if days have passed, not years. Gray tweed industrial carpeting. Interlocking chairs with blue plastic seats and chrome arms. Round clock. Magazine rack affixed to the wall. Square laminate-topped table littered with—even this early in the day—empty Styrofoam cups, most holding cold coffee. A *No Smoking* sign. A notice reading, *Please have your insurance information ready.* Off to the left, an alcove with vending machines for coffee and hot chocolate and cold drinks. Five years and not one single thing has been altered. Rose is faint with memory. She wills herself not to run.

WHEN THEY TOLD HER TODD WAS DEAD, SHE WOULDN'T believe it. She wanted to see him, asked to see him. Not now, Rosie. Ned said. Your husband's right, the doctor agreed. It would be better if you don't. She should have insisted. *Ned* should have insisted.

She fainted in the middle of the emergency room, the only time in her life she has ever passed out. They hustled her away in a wheelchair, swooped her off to a small room, made her lie down, whisked the curtains closed. So much activity. Such urgency. For what?

Overly solicitous nurses bustled around bringing water, a pleated paper cup that contained a pill. Left alone at last, she sat right up. Through the curtain she heard voices: the doctor talking to Ned, telling him that Todd had suffered so much brain damage that had he lived he would have been no better than a vegetable. *A vegetable.*

For days the words echoed in her head, giving her no rest, buzzing round and round like a fly trapped between glass and screen. After the funeral, Ned's sister Ethel put her arm around her and said, "It's terrible, Rose, but what with head injuries like that it's a blessing he went. Truly it is." As if *that* was supposed to console her. Truth is, she would have taken Todd if he'd been able to do nothing but drool. No more capable than a cucumber. Taken him and been glad for it. At least he would still be with her. At least she could have cared for him, tended to his needs. Kissed him. Smelled his hair. At least then she would have had a place to pour her love. If Rose knows anything it is this: To stay alive love needs a place to go.

A WORKMAN SITS ACROSS FROM THEM, CUPPING A HAND wrapped in a towel. Blood has already seeped through the folded terrycloth. A child with feverish eyes and flushed cheeks sleeps in his mother's lap. The woman's shoes are unevenly worn and misshapen.

Cheap shoes. It pays to take care of your feet, Rose thinks. Your feet and your teeth are no place to save money.

The double doors glide open with a pneumatic whoosh, and a young man dressed in athletic shorts and a U Mass jersey hobbles in on crutches, gives the receptionist his name and insurance card, is instructed to join the others in the waiting room. He gives Opal the eye.

The clock reads 7:30. It doesn't seem possible that only a half hour has passed since Ned left for the station. It feels like weeks.

FIVE YEARS AGO, WHEN THEY LEFT THE HOSPITAL—LEFT Todd—she made Ned drive her directly to the intersection at High and Church. He made a fuss about it, but she wouldn't back down. The pavement was still wet from the fire hoses. Near the curb, small fragments of glass caught the sun, mocking her with their resemblance to jewels.

A week later, the fresh scar on the elm—a spot of bare bark about the size of a dishpan—was the only evidence of what had occurred there. Rose had ripped down the plastic roses and crude crosses Todd's classmates had tied to the tree.

Day after day, she returned to the site, needing to stand at the last place her son had lived, had breathed. When Ned put his foot down and refused to take her there, she walked. More than once she went in the evening, staying until it was dark, staring up at the stars like an animal until she could stand to make her way home.

She was not surprised by the persistence of her grief. What surprised her was the idea that anyone *could* get over it. People thought grief was like the flu, something you got over. It wasn't. Oh, it ebbed for a moment—like a new moon tide flowing out—but then it rushed in and swept you away again. What surprised her was that the sky stayed blue.

Weeks after he died, she walked into the woods beyond the cul-de-sac and began to cry. Wrenching sobs, horrid, keening sounds you might make if you were wounded, your flesh pierced. If she had had a knife with her, she would have cut herself. You should be able to chop off a finger—something to express your grief—but they don't let you.

IT SEEMS LIKE ONLY MOMENTS HAVE PASSED, BUT WHEN Rose surfaces, it is 8:15. Although she is not aware of them having left, both the man with the injured hand and the feverish boy and his mother have disappeared.

Eventually, they come for Zack. He is rolled off in a wheelchair by a nurse who is all efficiency. Opal goes with them, murmuring reassurances to her son. Rose watches them disappear behind swinging doors.

A NURSE HANDED HER A PLASTIC BAG WITH TODD'S CLOTHES when they finally left the hospital. Ned assumed she threw them out, but she kept them. The blue jeans and plaid shirt, the navy T-shirt, his jockey shorts, each item torn and stained with what you could think was rust if you didn't know better. Fingering each article, she would mentally recite the autopsy report, which she knew by heart. Fractures of wrists and arms and ribs, brain ripped—pons from medulla—aorta ripped. *Ripped.* The single word summing up all the violence done to her son.

At home, she found his windbreaker hanging on the back of a kitchen chair. It smelled of him. She rolled it up tight and sealed it in a Ziploc freezer bag. Despite the bag, when she took it out months later his smell was gone.

Ned had wanted to cremate Todd's body, but she balked. It was unbearable to think of more damage done to him. Later she wished she had agreed. Then she would have his ashes. She could have sifted them through her hands, tasted them. *Ingested* them.

Taken him back into her.

"MRS. NELSON?"

Opal plops down next to her.

"How is he?" Rose asks.

"Who the hell knows?" There is a hard edge to Opal's voice. She is near her limit. "They think it's a fracture, but they won't know until they've taken X rays. In the meantime, they've got us sitting and waiting in some other goddamned hall."

Nearby, other patients look over. Opal is attracting the attention of the admissions staff. Rose wants to tell her to lower her voice. She is aware of Opal's too-short skirt, her bare legs. At least she's wearing shoes. She supposes that's something.

"Christ," Opal continues. "This is the most inefficient place I've ever been in. A fuckin' vet could do a better job."

Rose remembers how careful she had been. How quiet. How she had swallowed her own anger, nearly choked on her cries. *Be careful,* she wants to say. *Don't make them mad.* The spot on her stomach begins to itch again.

"Perhaps you should call someone? Your . . . your husband?"

"Who?"

"Your husband."

Opal looks straight at her. "Would if I could, but there ain't no such creature. I'm not married."

Lord, Rose thinks, what have I gotten myself into?

"Mrs. Gates?" A doctor approaches, looks from Rose to Opal.

"Miss Gates," Opal corrects.

"We've had a chance to read the X rays. Your son has a buckle fracture of the right wrist."

"Oh, God," Opal breathes. "Can I see him?"

"In a few minutes. Right now, we're putting a cast on. Normally we'd use a splint, but at his age, a fiberglass cast is the better choice." He pauses, looks down at his clipboard. "We need more information." He motions toward the alcove with the vending machines.

Opal holds her ground. "I want to see Zack."

"In a minute."

That's right, Rose thinks. You insist. Don't let them keep you apart. *It would be better if you don't.*

"They're putting the cast on. Then we're taking a few more X rays. While they're finishing up with that, I have a couple of questions."

"More X rays? Why?"

"Routine." He doesn't meet her eyes.

"It's his arm. That's all. You've already X rayed that. Why do you need more X rays?"

Again he motions toward the alcove. "I just have a few questions."

"So ask."

"How did it happen?"

Opal's gaze shifts. "What?"

"Your son's injury. What caused it?"

There is a slight hesitation. "He slipped. In the tub."

Rose can't read the doctor's expression, but even a blind man could see that's a bald-faced lie.

"In the tub?"

"Yes," Opal says, her voice more confident.

"There is a bruise on his upper thigh. Can you explain that?"

"Explain it?"

"Yes. A rather significant bruise on his left thigh. How did it happen?"

The college boy on crutches and an older couple are openly staring at Opal.

"How the hell should I know? He's a boy. He plays at the playground. Sometimes he falls down."

Boys bounce. In spite of herself, Rose feels a flash of satisfaction.

"Why the fuck are you asking me these things?"

"It's just routine. We have to fill out forms. Mandatory reports from the emergency physician, cases like this."

"Cases like this? What the hell does that mean?"

Rose can see from the doctor's expression that Opal's belligerence is not helping.

"Shit," Opal says. "What? You think I hurt my son? You think I'd do anything to hurt Zack? Are you crazy? Are you out of your fucking mind?"

"Relax, Miss Gates."

"He's my son. I wouldn't do anything to hurt him."

"Calm down."

Calm down. That's what the nurse told Rose when she asked if she couldn't see Todd. *Calm down.* They are in charge. You are at their mercy.

"No one's accusing you of anything. We're required to ask these questions. It's simply procedure we have to follow in cases like this."

"Like what? Why do you keep saying that?"

"Were you alone with your son when he fell?"

"Alone?"

"Yes. When Zack fell, was anyone else there?"

Opal sinks back into the chair. "This is crazy. You can't believe I'd hurt Zack. He's all I have. I *love* him."

"Were you alone?" he asks again. "Did anyone witness the accident?"

Opal doesn't speak.

"You have to answer these questions, Miss Gates." He scribbles something on the margin of his report. "Would you like me to call our social worker? All right, then. Were you alone when the accident occurred? Did anyone else see it?"

"I did."

Both faces turn to Rose.

"And you are?"

Having uttered two words—words that still seem to hang, to echo in the air—Rose is incapable of further speech.

"Your name?" The doctor waits, pen poised over clipboard.

"Rose Nelson." Opal takes over without missing a beat. "Mrs. Nelson is my neighbor."

Rose could just bite her tongue. What in the world had she been thinking?

"And you were there when it happened?"

"She just stopped by for coffee," Opal continues. "I had just finished giving Zack his bath and while I was answering the door, he got back in to get his boat. He must have slipped, because he started crying."

Rose is appalled at how easily Opal lies, how innocently she faces the doctor while lies just trip out of her mouth.

"Is that true?" he asks Rose.

What can she say now? *I wasn't there.* She doesn't know how to retract the words. She nods.

The doctor finishes jotting his notes, then closes the folder.

"I want to see him now," Opal says. "I want to see Zack."

Rose stares at her feet, unable to look anyone in the eye, as if she is the guilty one. Lord, she thinks again. What have I gotten myself into?

CHAPTER 10

❧ O P A L

THE TOTAL FOR THE X RAYS, DOCTOR'S FEE, AND emergency room fee comes to nearly four hundred dollars. Opal hands over her Visa. Lord knows how she'll pay it off. Naturally they've charged her for the additional X rays, pictures she didn't want and that revealed no other breaks or fractures, something Opal could have told them if they'd only asked. Like they'd believe her. Policy, they said. Well, fuck policy.

Earlier the doctor gave Zack something for pain and he's listless. Vulnerable. The sooner they're out of here, the happier she'll be. When she returns to the waiting room, Rose is nowhere to be seen. The ladies' room, Opal thinks. She could sure use Rose for moral support. The woman is as plain as a slice of bread, but there is something solid about her, something dependable that Opal needs right now.

"Mrs. Nelson called a taxi," the admitting nurse informs her.

Opal is disappointed. She wants to thank her for backing up her story with the doctor. Couldn't you just have flattened her with a poleax when Rose spoke up and said she had been there when Zack got hurt.

Opal knows for sure her own mama wouldn't have lied for her. Melva preaches honesty like it's her own special religion.

She doesn't want to be thinking of her mama just now. She can imagine what Melva will have to say about Zack's arm. Her mama would get her pinched-lip look and act like this is exactly what she would expect to happen. Like it was Opal's fault he fell. Like Opal isn't to be trusted with having a child. Just another thing she can't do right. She hates to think of what Melva would say if she found out she'd left Zack alone when he broke his arm. That would be something she would hold over Opal's head for the rest of her life. Like her pregnancy. Like her refusal to marry Billy. Another subject her mama just can't seem to get off of.

Don't you love Billy? Melva would ask.

How could she tell her mama that what she felt for Billy was lust, pure and simple. Can't her mama see love isn't supposed to be like what she and Billy had? Love isn't about accusations, about feeling less than. Opal is holding out for something more.

Right then, as she and Zack are leaving the hospital, Opal understands she can't go back to New Zion. Even if she wanted to, which she decidedly doesn't. In September when she threw that Monopoly die and headed north, she was choosing something else for her and Zack, even if she wasn't exactly clear on what it was. And that changed everything. There are lines in life that, once a person crosses over them, there's no going back to the other side. Trouble is you don't always know there's a line you're stepping over until you're already halfway across. That's why keeping an eye out for signs is so important. It helps prepare you.

She surely does not have the least idea of what kind of life waits for her here in Normal or in the next place she lands. She only knows she can't go back to the way things were in New Zion. This lack of resolution could be depressing, but she tries to think of it as hopeful. Even today, with Zack's broken arm, she believes in the possible. Anything can happen. Any wonderful thing.

Of course, this is another thing she and Billy disagree on. He expects the worst. The bumper sticker on his pickup reads, *Shit Happens*. She wouldn't have something like that on her car in a million years. Talk about asking for trouble.

All Opal knows is that she was *led* to Normal. She's traveling on faith here.

As they cross the parking lot to the Buick, the sky darkens. "Looks like a storm coming on, bud," she says to Zack.

"I have a cractured arm," he says, using this information as leverage to break the backseat rule and sit up front with her.

They haven't even gone a mile when his lower lip begins to tremble. "I don't want a cractured arm."

Opal could sure use some help here. Unbidden, Melva's voice takes up residence. *You made your bed, girl, you lie in it.* Another of her mama's cherished philosophies. Opal reaches over and pulls Zack across the bench seat, closer to her.

"Do you know what that means, bud? It means the bone got hurt. That's all. Like when I cut my hand on the broken glass at Melvama's." She takes her hand from the steering wheel and turns it palm up so he can see the thin scar. "Remember?"

"Yeah."

"Well, your arm got hurt, but it'll get better; it'll heal exactly like my hand did."

"It will?"

"It surely will."

"Why do I have to have a cast?"

"Oh, that's just a big old bandage. That's all it is."

"Okay," Zack says. He lays a moist hand on her thigh and huddles closer.

They barely drive two blocks when the rain begins to come down full strength, striking the windshield with the sharpness of hail. Opal circles past the library and continues down Main, her attention divided between the road and Zack. A familiar edginess strikes her, what Billy calls her "can't-hit-a-moving-target" mood. No way she feels like going home now.

She pulls into the Creamery's parking lot. "Want something to eat, bud?"

"Actually, the doctor said I'm not supposed to get my cast wet."

Lately he'd been starting every other sentence with that word: *Actually, I'm not tired. Actually, I want a Coke.* Opal doesn't know where he picked up the word, but she loves the way it makes him sound. Like a little professor.

She digs around the backseat until she retrieves a plastic grocery bag. "Here. We'll wrap your arm in this. Okay?"

"Okay," he says in a bitty voice.

Their waitress is dressed in just about the ugliest brown uniform on earth. A fluted cap sits on her head, one you wouldn't catch Opal wearing in a million years. It looks exactly like the cup Dr. Wallace's hygienist fills with mouthwash. The name badge identifies her as Tammy, which Opal flat out can't believe. Tammy is *her* baptismal name: Tammy Raylee Gates. For a fact, she knows this coincidence has to be some kind of sign, but she's too wiped from the morning to consider it right now. The only thing she knows is that of all the names on the planet, Tammy is the one she hates the most. Later, she will realize she should have gotten straight out of there the second she saw the woman's name. How could she have ignored an *obvious* sign? The irony alone should have alerted her.

"WHY'D YOU NAME ME AFTER HER?" SHE ASKED MELVA WHEN she was ten. "Tammy's a stupid name." Her mama turned vague, the way she did when she was avoiding unpleasantness and said, "Your Aunt Tammy is a good friend of mine." Like that was a reason to saddle a kid with a name like that. And—technically—Tammy Roscoe wasn't even her aunt.

And wasn't it just like Melva to do something really important like picking a daughter's name with less attention than you'd use to name a dog. Opal herself can't imagine saddling a child with a ditzy name like Tammy.

She supposes it could have been worse. When she went into labor, her mama could have been watching TV, one of those afternoon soaps she'd cut off a foot before admitting she's addicted to. Then later, when it came time to put a name on the birth certificate, she could have picked one from the show. One of those sappy, soap opera names. Opal could easily have been called Erica. Or Tiffany.

Opal was thirteen when she knew for sure she had to change her name.

"ARE YOU READY TO ORDER?"

Opal tucks the breakfast menu back behind the napkin holder. What is called for here is some serious sugar. "Can we see the dessert menu?"

The waitress looks at Opal and then Zack. "Aren't we a little early for dessert?" she says, pushing the comment through a totally phony smile that doesn't fool Opal for one minute.

"No, *we* are not." Like she cares what this waitress thinks. At least Opal doesn't walk around with a paper cup stuck on her head.

She orders the biggest sundae the place offers, with whipped cream and pecans. Zack gets a strawberry milkshake. How bad can that be? It has milk and fruit.

"You know what?" Zack says to the waitress when she brings their order.

"What?"

"I cractured my arm."

"You did," the waitress says. "You cractured it." She thaws slightly and smiles at Opal like, *Isn't that so cute.*

"Fractured, Zack," Opal says. "You fractured your arm, sugah." She peels the paper sleeve from the straw and sticks it in his milk shake.

"How did that happen?" Tammy asks.

"He fell," Opal says. Why the hell is this woman with a Dixie cup on her head questioning her? Just like the emergency room doctor. *Routine questions,* he'd said. As if anyone could even think she'd hurt Zack.

"Mama?"

"What, sugah?"

"I feel funny."

"Here. Drink some milkshake." They never did have breakfast.

"I don't *feel* good."

"Come on, bud," she says. "Come sit by me." She moves over, making room for him in her side of the booth. "Here. Try some of mine." She scoops up some of the whipped cream.

"I don't feel good," he says again. "I want to go home."

He does look pale. Opal signals for the waitress and gets the check. Seven dollars, plus tax. Jesus. What does the cream come from? Platinum cows?

"Mama," Zack whines.

"Okay, bud. We're going in a sec." She roots though her purse for her wallet. Shit. Shit. Shit. The bill compartment is empty.

"I don't feel good."

She *knows* she has a ten. She saw it yesterday when she paid Zack's preschool.

"Mama?"

It has to be there. Then she remembers. The box of eclairs, her impulsive donation to the fund for the young mother.

"Mama?"

"Just a minute, Zack."

She ferrets for change in the bottom of her bag, coming up with two quarters and a dime. She digs through gum wrappers, wadded-up tissues, a hair brush, lipstick, a roll of breath mints, finds another dime.

"Is there a problem?" Dixie cup stands over the table.

This she doesn't need. "I'm a little short."

The waitress waits, not smiling.

"You take credit?"

"No. Cash only. Or local checks. We'll take a check."

Opal makes a pretense of looking for her checkbook, although she can see it plain as day sitting back on the dresser in her bedroom.

"Wait here," Dixie Cup says, like Opal is going to take off. "I'll get the manager."

Immediately Opal can see he isn't going to be any better. He leaps right in before Opal can get a word in edgewise. "There a problem here?"

She knows how Melva would handle this. Her mama would fix her sweetest smile on the man and charm him into footing the bill. She has seen Melva do her act a kazillion times, but this is one behavior gene that missed her DNA. "I'm a little short," she explains. "I was certain I had a ten."

"Mama?" Zack pulls on her arm.

"Just a minute, sugah."

"You can't pay?" He says this like, *You've murdered your husband?*

Jesus. They're talking seven dollars here. Not exactly the national debt. "I can. I just don't have the cash with me. I live here. Over on Chestnut. Next to Rose and Ned Nelson." Opal has noticed that people get real sympathetic when Rose's name is mentioned, but if he's heard of her neighbor, the manager doesn't betray it.

"How short are you?"

"Seven dollars."

"Mama?"

"Seven dollars?" He says it like it's seven hundred.

"Yes." Fuck. Like what? She's trying to stiff them? "I'll bring it back later." She tries a smile that strains every muscle in her face. "Promise."

The man looks like he's debating whether or not to call the police. "Hi, Opal."

There—bigger than life—is Ty Miller. All duded up in tight jeans, suede jacket, and cowboy boots.

"Need help?" he asks.

"No," she says. This is one bad day going directly downhill to worse.

"This woman can't pay her bill," the manager says, like it's now public business.

"Well, shoot," Ty says. "No problem. Here. It's taken care of." He drops a ten dollar bill on the table.

"Please," Opal protests, but before she can say another word, Zack pushes out of the booth and vomits all over Ty's high-heeled boots.

Later Opal will play the whole day over and over. Zack's accident. The doctor's suspicions. Her lie about how he got hurt. The trip to the Creamery. No money for the check. Zack puking on Ty Miller. Each episode part of a larger, inevitable path that leads straight to a heart crushed flat.

CHAPTER 11

⊷ R O S E

ROSE HAS HEARD THIS ALL BEFORE. HALFWAY INTO THE regular season and the Patriots have already lost four games. "Same old story," Ned grumbles. "The quarterback can't do it alone. You've got to have a running game."

She looks up from measuring coffee to see Willard Scott sending off birthday wishes. A face flashes on the screen—dried apple face, all wrinkles, nose, and chin—a face so old it's impossible to tell whether it's a man or a woman. Rose has observed how when a person gets really old, all gender drops away. She can't imagine why anyone on earth would want to live to be one hundred anyway, robbed of everything, even gender. She certainly doesn't. A name—*Katherine Waite, 103, Courtland, Kansas*—scrolls beneath the withered face.

Ned sets aside the newspaper. "It's best if you don't get mixed up with that one," he says.

She stares at him. Why on earth would she want to get involved with a stranger living in Kansas?

"Her," he says, jerking his head to indicate the house next door. "The fruitcake. I'm just saying, it's wise to keep your distance."

"Oh," she says and pours water through the Mr. Coffee machine. The itchy spot on her belly starts up, and she gives it a quick scratch.

"Listen to me, Rose," Ned continues. "I know her type. She's the kind who makes a mess of her life and then expects other people to clean it up."

"I guess," Rose says.

"You guess? I told you the minute I saw her that she was nothing but trouble. Flouncing into the station asking to use our phone, spouting language that would make a trucker blush. A fruitcake."

"Yes," Rose agrees. Beneath her dress and slip and panties, the spot glows, halfway between an itch and a burn. Lymph nodes. Chemo, she thinks. Would it be so bad? What does she really have to live for?

"Dressing in clothes not fit for a twelve-year-old. She's got Ty so turned around he doesn't know a wrench from a pair of pliers."

Rose would just as soon not get started in on Tyrone Miller. She can't figure out how Ned developed such a soft spot for him or why, in spite of his background, Ned took him on at the station, giving him a chance when no one else would.

"Going to the hospital with her was one thing," Ned continues, "but you have to stop it now, nip it in the bud. Next thing, she'll have you baby-sitting. The best thing to do is just stay clear of her."

"You're right," she says. He doesn't have to lecture her. Despite yesterday's trip to Mercy Memorial, she has absolutely no intention of any further involvement with Opal Gates or her boy. The way lies just *tripped* off that girl's tongue. Rose wouldn't put anything past her.

She scrambles Ned's eggs, stirs them into the fry pan, cooking them until they are dry the way he likes them. Rubbery, to her taste. She prefers eggs fluffy and moist, but over the years has adjusted to eating them Ned's way. It's easier than cooking two batches. She spoons his breakfast onto a plate.

"I feel sorry for the poor son of a bitch who married her." Ned forks the eggs on a slice of toast and folds it into a sandwich, a habit that drives Rose crazy. "Any fool can see why he left her."

How can he be so sure Opal isn't the one who wanted out of the relationship? And wouldn't he go right through the roof to hear she isn't even married? Rose can only imagine what he'd have to say if he knew how she lied for Opal at the hospital.

"More coffee?" she asks.

"Half a cup," he says, holding out his mug, an oversized plastic cup, the interior discolored a deep nut brown. There is a toast crumb on the corner of his mouth. She wishes he would use his napkin. Thirty-six years of marriage and she still hasn't gotten him to use a napkin.

"You all right, Rosie?" he asks. There is unexpected concern in his voice, and he's looking right at her. The paper lies neglected on the table. Rose allows herself one weak moment when she nearly tells him all that she has locked inside. Not just about yesterday and how she'd told the doctor she was there when the boy got hurt, but about the mole on her stomach and about what happened at the writing class, and most of all about how she had refused to let Todd use the car, sending him off with Jimmy to die in that accident. This weight lies so heavy in her heart she can't even imagine the relief of setting it free. She very nearly sets it out on the table right then and there, spilling it like a blob of grease from one of the engines Ned is always repairing. Tell him and let him fix it. But the time for fixing things is long gone, and she allows the moment to pass.

"I'm fine."

"What's on your agenda today?" he asks.

She imagines the day yawning ahead, but before she can manage a word he has turned his attention back to the sports pages.

THROUGHOUT THE MORNING SHE HALF EXPECTS TO HEAR from Opal, and when the phone finally rings she picks it up without stopping to think. Ned doesn't need to worry. She isn't going to get further involved. She just wants to hear that the boy is all right.

When she hears the voice on the other end of the wire, she nearly drops the phone.

"Hello, Rose. This is Anderson Jeffrey. From the college." As if she could have forgotten. As if she knows so many men he needs to identify himself. As if she has shamed herself in front of so many of those men.

"Don't hang up, Rose. Please, don't hang up." He is speaking in one long breath so that it sounds like "fromthecollegedonthangup-roseplesedonthangup."

"Yes?" She is surprised to hear how normal her voice sounds.

"Hello, Rose," he says, slower now that he sees she isn't going to hang up.

"Hello," she parrots back,wondering how many times they are going to toss the greeting back and forth.

"How are you?"

"Fine. I'm fine."

"Really?"

"Yes," she says firmly.

"I'm glad." He waits, but she doesn't offer more. "I need to talk with you," he finally says. "Can we talk, Rose?"

A memory—his lips on hers—cuts off all possibility of speech. Her stomach is itching like crazy, and she pushes her fingertips against the spot, presses hard.

THE SECOND DAY OF CLASS, SHE SAT AT THE SAME DESK she had the first time, laid out her paper and pencil, got set to write out her grocery list. They were out of eggs, she knew. She planned on waiting until after class to tell him she was dropping out.

"We'll do more 'hot writing,' " he told them, "but this time we'll start with memory. Memory—this alluvial morass—is the territory of the writer."

Alluvial morass? Rose didn't have the slightest idea what he was talking about, but a shiver of unease rippled through her.

"Begin with this phrase: 'I remember.' And write a list of things."

"What?" She was so surprised by his directions that the question popped right out.

Anderson Jeffrey looked straight at her and smiled. *"I remember,"* he repeated. "Make a list of all the things you remember."

A second ripple of anxiety took hold, but she carefully wrote *I remember*. The others in the room were scribbling noisily, but she thought a moment and finally put down *picking strawberries with Momma*. This memory—surfacing out of nowhere—gave her courage. *Dad's work shoes*, she wrote next, amazed at how clearly she could see them. The creases across the instep, toes turned up, the mismatched laces. What a funny thing to remember after all these years. *Tootsie*, she wrote, thinking of the calico kitten she had as a child. *Orange Popsicles*. And then, before her mind had even grasped what was happening or could catch up with her hand, she wrote *Todd. I remember Todd*.

Once her hand set that sentence to paper, it refused to stop.

Her pen moved across that paper like she had been waiting five years to get this down. She wrote all about Todd and how she missed him and how one minute a person could be in your life, laughing and smiling and driving you crazy with their foolishness, and then the next, with no warning, they were gone. All the words you never got a chance to say would be locked up inside you, and whatever happened to words locked inside? Where did they go?

Then she started writing about Todd's friend Jimmy, who walked away from that crash with no more than a scratch. Really, a scratch. People said things like that, in exaggeration, but it was true. Jimmy had a small red scratch on his right arm, and Todd was dead. Today Jimmy was twenty-two and had two kids of his own. And then she wrote about how she hated Jimmy, and how Reverend Wills said it was a sin to hate and she needed to forgive. She said that she had reached forgiveness so as to please the Reverend and Ned, but the hate was still there. Sometimes she thought it was the only thing that kept her alive, and so she put that down, too. She wrote how at the funeral she overheard someone say it was a miracle that Jimmy hadn't died in the crash too, but it wasn't a miracle to her.

About this point in the writing, she knew she would have to burn that paper and everything she had committed to it. It wasn't "hot writing"; it was scalding—jumping and rolling all of its own power, like the pot of water when she sterilized canning jars or Todd's baby bottles when she prepared them for his formula, after she stopped nursing him.

Then she wrote about secrets and regret. Frightful secrets. Grim regret. She wrote about how after the accident people had consoled her. *It's not your fault. You mustn't blame yourself.* But the terrible thing was it *was* her fault. She should have let Todd take her car, and then he wouldn't have been in the truck with Jimmy Sommers. She would have to live with the pain and guilt of that for the rest of her life. She wrote about Todd's birthday and how the first year after he died she waited all day for Ned to say something about it, to mention it, but he never did. He just went on like it was an ordinary day like any other, and she realized then he had forgotten. She wrote about how for a while she thought about leaving Ned even though she knew she was just fooling herself. To leave someone, you had to have someplace waiting for you.

About this time in the writing, she became aware of Anderson Jeffrey standing by her. When she looked up, every eye in the room was focused on her. The professor had already collected the other papers and was reaching for hers. It never *occurred* to her he would want to take what they had written. Before she could object, she felt it gliding from her fingers to his.

In the cab, on the way home, she tried to figure a way to get that paper back. One more week, she vowed. She would go back one more time so she could get that paper back.

The following week, she planned on speaking to him after class. During the hour, she was careful to write about safe things, things like the history of Normal, things that wouldn't need to be burned after she wrote them, things that didn't come out of any *alluvial morass*.

At the end of the class, before she could say a word, Anderson Jeffrey asked to see her. He led her to his office, a small room with a plain oak desk like the one in Doc Blessing's office and a sofa so covered with stacks of papers and books that there wasn't an inch free to sit on. Immediately she saw that he was the kind of person who wouldn't keep a spare key to his car. The kind of man who automatically expected other people to take care of locked cars and dirty dishes. She wondered what he wanted and how soon she could leave, but he talked about her writing and what he called her raw talent. For an instant, something close to pleasure flickered inside, and she remembered her tenth grade teacher, Mrs. Finney, who had told her once that she was a "smart girl." But then the warmth faded. She let him talk, not listening to the words, only the slightly hypnotic voice that matched his clean fingernails. "I'll see you next week," he said when he opened the door for her, letting his arm brush against hers. "Yes," she answered, so grateful to escape she forgot to ask for her paper, forgot to tell him she wasn't coming back. The next week in class he paid special attention to her, although she wasn't the prettiest or the thinnest or, Lord knows, the youngest. And he asked her to come to his office again so they could discuss her writing, although she had no idea what in the world he could possibly find to say about it.

The second time she followed Mr. Anderson Jeffrey to his office, she noticed right off that the sofa was cleared off, revealing an ugly plaid fabric. She should have left right then, but she let him lead her over to the couch. She couldn't think or talk or even move. Paralyzed, she just let him kiss her. It was like drowning would be in the final moments after you stopped fighting it.

ROSE MANAGES TO PULL HERSELF TOGETHER ENOUGH TO tell Anderson Jeffrey that she can't talk now.

"Will you call me back?"

"Yes," she says, although she has absolutely no intention of doing this.

"Promise," he pushes.

"Yes," she says again.

"Do you have a pencil handy? I'll give you my home number."

She would rather strip naked on the Town Square in front of Colonel Normal's statue than take down his phone number.

At last she manages to get rid of him. She doesn't even want to think of why he wants to see her. Take care of who you let into your life, she says to herself. Take care of who you let in, because once you let someone in, it's not so easy to get them out. But it is Opal Gates, not Anderson Jeffrey, she is thinking about.

After she hangs up, she looks out toward the Montgomery place. In spite of herself, she wonders about Opal, wonders how Zack is.

At that moment, she sees Ty Miller pulling up the Montgomerys' drive. She watches as he crosses the lawn and climbs the front steps. Well, it seems as if that girl doesn't have to go looking for trouble. It will come looking for her.

CHAPTER 12

❧ N E D

N ED BURROWS DEEP UNDER THE HOOD OF CHUCK Winski's Nova. Something is off with the timing, something he suspects Chuck tried fixing himself to save a trip to the garage. Nice enough guy, but Christ, he can squeeze a nickel until the buffalo farts.

"You fool around under here?"

"Not exactly."

"Jesus, Chuck. You either did or you didn't."

"Well, I didn't but . . ." The hesitation gives him away. "Well, my nephew, you know, Janice's boy, he took a look at it."

It was always the nephew. People wanted to save themselves a buck or two, and then when it went sour, they laid it on the nephew. Hell, if nephews were responsible for all the cars screwed up by every cheapskate in Normal, there wouldn't be a kid in town who didn't wear a socket wrench in his back pocket.

"What'd he do?"

"Jeez, I don't know. Just looked at it. Maybe turned a screw or two."

"Park it out back between the tow truck and the green Chrysler. I'll try and get to it this afternoon."

Ned writes up the order sheet. In the service bay, Ty is whistling, working out some new tune, his mind more on music than transmissions, as usual. Ned has tried telling him to forget music and stick to cars. More money in it. Dependable money. He has even hinted there might be a bigger role for Ty at the station, has dropped hints about turning over the place to someone else once he moves to Florida. Ty isn't interested. He has bigger dreams, ideas that to Ned's way of thinking have as much chance of holding water as a rusted-out radiator.

At least he isn't a drinker. Most every mechanic Ned has ever known has a drinking problem. Except for not showing up every now and then, the kid isn't bad. Understands engines. And in spite of his history, he stays out of trouble. Ned doesn't regret giving him a chance—not for a minute. Out front, someone pulls up to the pumps.

It's an automatic habit to troubleshoot every car that drives up. Twenty feet away and blindfolded, he can diagnose a skip in an engine, the squeal of a loose belt. Now, even inside the shop, he picks up a tell-tale growling. Easy call, this one. Water pump on the way out.

He looks up and sees the gray Buick. It's his neighbor the fruitcake. The donut he grabbed earlier at Trudy's sits heavy beneath his ribs. He rubs a hand absently over his chest. He has to cut back on the grease.

As if operating on radar, Ty wheels his creeper out from beneath an Escort—leak somewhere in the exhaust—and crosses over to where Ned is standing. They watch Opal get out of the car, flashing legs naked up to there.

"Forget her," Ned says. Everyone in town has heard how Ty bailed her out at the Creamery, how the kid vomited on his boots.

He could have saved his breath. Ty is already out the door. Ned reaches for the bottle of Tums beneath the counter, takes two.

Seeing Opal reminds him of Rose. Okay, she was only helping out when she went to the emergency room with the kid, but he doesn't like it. He doesn't think things can get worse with Rose, but it sure isn't healthy, her spending time with Opal Gates. He'd like to forbid it.

At the pumps out front, Ty is hanging all over the Buick. While the tank is filling, he washes the windshield, spending more time than the job requires. Jesus, why doesn't he just drool on the glass?

Ned tosses his grease rag on the counter and decides to break early for lunch. He goes to the john, takes a piss, scoops some Glo-Jo out of the jar, works most of the grease off his hands. When he comes out, damned if Ty isn't *still* hanging over the Buick. "I'm going over to Trudy's," he shouts, making a point of ignoring the girl. The boy is in the backseat of the Buick. Cute little tyke. Ned has no grudge against him. He nods as he walks by.

The diner is near empty. He has beaten most of the lunch crowd. "You're early," Trudy says.

He takes his regular stool; she brings him a mug of high test.

Although she isn't much older than he is, Ned can't remember a time when Trudy hasn't been behind this counter. The place belonged to her parents, and when they died—it must be thirty years ago now— she took over. He wonders if she ever thinks about retiring, heading south. What keeps her going?

"BLT, toasted," he says.

"Fries or slaw?"

He thinks about his persistent heartburn. What the hell. He orders the fries. He has the place to himself, and in spite of CNN on the tube, there is a peacefulness here that suits him. Through the opening in the wall above the counter, he watches Trudy work the grill. She moves with economy, the way good workers do. No wasted motion. She lays out a half dozen pieces of bacon, puts two slices of white in the toaster, spills a portion of fries into the basket, lowers it into the fat. Not for the first time, Ned wonders why she never remarried after Jim passed on. His eyes fall on her hips, broad, the way he likes a woman's hips. No skinny-Minnie type for him. Give him something you can hold on to. Briefly he allows himself to contemplate what Trudy would be like between the sheets. In high school she had a reputation. It daunted Ned then, and it does so now. To be honest, it also excites him. He averts his eyes to the overhead television, stares at the stock market report, which doesn't interest him in the least, then watches a clip of Quayle making another error. The man can't keep his foot out of his mouth.

The vice president fades away, and a close-up of a woman's face fills the screen. Ned recognizes her immediately. Everyone in the country knows her by now. The woman who killed her kids. For a solid week she turned up on every morning show, crying and pleading with the kidnapper for the return of her kids when all along she killed them herself. He can't understand how someone could lie like that, fooling everyone. When the segment ends, he's relieved. Just looking at her gives Ned the willies. A mother killing her own kids seems like the most unnatural thing in the world to him. There should be something worse than the gas chamber for people like that.

When the whole story came out on the evening news, Rose got up, switched off the set and left the room. He heard her crying in the bathroom. He didn't know whether to go in and say something or stay put. Living with Rose is like walking on eggs.

He swigs the coffee and thinks about her. He feels like she is getting farther and farther from him. For days, he has tried to come to understand her lie about the college writing class being canceled. Why couldn't she just tell him the truth? He's put up with a lot from her in the past couple of years. He's tried sympathy, tenderness, even anger. Nothing helps. She refuses to go to Ethel's for the family's Christmas gathering. She won't drive. The lie about the college feels like the last straw.

He woke up sometime after midnight last night and watched her sleeping. Even in sleep she seems different, distant. Looking at her in the dark, he found himself thinking, I don't know how much longer I can go on like this.

This thought has played in his mind all morning. Never once, in the past five years, during all the hard days and weeks and months since Todd's death had he ever thought of leaving Rose. Somehow we will get through this, he always told himself. Eventually things will get back to normal. Last night, it occurred to him that maybe time wasn't going to cure things. Maybe Rose would always be this way, stuck in her grief. Maybe they would never get back to the way things were. He lay awake, frozen, afraid of what he might say if at that moment she woke.

This morning, the memory hangs on like the remnant of a bad dream.

Trudy brings the sandwich and fries, lights a cigarette, refills his coffee without his asking, and pours one for herself. She slides onto the stool next to his.

"How's Rose?" she asks.

For a minute he considers asking her advice, getting a woman's point of view. Of course, he says anything to Trudy and by the end of lunch hour, half the town will hear about his problems. The only thing bigger than Trudy's heart is her mouth.

"Doing fine," he says. "Just fine."

When he returns to the garage, Ty is gone. The Escort is still in the service bay. This day is turning into one long disappointment. Ned feels a headache coming on. Everything is spinning out beyond the reach of his hands.

CHAPTER 13

❧ O P A L

O PAL SWINGS INTO NELSON'S SERVICE STATION AND parks at the pumps. She has come directly from the bank, where she withdrew thirty dollars. Aunt May's money is just *evaporating*. It's already clear as crystal that the dolls aren't going to bring in enough to get them through the winter. She's hoping Maida Learned will hire her part-time at the toy store. At least until after the holidays.

She barely has time to switch off the ignition and get out of the car before Ty Miller comes out of the station, like he's been sitting there waiting for her arrival. He moves across the lot with the liquid gait of a long-legged, loose-hipped man. She plans to get some gas and give him the money for her bill at the Creamery. She's searching for the words to talk about his boots. Can you dry-clean boots? She doesn't have a clue. Best to stay off that whole subject. Course her mama would handle the entire matter in some clever way, but Opal is not her mama, a fact Melva never tires of pointing out. You got to think on your feet, Melva likes to instruct, but this is a skill Opal has no more mastered than the one on how to sweet-talk a man.

"Hello again," he says.

"Hi," she manages. A man walks like that, he's just got to know how to dance. Opal loves to dance. Billy hates it. Even when she insisted he take her to the prom, he refused to dance any of the fast ones and only two or three of the slow ones—if you could call what he did dancing.

He'd sway from one foot to the other, pressing his pelvis into hers. Stand-up fucking, he called it. Not the least thing romantic about Billy.

Tyrone takes the nozzle from her. "Fill it up?"

"Ten dollars."

Even sitting back in the car, her legs are all shaky. She feels about sixteen.

Tyrone ducks down and looks in at Zack. "How you doing, buddy? Got a bum arm there?"

Zack grins like they are old friends. "Actually," he says, "it's cractured."

"High test?" he asks Opal.

"Regular."

He strolls back to the pump as if he has all the time in the world and starts filling the tank. She could just die when he catches her watching him in the side mirror and winks. Then damned if he doesn't come around and start cleaning the windshield, staring straight through with the darkest eyes—eyes nearly black, and so beautiful they make a person almost forget about the scar.

"Check the oil?"

"No," she says. Even with the scar, he's good-looking—no getting around that. But good looks don't feed the hogs.

He's still working on the windshield, though it's so clean now you could let a baby eat off it. Next he cleans the wiper blades, swiping them dry with an orange rag. She looks at his hands—bold looking, long-fingered hands that are separated from her by no more than ten inches and a sheet of glass—and knows the confusion of wanting something and not wanting it, both in the same breath.

After he finishes with the wipers, Ty checks the oil anyway. When there's nothing left to do, he takes her money. With sense enough to feel the relief of a close call, Opal drives off.

She's halfway home before she realizes she has still neglected to pay back his ten bucks. Well, no way she's going back now.

THE PHONE IS RINGING OFF THE HOOK WHEN SHE GETS home. Three guesses who, and the first two don't count.

"Hello, Mama," she says.

"Where have you been? I've been calling on and off for two days."

Six states and four months away and she's still accountable to her mama. "Zack and I were out," she says. "Errands." She hopes Melva doesn't ask why Zack isn't in school. No way she's going to say one word about his broken arm. With her mama it's definitely a case of what she doesn't know won't hurt Opal.

"I mean Tuesday night." Melva's voice is hard with suspicion. "Where were you Tuesday night?"

"Tuesday night?"

"That's right. About eleven?"

Fuck.

"I must have let the phone ring twenty times," Melva says. "You're not keeping Zack out that late, are you?"

"No, Mama."

"What were you doing?"

Opal stalls for time. Her mama has a nose for lies. "Well, I was here," she says. "Maybe you dialed the wrong number."

"I did *not* dial the wrong number. I've never in my life dialed a wrong number, and I'm not about to start now."

"I was here, Mama," she repeats. Melva may have suspicions, but stuck in New Zion there's no way she can dispute Opal's story. She rips open a bag of Cheetos and dumps them in a bowl, which she sets in front of Zack.

"What do you want, Mama?"

"What do I want? I want to know when we can expect to see you again."

"I don't know."

"Raylee," Melva says in her bossy voice. "Raylee, I swore I wouldn't say anything, but this nonsense has gone on long enough. It's time you packed up and headed back here where you belong."

"We've been over this before, Mama."

"Not to my liking."

"Oh, Mama."

"The holidays are coming up," Melva barrels on. "We want Zack here for the holidays. I just can't abide the thought of him all alone up there at Christmas."

"He's not alone, Mama. He's with me."

"Well, you know what I mean, Raylee. He should be with his kin, not strangers."

Opal stares at the Chiquita sticker. South America is looking better all the time.

"If it's about money, Raylee, if you need the money, your daddy can send some."

"How is Daddy?" Opal asks. "Can I talk to him?"

"He's not here. He and Billy went over to Raleigh."

"To Raleigh?"

"Ed Bagley had a couple of season tickets he wasn't using."

Her daddy and Billy at a ball game? Her daddy doesn't even *like* Billy. She pushes aside the cereal bowls to make space on the table for Zack to spill out a set of Magic Markers.

"Raylee? You hearing me?"

"Opal," she says. "My name's Opal."

"Girl, you can call yourself any fool name you want, but our patience is wearing thin. It's time you brought Zack back home."

Before she can think of an answer, the doorbell chimes. "Listen, Mama," she says. "I can't talk now. There's someone at the door."

TY MILLER STANDS ON THE FRONT STEPS. BIG AS LIFE AND twice as exciting. "Here," he says, handing her a box of brownies. Not even a hello, just like it's an everyday occurrence, her opening the door, him standing there.

Zack runs in from the kitchen. "Hi," he says, not the least bit shy.

"Hey, scout," Ty says.

Zack giggles. "I'm not scout. I'm Zack."

"Well, Zack, this is for you." Ty hands him a bag.

Zack reaches out his good arm, takes the bag. "Open it, Mama," he says.

Opal pulls out a bunch of bananas, of all things. "Why'd you come here?" she asks, though it's plain as day to her why he's there, and she's not interested. Well, okay. That's a flat-out lie. She is attracted, no denying *that*, but she's not about to get *involved*, not about to *lose* herself. She has Zack to think of now.

"I got a cractured arm," Zack says.

"That so?" Ty ignores Opal's question.

"Want to write on my cast? Can he, Mama? Can he write on it?"

Somehow, before she can muster up an answer, Ty Miller is standing in her front hall. Well, it'll take more than a box of pastries and a bunch of bananas for him to worm his way into her life. "I forgot to pay you at the garage," she says. "I'll get your money."

"No hurry," he says, but she's already halfway to the kitchen. When she returns, he's writing on Zack's cast. He's drawn a line of musical notes with the black marker and is using the fine-tip yellow one to make a little harmonica. Zack is leaning against his knee with a smile so big Opal's heart could just split because she's so jealous.

When he finishes the last flourish, she holds out a ten. She readies herself for his refusal, gets set to tell him she doesn't take handouts from strangers. But he looks directly at her with those startling eyes and slips the bill in his jeans pocket, leaving her with a mouthful of argument and nowhere to spend it.

"Look, Mama," Zack says. "Look what Ty put on my cast."

"I see," she says, civil as can be.

"What's that?" Zack asks, pointing to the tiny drawing.

"A harmonica," Ty answers. "You ever see one?"

"Nope."

"Want to?"

"Yes."

"You wait right here."

It doesn't take him but two minutes to return. Ignoring Opal, he kneels down on the floor by Zack and begins to play. With the first dozen notes—just a quick riff up the scale—Opal can hear the sure, sweet sound of someone good. He slides up and down the mouthpiece a couple of times then hands it to Zack. "Here. Give it a try."

Before Opal can even collect herself enough to protest—she doesn't even want to *think* about where Ty Miller's mouth has been—Zack is blowing, creating wheezy, weak sounds.

"You do it," he says, handing the harmonica back to Tyrone.

Ty cups his hands around the harmonica and starts. He hasn't gone half a bar into the song when Opal recognizes an old blues number she's heard half her life: "Train Whistle Blues." In spite of herself, she closes her eyes. If she didn't know better, she could think she was back in New Zion with Mr. Moses sitting on the bench outside of Clark's hardware, nursing his Friday night hangover. She can picture him so clearly, elbows resting on his knees, hands cupped around his mouth, making that old mouth harp moan and cry and talk.

"Well, that was nice," she says when he's finished, hearing in her voice the cool, extrapolite tone Melva uses whenever she doesn't like someone.

"Thanks."

"Reminds me of someone back home."

"Where's home?"

"North Carolina."

"Never been there," he says, "but I'm going someday. It's home to one of my idols."

"Who's that? Jesse Helms?"

He laughs. "No. An old harmonica player. Brother Jones. The best."

Zack pulls on his arm. "Show me how," he says. "Show me how to do it."

"Tell you what," Ty says. "How'd you like one of your own?"

"Zack," Opal says. "Take these in the kitchen." She hands him the bananas. He starts to fuss. "Go on, sugah. Do as I say."

"You better go," she says as soon as Zack is out of sight.

"Did I do something wrong?"

"I just don't like people making promises to my boy. Promises they can't deliver on."

He looks her straight in the eyes. "I never say anything I can't deliver on, Opal."

In spite of all her best intentions, in spite of her vow to give up sex, she feels the arrow of desire shoot directly from her throat to her belly.

"I'm not a liar," he says. "Whatever else I am, I don't lie." Reflexively his fingers trace the scar on his cheek. "A man should keep his word, whatever it costs him."

Lord, is she heating up. If she even looks at him, she's sure he'll read it on her face.

"And you, Opal Gates? What do you believe in?"

"Look here," she says. "I guess what I believe in is my business." Just because he comes marching into her house with a box of brownies, a bunch of bananas, and a harmonica sweet enough to make a dead goat weep, that doesn't give him any claim on her.

Instead of being insulted, he laughs. "You like blues? I play weekends over in Springfield. Part of a blues band. Maybe you could come to hear us some night. You too," he says to Zack, who has reappeared.

"Can we, Mama?" Zack asks. "Please."

"We'll see," Opal says, a phrase she's heard from Melva half her life and swore she'd never say to her son. "We'll see."

"Guess I better quit while I'm ahead," Ty says.

"What makes you think you're ahead?"

He laughs. "I'll call you with directions."

After he leaves, Opal returns to the kitchen. And isn't the very first thing her eyes land on the Chiquita sticker. Well, fuck. Plain as udders on a cow. Of everything on earth that Tyrone Miller might have chosen to show up at her door with, he's picked a bunch of bananas. Right then and there, Opal knows she is in a heap of trouble.

"I'm getting a harmonica," Zack says. "Ty's getting me one."

"We'll see," Opal says as she pours him some Coke. She gets him settled with a brownie and then digs out *1000 Names for Your New Baby*. She flips to the T's. *"Tyrone,"* she reads. *"(Celtic) of uncertain meaning. Dim., Ty."*

She slams the book shut. For sure, the last thing she needs in her life is uncertainty. She marches straight back to the kitchen and peels the sticker off the door with her thumbnail. Zack watches her with interest.

She rolls it between her fingers until it forms a little ball and then throws it in the trash.

The fact is some signs need erasing before they can do much damage.

The heat in her belly takes a little more concentration to make disappear.

CHAPTER 14

✧ R O S E

ROSE IS IN THE FIRST-AID AISLE OF MAHONEY DRUGS, picking out medicated ointment for her itch—something with some potency to it. She squints at the lettering on the tube she is holding. Why the manufacturers don't make the print large enough for an ordinary person to read is beyond her. *Prescription strength relief,* she makes out. That sounds promising.

Too late, she looks up to see Mary Winski bearing down. Mary is a toucher, and if it's one thing Rose can't stand it's people pawing at her.

Plus she still can't forgive Mary for the scene she made at the funeral, carrying on loud enough to turn heads, as if Todd were *her* son. Now she has to brace herself for the overly solicitous hug. As she approaches, Mary's face just *melts* into a mask of pity. It's enough to make a person want to throw up.

Before Todd's death, the two of them hardly exchanged ten words a month, but after the funeral the woman just kept calling, insisting Rose come over for lunch or to swim in her pool. Rose would rather be dead. As if she'd even want to swim in that ridiculous pool or go to the parties Mary holds in her backyard, which she's strung with colored lights on anything that stands still. And those dreadful plastic Japanese lanterns. As if they had some big Hollywood pool instead of one of those aboveground ones that are as ugly as sin no matter how you try to disguise them with shrubs. If there's one thing Rose can't abide, it's someone who puts on airs.

Mary is dressed in fuchsia sweat pants two sizes too small and a pair of purple striped running shoes with Velcro straps instead of laces. At least Rose hasn't come to *that*. As Mary makes a beeline for her, Rose stiffens for the inevitable embrace.

"I hear that girl is seeing Tyrone Miller," Mary says, bulldozing right in.

Rose shrugs, noncommittal. She has no doubt everyone in Normal has heard about all the time Ty is spending over at Opal's. The girl is grist for the town's mill, and every single thing about her and her boy is fair game. Ned said that all anyone over at Trudy's could talk about for the better part of two days was the business about the boy's broken arm and the bruise on his leg and the emergency-room doctor's suspicions and the way that girl had no sooner left the hospital than she'd taken the child to the Creamery and fed him ice cream and how he threw up all over Ty's boots. He reports this to reinforce his argument that Rose should continue to have nothing to do with Opal.

"You've probably seen more than any of us," Mary says, her eyes all alight with the prospect of fresh news. "Living right next door and all. What's she like?"

"I don't know any more than you do, Mary," Rose says firmly.

Mary leans in, takes hold of her arm. "But you went with her to Mercy when the boy broke his arm. Isn't that right?"

Rose nods. Let's get off *that* subject. Every time she thinks about the lie she told the doctor, she feels faint. She lives in dread that somehow Ned will find out. "What in tarnation were you thinking of?" he'd say, and before she could even begin to explain, he'd trot her back to Mercy to straighten it all out. Ned can't stand a lie.

"I don't know any more than you do," she says as she tosses the medication into her cart with the Tums and Anacin and Crest. "And I don't like gossip." Before Mary can respond, Rose wheels off down the aisle. One thing about Todd's death, it set her free from caring about the good opinion of people like Mary Winski.

NED DROPPED HER OFF EARLIER ON HIS WAY TO THE STATION and now, as promised, Willis Brown is waiting in the parking lot to drive her home. As soon as he sees her, he scoots around the cab and, deaf to her protests, takes the package from her and opens the passenger door.

"I'm not an invalid, for heaven's sake, Willis," she says.

"Cold last night," he says as he slides behind the wheel. "They say it's going to drop to the low twenties tonight. Bet we get snow any day now."

"I guess." Rose doesn't give a hoot whether it snows or not.

"The walnuts are dropping off the tree over at Hudson's farm, covering the ground like a blanket. My grandpa always said that was a sure sign of a hard winter to come."

Rose's own father didn't hold much stock with the walnut method of foretelling a cold winter. The thickness of a fox's fur. The tightness of corn husks. That's what to look for. She doesn't share this with Willis.

"I remember when I was a kid we always had the first snow by Thanksgiving. Here it is December and we haven't seen a flake."

Willis isn't a day older than she is but acts as if he were born in the last century. Same conversation every time she takes his cab. He and Ned are a pair of stuck records.

She falls quiet and stares out the window as the cab continues down Main. Creeping change is coming to Normal. Three new shops have opened in the past year. One is a wine and cheese place. Imagine. An entire store just for wine and cheese. A bank has set up credit card headquarters over in Hallway, and entire tobacco fields on the outskirts of town have been leveled to make way for ugly subdivisions. Even isolated by grief, Rose feels the change; she doesn't like it.

When Willis pulls up to her house, she has her hand ready on the knob, all prepared to open the door before he can get it for her.

As he pulls away, giving a little toot, she peeks next door. No sign of Opal Gates.

She unlocks the door, takes the day's mail from the box. She sets her bag on the kitchen table, puts the pile of mail at Ned's place. Bills and junk mail is about all they get, and she's happy to have him deal with it. She's turning away when the top envelope catches her eye. Handwritten address on the front. It doesn't look like a bill.

She holds it at arm's length, squinting. Bifocals will be next.

Raylee Gates, she reads. It's a moment before she realizes Bert Green has made a mistake and mixed a letter intended for next door in with their mail. She suspects these things happen a lot more than the post office lets on. She'll point out his error tomorrow.

She drops the letter on the counter, separate from the others, and carries her purchases upstairs. She tucks the ointment in the middle drawer of her dresser under a slip where Ned won't see it. Not that he'd have cause to be looking through her bureau, but it's best to be on the safe side. The rest of the things she stores in the bathroom cabinet. It's nearly noon. Time for lunch.

First thing her eyes rest on when she gets downstairs is the envelope. Bert should be more careful. Something like a person's mail should be *secure.* He's just lucky it didn't land up with someone else's mail. Mary Winski would probably be heating a kettle to steam it open right now.

The postmark is too blurry to make out; she gets Ned's magnifying glass from the desk. *New Zion, North Carolina.* New Zion. Just right for a southern town. As far as Rose can decipher it was posted two days ago. She reexamines the name.

Raylee Gates. The *Ray* and *lee* all scrunched together like one word. The boy's father? Didn't Opal say she wasn't married? Why the same last name?

Curiosity killed the cat, her mother used to say.

IT TAKES THREE RINGS BEFORE OPAL ANSWERS THE BACK door.

"Here," Rose says, thrusting the envelope at her. "This was mixed in with our mail." She can see beyond the girl's shoulder that the kitchen is a mess. Sink full of dirty dishes and the whole place no cleaner than you'd expect. Louise would have a conniption fit if she saw her kitchen in this condition. There is a spidery drawing held to the refrigerator by magnets: two stick figures with wide smiles. The big one has red bolts flaming out from the head. The small one has matching bolts. No sign of any father. No sign of any Raylee.

"Rose," Opal says, pleased. "Come on in. Want a cup of coffee? A muffin?"

Rose spies a plate of misshapen muffins.

"Blueberry. I made them myself."

Well, a person could tell that just by looking. Probably a mix.

"I think this letter's meant for you," Rose says, ignoring the invitation. "The last name's the same and all, but it was addressed to a man, Raylee Gates."

"Oh," Opal smiles brightly. "That's me."

"You?"

"Yep. Raylee was my name before I changed it to Opal."

"You *changed* your name?" Rose has never heard of anyone changing names, except maybe criminals.

"Four years ago," Opal says. "Raylee was my middle name, after my daddy's father. I think he always wanted a boy, but I was what he got."

"Well, Opal's nice," Rose says. If she were going to change her name, she'd certainly pick something prettier, not so old-fashioned.

"It means 'jewel,'" Opal says. "And opals are my favorite stone. The way they look so soft and pretty but hold fire inside."

"Is it legal? Changing your name like that?" She can't imagine a person can just up and change her name like that.

"Well, I had to go to court. Before a judge and all. But it's important that your name fits you." She smiles at Rose. "I looked up your name in my name book. It means just what it is—a rose. Just right for you."

"I don't know about that," Rose says, twisting her hands in embarrassment.

"For a fact, names are important," Opal says again. "I must've spent a hundred hours trying to decide what to name Zack. Billy wanted to name him after him. Fat to no chance of that. Zackery means 'the Lord's remembrance.'"

Rose realizes she hasn't the slightest idea what the meaning of "Todd" is. She never gave a minute's thought to the meaning of it when she and Ned chose it. She would like to ask Opal to look it up in her book.

"How did you land here in Normal?" she asks.

"It's where I was when I used up three tanks of gas," Opal says. "Listen, don't stay here standing. Come on in." Next thing, Rose is hearing all about the die from some Monopoly game and how this was Opal's sign of how far she should drive.

"Really. Three tanks," she says, as if throwing a die is a perfectly sane way to arrive at a destination. She's glad Ned isn't around to hear this.

"I pay attention to signs," Opal says. "Don't you?"

"No," Rose says. She knows better now than to trust in such foolishness.

"My Aunt May says signs are the Lord's way of letting you know He's always making plans for you way down the road, plans you can't even imagine. I'm not so sure about the Lord part of it, but I do believe there are signs giving us information. There's meaning to things. We've just got to have patience to find them."

Patience. This girl doesn't have the least idea what patience means. Sitting for hours—day after day—holding a pair of your dead son's socks in your hands and waiting for some indication he isn't lost to you forever. That's patience. For all it's worth.

"And random acts," Opal is saying. "Things that look purely accidental—like me ending up here in Normal—all end up making a pattern. If you pay attention, in the end, taken together, these random acts all make a kind of sense."

Rose thinks this over. "Like a quilt," she says.

"Exactly," Opal cries. "Exactly like a quilt."

"Mama." The boy comes into the room. No shoes. A thin shirt. Rose wonders if he has winter clothes. A day like this calls for a sweater to cover those thin arms. The cast is a total mess. Someone has let the boy loose with a box of markers.

"I want a muffin," he says. He gives Rose a shy smile.

"Coming right up," Opal says.

"Can I eat in my tent?" he asks.

"Sure can, bud." She turns to Rose. "He's got this tent he set up in the living room. He likes to eat inside."

"I see," Rose says. *That* will lead to crumbs all over the house.

While Opal gets the boy a muffin, Rose notices a ballerina doll sitting on the counter. "Is that one of the dolls you make?" she asks when the boy has left.

"Sure is," Opal says. She hands the doll to Rose.

"It looks real lifelike," Rose says.

"The trick is the face. You've got to put the features low. Lower than you'd think. Most people put them way too high."

Rose fingers the length of tulle skirt, the narrow rhinestone straps. "You make the outfits, too?"

"Yes."

The seams are double stitched. Tiny stitches. "By hand?"

"Until I can afford a machine."

Rose thinks of the Singer standing idly in one corner of her dining room. Of course she keeps her mouth shut.

"Billy thinks they're dumb."

"Billy?"

"Zack's daddy. He thinks making dolls is a pure waste of time."

Rose can see why Opal wouldn't marry the boy. If a person can't see the beauty in these dolls, they don't deserve marrying.

"I wouldn't marry him if he was the last man on earth," Opal says, exactly as if she has read Rose's mind. "I can't figure out why my mama's pushing this again. She never has liked the first thing about him. But now, all of a sudden, she acts like he's hung the moon." Opal gets up and retrieves her tote from the counter. She takes out a wallet and slips out a photo that she passes to Rose. "That's Billy."

Rose holds the photo back until it comes into focus. The boy is dressed in a basketball uniform, and although it's hard to judge from a snapshot, Rose isn't impressed. His smile looks self-satisfied. "Nice looking," she says.

"Good looks don't feed the hogs," Opal says.

Rose hasn't the faintest idea what that means.

"Emily says I look for love in all the wrong places," Opal goes on. "She says they could have written that song just for me."

Rose immediately thinks about Tyrone Miller. "Who's Emily?"

"My therapist."

Good heavens. For a young girl, Opal has a complicated history. Name changes, therapists, boyfriends. Someone, she thinks, should warn her about Tyrone, especially with the boy in the house. She makes up her mind then and there to tell her.

"Rose," Opal says before she can say a word. "Rose, I'm real sorry about Todd."

Most people act like they would rather eat snake, would rather have their tongues pierced with a dinner fork, than mention his name. Opal says his name like it's the most natural thing in the world. "Dorothy Barnes told me about the accident. Shit. I can't imagine what it'd be like to lose your child."

I can't imagine. You don't want to. You most certainly don't want to.

The mole on her stomach, the spot that hasn't bothered her all the time she's been at Opal's, doesn't just begin to itch—it burns. All thoughts of warning Opal about Ty just vanish into thin air. She flees before Opal can say another word.

CHAPTER 15

∾ O P A L

THE SUN IS SHINING—UNSEASONABLY HOT FOR December—and Ty has stripped off his jacket. From her perch on the back steps Opal watches the muscles of his shoulders and arms move beneath his shirt.

It turns out that Ty Miller is not a man easily put off. Today he's giving the Buick a tune-up, and she has that hard scratchy feeling in her chest she gets whenever someone does something nice for her.

He refuses to take money for the labor, just for parts. "I'm not a charity case," she told him last week when he replaced the fuel pump, but he just gave her that wide smile and said, "No one could ever think you were, Opal. There's not the least thing needy about you."

He hasn't made a real move yet. Hasn't suggested a real date or even as much as touched her, anything that would cause her to out-right reject him, but she's nervous about the way he's barreling into her life. And she's troubled by Zack's affection for him. The second time Ty stopped by he brought the promised harmonica. Not a cheap plastic toy either, but a real chrome one. Opal doesn't want her son to become attached to this man who for dead certain—no matter what the Chiquita sticker might signify—will have no place in their lives. One thing about Opal, she doesn't need to see a mule on the tracks to know there is a train wreck coming, and she has no intention of being involved in another collision with a man, no matter how he cares for her car or how many harmonicas he buys for her son. No matter how *hot* she gets every time he turns up. She has no place for a wannabe cowboy in her life and a Yankee to boot.

"The timing's off," Ty tells Zack. "What we got to do here is adjust the idling; then we'll reset the points."

"We'll reset the points," Zack repeats. He is holding his body in exact imitation of Ty, who ruffles his hair before he bends over the fender of the Buick and disappears beneath the hood.

His tight jeans and cute ass aren't doing a thing to calm her nerves, which are high-wired. She's been jumpy all morning, and Ty is only partially to blame. For one thing, five days have passed since Melva has called, and as much as this should be a relief, the silence doesn't feel like good news. She'd like to believe her mama has given up the crusade to get her to return to New Zion for Christmas, to get her to return and settle down with Billy, but past experience indicates Melva's silence means trouble is brewing. She consoles herself with the fact that her mama is six states away. How much damage can she do?

As for going back to New Zion, there's no way Opal will let herself be talked into it. For the first time in her life, she feels like she has independence, which is turning out to be both scary and exciting. What Emily would call empowering. One of the things she is discovering is that she is stronger than she thought.

A movement over at the Nelsons' draws her attention. A curtain shifts in an upstairs window. Rose is looking out the window.

Her neighbor is a mystery. After Rose lied for her at the hospital, Opal thought they might become friends, but it's clear as day Rose is avoiding her. When Opal brought a cake over there to show her appreciation for the help Rose gave her when Zack broke his arm, a gesture her mama would have approved of, Rose wouldn't even answer the door, fuck you very much.

Then last week, when Opal had given up on any chance of friendship, didn't Rose appear with that letter from Aunt May and agree to stay for coffee, although she hardly spoke two words. Opal is used to being around women like her mama, women who can't abide a conversational vacuum, who fill up every idle moment with so much chatter that Opal's teeth nearly ache with the memory of it. When it comes to conversation, her mama is stuck on one speed: wide open. Being quiet is a practice more people could make use of. Rose's silence is relaxing. Also it makes it easier to tell her things.

Rose did not laugh or poke fun when Opal told her about her belief in signs and how you had to look for them. She didn't say, "Jesus, Opal, when are you going to grow up?" the way Billy did. And when she told her about throwing the Monopoly die and the three tanks of gas it took her to come to Normal, Rose only said, "Really? Three tanks," and then nodded as if this was the only sensible way to arrive at a destination.

Try to talk to Billy or her mama about something like that and Opal might as well be talking to a telephone pole.

"You want anything?" she calls to Ty. "Coke or something?"

"We're all set," he says. "Right, buddy?"

"Right," Zack says. "We're all set."

Opal decides she might as well use this time while Zack is occupied to catch up on her work. She's pushing a deadline on a birthday order for an astronaut doll. And she has less than three weeks to fill the Christmas orders. Plus Maida's put her on part-time. She's grateful for the job, even if it does eat up most of the time Zack is in school. She's supposed to stay on until January, but there's a chance it might develop into something more. Yesterday Maida asked Opal if she ever thought about writing little stories to go along with the dolls, personalizing each one with the child's name. She said that kind of thing appeals to children. The idea that someone would think about her, enlarging on possibilities, amazes her and opens her mind to the fact that there is more potential than she realized when she was stuck back in New Zion. A whole world of promise and potential and possibilities for her—and for Zack.

She has been sewing for about an hour when she hears the sound of Ty's harmonica. The notes float in from the backyard. Her hands slow at their stitching. No question about it, he can flat out play that thing. The tune is slow and sweet, with the right touch of loneliness every good blues song holds in its bones. It reminds her of home and train whistles and Mr. Moses sitting on his bench working off a hangover. It's dangerous music, music that could get inside her and crack open her heart if she let it.

"Wailing blues," her Aunt May calls it. She should know.

May's first and third husbands were guitar players, and from the time Opal was thirteen, her aunt advised her to stay away from musicians. "Might as well move directly on over to Heartache Hotel as lose your heart to a musician. They're born with nervous feet, feet that can't settle down."

Not that Opal is about to settle down with anyone. For dead certain not a part-time mechanic who plays in a second-rate band. No way. She has bigger things in mind for her and Zack.

Out in the yard, the song of the wailing blues plays on.

CHAPTER 16

❧ R O S E

ROSE HAS COME UPSTAIRS TO PUT MORE OINTMENT ON her stomach. Several days ago, when the itch about drove her crazy, she got as far as picking up the phone, but before her fingers even hit the first digit of Doc's number, she replaced the receiver. She can't face the prospect of seeing him, being fussed over.

Through the window she hears noises from the yard next door. Tyrone Miller is there again. She could do with a hedge between the houses—privet or something. When Louise lived next door there was no need, but now a hedge would be a plus. She goes over to pull the blind.

Tyrone's lower body extends from beneath the hood of the girl's car. The boy is at his side. Opal is sitting on the stoop watching them.

What was it the girl told her the therapist said? She went looking for love in all the wrong places? Well, it's clear as day she doesn't have to go about doing much looking. Trouble has found her. Tyrone Miller is about as close to wrong as you can get and not break the law.

Ned is about the only soul in town who has much good to say about him, always telling people what a good mechanic he is, how well he's turned out considering he's been on his own since he turned fourteen and his stepfather kicked him out of the house. Of course, Ty claims to be a musician, but the harmonica is not really an instrument you can take seriously—not something you would fancy up by calling yourself a *musician*.

She thinks someone should tell the girl about Tyrone's history. Not that she's about to take on that task. She can't imagine what got into her that she almost said something last week when she took the mis-delivered piece of mail over there. It isn't her place to interfere. No matter how young she looks or how immature she acts, Opal Gates is an adult. She is old enough to go before a judge and change her name. Old enough to have a child and leave her family. Old enough to run her own life in spite of all her foolish talk about signs.

For certain, there are no signs to point one's way in life. If there were, then surely, Rose would have been given an omen that September day when Todd drove off with Jimmy Sommers. Surely, if signs were being handed out, she would have been warned that within the day his laughter would be replaced by the sober voices of doctors and undertakers, that his dimpled grin would be gone forever, replaced by the righteous faces of the members of the Congregational Church Caring and Concern Committee as they dropped off their lemon chif-fon cakes and meat loafs, their molded salads and their green bean casseroles topped with canned fried onions.

No, that sunny September day when she saw Todd for the last time, there had not been the least hint of the calamity to come. Nothing. Of that she was sure.

Right after he died, she did look for some indication that a part of him was still here. Once a blue jay swooped across the yard and perched on the windowsill above the kitchen sink. Crested head cocked, it stared directly through the pane, stared straight at her. Des-perate for a sign, she thought, It's Todd. Or a message from Todd. But the bird never returned, and after a while she began to think she exag-gerated the whole thing. And why a blue jay? What could that possi-bly have to do with Todd? It didn't make sense. The cold hard fact is that Todd is gone and all the searching for signs and wishing for mes-sages won't bring him back.

No. No matter what Opal or *Raylee* wants to believe, life is filled with bewildering and unexpected and hurtful events, and no one is ever handed a road map to prepare for them or aid in avoiding them or ease the way after they've hit. Sooner or later the girl will learn that.

Across the way, the girl looks straight up at the window. Rose pulls back. She's getting to be no better than Mary Winski, spying on them like an old gossip. It's not her business. Nothing that happens over there has anything to do with her. It's certainly not her job to rob the girl of her notion about signs, or to tell her she should take the boy and head back to North Carolina. Or to fill her in about Tyrone.

Turning from the window, she loosens her waistline and adjusts her skirt so she can check the red-rimmed mole. The circle of inflammation looks larger to her, although the constant scratching could cause that. She takes the top off the tube of ointment and dabs some over the spot. When she is done, she tucks the tube safely away in her dresser drawer. She is overtaken with weariness. Just a nap, she thinks, and although it has been months since she slept in the afternoon, she stretches out on the bed. In the first year after the accident, she spent a good part of each day sleeping. She had no idea a body could sleep that much. When Ned came home in the evenings, he would find her stretched out on the sofa.

Now, she drifts off to the sound of a boy's laughter.

SHE WAKES SWEATY AND ANXIOUS. WISPS OF A DREAM FLOAT overhead, escaping into the air: She sits on a plaid couch, naked as a baby. There is a black cabbage rose growing out of her stomach. Flat—like a tattoo—it has thin dark tendrils that curl up around her waist and down over her hips toward her groin.

She presses her palm against her abdomen, presses the dream away. Visions of the spreading black tendrils persist. She is not a person who gives much thought to the meaning of dreams—dreams are just dreams—but this one has unnerved her. Those spreading tendrils. She thinks of disease. *Chemo. Radiation. Surgery.*

She lies still, concentrating. The mole is not itching now. If there were something serious going on there, wouldn't it take more than a medicated ointment to quiet things down?

She hears, from a distance, the sound of music. Notes rise and fall like a train whistle. Tyrone and his harmonica. Such a lonely sound, she thinks.

She checks the bedside clock: 4:00. She should get up, should think about starting dinner.

Her mind drifts off, and when it finally settles down it lands on Opal. Not that she approves of the girl, but there's no denying that for such a slip of a thing, she's full of surprises. Leaving home, raising her boy alone, changing her name. She is someone who takes chances.

For the second time since Opal moved in, Rose recalls her sixteenth year and Rachel's cousin, the boy she slipped out to meet. That entire summer, he was all she thought about, an obsession that led to risks, unusual for her even then. That risk-taking girl feels distant, like no one she knows. Someone more like Opal.

Tyrone Miller's harmonica wails on, and a heaviness weighs on Rose's chest. She can't say for sure if it is longing or grief.

CHAPTER 17

↬ O P A L

There's a storm in the air, the temperature cold enough for snow. They'll need warmer clothes. The furnace rumbles on. Money literally burning up, going up in flames.

The five thousand dollars Aunt May gave her seemed immense when she was living rent-free in one of her daddy's apartments. Now she's amazed at how quickly the money goes, how it just *melts* away. One thing for dead sure, she isn't about to ask Melva for help.

Opal does not know what went wrong between her and her mama. She has a distant memory of being a child. Of her mama combing her hair, taking more time than you would think necessary to get the snarls out so it wouldn't pull. She recalls a time when Melva had *patience* with her. A time when her mama played with her. A time when her mama *liked* her.

Then one day, it just seemed like Melva was always angry and everything Opal did was wrong. In Melva's opinion, she couldn't dress right or talk right or act right. Whatever Melva's expectations were for a daughter, Opal sure didn't meet them. Her mama would have liked her to take part in beauty pageants. To be *demure*.

"All we wanted is the best for you. Only the best. From the day you were born," her mama would say, her mouth holding prim in that thin, lemon-sucking look and acting like it was Opal who wanted less than the best. But what was the best? Being a majorette, twirling a baton?

Joining the Junior ROTC? Upgrading yourself by the calculated choice of a husband?

"You're just a disappointment that keeps on growing," Melva would tell her.

How does she disappoint? Looking back on it, Opal is aware that somewhere along the line, she decided she could please her mother or herself. No choice there.

She keeps hoping that her mama will change, that one day she'll say, "I love you, Opal. I'm so proud of you," and all the other things mamas are *supposed* to say, all the things Opal says to Zack. She wants to believe Melva *feels* them, but just doesn't know how to show it.

One thing she knows right from the get-go is that her mama for sure wouldn't approve of any harmonica-playing, wannabe cowboy with a scar across his face coming into her life. Facing her about Billy had been bad enough.

"How could you?" her mama said over and over throughout Opal's pregnancy. "I'm so embarrassed I can barely hold my head up in front of a living soul." Her mama carried on and on until somehow the whole shameful thing became all about Melva. No, she doesn't want her mama to know anything about Ty. Not that there's anything to tell.

As if her thoughts have conjured him up, she hears the sound of Ty's truck turning into her driveway. She isn't exactly surprised since he's been showing up regular as watermelon, but this is the first time he's come while Zack's at school.

She presses her palms against her chest, trying to calm the flutter. She wishes she had washed her hair, worn something else—thoughts she recognizes as dangerous.

"Hi," she says.

"Hi."

"Zack's not here," she says, as if that's why he has come.

"I figured."

After a moment's hesitation, she steps back and allows him in. She wishes he weren't so good-looking. She wishes Zack were here to defuse the tension. She wishes she had washed her damn hair. She wishes she had shut the door to the dining room. Her dolls are spread out all over the place. She's used to her mama and Billy thinking she's the next best thing to retarded for spending her time sewing them, but she doesn't want Ty thinking that.

Of course, as if her thoughts have guaranteed he'll notice them, he looks over her shoulder straight at the table.

"Those the dolls I've been hearing about?"

"I guess." Who's he been talking to? What's he been asking about her?

"The ones you make?"

Fuck. "Yes."

He crosses to the table, starts to reach for one, stops short and takes a look at his hands. "Be right back," he says, and heads for the downstairs bathroom. She hears water running in the sink. It takes her a minute to realize he's washing up. He's *cleaning up* before touching her dolls. Whatever Ty has done or might think to do, this simple act—the respect of it—threatens all of her defenses, all of her declarations to stay clear of him. What she needs is some distance here, she thinks as he returns, some perspective. Some *resolve*.

She's still working on the astronaut doll and has just attached a little NASA patch on the flight suit.

"You made this?" he says.

"Uh-huh."

He takes his time looking at it, paying attention in a way that isn't fake or polite. A person can tell the difference.

"It's great. It's amazing."

"Thanks." She works to keep her voice casual.

"No. I mean it. It's really something."

"You want a Coke or something?" *Distance. Resolve.*

"Nah," he says, setting the doll back on the table. "I just came by to give you this."

"What is it?" She takes the envelope he holds out.

"Ticket. There's a blues night in Northampton in two weeks, and the band's going to be playing."

She opens the envelope, slides out the ticket.

"It's a pass," he says. "Gets you in free. I wanted to get it to you now, 'cause I'll be out of town for a while. We've got a gig in Cambridge."

The price is printed right on the stub. Twenty dollars. "Doesn't look like any pass to me. Looks like a ticket."

"It's free. They give them to the band."

She holds it out to him. "Like I told you before, I'm not a charity case."

"Never thought you were," he says, ignoring the ticket.

"Well, stop treating me like one then. Coming here with your gifts, doing favors." She remembers her mama's church group in New Zion, and the righteous looks on their faces when they delivered the food baskets to the poor. *She* isn't anyone's charity case.

Ty looks directly at her. "Maybe I'm going about this the wrong way," he says. "Maybe they do it different where you come from. Thing is, I like you. I'm just trying to show it in the only way I know how. Maybe I've made a mistake, but it wasn't 'cause I was trying to. The thing is, I'm not the enemy, and you keep treating me like I am."

"I appreciate—" She swallows, tries again. "I appreciate all you've done for me. How you've fixed the car and all."

He runs a finger over the scar on his cheek. "Opal Gates," he says with a laugh. "I've got to say you're different from most girls I know."

Opal gives a snort. "That's what Zack's daddy used to say. Told me he loved me because I was different, but as soon as he could, he started working to change everything about me that was different."

"Sounds like a man who doesn't know a good thing when he's got it."

"Something you should know, Tyrone Miller: Sweet talk doesn't go far with me."

"Never thought it would." He grins. "So are you going to take the ticket or not?"

He looks so hopeful she has to smile. "Okay."

"Then you'll come?"

"Maybe. I'm not saying yes and I'm not saying no." She has no grounds to feel so happy. It's just a ticket. It's not like it would be a date or anything. Not like she's signing up for anything.

"I didn't know if you'd made plans yet or not."

"I'm not much for planning ahead."

"I mean, because it's New Year's Eve and all."

"New Year's Eve?"

"Right."

"You mean this is like a date?"

"Not if you don't want it to be."

"I don't know. I'd have to get a sitter for Zack."

"You could ask the Nelsons if they'd watch him."

"You've got everything all figured out."

"If there's one thing I don't have, it's everything all figured out. So you'll come?"

"Maybe."

"There'll be dancing. Do you like to dance?"

"I used to." It's been what? A hundred years since she's gone dancing.

"It's not something a person forgets."

"No. I guess not."

He starts humming—a James Taylor song—and reaches for her hand. The charge jolts straight through her. The hot weight of wanting settles in her belly, spirals up to her throat, spreads down to her thighs. *Distance. Resolve.* She pulls her hand back. "I've got to go get Zack."

SHE WATCHES HIM STRIDE DOWN THE STEPS IN HIS LOOSE-hipped walk. She closes her eyes and recalls the heat of his hand on hers. She isn't sure what's ahead, but she feels a promise of something like joy hanging in the air, as sure as mist over May mountains.

This sense of pleasure stays with her all the way to the day care, and nothing, not even the disapproval on the teacher's face, can spoil it.

"We need our parents to be prompt," Mrs. Lloyd says.

"I know. I'm sorry."

"This is the second time this week we've had to wait for you."

"I know." She'd like to tell the woman to shove it, but she needs this school for Zack.

"You know our policy. The children must be picked up promptly."

"It won't happen again."

"I hope not. We'd hate to have to disappoint Zackery."

"SHE WAS MAD," ZACK SAYS AS THEY GET IN THE CAR.

"Tough titty."

"She whispers about you to the other teacher."

"She's an old cow." *He washed his hands before he picked up her doll. He said it was great. Amazing. Really something.* "Let's forget about her."

"But what if they won't let me go back?"

"Don't worry about it, Zack. Hey. You know what? In seven days it's Christmas and we haven't even bought a tree. What say we go get one right now?"

"A big one?"

"The biggest one we can find." Fuck the money. It's Christmas. Their first totally on their own. Wouldn't be Christmas without a tree. And not one of those fake silver ones her mama sets up. *He likes her. That's what he said.*

Speeding through the winter twilight, caught in the magic of lights strung on trees in front yards, Opal allows herself to believe that at last everything is going to be all right. That the worst part of her life is behind her.

❧ WINTER ❧

CHAPTER 18

❧ O P A L

AN-END-OF-THE YEAR STORM HAS SHUT DOWN HALF
the state, and now Opal is marooned in Northampton with
Ty. The concert canceled, the band has moved on to their
own private New Year's party. Nothing about the evening is turning
out like Opal expects.

"You sure we can't get back to Normal?" she asks. They are in the
kitchen of the house two of the band members rent.

"Not with this storm," he says, brushing the hair off her forehead,
tracing a finger down her cheek.

"I shouldn't have come. Zack will be worried."

"Zack will be fine. Rose is probably making him hot chocolate
right now."

How can she expect him to understand? One of the few things her
mama is right about is that you have to have a child to know what it's
like. "I better give her a call."

"Okay." He smiles, trails his finger along her jaw, down her throat.

"The phone," she manages. "Where is it?"

"Upstairs." He smiles again. "Tell her we'll be home in the
morning."

She heads up the stairs just about torn in two. Of course she's worried foolish about Zack. He's never spent a single night apart from her.
But a part of her—the part that always seems to be landing her in trouble in spite of her best intentions—is dancing with danger. That part

is *excited* in a nervous kind of way to be snowbound with Ty, a man who has the power to suck the air straight out of her lungs with the simple touch of a finger on her throat.

From below she hears the sound of a man's laugh. She thinks it's Wesley, the bass player. The other two, Anthony and Ben, play guitar. They're black, a fact Ty hadn't seemed to think was important enough to mention. Their girlfriends, also black, are dressed up like it's the senior prom instead of New Year's, all bright red, purple satin. Total attitude. They keep throwing looks her way like she's white bread. Like she cares.

She can imagine what her mama would say if she could see her. "I'm not prejudiced," Melva always says, "but folks should stick to their kind." Opal giggles, whether from the two beers she's had already or the picture of her mama's outrage she doesn't know. What she does know as pure fact is what her mama would say about her being here. She'd make her feel like trash.

A Janet Jackson song drifts up the stairs. The *Rhythm Nation* album. What's so wrong about wanting a man? Why is it such a crime in her mama's eyes? That's what she'd like to know.

She picks up the phone, hears the hollow echo of a dead line.

"Everything okay?" Ty comes up behind her. He carries two fresh cans of Miller, hands one to her.

"Phone's dead." There's nothing she can do now except hope the storm lets up so they can try and get back to Normal. She crosses to the window. "When do you think it'll stop?"

"Probably sometime tomorrow morning."

A plow goes by and then a sander. Below, trees are transformed into white sculpture.

"Is the snow always like this? So heavy?" She asks. Ty comes up behind her, wraps his arms around her neck, holds her close. She has to remind herself to breathe. There is something about the storm that makes everything seem unreal. Another world. A world where her mama's rules don't apply. She is aware of the bed behind them. King-sized. Unmade. The plow moves on, leaving in its wake perfect silence.

"What? You don't have snow in North Carolina?"

"Not much." Even with the streetlights, she can't make out the house across the road. "You sure we can't get back tonight?" She's not sure if she's hoping he'll say yes or no.

"Don't worry. Zack'll be fine. No place he'll get better care than with Rose and Ned."

Of course this isn't true. He'd be best off with her.

Downstairs someone has put on another tape. Bonnie Raitt. Outside everything is gray and white. Shadows and light. "It's like a fairy land," she says and, feeling foolish, sips her beer although she's already had too much.

He takes the can from her hands, sets it on the floor, pulls her to him, cups his hands over her ears, his fingers cold from the beer. "Jesus, but you're small," he says.

Please, she thinks, don't let him be a good kisser.

But he is. His kiss is long and soft and deep, with just the right edge of insistence behind the gentleness. She opens her mouth to him, takes his tongue.

"Well, shit," he says when he finally pulls back.

Besides the two of them, the oversized bed seems like the only other thing in the room.

He leans over, kisses her forehead. "Come on," he says, surprising her. "Let's go down and dance."

Downstairs, they've separated into couples. Anthony is with the girl named Darlene. Sylvia hangs all over Wesley. Ben and the third girl have disappeared. The smell of pot fills the room. Prince's "Purple Rain" is playing.

Without a word, Ty draws her to him. He waits an instant, just holds her still, his cheek resting on her head; then he begins to dance. Well, clear as day *this* is no stand-up fuck. This is all prelude. She follows his lead, light-headed yet aware of everything: his hand on the small of her back, his breath against her hair, his thigh against her hip, her breasts against his ribs, her cheek against his chest. Her belly is hollow with wanting. She wonders if it is possible to come just by dancing. She wonders if it is possible for a life to change in such a short amount of time.

The cassette flicks off, and after a minute, Wesley goes over and slips another tape on. Ty doesn't release her. His thigh presses against her. She presses back. Outside, the plow makes its return route, scraping clear the other side of the street.

She wants to reach up and touch his scar, ask him how he got it, but she doesn't. Every girl he's ever been with must have asked that question. You're different, he had said. She wants that—wants to be different for him. It's a dangerous wanting. No future here. Aunt May's warning echoes somewhere in the depths of her brain.

Without letting her go, Ty crosses to the couch, draws her down on his lap. She feels the hardness of him against her legs. Sweet Jesus, she's already wet. She welcomes his kiss. His palm brushes her left breast, circles over her nipple. A moan—involuntary, deep—escapes her throat.

He stands and, carrying her as if she were no heavier than Zack, he heads upstairs.

"You okay?" he asks

"Yes," she says. She's dizzy. From beer and wanting him.

"Happy New Year," he says.

"You, too." She hasn't done a lot right in her life. It's important to do this right.

"You sure you're okay with this?"

"Yes."

He carries her to the bed.

CHAPTER 19

❧ R O S E

IT'S BEEN SNOWING SINCE LATE AFTERNOON, AND A STAR-
tling mantle of white covers the yard. In the glow cast by the
porch light, Rose notes that it's already built up in the crotch of
the old maple. The forecast was for four to six inches, but they've got
at least that much already. It's the fine, steady kind of snowfall that
always leads to serious accumulation. They're in for at least two or
three feet.

Ned and the boy are watching TV. Rose is in the kitchen pouring
her emotions into a piecrust. She hasn't heard one word from Opal.
You'd think the girl would show some concern about Zack. About the
storm. She mentioned this to Ned, but he immediately defended
Opal, said the lines were probably down. If this keeps up, I wouldn't
expect them back until morning, he said. Snowstorm or no snowstorm, Rose doesn't approve of the girl spending the night with
Tyrone. She doesn't even want to think about what they're up to.

Earlier in the week when Opal came over and asked if she'd baby-
sit, Rose was caught completely off guard. Before she could even think
straight enough to come up with an excuse, she found herself agree-
ing. She was sure Ned would hit the roof, braced herself for his disapproval, but he didn't say a word. Now he and the boy are curled up in
the recliner—the boy in Ned's *lap*.

The sight of him sitting there with the boy was more than she
could handle. She headed for the kitchen. She can't understand Ned.

Whatever his feelings about Opal—which he's made pretty clear in the past—he holds no grudge against the boy. Fine with Rose, but no need to go *overboard*. No need to sit with him on your *lap*.

She spoons out flour, cuts in lard, sprinkles in some water, works the pastry until it's ready for rolling, but not overworked. Not tough. Rose is proud of her crusts. Back when she used to do things like work on the church's holiday fair, her pies were always the first to be sold.

She rolls out the dough, transfers it to a pie plate. New Year's Eve or not, it was a mistake to say she'd watch the boy. Now with the storm, looks like they're stuck with him for the night.

Earlier, Rose went next door to get the boy's pajamas. Place was a mess, of course. Beds unmade. Clothes all over the floor. All she could find was a pair of summer pj's, so she'd grabbed one of the boy's sweatshirts and a pair of socks as well. There was a stuffed tiger lying on the bed, and she took that too. Todd had slept with a panda bear. Before she could stop herself, she held the toy to her face and inhaled. The smell of it, the sweaty sweet smell of boy, triggered memories. Inside her chest, her heart actually *hurt* from them.

In the living room, Ned has switched to the weather channel. "They've changed the forecast," he calls to her. "Now they're saying four to six feet. Maybe more. Better get out some candles just in case."

She opens a can of Comstock's blueberry filling, pours it into the pie shell. Ned comes into the room. He goes to the catchall drawer, opens it, ruffles through the accumulation of junk—notepads and screw drivers, elastic bands and paper clips—shuts it.

"Candles aren't in there," she says.

"Not looking for candles," he says. He goes back to the living room. She hears the desk drawers slide open, then close. He's driving her crazy. Probably looking for batteries for the transistor. He likes preparing for storms.

"Rose?" he calls.

He can't locate the hand at the end of his wrist if she isn't there to point the way. She slides the top crust on the pie.

"Rose?" He returns to the kitchen. "You know where the cards went to? I can't find a deck anywhere."

Rose's hands freeze at their work. "I don't know," she says in a voice gone flat as a pillow slip.

"Used to be a half dozen decks around here."

There are two decks in the bottom drawer of the sideboard in the dining room, but she would eat soap before telling him this.

He paws through another drawer. She is so mad she could spit. What's the matter with him? What's he *thinking* of?

She crimps the crust, cuts vents in the center. Just as she slides the pie into the oven, she hears him in the dining room, opening drawers.

"Found them," he calls out. Then, right before her eyes, he brings the boy into the kitchen and sets to work. "Ever see a house built with cards?" he asks the boy. He takes two cards and forms a little steeple in the center of the table, then takes four more and boxes it in. He's better at this than you might imagine. Once he and Todd constructed a house so big it stood seven levels high, covering most of the dining room floor and taking seven decks of cards. There is a picture of that structure somewhere in the photo albums stored in the attic, albums Rose can't bring herself to look at. She cannot believe he is making a house of cards with this boy. What's the matter with him?

"Okay," he says, handing a card to the boy. "You next. Just set it against my card."

She wipes off the counter in a fury, her back stiff with protest. She tries to block out their laughter. How *could* he?

"All right," she says to the boy when she's cleaned up. "Time you were getting to bed."

Over his protests, she takes him to the bathroom, strips off his clothes. He needs help putting on the pajamas.

"Actually, I don't wear that in bed," he says when she pulls on the sweatshirt.

"It'll keep you warm tonight," she says, in no mood to argue. She's forgotten to get his toothbrush, if he *has* a toothbrush. Well, one night won't cause decay.

"When's my mama coming back?"

"She'll be here in the morning," Rose says.

Back in the living room, Ned watches while she makes up the couch.

"Don't you think he'd be more comfortable upstairs?"

What is he suggesting? The house of cards was bad enough. To think she'd even consider letting the boy sleep in Todd's bed . . . What's *wrong* with him? He should know there's no way that will happen. No way in hell any other child is *ever* going to sleep in her son's bed.

"This will be just fine," she says. She settles the boy in, then flicks off the television, switches off the lamps. She goes to the kitchen to check on the pie.

"Zack," she hears Ned say, "you want me to leave a light on in the hall?"

"Yes, please," the boy says.

"Okay," Ned says. "You all set now?"

"My mama'll be here in the morning?"

"She'll be here."

"Night."

"Good night, son."

Son.

The pain just takes her breath away.

CHAPTER 20

⋄ N E D

NED WAKES BEFORE FIVE.
"You stay put," he says to Rose. "No sense both of us getting up."

"Plowing?" she asks.

"Yup. Might as well get started. There'll be a full day of it."

"I'll make you breakfast."

"No need." He reaches over and pats her shoulder. Last night she
hadn't let him touch her. When he wished her Happy New Year, she
nearly bit his head off. Course she'd been mad all evening. Taking it
out on him. And the boy.

He can't believe Rose put the boy on the couch all night. Wouldn't
have hurt to let him be in Todd's room. Might have helped. That room
is like a wound that doesn't heal. He has never in his life met someone
who holds on to grief the way Rose does.

"I'll stop by Trudy's and grab something."

He's at the door when Rose stops him.

"Don't wake the boy going down," she says.

He nods, eager now to escape Rose's grief, her anger. He can't wait
to get outside, to start the plowing, to do something he can control.
He likes early-morning work. Always has. Enjoys being up when
everyone else is still asleep. It's like he has the world to himself, at
home in the cab of the tow truck, traversing deserted streets.

"Christ." He jumps a foot when he sees the boy. "You near scared me to death."

Zack sits in the dim kitchen. He's already dressed and holds his pajamas and stuffed toy in his lap.

"I thought you'd still be asleep," Ned says.

"Can I go home now?"

"It's a little early for that. You and I are probably the only ones up." The salt tracks of dried tears trace down the boy's cheeks.

"I want to go home. When's my mama coming back?"

"Pretty soon." Ned says, hoping this is true. He trusts that girl has some sense of responsibility, all evidence to the contrary. "You want me to turn on the television?"

"No." The boy's lip starts to tremble. "I want to go home."

"Rose will be up soon. She'll get you something to eat." He laces up his boots. "I've got to get to work now. You want some juice or milk before I go?"

Zack shakes his head.

"Sure?"

"I want my mama."

"Well, like I said, she'll be here before you know it." He zips up his old parka, heads for the door. "You want something, you go up and tell Rose. Okay?" He takes the silence for assent.

Off to the east, the blue-gray sky is streaked with pink. The snow crunches under his boots; his breath mushrooms in the frigid air. It must be in the teens. No wind. That's a help—no drifting.

He begins shoveling a path out to the truck. A good eighteen inches of accumulation. Before he's gone five feet, he's breathing hard. He stops to rest. He can remember when he could shovel the entire drive and not break a sweat.

It takes a while to clear the windshield. A coating of ice lies beneath the layer of snow, and he works methodically. His breath is ragged. Up at the kitchen window, the pale oval of the boy's face stares out at him. He waves and smiles, but Zack doesn't smile back. Such a serious child.

He hops into the cab, engages the four-wheel drive, starts backing down the drive. When he checks again, the boy is still at the window.

"Christ." He hesitates, then pulls up and—engine running—heads back into the house.

"Ever been in a snowplow?"

"No."

"Well, I'm heading out now. Got some driveways to plow. You interested in coming along?"

He shakes his head. "I'm waiting for my mama."

"You know about plowing?"

"No."

"It's an important job. First you got to attach a snowplow to the front of the tow truck. Then you clear the snow off people's driveways. When my boy Todd was about your age, sometimes he'd come with me."

"He did?"

"Uh-huh. And I let him help push the lever that lets the plow go up and down. You think you could handle something like that?"

"I think so."

"I could use the help."

"Okay."

"Well, lets find you some working clothes." He helps the boy pull on the sweatshirt, finds an old wool sweater of his, Rose's windbreaker, a pair of his gloves that swim on the boy's hands. "That should do it," he says. "You hungry?"

"Uh-huh."

"What say we stop by the diner and get ourselves some breakfast. You like pancakes? My boy, he used to love pancakes. With plenty of maple syrup and a big glass of milk on the side."

"Actually, I like butter."

"Butter's good."

"And sugar."

"After we have breakfast, we'll go by the garage and pick up the plow, and you can give me a hand with a few driveways. You want to do that?"

"And I push the lever?'

"You betcha."

Before they go he remembers to leave a note for Rose telling her he's taken the boy.

"Will she be mad?"

"Who? Rose?"

Zack nods.

"Nah. Why'd she be mad?"

"She got mad last night when you were making the card house with me."

Not much slides by this kid. "Don't you worry about Rose. She's not mad at you, just mad at the world."

"Why?"

"It's a long story."

"Because your son's dead?"

Ned pauses. "You know about Todd?"

"My mama told me."

Ned wonders if Rose can hear them upstairs. "Come on," he says. "We got some plowing do to. Let's head over and get ourselves some pancakes."

"Ned?" Zack says as Ned buckles the seat belt around him.

"What?"

"Todd was your little boy."

"He was, yes."

"Are you mad at the world, too?"

CHAPTER 21

∻ ROSE

FROM THE LOOK OF HER IT'S CLEAR AS DAY WHAT THE girl's been doing all night. Circles under her eyes. Whisker burn all over her face. Rose purses her mouth in disapproval.

"I really appreciate your keeping Zack," Opal says.

"They should be back soon," Rose says, ignoring the thanks. Girl might as well be wearing a sign. Rose isn't a prude, but there are *standards*. She did not watch that boy all night so Tyrone could get in Opal's pants. She busies herself resetting the clock, catching up the half hour they lost when the power failed.

"I hope he wasn't any trouble."

"No trouble," Rose says. Which does not mean that Opal can drop the boy off here anytime she wants. She'll nip *that* thought in the bud.

"How much longer will they be?"

"No telling," Rose says. "You're here. Might as well have a cup of coffee."

"Thanks." Opal plops herself at the table.

"Want some breakfast?" The words are out before she can stop them. What the devil has gotten into her, inviting chaos into her home? "Cold day like this, I always want to make a batch of pancakes. That be all right?"

"Perfect," Opal says.

Todd liked pancakes. Nothing I said would persuade him to eat waffles. Rose is so close to saying this she can feel the words in her mouth, hard and smooth as marbles against her tongue. She feels a shifting inside, dark and dangerous, black water beneath ice. She gets out the Bisquick, stirs in water, tests the skillet. When she's sure it's safe to speak, when she is sure no treacherous words will slip through her lips, she says to Opal, "There's syrup on the refrigerator door. Plates are in the cupboard over the dishwasher."

She spreads a thin sheet of butter on the griddle, spoons out the first pancake. Spoons out another. When Todd was little, she would form animals for him with the batter. Rabbits and kittens and snakes. Sorrow is endless.

"Rose?"

"Ummmmm?"

"How did you and Ned meet?"

"Oh, I don't know. Seems like we've always known each other."

"You were childhood sweethearts?"

"No. We didn't start dating until I was in my junior year. Let's see. I was sixteen. He was a few years ahead of me in school."

"How did you know?"

"Know what?"

"That he was the one. That you wanted to spend the rest of your life with him."

"I don't know. Just seemed natural." Rose's face softens as she pictures a young Ned, his full head of black hair, his wide grin. How shy he was. He hadn't been able to look her in the eye the first time he asked her out. She remembers nights after a movie or ice skating, how they would sit in his old car, steaming up the windows. She recalls the urgency of desire. Marriage couldn't come soon enough for them. This is nothing she will share with Opal. Folks want to blurt out private matters on *Oprah* that's their business. Some things should remain personal.

"How long have you been married?" Opal asks.

"Thirty-five years." That was 1955. Eisenhower was president. Hope was in the air. They had eloped, saving the wedding money to put down on their first house, a four-room place over on Easton. Jim and Nancy Powers had stood up with them. There're pictures in an old album. Rose wore a royal blue suit she had made herself, with a hat of matching fabric. French seams. Fully lined. Ned wore a gray suit. He had a new haircut that bared a swatch of white skin at his hairline. That narrow band of pale skin had raised the tenderest feeling in

Rose. Just turned her heart right over. None of this is anything she wants to share with Opal. She flips griddlecakes onto two plates.

"But how did you know you could . . . Well, that you could trust him?" Opal leans in toward Rose, her face serious.

Tyrone, Rose thinks. She's asking about Tyrone. "I felt safe with him." That was the truth, plain and simple. Back then she felt like nothing bad could ever happen as long as they were together. They were what? Nineteen and twenty-two. How could they have known there is nothing and no one that can keep a person safe?

"I never really felt that way with Billy."

"Is that why you didn't marry him?" One good thing about conversing with Opal, you can say whatever pops into your head.

"I didn't love him."

So you just hop in bed with someone you don't love, Rose thinks. She hears young people today do that sort of thing. Opal isn't careful, she'll find herself carrying again. Before she knows it she'll wind up in a trailer park.

"I *thought* I loved him."

"You didn't?"

"Fuck, no."

Rose lips tighten. A trailer park, for sure.

"Oh, at first I did, I guess. Emily—my therapist—"

Rose nods. She knows about the therapist.

"She says I was looking for love. She says I had a hungry heart."

This is one thing Rose can understand. She knows about the hunger of an empty heart.

"But it was mostly physical."

Rose certainly does not want to hear anymore. She pours syrup onto her cakes, cuts them into wedges.

"And he bored me. With Billy there were no surprises."

This sounds good to Rose. A life with no surprises. Like sending your son off one day and expecting him to come home as usual, except he never does.

"And we were always fighting."

"About what?" She takes a mouthful, chews.

"Any damn thing. The baby shower, for instance. Sujette—she's my best friend—she wanted to have a shower for me. My mama said no. She said you couldn't have a baby shower until you have a bridal one. She said it's a rule. My mama's big on rules."

Rose can sympathize with Opal's mama. Raising a girl like Opal would be a trial.

"Course Billy sided with her. And he's always making fun of me for believing in signs. He doesn't hold much truck with that stuff."

Rose can see how someone would have to believe in signs to be married to Opal. Well, Billy's right. There are no such things as signs foretelling what's to come. And maybe that's a good thing. No matter what Opal likes to think, maybe it's best that you can't see what's coming. A person might think it would help her get ready, but there are some things there's no way of preparing for. The best you can hope for is to survive. And sometimes you don't even want that.

"And he got real mad about Zack's name. He wanted to name him William."

They named Todd after Ned's brother who died when he was three. They should have named Todd something else. She sees now that it was not a good omen to name their son after a boy who had died in infancy. Maybe if they had named Todd something else, he would still be alive. She would like to ask Opal what she thinks about this, to have her look up "Todd" in her name book and see what it means.

They are just finishing up when the phone rings. She stares at the receiver, unable to believe he'd call on a holiday when Ned could very well be answering. She sets the dishes in the sink, begins to rinse them, ignoring the phone.

"Want me to get it?" Opal says.

There's no avoiding it. Rose wipes her hands and lifts the receiver. Heat creeps up her neck, floods her cheeks.

"Hello," she says, careful to keep her voice even.

"Hello, Rose," Anderson Jeffrey says. "Happy New Year."

"Happy New Year," Rose responds.

"Have I called too early?"

"No," Rose says, "but I have company right now."

Opal makes a don't-pay-attention-to-me, go-on-talking motion with her hands. She pours herself a second cup of coffee, sits back down.

"I need to talk to you, Rose."

"I'll call you back," she says. "Tomorrow."

"You have the number?"

"Yes," she says, although she doesn't.

"Let me give it to you anyway."

She finds a pencil, takes it down. This man is not going to go away.

How did everything get so complicated? Why can't people just leave her alone? She looks across her kitchen at Opal, who is stirring sugar into her coffee and settling in. Take care of what you let into your life, she says to herself. Take care of what you let in, because once you've let them in, it's not so easy to get them out.

CHAPTER 22

~OPAL

PAL CAN'T SIT STILL.

"I'll talk to you later," Ty said earlier when he dropped her off. So she's spent all day watching the clock and waiting on the phone. Can't even take a shower in case she misses the call. Shit. Might as well be back in high school.

She's tired as hell. They got—what?—two hours of sleep last night. Total. Just the memory is enough to start her blood heating. And now here she is left hanging.

She needs a nap. And a shower. And to hear from Ty, damn him. She wanders into the kitchen to check on Zack. He's been drawing for more than an hour, each picture the same. A big truck with a block of black on the front. A snowplow, he's informed her.

He looks up. "Now?" he asks. "Can we do it now?"

Opal checks the clock. Four o'clock. About a half hour of daylight left. "Pretty soon," she says.

"You promised," he reminds her.

"I know. Pretty soon."

What had Rose said? If a person's right for you, it feels natural; you feel safe with him. Does she feel safe with Ty? Last night she had. Once, when she'd drifted off, she woke to find him drawing a finger over her shoulder, touching her like she was something breakable, something that could stain. "You are one beautiful woman, Opal Gates," he told her. In spite of her best intentions and her suspicion of sweet talk, his words wiggled right into her and settled in, spreading warmth.

Billy wouldn't say something like that with a gun to his head. Or her mama. Melva's not prone to compliments. Her mama believes praise of any kind swells your head.

Why hasn't he *called*?

She can't call him. Even if her pride allowed, she doesn't know his number. She doesn't even know where he lives. Hell, come to that, she doesn't know the first damn thing about Tyrone Miller. Doesn't know if he has a girlfriend hanging around in his past—or in his present. A man who can kiss like that, who can play a tune that melts a girl's heart and every other part of her anatomy, wouldn't be surprising if there were other girls hanging around. The thought of Ty with other women makes her just *sick*.

Fuck him. Bringing gifts to Zack. Fixing the Buick. Like he was doing her some big favor. Pouring sweet words into her ear and now, one night of sex and he can't be bothered to pick up the phone. Fuck him. Which is, unfortunately, precisely what she would like to do.

In the past, she'd have picked up the phone and called Sujette, told her all the sordid details, but they haven't talked for weeks. The last time they spoke it was clear as day Sujette was distracted. She's finished college and works as an aide at some law firm. Dating a paralegal. Her life is going down a nice straight road—away from Opal.

And even if she could talk to Sujette, could sit down and tell her all about Ty, she knows full well what she could expect.

Sujette would shake the shit out of her. *Wake up. Haven't you learned your lesson?*

Who else is there? Aunt May. She'd be worse. "Didn't I warn you, girl? Stay away from musicians. They attract women like flies to a jam jar. Just traveling feet and trouble, that's all they are." No, she can't say she wasn't warned. She shouldn't have gone out with him. She definitely shouldn't have slept with him. Well, that's water past the bridge.

"Okay," she says to Zack. "Let's go."

She has never in her life made a snowman, but how hard can it be?

Harder than you'd think, as it turns out. The snow is dry, and no matter how much she packs it into a ball, it dissolves into flakes as soon as she uncups her hands.

"Snow angels," she finally proposes to Zack. "Let's make us some snow angels."

IT'S DARK BY THE TIME THEY GO INSIDE, BOTH SO COLD they can barely feel their toes.

"How about some cocoa, bud?" she says, peeling wet layers off Zack.

"With marshmallow?"

"You bet." His fingers are bright red, his cheeks red with white spots. Frostbite? She rubs them with a towel until the white spots fade.

"Come on," she says. "Let's get us something to eat." She and Zack are fine together. They don't need anyone else.

SHE LETS ZACK STAY UP UNTIL NEARLY TEN — NO SCHOOL this week—and she's grateful for his company. The silence grates on her nerves. Budget or not, she's going to order cable. The only books in the house are a row of Reader's Digest Condensed Books on a shelf in the living room. Opal's been going through them systematically. So far her favorite is *The Snow Goose*. After she finished it, she wondered what parts were left out. One of these days she's going to go to the Normal Public Library and get a real copy. Read the whole thing.

She's in the kitchen getting herself a Coke when she hears a truck pull up. Of course her heart does that funny little thing it's learned to do whenever she thinks of Ty. She's wearing her pink robe. Not a color most people would think a redhead could wear, but Aunt May gave it to her when she went to the hospital to have Zack, and it becomes her.

She hears the engine die, the truck door open. She has a quarter mind not to answer the door, pretend she's asleep. Let him see what waiting feels like. She looks over at the new Chiquita sticker she has applied to the cupboard door, remembers the bananas he brought Zack. Between the sticker—such a *clear* sign—and the memory of last night, her rebellion dissolves before she can even build up a head of steam.

It's late. After ten. She wonders if the Nelsons are still awake. Or the family across the street. Coming here in the middle of the night, why doesn't he just announce to the world? Well, people are going to talk no matter what you do. If it's one thing she learned about when she was pregnant with Zack, it was the human desire for gossip.

Well, let them talk, and fuck all consequences.

Of course, too late, she will learn that consequences are never what you prepare for or predict, never what you can possibly imagine they might be, no matter how many signs you believe with all your heart you see.

She pads across the floor, cold beneath bare feet, and reaches the front door just as she hears the heavy fall of his feet on the porch. She swings open the door before he can even knock.

"Hey, Raylee," Billy says.

Her smile freezes, fades. "Hi, Billy," she says. He looks *almost* the same. It takes her a moment to realize the difference. He's wearing his hair shorter. That must please her mama. "I can't believe you were foolish enough to get yourself in trouble," her mama repeated in the days following Opal's declaration. "Pregnant with a boy who has yet to develop a nodding relationship with the barber."

"That why you don't like him? Because he needs a haircut?"

"Watch your mouth. Don't you go sassing me."

Opal can only imagine what her mama would say about Ty's ponytail. Probably need smelling salts.

"What're you doing here?" she says.

"Shit, Raylee."

"*Opal.*" Clear as river water he's been spending time with Melva.

"I drove all day and half the night and that's all you got to say? 'What're you doing here?' "

She draws the robe tighter.

"Ain't you even going to let me in?"

She steps back, shuts the door behind him.

He looks around. "Where's Zack?"

"Asleep." Where the hell does he think Zack is at this hour, in school? He checks out the living room. The light is off in the dining room. No way he can see her dolls. He swings his arms, rubs his hands together. "Cold as a witch's tit," he says. "How do you stand it?"

"You get used to it. So why'd you come?"

He smiles, the smile he used to get out of trouble in homeroom or with the coach. The smile he used to get her *into* trouble. The smile, she is amazed to realize, which is having about as much effect on her as a single flea on a junkyard dog.

"Figure, you wouldn't come to me, I'd come to you. Figure that's what you're waiting on." Like he's doing her some big favor. "So you win. Here I am."

"It's not about winning," she says.

"Well, what's it about, Raylee? *Opal.* Why'd you run away? And don't go giving me none of that sign crap. What the hell is it about?"

What *is* it about? Nothing Billy would understand. It's about *choices.* About there being more to life than getting married to a boy who got you in trouble when you were fifteen. It's about life and daring to go looking for it.

"You want to go fuckin' up your life, that's your business, but you got to think of Zack."

What she's hearing here is Melva's voice. Blah, blah, blah.

"You got no right to take him away from me, from his kin."

This from a man who didn't want her to have the baby. "When did you get so all-fired hot on being a daddy?"

"I thought we could work this out."

"There's nothing to work out."

"Dammit, Opal, that's where you're wrong. No woman walks away from me. No woman takes my child."

"No man gives me orders. Is that what this is about? Male pride?"

"You think you're smarter than everyone. You think you've got the answers. But you're wrong, Opal. As wrong as you can be."

"Well, what if I am? It ain't no concern of yours."

"But Zack's my concern. And you can't keep a boy from seeing his daddy."

"You ain't his daddy. A daddy does his share." A daddy brings bananas. "You're just a mistake that planted the seed."

"Yeah? Well, this *mistake* is coming back here tomorrow. I drove for two days to see my boy, and I'm not going back home until I do. There's no way you're going to stop me, Raylee. You got that clear? No way in hell."

HE'S GONE A HALF HOUR WHEN THE PHONE RINGS. THE USUAL pattern. He's calling to continue the fight.

"Listen—" she begins.

"Opal?"

She falls silent.

"You okay?" Ty asks.

"Yeah. I'm just dandy."

"Sure? You sound funny."

"I said I'm fine."

"God," he breathes. "It's good to hear your voice. I was about crazy all day. Thinking of you. Remembering last night."

You got a funny way of showing it, she almost says; then she thinks better of it.

"What about you?" he asks the silence. "You have a good day?"

"Perfect," she says. Damned if she'll tell him how crazy she's been. "Best day of my already perfect life."

"What'd you do?"

"Zack went plowing with Ned. I had breakfast with Rose. Then we came home. I worked a little. Zack took a nap, drew some pictures."

"Sounds cool," he says. No explaining where he's been all day, and she'd cut out her tongue before she'd ask.

He waits. The silence is uncomfortable.

"You sure everything's okay?" he says. "You seem different."

You asshole, she thinks, spoiling for a fight. You darling, she thinks, caring for me.

"Just wanted to let you know," he says. "I came over earlier."

"You came over here?"

"I wanted to see you, but there was a truck in the drive. I figured you had company."

"Billy," she says.

"Oh," he says.

"Zack's daddy."

"Oh," he says again, his voice gone all formal. "Well, I won't keep you then."

"He's gone."

"You alone?"

She curls up in the chair, pulls her legs up under her robe. "Yeah."

"All ready for bed?"

"Just about."

"I suppose—"

"What?"

"Well, I suppose it's too late for me to be coming over."

She's leaping straight from the pan to the fire here.

"No," she says. "It's not too late at all. In fact, it's high time."

CHAPTER 23

❧ R O S E

THERE'S NO GETTING AROUND IT. ANDERSON JEFFREY will keep calling until she caves in and talks to him. Rose fears one of these times he's going to call when Ned is home. Then she would be . . . Well, as Opal would say, she'd be *fucked*. She is shocked how easily the word slips into her mind.

How did she manage to get herself into such a fix? She dials, half hoping he won't answer, but he picks up on the very first ring, as if he's been standing there waiting for her call.

"Thanks for calling, Rose," he says when he hears her voice.

"You're welcome," she says, polite as can be.

"I have to see you."

She has no response for this.

"There's something I need to tell you."

There is nothing on earth Anderson Jeffrey can say that she wants to hear.

"It's about the piece you wrote in class."

The piece she wishes she had never written, the hot spilling of rage and loss and guilt. Who knew writing could get a person in such trouble? And how had she come to pour it all out anyway? The relief of it, she supposes. All these years when there was no one to talk to about Todd. No one to remember with. No one to help keep him alive.

"It's important," Anderson Jeffrey says.

He suggests they meet somewhere in Normal—more convenient for her—but she wants no part of that. They settle on a café near the college. At least she's not likely to run into someone she knows there.

Fuck, she thinks after they hang up. She tries the word out loud. Once the shock of hearing it fly out from her lips passes, she is surprised at how satisfying it feels on her tongue. *Fuck*. Lord, Ned would die if he heard her. If her mother were alive she'd use up half a bar of soap washing out her mouth.

ROSE TAKES THE PIONEER BUS SYSTEM TO THE COLLEGE. AS she pays the fare, she misses the slot and the token falls to the floor, rolls the length of the bus. The driver sighs, impatient. She fishes out another token, finds a seat, stares out at the winter landscape.

What does he want with her?

Whatever it is, it was set in motion by the words she spilled out on paper the second day in class. The "hot writing." All the things she wrote about Todd and his death. In that class, something was set in motion, and she can't go back now and change it. If she could, the first thing she would change is the last time she saw Anderson Jeffrey.

If it had stopped with the kiss, that would be shameful enough. Her face flushes with the recollection. The rest of the memory is at a distance, surreal, like a dream. It has that weird underwater feel to it. Sometimes she can actually make herself believe it *was* a dream, that it couldn't have really happened. Maybe she's turning crazy. Like Bernie Feldman who was normal as blueberry pie until the day she started accusing half the men in Normal of raping her. What seemed at first like no more than a joke turned mean when she kept filing reports with the police. Then she said the KGB was trying to recruit her, that she was receiving coded message on the radio. They finally shipped Bernie off for shock treatments.

Rose thinks what happened between her and Anderson Jeffrey was real. It just seems like a dream, which, Lord knows, she would prefer.

After he kissed her, she wanted to flee, but she closed her eyes and stayed there, sitting up straight on that ugly plaid couch. Her legs wouldn't move. "You break my heart, Rose," he told her. Paralyzed, she kept her eyes closed all the time his fingers unfastened the buttons on her blouse—a blouse she has since burned with the trash. That part is definitely true. She knows she burned it. She saw the ashes as proof. Would a person go so far as to burn a perfectly good blouse if she were only remembering a dream?

When he pulled up her skirt—*in the dream?*—she could have died. Her old cotton panties, her thick stomach, the three scars that trisected her belly like the puckered ridges on a road map: one from an appendectomy when she was twelve, another from the cesarean when she was thirty-three (long after she had given up all hope for a child), and the last from the hysterectomy when she was forty-two. He traced a finger over them. She moved her hand in protest, but he pushed it away. "Battle scars," he said. She remembers the terror. Of him, of someone coming in. "Battle scars of life," he continued. "Honorable scars." Even in her fear, she thought, This man doesn't have a clue. The worst of her scars don't show at all. If she had a scar for losing Todd, it would be one of those angry red ones that cuts from throat to groin, like the worst kind of open-heart surgery.

Slowly he pulled down her slip, her skirt. "Thank you, Rose," he said. "Thank you for letting me see your pain. Your scars."

Was it a dream? She wonders if she is going crazy. Grief can do that to a person.

Well, she must be insane to meet him. She thinks again of Bernie Feldman. Next thing, she'll be getting messages on the old Magnavox.

She'll just turn right around and go home. And the next time he calls, she'll tell him flat out to stop bothering her. It's what she should have done the first time. But when the bus pulls up to the curb, he's there waiting for her, offering her no escape. She brushes by him, avoiding his eyes, ignoring his hand.

"Thanks for coming," he says. "How about a cup of coffee? Would you like that?"

What she would like is never to have met Anderson Jeffrey, but she allows him to lead her to a café. He selects a small round table by a plate glass window. The street and sidewalk outside are edged with piles of gray snow and frozen slush pushed aside by plows. They are the only customers.

He orders two cappuccinos—a drink that sounds foreign, unpleasant. "This place is usually busier," he says. "It's semester break."

"Oh," she says.

"Not much for small talk, are you?" He laughs, a short bray of a sound that she finds disagreeable.

Fucking disagreeable. Lord, she hopes she's not getting that disease where a person comes out with all sorts of horrid things. She's read about it. Some kind of syndrome. You blurt out the nastiest things. This is not her. It's someone else. Opal seems to have taken up residency in her head. Say what you will about the girl, one thing about having her sitting in your brain, it gives a person courage.

"What do you want from me?" she says. "Why do you keep calling me?"

He gives a nervous little chuckle and looks around, although there is not another living soul within earshot. For the first time she thinks that in spite of being a teacher, in spite of soap-clean fingernails, which she now notices are bitten to the nail bed, the man is not so sure of himself.

"I have been teaching writing for twenty-five years," he tells her, "and writing for longer than that."

He's older than he looks.

The waitress brings their drinks, small cups of something with white foam on the top. He sends her off for biscotti. *Another* foreign food.

Rose sips the drink. Beneath the foam, it's bitter.

"No student has ever touched me the way you did, Rose," he says. "Your willingness to go so deep—to write from such pain, without self-consciousness. That's why that day in my office . . . Well I want to apologize for what happened."

What did happen? A kiss? Or something more? Something she continues to hope happened in the privacy of her dreams. She'll just finish the coffee and catch the next bus back to Normal.

"The piece you wrote about your son," he says, "about Todd. It's one of the most articulate pieces of writing about grief I have read."

Articulate? There is nothing *articulate* about grief. Grief takes your tongue, robs your brain, makes you mute.

"I tried to tell you on the phone, when I called earlier this fall," he is saying. "I submitted your essay to a magazine."

"A magazine?"

"A journal, really. *A literary journal. The Sun.*" He says this like he's saying *The Holy Bible.* "They've accepted your piece." He delivers this news with a wide smile, like she should be delighted. "They need your permission to print it."

"A magazine people read?"

He laughs. "That's the idea. Each issue has a theme. They want yours for an issue on grief."

Rose is truly horrified. "No," she says.

"Don't answer now. Think about it."

"No."

"If you need to reread it, I kept a copy I can get to you. I'll mail it."

She doesn't need a copy. She knows perfectly well what she wrote. Everything.

She rises, buttons her coat.

"No," she repeats.

"Just think about it. Promise me you'll think about it."

She just manages to catch the bus, flings her token in the slot, sinks into a seat. She could ride on the bus forever, keep going through town after town. She understands why Opal traveled all the way to Normal. Sometimes a person has to run from the people who want too much.

Anderson Jeffrey wants her to say yes to allowing strangers to look into her heart, to read everything about Todd, things she hasn't even told Ned. Ned? He wants her to forget all about Todd, to return to herself, to move to Florida, to stay away from Opal Gates. And Opal wants to be her friend, to have her sit the boy.

Can't they all see they are asking more than she can give?

CHAPTER 24

❧ N E D

S TU WESTON'S MERCURY HAS BROKEN DOWN OVER IN
Pellington, a setback Ned doesn't need on the schedule. From
Stu's description, it sounds like a dead battery. Probably all
that's called for is a set of cables. How a man can live to be in his fifties,
run a business, and still not know enough to carry a set of cables is
beyond him. Then the same man will decide to save some money and
do his own oil change, cross-threading the drain plug in the process
and expecting Ned to fix it. Naturally Ty has taken the morning off
again. Probably over at Opal's. Dogs in heat, those two. Nothing for it
but to post a notice on the door, close the shop, and head over to
Pellington.

He backs the tow truck out onto the street. This time of year, he's
called out half a dozen times a week. If it's not dead batteries, it's someone stuck in a snowbank. Ned has never been that fond of winter, and
lately he's been sick to death of it. It's hanging on like a disease, dragging him down, making him tired. He can't wait for spring.

That's another appealing thing about Florida: no snow. Ned pictures a new life down there, somewhere on the west coast below the
panhandle, by the Gulf. Somewhere away from winter. Away from a
house that holds grief.

The Sox have a spring training camp down there. He could catch
some games, go fishing every day, maybe buy a little outboard—
something with a little zip. A two hundred horsepower Mercury

would be nice. He can almost *taste* this life. The salt breeze. A cool beer. Marlin on the grill. A man can dream, can't he?

One of these days he's going to give Joe Montgomery a call. On their Christmas card, Louise invited them to come down. And why not? Maybe he'll just go ahead and buy the tickets. Surprise Rose with a trip to the Sunshine State. If he already had the tickets she couldn't refuse. They'd go for a week, sit in the sun, collect shells, do a little fishing. They'd have dinner out a couple of times with Joe and Louise at one of those shrimp places: Early Bird special, all you can eat. And Rose would come to see the appeal of the place. Maybe they'd look around at real estate. A man can hope, can't he?

STU DOESN'T EVEN HAVE THE GRACE TO LOOK SHEEPISH WHEN the tow truck pulls up.

"What you got here?"

"It was fine this morning."

"Started right up?"

"Well, maybe it was a little sluggish. Took a time or two to get her to turn over, but then she was fine."

"Let's take a look."

Ned slides behind the wheel, turns the ignition. Nothing. Battery's dead, all right.

"How long she been sitting here?"

"Couple of hours. Maybe three. I spent most of the morning in meetings, and when I came out, she wouldn't start up."

Ned checks the dash. Just as he thought. "Left the lights on," he says.

Stu roars, like this is the funniest thing he's heard all week. "What'll it take for you not to tell Dottie?" he says.

Doesn't take more than ten minutes to get the Mercury started and Stu on his way. Ned stores the cables back behind the cab and pulls away from the curb. No traffic. This time of year Pellington is pretty quiet, most of the students gone home on semester break.

It's well past noon, and he can't decide whether to grab a bite at the local coffee shop here or shoot back to Normal and stop at Trudy's. Trudy's is dependable—no telling what he'll get here—but he's hungry. As he drives by the restaurant, he slows the truck and glances in the plate glass window, checks to see how crowded it is. He gives a quick glance, then another. Impossible. The woman sitting at a table inside is the spitting image of Rose. Of course, he *knows* she's home, but he'd swear on the Holy Bible she's sitting at that table. When he gets home, he'll have to tell her she has a twin. He presses his foot against the accelerator and is passing by the place when he recognizes the coat: Rose's coat. The blue one he gave her last Christmas.

He executes a U-turn and drives by again. It *is* Rose. She's sitting with a man who looks vaguely familiar—someone he knows but can't pin down because he's seeing him out of context. Not a customer. A moment later it hits him. The professor from the college. Before Rose can look out the window and see him staring, he plants his foot on the gas and takes off, as if he were the one caught doing something wrong.

How the hell did she get over to Pellington? And what is she doing here? And why is she with that writing professor? The questions are giving him a headache.

Back in October, the day after he stopped by the college to check on the refund, Ned quizzed Rose over dinner. "That teacher over at the college," he said. "You say he left town?"

There was a long beat while Rose chewed a mouthful of food; then she looked straight at him. "Yes," she said. "He was called out of town." Her eyes were direct, guileless. He would have sworn she was telling the truth. In spite of the fact that he had *talked* to the registrar's office, had, in fact, seen the man *teaching* the class, he was momentarily unsure of his facts. Why? she asked. Just wondering, he said. He wondered how far to push. Had she lied like this in the past? He would not have believed it possible. Not his Rose. But how could he know? He let it drop.

NOTHING IS CERTAIN ANYMORE. ALL THE THINGS HE believed in and counted on are in question. He'd like to turn the truck around and go into the restaurant and confront Rose, ask her what the hell is going on. Which is, of course, impossible.

He heads directly to the station. He's lost his appetite.

He makes a note in the book to bill Stu, then gets to work on a transmission. He deliberately puts all thoughts of Rose out of his head. But he can't get his heart into his work. Twice he has to start a lube over.

He closes shop early. Outside he sits in the cab of his pickup. He doesn't want to go home yet, doesn't want to face Rose.

At last he switches on the ignition. Minutes later, he pulls up in front of Trudy's, catching her just as she is locking the front door.

"I was just about to close up," she says.

He nods and turns back to the truck.

"Oh, for heaven's sake, come on in," she says. "I still have half a pot of coffee left. It'd be a shame to throw it out."

Inside, it's quiet. Trudy slips behind the counter. She's dressed in jeans, as usual. Rose once told him that Trudy would wear jeans to the Inauguration.

"You want anything with this?" she asks as she pours his coffee.

He's got a headache—never did have lunch—but he doesn't want her to fuss. There's a powdered donut left under the plastic dome. "I'll take that."

She puts it on a plate. "If you sit in that booth where I can put my feet up, I'll join you."

He carries their mugs over, slides onto the bench. She sits down with a sigh. "We're not getting any younger," she says. He notices how tired she looks. She opens at 5:00 A.M. On her feet all these hours.

"Not that I'd want to," she adds.

"What?"

"Get younger."

"You wouldn't?"

"Hell, no. Once around is enough. What about you? Would you like to go back twenty years? Live it over?"

If it would turn out differently, he wants to say. If Todd doesn't die. If Rose doesn't turn into this stranger. He wants to tell Trudy about seeing Rose in Pellington, about her lying about the college class, but mention it to Trudy and he might as well take out an ad in the *Banner*.

"To want to live it over means you have regrets," she says. "I don't even have regrets. Only about Jim."

"Nothing else?" He thinks about the reputation she had in high school, thinks about how she never worked anywhere but here, never had a chance to pick a different life.

"Oh," she says, "if we lived our lives again, I think we'd just go on making the same choices. Same mistakes. I don't think we'd be any smarter."

Is this true? Was it all foretold? Or would a person choose a different route, marry someone else? And what would have happened if he had married someone else instead of Rose? Someone like Trudy.

"You know," she says. "I've always been a little jealous of Rose."

"Of Rose?"

"But if I did it all over again, I still don't think I'd be smart enough to latch on to someone steady. Someone good. Someone like you."

Trudy's words leave him completely tongue-tied.

❧ S P R I N G *❧*

CHAPTER 25

↣OPAL

Opal opens the kitchen door. Person's got to be dead not to smell spring. Perhaps even the dead smell spring in their earthen beds. On the far side of the lot, a gray squirrel leaps, bounding—all four feet in the air at once—like a child's toy. She looks across to the small oval of earth Ty has tilled.

According to him, March is still too early to be planting most things. You can't count on the last frost until late May, he says. April is soon enough to plant. Patience isn't a suit in any deck Opal owns. She picks up a packet from the counter. *Sweet peas.* She would have bought them just for the name.

The soil in New England is the darkest she has ever seen, like strong coffee. Nothing like the rust red earth of New Zion. It looks like things could jump straight up overnight. Ty arranged for a farmer to drop a half load of cow manure, and yesterday she forked it in. Even aged, you can smell it a good twelve yards away, surprisingly pleasing for something that is shit. She reads the directions printed on the back. *Depth to Sow: one to two inches. Seed Spacing: One to two inches. Row spacing: One and a half feet. Days to germination: Seven. Days to harvest: Fifty-five.* Seems straightforward enough.

With a stick, she draws a furrow, then rips open the packet and dumps the seeds into her palm. They look like withered pebbles. Like pale, dimpled old men. It's amazing that something so *dead* looking can hold the promise of life. It's almost enough to make a person believe in God. Almost.

She drops each one in the furrow, using her hand to measure distance from seed to seed. How precise do you have to be? She smooths the earth back over them, patting each spot with her fingers, like she's putting them to bed. How has she managed to live until now without planting something in the earth? Except for her roses—a flower greatly overrated in Opal's opinion—her mama wasn't much for gardening. Melva doesn't like to get her hands dirty or damage her manicure. *Water after planting*, she reads.

She finds a jug in the kitchen. It takes three trips before she has watered the entire row. She'll need to buy a hose. And a chair for sitting—one of those wooden ones with arms wide enough to hold a glass of lemonade.

"Hi." Ty holds out a bag. "Lunch?"

Opal lights up like a bulb. No use pretending otherwise. He only has to look at her and her hormones go into double time. Triple time. Shit, they run the three-minute mile. "Didn't hear the Jeep."

"Don't have the Jeep. Rode my bike."

"Didn't hear any motorcycle either."

"My bike," he says, pointing over to the drive where a beat-up Raleigh drunkenly leans on its kickstand.

"You ride a bike?" she says. The sight of Ty pedaling all over Normal sets her giggling.

"Something funny about that?" he says in a mock mad voice that only makes her laugh harder. He grabs her around the waist, rolls her to the ground, tickling her until she shrieks.

"You think it's funny?" He's pinned her beneath him.

"No," she manages, still laughing.

His legs straddle her hips, his hands pin her wrists to the ground.

"You finding something funny?" he says again, his voice now husky, low.

"No," she whispers. The sun hangs over his shoulder, and she closes her eyes against the glare of it, against the brightness of him. His breath brushes her face. Her legs open to the weight of him. "Nothing funny at all." And Lord help her, now those hormones are striding flat out, marching straight through Georgia.

"WHAT'S THE BRAVEST THING YOU EVER DID?" TY ASKS HER.

She loves this, lying in his arms after they do it. Every muscle unlaced, every worry banished. Satisfied six ways to Sunday. Played out and flat done in. Just lying and talking lazylike, saying the first thing that pops into your brain.

"Bravest?"

"Yeah."

"I don't know." Having Zack? She thinks of how scared she was toward the end when her belly was swollen out hard, knowing in weeks she was going to be giving birth to a baby, a real baby weighing more than seven pounds, a baby she was going to have to push through that tiny hole between her legs—the actual size of which she knew because she had made the mistake of checking, first with her finger, then in a hand mirror—and how she couldn't even think about the pain that lay ahead. But by that time in the whole procedure, she couldn't exactly turn around and go back, so how could you use that as an example of courage? To be truly brave, a person has to have a *choice*. They have to decide to go ahead and do what it is they are afraid of. "Once I swam in a lake when there were copperheads swimming real near," she says, knowing it really doesn't count. She was only about eight, without sense enough to be scared. "What about you? What's the bravest thing you ever did?"

"Easy one," he says. He reaches over and gets a chip from the bag on the nightstand, feeds it to her, then licks the salt from her lips. She loves the way he'll eat in bed, like it's a party. "Christ, Raylee," Billy used to say when she brought a sandwich back to bed. "You're getting crumbs all over the fucking sheets." The only thing Billy ever wanted to eat in bed was her.

"Well, what was it?"

"Bravest thing was coming back here after you were so cold to me."

"I was not."

"Were too." He feeds her another chip. "You were pure ice. Lady, you were mean."

"Was not," she says, pleased.

His finger is now drawing salt on her left breast, which he tongues off. She feels herself grow wet. *Again.* Is there something wrong with her? Is she a nympho? Back in New Zion this is about the worst thing you can be. Most of the girls back there would rather drink lye than admit they *like* sex. For her it's like a drug, like she was born to fuck—

an attitude that made Billy so nervous he conveyed the opinion it wasn't natural for a girl to be so enthusiastic about sex. Ty doesn't seem to have this problem.

But how can a person tell love from lust? Lust gets a person in a heap of trouble, but love can land you in a pile of shit. You're not careful, it can land you in marriage, a state Opal is none too anxious to enter. Just think. If she had married Billy, by now she'd have been married, a mother, *and* a divorcée.

During the winter, Melva informed her that Suzanne and Jitter were getting divorced. Well, duh. No shit. From day one it was clear as crystal that match wasn't made in heaven. Jitter only married her because she was pregnant, and she only *got* pregnant to escape her crazy family. It's just as easy to marry someone who wears well. A person can make a point without slitting her throat.

Not one thing Opal has seen to date makes her the least anxious to say *I do*. She has no intention of getting married until she is good and certain she's found the man for her.

"I love you, Opal."

"Mmmmmmm." She cuddles closer. Before she says a thing like this again, she is going to be *sure*. She'll have to see a sign bigger than a billboard before she'll make that leap.

He lifts his arm from her stomach, checks his watch.

"What time is it?"

"One. What time do you get Zack?"

"Two-thirty."

"Want me to get him?"

"What? You don't work anymore?"

He runs a hand over her breast, which—if she can believe what this sweet-talking man says—is perfect. "Taking a few days off."

She waits.

"Going down to Cambridge." He moves on to her other breast. "There's an open mike at a coffeehouse there. Ant has some connections. We might do a taping."

"Oh," she says, drawing away the tiniest bit. *Musicians have traveling feet.*

He pulls her back. "You could come."

"Can't," she says.

"Zack could come, too," he says, reading her mind.

"He's got school."

"Fuck school. Take him to the science museum, the aquarium."

"I can't." And there's work. Since Christmas she's only on two days a week, days she can't afford to take off. And Ty is not exactly swimming in cash.

"You don't want to go?"

"I do."

"Well, come. It's simple."

Nothing is ever as simple as it seems. The doorbell cuts off the conversation.

She can't imagine who'd be ringing her bell. Rose? She gets up, pulls on her shorts, Ty's shirt. On the way down the stairs it hits her Billy might have come back. Would he dare show his face again? Except for the checks he's been sending since February, he hasn't been in contact. She peeks out the window to see if there's a black Ram pickup. What she sees is a police cruiser pulled up to the curb.

"OPAL GATES?" THE OFFICER SAYS.

"Yes." Her tongue turns to cotton.

He holds out an envelope. "Here," he says. "I have to give you this." He thrusts the envelope into her hands.

"What is it?'

"Court order."

He looks down at the paper he is carrying and rattles off something about a summons and a motion. Words she can't take in float in the air. *Domestic relations. Temporary service.*

"If you'll just sign here," he says.

She freezes. She has no intention of signing anything.

"Right here," he says, pushing a pen into her stiff fingers. "To show you've received the papers."

"I don't understand."

"Look," he says, not unkindly. "These papers have been filed in the district court, and I'm serving you with copies. There will be a hearing. You have twenty days from today to file an answer with the court."

"The court?"

He shuffles through the papers. "The hearing date is set for March twenty-eighth."

None of this makes sense to Opal.

"Do you have a lawyer?"

"A lawyer," she parrots. Her mind brays, A lawyer, a lawyer.

"An attorney. My advice is to get one. You'll need one for the hearing."

His voice is hollow, as if she is listening from underwater. "Hearing?"

"At the district court. For custody."

Custody. The word strikes Opal with the swiftness of a snake. One summer, when she was five, during a trip to Virginia Beach, she was knocked down by a wave. Before she could get up, a second wave roared in, slamming her down in the surf. She wasn't in real danger. Her daddy was there within seconds, scooping her up in his arms, but in the moments before he reached her, she felt panic cross over to terror. This is how she feels now. The cold shock of disbelief, then sheer and burning fear.

"Get off my porch!" she screams. "You get the fuck out of here!"

"Opal," Ty calls from inside. "Something wrong?"

"No sense getting upset, Miss Gates," the cop says. He's delivered papers like these before. "I'm just doing my job. As soon as you sign I'll leave."

Opal's hand shakes as she scrawls her name.

"What's the matter?" Ty is by her side.

"It's Billy. That asshole is serving me with papers. *Papers.*" She opens the envelope, but the print on the page swims. "He's trying to get Zack."

"You sure?"

"That's what the cop said. He said *custody.* And I'm standing here holding the damn things, aren't I? Jesus." She's falling into a fast rage. "Well, here's what he can do with his fucking papers." She tears the first sheet in half.

"Hey. Take it easy."

"You take it easy. What do you care anyway? What's it matter to you?"

"It matters."

"Why? Zack's nothing to you."

"That's not true, Opal. You know how I feel about Zack."

"But he isn't your son. He's mine. He belongs to me, and no one—least of all that for-shit Billy Steele—is going to take him from me."

He kneels and starts picking up the papers. "Settle down."

"Just leave," she says.

"What?"

"Leave. Just go on. Get out."

"You want me to leave?"

"Yes."

"You always do this, you know."

"Do what?"

"Make me the enemy. When you're scared, you make me the enemy. But I'm not. I love you, Opal."

"Just leave."

"You sure?"

"I'm sure."

He looks at her sadly, then bends down and kisses her. She doesn't give in.

"I'll call later," he says. "And I'm here, you know. You want me, just call. I'll be here."

Which is a fucking lie. He won't be here. He'll be in fucking Cambridge, making a fucking recording.

LATER, AFTER SHE'S GOT ZACK TO BED, HE CALLS.

"How you doing?" he says.

How the fuck does he think she's doing?

"I've got a name for you. A lawyer. You're going to need one, and she's good."

A lawyer. Money. Shit.

"She's over in Springfield. Works alone. Charges the lowest fee around."

Great. Probably on the edge of getting disbarred.

He gives her the lawyer's name and number, tells her he loves her.

Words are cheap, she thinks.

After they hang up, she retrieves the court papers.

According to the first page, Billy wants to be adjudicated Zack's father. This she doesn't understand. She's never denied Billy is Zack's daddy. It's on the birth certificate, for heaven's sake. Everyone *knows* he's the daddy. Why is he taking her to court to prove something everyone knows is true in the first place? What's wrong with him?

She continues reading. The second page is a petition for the court to appoint a guardian ad litem—an individual, she reads, whose purpose is to evaluate the family and specifically investigate issues relative to custody.

Relative to custody.

No way he can do this, she tells herself. No fucking way Billy's going to get Zack. No way a judge will take a child from his mama and give him to a man she isn't even married to, a man who didn't want him in the first place.

Will he?

CHAPTER 26

∿ R O S E

OPAL'S OUT THERE WORKING IN THAT GARDEN—NOT that you could call a puny plot like that a real garden. Her skinny little body is cloaked in a man's shirt—Tyrone's, most likely. The two are thicker than thieves. The girl's probably fixing to ask him to move in. Rose wouldn't put anything past that one. She pulls the shade down and returns to the kitchen.

Today's the day. She can't postpone it any longer. Much as she'd like to ignore the mole, no ointment she's bought to date has done one thing to relieve it. She's going to have to see someone. Doc Blessing is out of the question. He'd feel bound to tell Ned.

She finds the phone book, flips to the yellow pages. Lord, but there's a lot of doctors. Who would believe six pages of listings? She points a finger, lets it land on the page. Dr. Alan Magneson. General Practice, says the fine print after his name. This sounds like what she wants. Springfield is far enough away so she shouldn't run into anyone she knows.

She copies out the number. She'll call after lunch.

She's mashing up the eggs for a salad when she hears screaming from the yard next door. She practically drops the bowl getting to the window. There's the two of them—Tyrone's shown up since she last looked over—and they're rolling in the grass. Right there in open view of anyone who cares to watch, Tyrone is on top of Opal. Next thing, they're kissing. Well, why don't they just *do* it right out in plain sight? No better than a pair of mating dogs.

She returns to the eggs, but finds she's lost all appetite for lunch. She refrigerates the salad, pours herself a glass of iced coffee. Finally she dials the doctor in Springfield.

"Dr. Magneson's office," a voice says.

"I'd like to make an appointment with the doctor."

"Are you a patient of his?"

"No."

"I see. Do you have a referral?"

The question throws her. "No," she finally says.

"I'm sorry, Miss—"

"Mrs. Nelson."

"I'm sorry, Mrs Nelson. The doctor isn't taking new patients at this time. We can't see you without a referral."

"Oh." Rose doesn't bother with good-bye. Referral? This is going to be more complicated than she thought.

At the end of the Physicians listing she reads: *Also See Health Clinics.* She flips back to the Hs, finds an ad for "Health Connections," which doesn't sound very medical.

Women's Health Services of Springfield another ad proclaims. *Services. Connections.* Are these people doctors or repairmen?

She dials the "Services" number.

"Women's Health Services of Springfield," a bored voice recites. "Health care for women."

"Yes. I'd like to make an appointment with a doctor."

"Gynecology?"

"What?"

"Do you want to see a gynecologist?"

"No. Just a regular doctor." She's not about to go into detail with some stranger.

"Is this urgent?"

Is it? She supposes not.

She is given an appointment for three weeks from today.

When she thinks to look outside again, Tyrone and Opal have gone inside. She's thankful for that.

IT'S 2:00 A.M.

Rose is sitting in Ned's recliner, staring at the TV. With the money these people have to spend, you'd think they could come up with something better than the garbage that's on.

She hits the remote, sees a muscular blond woman in a bathing suit and Nikes jumping on and off a platform. Her ponytail swishes from side to side as she bounces up and down. Her smile shows a lot of teeth, so white they look unreal. Behind her, two men and two women are also stepping on and off platforms, clapping their hands to what must be music, although Rose doesn't know for sure because she has the sound turned off. She doesn't need Ned waking up.

She clicks the channel button. Another blond, this one demonstrating a comb that makes her hair look fuller. A number flashes on the screen. You can order by a credit card. for $19.99. For a *comb*.

Click. Another actress who looks vaguely familiar peers out at Rose. She smiles, revealing a set of impossibly white teeth. Dentists are becoming rich off these women. Before and after pictures of other women appear on the screen. The actress is promoting a line of cosmetics. Rose adjusts the sound so she can hear. The whole kit— foundation, blush, lipstick and lip liner, two kinds of shadow, eyeliner, mascara, something called a "concealer"—costs $119. Imagine. She turns the sound back off.

Click. A man demonstrates hair products for men.

Click. Another nearly nude body. A man with grotesquely developed muscles—you can see the veins—speaks into the camera while a blond girl in next to nothing demonstrates a machine that as far as Rose can make out from their gestures is supposed to reduce your stomach.

Her own stomach is beyond help: soft, doughy, scarred. With a mole that is not going away but is probably nothing. Probably.

And what if it is something? *Cancer.* There, she thinks it. The big C. "Cancer," she says aloud to the blond who is now performing an apparently unlimited number of sit-ups. She has a stomach with muscles you can actually see. With no moles. The woman screams health.

Click. And if it is cancer? She makes herself say the word again. Will she get treatment? Chemo? All that poison they pour in your system that makes you go bald? Will she tell Ned? Well, she'll cross that bridge when she comes to it.

She hits the remote again. An old black-and-white movie floods the screen. As far as she knows, there's no cancer on her side of the family. Heart is what she thought she'd have to watch for. Her father at sixty. Her mother at fifty-eight. One minute ironing the Thanksgiving tablecloth—the large damask one—and the next collapsed on the floor. Dead by the time the rescue squad even arrived.

Women's Health Services. She doesn't like the sound of it. Probably for people on welfare. Black people. A sudden thought horrifies her. Lord, she hopes she hasn't gotten herself involved in some abortion place.

On the screen, the scene is so dark Rose has to squint. She stares at the actor. Someone she had never liked, though she can't for the life of her think of his name. Big beefy man. He's wearing a uniform. World War II movie. Nothing she wants to watch. The name comes to her as she points the remote, removing him from the screen. Robert Mitchum.

Click. The Shopping Channel. It amazes Rose the things people will buy. Shapeless sweat suits in lavender and aqua. Sweaters. All kinds of tasteless jewelry. Absolutely no guarantee about quality. The camera zooms in on a doll. A collector's item, according to the text scrolling on the screen. A limited edition.

Opal makes better dolls that that.

Opal.

Rose can hardly stand to think of the girl. By suppertime, it was all over town she'd had papers served. Matters like that are supposed to remain confidential, but little chance of that in Normal. Rose herself saw the police cruiser in front of the house. Of course at first she thought they'd come for Tyrone and felt guilty she had never warned the girl. But it wasn't about Tyrone at all. The boy's father was going to try and take him away. Opal isn't the most stable girl to have a child, but she is Zack's mother. Rose knows she loves the boy.

After they'd eaten, Ned—Ned, for heaven's sake—suggested she go over there and let Opal know they were here if there was anything they could do, but she didn't. She couldn't look Opal in the face. Couldn't take on more sorrow. She had more than enough of her own.

A noise from outside draws her attention, and she pulls the drapes aside to see a glimmer of light on metal. A car has pulled to the curb halfway between their house and Opal's. She cannot see the driver, but imagines him staring up at her. She feels a fluttering beneath her heart. The streetlight pools wetly on the car's roof, its hood. She thinks it's black, although she's not certain. It could be dark blue, even green. If the police should question her, press her to identify the color, the make, if it is American or foreign, she knows she could not say, although Ned would know in an instant. It's male, this ability to pick out the make and year of a car a mile off, identify it just by the shape of the front grill. But why is she thinking of the police?

When she checks again, although she has not heard an engine start up, the car is gone. As if it has never been there, as if conjured up out of her own guilty mind. She stares at the curb, as if there she will find evidence of its existence. The night is quiet. In the distance she hears a dog howling.

CHAPTER 27

⟿ O P A L

O PAL CHECKS THE ADDRESS SCRIBBLED ON HER PAPER, hoping there's a mistake. The building is run-down. A dump. The lawyer's office is sandwiched between a storefront tax service and a shoe repair shop. *A shoe repair shop.* Not a good sign. You don't need to be an Einstein to see that.

She slows, scans the street for a parking spot. It's metered parking here. Parallel. She hates to parallel park. The rear end of the Buick always ends up half in the street. Shit.

She finds a place on the next block, backs in, cutting the wheel sharply, but ends up three feet from the curb. She pulls out, backs in again. Sweat trickles down her ribs. She's already late.

Lucky for Billy he's in New Zion, out of range. If he were here, no telling what she would do. She's fit to be tied. Mad as a wet hen. Pissed off. En-fuckin'-raged.

When she thinks of him back in January, standing right in her front hall and giving her all that sweet talk about wanting them to be a family, saying he loves her when all the time he's been planning to try and take Zack from her . . . Well, when she thinks about this she could spit bricks. No way it's going to happen. No way she's going to lose Zack.

She has tried calling but has only been able to reach his answering machine, his low, lying, Southern voice. "Listen, you sorry son of a bitch," she shouted into the tape, "if you think you're going to take my son away from me, you're as wrong as a man can be."

One thing for sure, she's not going back to New Zion. She'll drink ground glass before going back there. The farther she and Zack are from Billy, the safer she feels. Maybe she'll sue *him*. See how he likes being served with papers, having to get a lawyer.

Inside the tiny entry, she finds a door marked *Vivian Cummings*. She has looked the lawyer's name up in her baby names book. It means "lovely, full of life." A good omen, she thinks, although doubts sweep in when she opens the door.

There are a couple of straight-back chairs. One scarred table holds an overflowing ashtray and a tabloid newspaper. Despair and defeat huddle in the air.

A second door bisects the far wall. She hears a phone ring behind it, the muffled sounds of a conversation. Silence. She pictures Vivian Cummings. *Lovely. Full of life*. And blond. Vivian is such a blond name. She wonders how Ty knew of her. Is she an old girlfriend?

She taps her foot impatiently. It's not like there are clients lined up. Finally a woman opens the door. She's overweight, gray haired, and wears a suit Melva wouldn't see fit to give to charity. This woman is a long way from lovely. Certainly not anyone Ty would have dated. Opal recognizes a misfit when she sees one. Jesus. She could just *kill* Billy.

"Opal Gates? I'm Vivian Cummings."

Well, duh. She shakes hands and follows the lawyer into the inner office, a space that reeks of cigarettes and is only marginally larger than the waiting room. Opal is no health freak, but a person's lungs could contract disease just walking through this place.

Vivian lowers herself into the desk chair. "You said on the phone you were served with a summons?"

"Yes."

"Got it with you?"

Opal opens her tote, takes out the papers, hands them over. She consoles herself with the thought that Ty said this woman is good.

Vivian picks up a pack of Winstons, shakes one out, lights it, takes a deep drag that she holds for a beat before exhaling. As if her craving is momentarily satisfied, she takes up the papers and scans them, frowning when she's done. "Not a lot of time before the hearing," she says. "It's scheduled for the twenty-eighth."

As if she can't read. She doesn't need to pay God knows what an hour for this nicotine-fixated bitch to tell her things that an idiot could read on her own.

"I'll need some background," Vivian says, taking another deep drag. "You're not married to this—" She refers to the papers. "—William Steele. Correct?"

That is one mistake she's avoided. "No."

"And you've never been married to him?"

No matter what Ty said, this woman is not the fastest engine rolling down the track. "No."

"Let's start with the paternity issue. Is there any question that William—"

"Billy," Opal says.

"That Billy is the father?"

"No."

"Do you have any formal arrangements with him?"

"Arrangements?"

"Visitation rights. Things like that."

"No."

"Has he ever mentioned anything about formal custody arrangements? Anything like that?"

"No."

"And he's never denied he's Zack's father?"

"No. That's why this doesn't make sense. Everyone knows he's Zack's daddy. Why is he making such a big deal about it?"

"Well, one reason is that establishing paternity is the first step in requesting custody, and it looks like he wants to gain custody," Vivian says.

"But he can't do that, can he? I mean, there's no way he can get Zack, is there? I'm his mama. How could he even think he could get custody?"

Vivian takes another drag, using the time to study Opal. "Let's back up a little before we get to that question. First thing. House rules: I need you to tell me everything. No secrets. No lies."

"Why would I lie?"

"I could come up with an easy dozen off the top of my head, but let's not waste time. You agree? No lies?"

Opal nods.

"Okay. Let's start with your move to Massachusetts. When did you relocate here?"

"Last September."

"And why did you leave North Carolina?"

Fuck. She might as well be back in school, or talking to Melva. "It's a free country."

The lawyer leans back in the swivel chair. "Two pieces of advice: Get used to answering questions because, believe me, it's just beginning. And get the chip off your shoulder. It won't help you here, and it sure as shit won't help you in front of a judge."

Get the chip off her shoulder. What is this woman? Melva's clone?

"Understand?" the lawyer asks.

"Okay."

"So why did you move here? Did you have friends or family here? A job?"

"No. Nothing like that."

"So how did you land here?"

Opal doesn't mention the three tanks of gas or the importance of signs. This woman has as much imagination as a basket of chips. "I've always wanted to live in Massachusetts," she says, making her voice soft and sweet. "Since I was a little girl. I thought there would be more opportunities for Zack. Down the road. College and things like that. I like to think ahead."

The lawyer leans back and squints at her through a stream of smoke. Opal fears she's overdone it. She'll have to be careful.

"No question, the fact that you left North Carolina complicates things. Under normal circumstances, a father can't be denied the rights of paternity. By moving here, Billy can make a case that he's being denied his rights."

"But he didn't even *want* Zack. He wanted me to have an abortion."

"Well, he wants him now." She refers again to the papers. "It's in your favor that he waited six months to file. Otherwise you'd be heading back to North Carolina to have the case heard there. The thing that concerns me is that he's asking for full custody, not shared. That means he's prepared to fight."

"Billy always wants what he can't have."

"To get sole custody, he will have to prove Zack would be better off with him, that he is the more fit parent. Is there any reason a judge would rule that Zack would be better off with him? Because that's what he—or she—will be looking for."

"That's flat-out ridiculous." No one could take better care of Zack than she does. Certainly not Billy. Opal can't even imagine him *trying* it: making meals, doing laundry, listening to him, tucking him in every night. Jesus.

"Here's the picture. The court's job is to determine what's in Zack's best interest. The system is set up to protect the noncustodial parent—in this case Billy—from changes like a move out of state. Like it or not, Billy, as Zack's legal father, has rights, and the system is designed to shield those rights. Now, it's not as cut and dried as it seems. They'll take into consideration Zack's current relationships with both you and Billy. Although the relationship of the noncustodial parent is not necessarily the determining factor in deciding best interest, it's definitely something they'll be looking at. Does Billy have an ongoing relationship with Zack?"

"He's seen him once in the past six months. Not exactly what you'd call ongoing."

Vivian scribbles a note on her pad.

"What about before you left North Carolina? Were you and Zack living with Billy then?"

"Shit, no."

"And did he have a relationship with Zack then? Did he see him regularly? Share the care of him? Have him visit overnight?"

"Occasionally. If it didn't interfere with his life." She's tired of the questions. She wants this woman to tell her there is no way she's going to lose Zack, no way Billy is going to get custody. That the idea is ridiculous. She wants *reassurance*.

"What about his parents? Did Zack spend time with them?" Vivian stubs out the cigarette, lights another.

"No. They didn't want anything to do with Zack or me." As far as Billy's parents are concerned, she is Satan incarnate.

"What about support? Does he give you money toward Zack's expenses?"

"Only for the past two months. He's sent a couple of checks. I thought he was feeling guilty." Now she understands. How could she have believed they came without a reason?

Vivian adds another note to the pad. "And at present there aren't any formal arrangements for visitation rights?"

"You aren't getting the picture. Billy never asked for any. I told you, he never even wanted me to have Zack."

"Was he ever abusive? Ever hit you or Zack?"

"No."

"Drink heavily? Take drugs?"

"No."

She scribbles out a few more sentences. "Anything you want to add? Anything you think might help? Anything we haven't covered?"

"What will happen at the hearing?"

"The judge will listen to the petitions. He'll appoint a guardian ad litem."

"A guardian." Opal's heart actually stops. "For Zack?"

"That's the name, but try and think of it as an advocate. Someone who will investigate; talk to you and Zack and Billy, maybe friends and coworkers; try and get a picture of Zack's life; and then report the findings—along with a recommendation—back to the court. Hold on. Let me check something."

She flips through a calendar, runs a finger—nail-bitten, Opal notices—along the page. "One piece of good news for you. Judge Carlyle is sitting that week."

"That's good?" Opal clutches on to the first hopeful thing to come out of this woman's mouth.

"She's fair. Won't come in with a bias. Hearing custody cases really is a job for Solomon. I won't go so far as to say Judge Carlyle is the wisest judge in the county, but she really tries to be fair."

This is the best thing Vivian Cummings has said so far. Anyone who's trying to be fair, who's concerned about Zack's best interest, that person would *never* take Zack away from her.

"We'll meet again before the hearing. Go over everything."

"One thing," Vivian says as Opal prepares to leave. "From here on in, assume you're being watched."

"Watched?"

"Billy's probably hired an investigator. That's what I'd tell him to do if he were my client. Custody cases have a way of turning nasty. What about you? Do you drink?"

"No. Only a beer every now and then."

"Do drugs?"

"No."

"That's two things we won't have to worry about muddying the waters and prejudicing the judge. And Zack's healthy? No illnesses. No accidents?"

Opal sinks back into the chair.

"What?" Vivian says.

"There was an accident. He broke his arm."

She makes a notation on the pad. "When?"

"Last fall."

"How?"

House rules: No secrets. No lies. "He fell," she says without the slightest hesitation. "In the tub."

"Where were you?"

"Downstairs."

"Were you alone with him?"

"What the hell are you suggesting?" This was the hospital all over again.

"I'm not suggesting anything. I'm getting information. Information you can bet Billy will have. Were you alone with Zack when he broke his arm?"

"No. My neighbor was there. Rose Nelson."

"Lucky for you. We'll have a witness if they try and make a case for neglect." Busy writing down Rose's name, Vivian does not see the fear on Opal's face.

SHE PICKS UP ZACK ON THE WAY HOME. NOT LATE. SHE'LL BE on time from now on. Every day. She'll do everything absolutely right. She'll be a great mother. A perfect mother.

"Look," he says. "We made puppets." He holds a brown paper bag out to her. His fist is inside, making the bag bob up and down. "Guess what it is?" He's giving her his biggest smile. Even the *idea* that Billy could take him pulls the breath right out of her.

"It's great, Zack."

"But guess what it is."

She takes her eyes from the road long enough to study the bag, sees the jagged fringe along the top, the red-and-orange bolts beneath the nose. "A dragon," she says.

"Right," Zack says. "You guessed."

No way Billy would have known. Not in a million years. He wouldn't have a clue. She hugs this small victory close.

"MAMA? IT'S ME, OPAL." SHE PAUSES, WAITING FOR SOME sign that her mama will comfort her. Lord knows, she could use some comfort. Through the connection, she hears Melva's tired sigh as clear as if they were in the same room, as clear as a pin dropping, like that advertisement for the long distance company.

"How is everyone?" she asks, searching for an opening to tell Melva what's happening. "How's Daddy?"

"We're doing fine. It's not us you need to be worrying about."

Shit. There's no mistaking her mama's tone. "You've heard? You know what that asshole Billy's gone and done?"

"Watch your language, Raylee. You know I won't stand for cursing."

"But you know what he's done? Right?"

"We know he's trying to bring our boy back where he belongs. That's what we know."

"Where he *belongs*? He belongs with me. That's where Zack belongs, Mama."

"That's a matter of opinion."

"Well, Billy's dead wrong if he thinks he can make me come back there by blackmailing me with the threat of custody."

"I don't think Billy is the least bit interested in bringing *you* back here, Raylee. I think you've tried his patience on that matter. You've wrung the last bit of patience out of all of us."

"I thought you'd be on my side, Mama. I'm your flesh and blood."

"Zack's our flesh and blood, too. We're backing Billy one hundred percent on this. Until you get some sense in your head, I've got nothing more to say."

"No one's going to take Zack from me. I'm his mama."

"You're stubborn and foolish. That's what you are. That always was your mistake. Now you're heading for trouble, and I swear I won't shed a tear. The way you're heading, you're going to end up just like May."

"Why is it always me, Mama? Why am I always the one in the wrong?"

"Don't you be getting sassy with me. And if you think we'll just sit by and do nothing while you ruin Zack's life, you are sadly mistaken."

"I'm not ruining anyone's life. Zack and I are doing just fine."

"I don't think so. I think you've got your head turned round and you wouldn't know straight if it walked up and bit you."

"That's not true, Mama. We're happy here and things are fine. Why can't you see the truth?"

"The truth? Since when did you become reacquainted with the truth?"

"I can't talk to you when you're like this," Opal says. "I'm going to hang up, Mama." No sense talking anymore. No sense in trying to get the last word in on her mama. No one ever has.

CHAPTER 28

⌖ ROSE

"So," ned says. "what's on the agenda for today?"

"The dentist," Rose tells him. She waits, takes a breath, and plunges in, "Then I thought I'd take the bus over to Springfield."

"Springfield?" Ned gives her a sharp look. If he were a suspicious man, Rose would have cause to worry.

"I thought I'd do a little shopping at the mall. Maybe buy a new bedspread. Ours is worn thin. The fact is we could use some new towels, too." She can barely look at him.

But now he is smiling like a crazy man. He's already looking ahead: She's back working at Fosters, measuring out seersucker and calico, selling pink satin for prom dresses, bringing home the odd yard or two at the end of a bolt, sewing herself a skirt.

"That's great, Rosie," he says. His pleasure, his *hope* shames her. "Do you need money?"

When she called the Women's Health Services she hadn't asked about fees. She hasn't the slightest idea what it will run, and she can't go by what Doc charges. Doctors now charge an arm and a leg. She can't use insurance. That would lead to forms coming to the house. Paperwork Ned might see. If things get complicated—if it's *malignant*—there will be plenty of time for insurance.

He pulls out his wallet and insists on giving her a twenty.

"What time's the appointment?"

"Appointment?"

"The dentist."

"Ten o'clock." For a terrible moment she fears he's got it in his head to drive her.

HE LEAVES, WHISTLING, HAPPY AS A LOON 'CAUSE SHE'S GOING off to shop for a bedspread, the first step down the road to being her old self. She skips most of her regular chores, using the time to shower and change into panty hose, a dress. She's ready early, waiting in front of the house for Willis to show up with his cab.

"Federal Savings," she tells him.

Years ago, when she was pregnant with Todd, she started a bank account. Every week she'd slip something in from the household money. Tight weeks no more than a dollar. Other times as much as a ten. And the birthday and Christmas envelopes from Ned—*I never know what you'd like, Rosie, so take this and get yourself something you want*—all those crisp twenty- and fifty-dollar bills went straight into the account. Her dream account. What she was dreaming of was a good start for Todd. College, if scholarships didn't cover everything. Anything left over, she and Ned would take a vacation. Travel to different parts of the country. Her whole life she's wanted to see the Grand Canyon. Those dreams are so far in the past, they belong to a different woman.

It has been five years since Rose has made a deposit, and it takes a few minutes for the computer to tally all the interest she's accrued. It nearly fills the whole passbook. When she slides it through the window, Rose can hardly believe what she sees: $10,434.50. *Ten thousand dollars.* For dreams that are dead. She withdraws one hundred. She can't imagine it will cost more than that for a doctor to take a look at her mole. The whole thing shouldn't take more than fifteen minutes. What could they charge for that?

The bus is on schedule. She recognizes the driver, the same man who drove the run to Pellington, and she concentrates on getting the token in the coin box. The bus is nearly empty, no more than a dozen passengers—mostly students and middle-aged women like herself. She walks to the rear, takes a seat, plops her handbag down on the space next to her. She doesn't want any chatty Kathy sitting down and making conversation all the way to Springfield. *Do you have children?* How does she answer? *No.* And erase Todd, as if he's never been. *Yes.* And leave her open to more questions. *One. A boy. He would have been twenty-one. Accident. Sixteen.* And suffer the inevitable, suffocating sympathy.

There should be a name for people who have lost a child. If your husband dies, you're a widow. If your parents die, you're an orphan. But there is no word in the dictionary that can be used to describe the limbo of losing a child. Maybe in another language. One of those tongues that has seventy words for love, one hundred words for snow. Maybe the Eskimos have a word to describe a person who's been robbed of her child.

SHE CAN SEE AT ONCE THAT THE CLINIC IS A MISTAKE. IT'S located in a storefront on the edge of the downtown district. The floor is covered with that cheap indoor-outdoor stuff they use that wears like iron and doesn't show stains. Ugly as sin. The place is filled with pregnant women and kids with colds. Most of the children are sprawled on the filthy carpet playing with a crate of toys. There is a poster on the wall promoting flu shots and another says something about AIDS. Heavens.

"Can I help you?" The receptionist has yellow hair straight from a bottle—the cheap color that should come with a free pack of chewing gum attached. A placard on the counter advises that all bills must be paid at the time service is rendered.

"I have an appointment," Rose says.

"Name?"

"Rose Nelson." She waits while the woman checks the schedule.

"New patient?" She hands Rose a clipboard. "Have a seat and fill out this form. Front and back."

Rose scans the form. *Personal medical history. Family medical history.* What does it matter if she had chicken pox when she was eight or that she never had mumps? Venereal disease? Even if a person had it, Rose can't imagine anyone actually checking that off. She's stuck at *Reason for appointment.* Inflamed mole? Skin condition? Rash? Finally she settles on "skin irritation."

She returns the papers to the desk.

"Insurance?"

"No."

The receptionist taps the sign with the eraser end of her pencil. "We require full payment at the time of your visit."

Rose nods.

"Have a seat. We'll call you."

One of the pregnant women makes room for her on a wooden bench. Rose sits, leaving space between them. The outer door swings open, and a skinny woman enters. She has the vague, floating walk of an ex-drinker. Rose stares straight ahead. She doesn't touch the magazines. She can imagine the germs.

At a quarter to eleven, she approaches the desk. "Will it be much longer?"

The woman checks the schedule. "Shouldn't be more than another ten or fifteen minutes."

"My appointment was at ten-thirty."

"I know. We're running late."

Twenty minutes later she is called. She rises, embarrassed by the sound of her name still echoing in the room, and follows the nurse down the hall to a small examining room. She sits while the woman takes her temperature—98.6, right on the dot—and blood pressure.

"One hundred forty-six over ninety. Is that about normal for you?"

Rose has no idea. "Yes." Why they need all this is beyond her. She's here for a mole on her stomach.

"When was your last exam?"

She hasn't been to a doctor since right after Todd died, when Doc gave her those pills. Why can't they just look at the itchy mole and let her go? "Last year," she says.

"Regular mammograms?"

She hasn't had one in years. Apparently it isn't her breasts she has to worry about. "Yes."

"Generally, would you say you're in good health?"

"Yes." She's healthy as a horse. Except for the itch.

"And let's see—" The nurse checks the form she's filled out. "You're here about a skin irritation. Is that right?"

"Yes."

"Where is it?"

"On my stomach."

She's handed a smock. "Put this on. It ties in the back. The doctor will be right in."

Rose folds her dress and slip and places them on the chair. She rolls down her panty hose, folds them, and tucks them out of sight beneath the dress. The tile is cool beneath her feet. Should she remove her bra and panties? She slips the smock on over them, then sits on the edge of the chair, avoiding the paper-covered examining table.

There's a wait of several more minutes before there is a brief rap on the door.

A woman enters, extends her hand. "Hello," she says. "I'm Dr. Nutt. Two Ts."

A woman doctor? Thank God she's kept the panties on.

The doctor looks over her chart. "You've come about an itch?"

"Yes. On my stomach."

"Well, let's take a look." Dr. Nutt pats the table. "Have a seat here."

The paper makes a crinkling sound when Rose sits down. Her pulse pounds.

The doctor takes a minute to wash her hands in the little sink. She dries them, then rubs them together briskly. "Okay," she says. "Lie back while I have a look." When she touches Rose, her fingers are warm. Rose remembers all the times she's jumped from Doc's cold hands.

Dr. Nutt runs a fingertip over Rose's mole. "How long has this been bothering you?"

Rose counts back to the fall. To September. Seven months. It doesn't seem possible.

"And has it been inflamed all that time?"

"You mean red? Yes."

"Has there been any pain?"

"No. It just itches. I bought something at the drugstore, but it didn't really help."

"And has the diameter of the inflamed area increased?"

"Maybe a little."

Dr. Nutt palpitates the area. "Is this sensitive?"

"No."

She adjusts the smock, checks over Rose's entire abdomen and chest. "Okay. You can sit up now." She slides an arm behind Rose, helps her up. "Why don't you get dressed, and then I'll come back and we can talk."

"I think it was smart to come in," Dr. Nutt says when she returns. She looks down at Rose's chart. "There's been no history of melanoma in your family, which is good, but there's definitely something going on around that mole. What I'd like to have you do is see a dermatologist, get a biopsy. Just to be safe."

Biopsy.

"Do you know someone you'd like to use? Or if you prefer, we can make a recommendation."

Rose feels faint. "A recommendation, I guess."

"I'd suggest Dr. Murphy. He's the best in the area. If you like I can have the desk call over and make an appointment before you leave."

Rose wants Ned. He'd know what to do. She could lean on him. It was a mistake to have come alone.

CHAPTER 29

❧ O P A L

T HE PROBATE COURT IS NEW. A BRICK BOX OF A BUILD-
ing, soulless as a shoe box. Opal is late and so sweaty her blouse
sticks to her skin. She is dressed according to Vivian's direc-
tives. Think *mature*, think *responsible*, the lawyer advised on the phone
earlier in the week. What Opal thinks is that she looks as if her mama
picked out her clothes. The white blouse and navy skirt are drop-dead
boring, and the panty hose and black flats don't help. Her hair, also
tamed according to the lawyer's instructions, is held back in one thick
braid. She feels like she's wearing someone else's skin.

"How do I look?" she asked Ty before she left the house.

"Great," he said. "You're going to do just fine."

When she gave Zack a final kiss and warning to be good for Ty, he
reached up and patted her cheek. "Don't be scared," he said, which
just about killed her.

He thinks she is going to a meeting. She hasn't told him anything
about Billy wanting custody, but she wonders how much he's overheard. She's doing her best not to bad-mouth Billy in front of him.

SHE THREADS HER WAY PAST THE SMOKERS CLUSTERED AT
the entry.

Inside, the corridors are crowded. She scans faces, each looking
sorry-ass or lost. Or angry. Attorneys and clients cluster in last-minute

conferences, and as she makes her way down the hall Opal catches phrases of their conversations. *Restraining orders. Drunk. Custody. Bastard. Deposition.* There is a whole Nashville of songs in this one corridor.

She gets directions to the courtroom where their hearing will be held and spots Vivian.

The lawyer, dressed in a pantsuit that looks like it was born wrinkled, nods her approval at Opal's appearance. "How you doing?" she says. "You okay?"

"Just tell me there's no fucking way he's going to get Zack," Opal says. "That's when I'll be okay."

Vivian takes her arm, leads her to a vacant corner. "You want to win this?"

"Of course."

"Then clean up your language. Swearing doesn't make you an unfit mother, but it will prejudice the judge against you. She's a stickler about comportment in her courtroom. Got it?"

"Yes."

"Okay." She checks her watch. "Let's run over it one more time before we go in. I'll do most of the talking. If the judge asks you a direct question, you respond, but keep it short. Don't ramble. Don't give extra information. Answer just what she asks. That's where people get in trouble. If you're not sure, keep quiet. And don't attack Billy. You want to look like the rational one here."

They've been over this ten times already.

"Remember, this hearing is only to present the petition. Nothing's being decided here. It's just the first step."

"*He threatened me,*" Opal hears a woman say. She turns to look at the speaker, a hard-faced woman in jeans. Another woman, an older version of the speaker, enters the conversation. "That man has intimidated the whole family. We can't take a breath without being afraid. She should have left him years ago." The lawyer—a moon-faced woman who already looks tired—takes notes on a yellow pad.

"And remember," Vivian is saying, "no matter what the opposing council says, keep your temper."

"Okay."

"We're second on the agenda, which is good. We won't have to wait around getting nervous."

As if her last nerve isn't already shot.

"The first petition—the paternity issue—is straightforward. We're not disputing that. On the custody petition, today is just the first step. There won't be a ruling on that. The judge will listen to the petitions, set a date for the trial, appoint a guardian ad litem."

"Fuck that!" a woman shouts. Heads turn. The frazzled-looking woman starts crying.

Vivian rechecks her watch. "Need to use the bathroom before we go in?"

"Oh, God."

"What? What's wrong?"

Of course she should have been prepared, but she isn't. No way. "It's them," she says.

"How do you want to handle this?" Vivian asks. "Your choice. You want to talk to them?"

"Not Billy." Talk? She wants to kill him. There are five of them: Billy, her parents, and two others, a man and a woman, both well dressed. Attorneys.

Before she can even think, her daddy is there, holding her.

"Hi, Opal," he says.

"Hi, Daddy," she says. She inhales his Old Spice, is comforted by the familiarity.

"Raylee," Melva says. One word that says it all as far as Opal is concerned.

Billy and the lawyers don't approach.

"It's time to go in," Melva says.

The courtroom is cavernous, with high ceilings and blond veneer walls. A bank of narrow windows looks out on a lawn and, beyond that, the parking lot. The judge's bench, flanked by two flags, occupies the front of the room. In front of the oak benches—pews, Opal thinks, like church—there are two long tables. Two officers in uniforms stand at one side laughing about something. Pagers and holsters are strapped to their belts.

There are already more than two dozen people in the room. She had not realized the hearing would be open, that strangers would be there, listening. Until now—in spite of the legal papers, the meetings with Vivian—it hasn't seemed serious. She has been thinking of it as a private matter between her and Billy—a direct and sorry result of Billy's mule-headedness.

The assistant clerk, a balding man in a worn gray suit, enters and takes his place at a small table directly beneath the judge's bench. He leafs through a pile of papers. Except for the muffled conversation of the officers, the room is deathly still.

"All stand," one of the officers says as a man in a black robe strides in through a door behind the bench. He has black hair and a trim beard and is younger than Opal had expected.

"Shit," Vivian mutters.

"What?"

"Wait here." She slides out, approaches one of the court officers, whispers, and a moment later is back beside Opal.

"What's the matter?"

"They've shifted schedules. Judge Caryle had a family emergency. Judge Bowles is sitting today."

"Is that bad?"

"It isn't great."

Opal looks at the judge, who is conferring with the clerk. He looks impatient, tired. The room has grown so still she can hear the sound of the flagpole lanyards clanging on the lawn outside.

The first case is called. *Vierra versus Vierra.* A matter of unpaid alimony. While the lawyers begin, Opal studies Judge Bowles. He seems alternately bored and impatient. She wonders if he has children and what kind of father he is and if being a man will prejudice him in Billy's favor. Judges are supposed to be impartial, but she doesn't think that's possible. They're human. A woman judge would be better. But maybe not. Most women have a built-in prejudice against her, and she doesn't know if a judge would be any different.

She sneaks a look over at the other table. Opal can't believe how much it hurts to see her daddy there, taking Billy's part. Her daddy. Another man against her.

But of course it is Melva who is behind this. She can see her mama's hand at work, clear as crystal. She can just imagine the arguments her mama and daddy have had over this. Why should she be surprised that her mama won? Melva holds all the currency in their marriage.

What do they all want from her? Why can't they leave her alone? Do they really think she will return to New Zion? Melva won't be happy until she's back there *behaving* herself. Her mama probably will ask the judge to make her change her name back to Raylee Gates. To Tammy Raylee Gates.

Tammy Gates.

Opal was twelve when she decided to change her name. She was in eighth grade at New Zion Middle School, and Sujette Davis was her best friend. They both had a killer crush on John David Elwood. It was late October and someone—they later discovered it had been Suzanne Jennings's older brother Willy—had called in a bomb threat. Since there was only one full class left, they let everyone out early. Sujette wanted her to come home with her, but Opal had her bike and decided she'd ride over to her daddy's office and surprise him. Sometimes he let her hang around there, and if he could get away, he'd take her to the soda shop for a sundae. This is what she had in mind when she pedaled over to his office, her book bag swinging on the handlebars, the air charged with unexpected freedom.

She left her bike leaning against a parking meter in front of his building and went right in, but the place was empty. Her daddy's door was closed. She slung her book bag on a chair and wandered over to the bulletin board. The board covered most of the wall and held photos of all the property for sale in New Zion and the surrounding county. She could remember always staring at those houses, trying to decide which one she wanted. She used to think her daddy owned them all and if she wanted one all she had to do was ask and he would give it to her.

Would she choose a farmhouse—a big, sprawling place that came with a barn where she could keep horses? Or one of the ranch houses with a pool in back? Or a brick colonial all neat and precise, with tall windows on the front? Each house suggested a whole life that matched it.

She was inspecting a small wood-frame house with a porch on the side, a porch that would get just the right amount of shade from the overhanging limbs of a copper beech, when she heard a sound from behind her daddy's door.

"Tammy," her daddy said.

At first she thought he had heard her in the office and was calling to her, but his voice was thick and choked, like he was swallowing food and trying to talk at the same time. The sound of it made the hair on her arms stand straight up.

He was groaning. Maybe he was having a heart attack. Melanie Scott's daddy had had a heart attack, and he was only forty—two years younger than her daddy.

She would *save* him, she would be the heroine, everyone in New Zion would be talking about how lucky it was that she had gone to her daddy's office instead of home with Sujette and how brave she had been and how she had saved her daddy's life. She was crossing to the door, all these thoughts swirling through her brain, when she heard another voice: a woman calling out her daddy's name. Then she heard more of the moaning noises and the woman making little puppy-like yips.

She backed away, face suddenly hot. For months, sex had been the primary topic of conversation between her and Sujette, and they both agreed it was totally creepy to think of their parents *doing* it, that they probably didn't *do* it anymore. Now here was her daddy, *doing* it with Tammy Lee Roscoe, her mama's old friend and a woman so plain no one could believe she was married to that good-looking Vance Roscoe, the town druggist, even if she was rich.

She fled, pumping the bike so hard that her calves were sore for three days after. She sang an old Elvis song over and over—the hound dog one her Aunt May loved—practically screaming it. But it didn't stop the chatter in her mind. Her mind just wouldn't shut up.

When her daddy came home for dinner, he carried her book bag. She stared straight at him, but he looked the same as always. Her good-looking daddy who most folks said could charm the legs right off a fly leaned over and kissed her mama on the top of her head and sat down to eat just as if it were a regular night. Her mama recoiled just the tiniest bit, and Opal understood her mama knew about her daddy and Tammy Roscoe.

The next day she demanded to be called Raylee. And she began to keep a list of possibilities for later, when she was old enough to change her name entirely.

WHEN HER ATTENTION RETURNS TO THE PROCEEDINGS, THE judge is ordering Mr. Vierra to pay five thousand in back alimony.

"I can't, Your Honor," he says. "I don't have it."

"If you don't pay it, I'll have to find you in contempt of court. If you're in contempt, I am going to sentence you to fourteen days in jail. Do you understand?"

"Yes, Your Honor. But I can't pay what I don't have."

Right in front of his ex-wife and everyone in the courtroom, the judge sentences him to fourteen days in the county House of Correction. The man is handcuffed and led away. This judge is no one to screw with.

The clerk checks through his stack of papers. "Docket number 5P754," he says. "*Steele and Gates versus Gates.* Appearances?"

Opal can't move.

"Come on," Vivian says, taking her hand, leading her to the table vacated by Mrs. Vierra. She sets her briefcase on the table, motions for Opal to take a seat. Four feet away, her parents and Billy and the two lawyers stand at the other table. There is a momentary wait while one of the officers brings over a fifth chair. Billy stares straight ahead, ignoring her completely. She might as well be on Mars as far as he's concerned.

"Vivian Cummings here," Vivian says. "Appearing on behalf of Opal May Gates. Miss Gates is present."

At the other table, the woman does the talking. "Appearing are William Steele, Melva Gates, and Warren Gates, and on their behalf attorneys Steven Lodge and Carla Olsen."

Opal takes in the smooth voice, the shiny shoes, the woman's perfect helmet of blond hair. No chain smokers there. No wrinkled suits. And she's damn sure they don't operate out of a rundown storefront office. These people mean business. A cold nugget of fear lodges directly beneath her breastbone.

She feels the judge sizing her up and is relieved when his gaze travels to the other table and lands on Billy. "Let's begin," he says.

Everyone nods.

"This is the mother?" he asks, looking again at Opal.

"Yes, Your Honor," Vivian says.

"And the father? And—" He checks his notes. "—the grand-parents?"

"That's correct, Your Honor." Again it's the woman, Carla Olsen, who answers.

The side door opens, and a wiry woman in a pantsuit enters. She begins chatting with the bailiff.

The judge leans forward, removes his glasses. "All the parties involved are aware that this is not a trial," he says. "It is a hearing. A preliminary hearing. We are here to determine—" He looks down at the papers. "—the matter of paternity and to appoint a guardian ad litem for the child in question."

"Your honor," Carla Olsen begins, "Mr. Steele seeks full custody of his son."

"I am fully aware of what Mr. Steele is seeking," he says. "Let's not get going so fast here that we put the cart before the horse. The first motion is the matter of paternity. Mr. Steele," he says directly to Billy, "you maintain you are the father of Zackery, the son of Opal Gates?"

"Yes, Your Honor," Billy says.

"Miss Cummings, does your client deny Mr. Steele claim of paternity?"

"No, Your Honor."

"Everyone agrees?"

Billy *is* Zack's father, but Opal feels she is giving away something important. Until now it has been her and Zack. Now Billy will be a legal part of their life. She glances over at him, but he continues to look straight ahead.

"Paternity is granted," Judge Bowles says. "The next order of business is to appoint a guardian ad litem. Mrs. Rogers?"

The wiry athletic-looking woman cuts off her conversation with the bailiff and crosses to a table by the recorder.

"Yes, Your Honor?"

"You've agreed to take the case?"

"Yes, Your Honor."

"Miss Gates, Mr. Steele," the judge says to her and Billy. "Mrs. Sarah Rogers will be, in effect, the voice of your son in the proceedings. She will be his advocate. She, or someone from her office, will be contacting you. They will conduct an investigation and report their findings back to the court. Is that clear?"

"Yes, sir."

"Yes, Your Honor."

"I'm going to set a hearing for ninety days from today. At that time Mrs. Rogers will have completed her investigation and will make her recommendations to the court. I will then hear testimony from all concerned parties and deliver my decision. Any questions?"

"About current custody, Your Honor," Carla Olsen says. "Mr. Steele and Mr. and Mrs. Gates—the child's maternal grandparents—are deeply concerned about the child's welfare in the interim. Until the evidentiary hearing, the father wishes an emergency custody order. We have serious concerns about the boy's well-being while he is in his mother's care."

"We contest," Vivian says. Beneath the cover of the table, she squeezes Opal's arm. Stay cool.

"So I'd expect," the judge says.

Opal is on her feet. "He can't do that. He didn't even want Zack. He wanted me to have an abortion."

"Miss Cummings, please tell your client to sit down and be quiet." Opal sinks back.

"Your Honor, this is outrageous," Vivian says. "On what basis are they seeking temporary custody?"

"A good question, Miss Cummings. Miss Olsen?"

"It is in the child's best interest, Your Honor."

He sighs, laces his fingers behind his head. "How does Mr. Steele feel that that will best serve the interests of Zack?"

"He is better suited financially to care for the boy. And he will have the additional support of the boy's grandparents, who will share in the daily care."

Melva taking care of Zack? It kills Opal to think of him in the tightly controlled world of her mama's house. Kills her. Feet off the furniture, elbows off the table. Rules for everything. Finish your dinner or no dessert. Everything in its place.

"Miss Cummings?"

"We oppose the petition, Your Honor."

"Your Honor." Carla Olsen again.

A flash of irritation flits over the judge's face at being interrupted. Opal allows herself to feel hope.

"There is also the question of ensuring that the boy will still be here in Massachusetts in ninety days. Last September, with no advance warning, Miss Gates removed the boy from his home, from his grandparents and his father, and left town, thereby depriving them of their rights."

"Is that right?" he asks Vivian.

"No, Your Honor. While it is true that Opal relocated from North Carolina, she in no way prevented the boy's father or grandparents from visiting. In the past six months Mr. Steele has seen fit to enter the Commonwealth only once, and the grandparents have never been to visit either their daughter or their grandson."

"Mr. Steele?"

Billy stares at the table.

"Mr. Steele, is it true that you have only been to see your son once since Miss Gates moved to the Commonwealth?"

"Yes," Billy mumbles.

"Mr. and Mrs. Gates? You have never visited?"

"Your Honor," Carla Olsen begins.

"A simple question. Will your clients please answer?"

"It's not that simple," Melva says. "We asked Raylee—"

"Raylee?"

"That's Miss Gates' birth name," Carla Olsen says. "Several years ago Miss Gates changed her name."

The judge makes a note. "I see. Go on, Mrs. Gates."

"We asked her to come home for the holidays. She refused."

"And did you then take it upon yourself to visit the child?"

Melva doesn't answer.

"Your Honor." The male attorney stands. "The point is, my clients think the boy will be better off with his father and grandparents."

"On what basis?"

"Miss Gates is not stable. Who can say she won't get it into her head to move to California next?"

"Miss Gates, are you planning another move?"

"No, sir."

"Miss Cummings, can you guarantee your client will remain where she is for the next ninety days?"

"Yes, Judge."

"I'm going to deny Mr. Steele's request. If Zack has stayed with Miss Gates since last September with no attempt on the part of the other parties involved to either see the boy or guard his welfare, I see no reason to change things now. Are there, at this time, any formal visitation rights in place?"

"No, sir."

"Miss Cummings, what is the boy's current situation regarding schooling?"

"He attends preschool half a day for five days a week until June."

"While taking into consideration the law's incapacity to manage family relationships, I am going to grant temporary visitation rights for Mr. Steele. I am ordering a two-week period of visitation for Zackery to visit his father between now and the hearing."

"Thank you, Your Honor," Carla Olsen says. She smiles widely, like this is a big victory.

Opal can't imagine Zack gone for two weeks. Her stomach feels hollow.

"One more thing," Carla Olsen says. "We are seeking an injunction preventing Mr. Tyrone Miller from having anything to do with the boy."

Opal's mouth drops wide open. She looks over at Billy.

"Who is Mr. Miller?"

"Miss Gates' current boyfriend."

Opal's knees turn buttery. What has Ty got to do with anything? She isn't married to Billy. She's a single woman. Why are they bringing this up?

"Relevance, Your Honor?" Vivian asks.

"Miss Olsen?" the judge asks. "On what grounds?"

"We are concerned, Your Honor. In the past, drug charges have been filed against Mr. Miller. Possession and intent to distribute."

"What? What is she talking about?" Opal turns to Vivian, who is on her feet.

"Your Honor," Vivian is shouting. "This is outrageous. I am personally acquainted with Mr. Miller. Those charges are ancient history. They have no relevance whatsoever. This is an obvious attempt to discredit my client and to prejudice the court."

"Approach."

Opal, sickened, watches while Vivian and the other attorneys cluster at the bench. The judge calls over the guardian.

Melva looks over at Opal, her face smug as a cat full of cream.

OUTSIDE, IN THE CORRIDOR, VIVIAN REACHES FOR HER ARM, but Opal shakes her off.

"Judge Bowles' denial for their injunction is a good sign. He isn't going to be swayed by anything that they can't substantiate by fact."

As far as Opal is concerned the judge might as well have ruled against Ty. She isn't going to let him *near* Zack. She can't take any chances. "Why the fuck didn't you tell me about Tyrone? Why didn't you warn me? Jesus, he's watching Zack right now."

Vivian grasps her arm, faces her. "Number one, you didn't tell me you were dating him. Number two, as the judge ruled, it doesn't pertain. As far as the court is concerned, he's clear and clean."

"Well, I can guarantee that's not what my mama's thinking. 'Where's there's fumes, there's fire,' in Mama's mind. How did she learn about Ty anyway?"

"Probably hired a detective. It definitely looks like they're ready to play hardball. Obviously they're planning on using anything they can find to prejudice the judge. Here's my advice: For the next ninety days live like a monk. Behave as if everything you do will be reported to the court. And start thinking about who you want us to call as character witnesses. We have to counteract the weight of your parents sitting there at the other table."

"The judge won't really give Billy custody, will he? He can't do that. I'm his mama."

"That's what we're hoping for." She gives Opal a quick hug. "Remember. Like a monk. The perfect mother."

WHEN SHE PULLS ONTO CHESTNUT STREET, SHE CAN'T BE-lieve her eyes. Ty has Zack out in the street—in the *street*—playing hockey.

"Zack," she says as she gets out of the car. "In the house."

He looks up at Ty, his smile fading.

"Don't look at him!" she screams. "I said get in the house."

"Hey, Opal. Calm down."

"What the hell were you doing in the street? He could have been hit."

"Hey, baby. Lighten up. It's a dead end here. We can see a car com-ing. We were careful." Out of Zack's earshot he says, "Don't yell at him. It was my fault. If you want to yell at someone, yell at me."

She turns away and heads toward the house. "I wouldn't waste my breath on you."

"What's going on here? You're being kind of rough, aren't you?"

"Just go home. Go home and leave me and Zack the hell alone."

"What's going on, Opal? What happened at the hearing?"

"What happened? I'll tell you what the fuck happened. Billy and my parents sat there looking concerned as their lawyer asked the judge for a restraining order. A restraining order to prevent you from having anything to do with Zack."

"Me?"

"You. Tyrone Miller. The drug pusher."

"Jesus. What happened?"

Opal is exhausted now. "Just go."

"But what did the judge say. What happened?"

"Oh, he denied the request."

"So there's no problem. Right?"

"Wrong. You're the problem."

"Damn, Opal, be reasonable. Don't do this. I can help."

"I don't need anyone's help. Least of all yours."

"The whole thing with the drugs happened a long time ago. It was a mistake. Okay?"

"I can't afford any mistakes. You hear me?"

"What are you saying?"

"I'm saying I want you to go."

"Jesus, Opal, I can understand that you're upset, but you're not thinking straight."

She turns on him, and her question comes out with all the sadness of her tired soul. "Why didn't you tell me about being arrested?"

"I was a kid. It was a mistake. Haven't you ever made a mistake?"

"I can't afford a mistake, Ty. I can't afford your mistakes. I can't afford you."

"Wait. Listen to me, Opal. Let me explain."

"Explain nothing. I can lose you. I can't lose Zack."

❧ SUMMER ❧

CHAPTER 30

⊸ N E D

J UST AFTER FOUR, NED LOWERS THE LIFT. AT THE SER-
vice desk, he notes the time in an appointment book thick with
order forms and assorted sheets of paper. The page is greasy
with thumbprints. Tyrone's been telling him he should get a computer,
but the thought is enough to bring on a headache. Why put any
money into something like that? As soon as he can convince Rose to
head south, the place is history. This isn't the time to be investing in
new equipment.

What is it the time for?

Ned never has given much thought to the patterns at work in his
life. He expected his life to be as predictable as his father's had been:
School, work, retirement. Time to fish. Maybe take that trip to the
Grand Canyon Rose used to talk about. But now his life is off
course, and he has no idea how to get it back on track. He has no
answers and no one to ask. The only one he sees regularly, besides
Rose, is Ty—not that he'd confide in him. The mechanic has been
moody lately, mooning around ever since Opal ditched him. Good
riddance, is what Ned thinks, but he knows enough to keep his
mouth shut.

Officially, there's another hour before closing, but as he has every
day for the past three weeks, he crosses to the door, switches the sign
from *Open* to *Closed*, and heads over to Trudy's. Without knowing

exactly how it came about, he has gotten in the habit of going over and sitting at the counter for a mug of coffee while she closes up. He finds a certain peace in watching her wipe the counters clean, refill the sugar bowls and catsup bottles, scrape clean the grill. The television behind the counter is usually on. *Oprah* turned low, although every now and then Trudy cranks up the dial and enters into the discussion just as if she's part of the studio audience.

Even though she officially closes at four, as soon as he walks through the door, she puts on a fresh pot. He looks forward to this time, but he can't shake the feeling that he's doing something wrong.

Today she sets out a slice of apple pie. "One slice left. You might as well finish it up." She makes it sound like he's doing her a favor.

Yesterday it was Boston cream. His favorite. He knows he shouldn't be eating this stuff. He's been putting on weight. It spoils his appetite for dinner. Not that Rose notices.

"You want a scoop of vanilla on that?"

What the hell, he's not going to live forever. Might as well enjoy what time he has left. He's fifty-seven. Not getting any younger, that's for sure. Sorrow tightens his chest. He can see all the promise of the future fading right before his eyes. "Sure," he says.

Trudy pours herself a cup and joins him at the counter. Today Oprah has some guy on talking about how a person can heal his life. Forgiveness is the key, he tells the audience.

Trudy snorts. "Forgiveness," she says, "is a bunch of crap. There are some things a person can't forgive." Her daughter Phyllis has just gone back to her husband, making it the couple's third or fourth reconciliation. There's plenty of talk around town that Jeff gets physical when he drinks. Trudy would like Phyllis to get a divorce and be done with it.

"I wouldn't put up with that shit for a minute," she told Ned last week. He does not doubt this. Trudy is not a woman to put up with anyone's bullshit.

"That's pretty," he says, pointing to a beaded band on her wrist, and then he feels embarrassed to be paying her a compliment.

"Thanks," she says, pleased. "Lorraine sent it."

Four years ago, Trudy began sponsoring a child on a Lakota reservation in South Dakota. On holidays, she puts out a carton for people to make donations to the tribe: clothing, canned goods, toys. Her dream is to make the trip out there to meet the girl in person. Ned wonders what the fishing is like in South Dakota.

"How about people like Hitler?" a woman is asking Oprah's guest. "Should we forgive people like that? Do they deserve our forgiveness?"

"Enough of this," Trudy says, hitting the mute button. Her favorite shows are when there is a movie star on. Like Julia Roberts or Cher.

"How's Rose?" she asks.

"The same," Ned says, which is as close as he can come to telling anyone about how bad things are at home.

Rose has reverted to that vague, floaty state he remembers from the year after Todd's death. She doesn't hear half the things he says to her. He might as well be living alone.

The cruel thing is that he thought he was getting her back. That day she said she was going over to Springfield to shop, he really took it as a sign she was returning to her old self. He allowed himself to hope.

That night, when he got home, he planned on surprising her and taking her out for dinner to that Italian place she used to like. But as soon as he walked through the door and saw her sitting and staring into space, he saw all his plans going up the flue.

What the hell is going on? he wanted to say. He wanted to get everything out in the open. When could he expect her to get on with life? How long was she going to keep grieving Todd? Not that he expected her to forget, but Christ, enough is enough. You can't expect a person to climb in the coffin and die too. And while he was at it, he wanted to talk to her about the professor he had seen her with in Pellington. He wants to tell her that he opened the letter Anderson Jeffrey mailed to her. He knows all about the piece she wrote for the writing class last fall. It was hard reading—all that stuff about Todd dying and Rose's guilt about not letting him use the car. Her *anger* at everyone. He had no idea.

He is ashamed he's read her mail. He's hidden the envelope in the back of the desk. He'd like there to be an opportunity to let her know he's read it and to tell her he doesn't blame her for Todd's death and she shouldn't blame herself. *Forgiveness is the key.* He wants to tell her he loves her. He wants to clear the air of secrets.

Well, now he has these afternoons with Trudy. His own secret. And two people who have spent most of their lives sharing everything now drift like dandelion fluff in a field of secrets.

Is that the way it is with secrets? One leads to another.

And another.

CHAPTER 31

❧ O P A L

"AUNT MAY? IT'S ME, OPAL."

"Opal, darling, how are you?"

Opal chokes back tears. "I'm sinking here, Aunt May."

"Hold on a sec, darling, can you?"

She hears May telling whatever guitar-picking man she is presently with to get going. A man's laugh floats through the wire, then the sound of a kiss—wet and long. Men love May, and she returns the compliment. Finally, her aunt picks up the receiver again.

"What's going on, child? Tell your Aunt May."

Instantly, Opal is catapulted back to her childhood, to the number of times she would ride her bike over to May's for consolation and understanding. *Tell your Aunt May. Give me a kiss.* Opal cannot imagine two women more different than May and Melva. Melva all tight-lipped and hard-edged; May full of laughter and ready to take love anywhere she finds it. You wouldn't believe they were sisters. Opal is no different than May. You wouldn't take her for her mama's daughter.

"Have you talked to Melva?" she says. "Has she told you Billy is trying to get custody of Zack?"

"She told me. I laughed out loud. I mean, the whole idea of Billy getting Zack is a joke."

"Well, I'm not laughing, Aunt May. I'm sitting on my last nerve here. The woman the court appointed is due here in an hour. She's coming for an interview, and I'm definitely not laughing."

"Well, anyone would be nervous about that, child, but you try and relax. Don't think of her as your enemy. She's just another woman, sugah. That's all. Just another woman with a job to do. You don't have anything to worry about. Any fool with two eyes can see that Zack's place is with you. Just look her straight in the face like you've nothing in God's world to hide. Be friendly."

How can you act friendly when a person is prying into your life, deciding whether or not to let you keep your son? "Do you know Mama and Daddy are on Billy's side?"

"Melva made that clear. She's turned pure crazy on this subject. I swear, sometimes I don't know what's the matter with her."

What *is* the matter with her mama? What's gone so wrong between them? "Why does she hate me so, Aunt May? Why does my Mama hate me?"

"Oh, sugar, she doesn't hate you."

"She does. She doesn't even like me."

"Now don't you be saying that. Don't you even think it."

Opal settles back and stares out the window, traces the progress of a squirrel up the trunk of the maple over in Rose's yard. What *is* she to think?

"Do you remember when I was in the high school play?"

"*Our Town?* Sure do." Opal can almost *hear* May's smile though the wire. "Lord, but you made me proud."

"Mama didn't even come."

"Oh, surely she did, child."

"She didn't. Not for one performance. She got one of her sick headaches. She didn't want to see me." She rushes on before her aunt can reply. "And she missed every single one of my dance recitals."

"Surely she didn't."

"And when I was having Zack, Mama didn't even show up at the hospital. Do you know where she was? Do you, Aunt May? She was getting her hair done. I was in the hospital having a *baby*, having her grandchild, and she was getting a dye job. Jesus."

"Try and understand, Opal."

"Screw understanding. I'm sick of being told to understand. And why are you defending her? Everyone always defends her. All I know is that she hates me."

"She doesn't hate you, Opal."

"She does."

"She's jealous of you."

"What?"

"Jealous, honey. Your mama's always been jealous of you."

"Of me? How can you be jealous of your own child?" She can't imagine being jealous of Zack. She thinks of how Melva is all the time saying, "We only want the best for you." How can you wish the best for someone and then be jealous if she gets it?

"Opal, Melva's afraid of you."

"Afraid of me?"

"You remind her of too much. She sees herself in you."

"I'm nothing like Mama." Outside, two squirrels are playing hide-and-seek in the branches of the maple. "There's not one thing Mama and I have in common."

"But she *was* like you. Not the way she is today. Back when she was your age, she gave our mama a run for her money. About drove her crazy. They had some fights those two."

"Mama did?"

"She surely did. If Papa hadn't kept the guns locked up, I think one of them would have killed the other."

"I can't picture that."

"Let me tell you, I was witness to the battles. Opal, honey, don't be too hard on your mama. She's just trying to make up for the mistakes she's made in life."

"Mama never made any mistakes. Don't you know that? She's perfect."

"Your mama's no different from anyone else. She has her share of regrets. That's why she's so hard on you."

"Right."

"Opal, I'm going to tell you something I've got no right telling, but I'm going ahead anyway. It's something that may help you understand about your mama and the guilt and regrets she lives with and why she's so hard on you and why Zack is so important to her."

Opal rolls her eyes. Nothing May can say will soften her heart toward Melva.

"When Melva was fifteen and just about the prettiest girl in New Zion there was a boy we were all crazy about. One of the Munford twins, Henry James. Lord, Lordy, was he good-looking. And smart. He went up north to school. Rhode Island, I think. One of those Ivy League schools. Anyway he came home for the summer, and right from the start he settled on your mama, cut her off from the rest of us and swept her off her feet. He brought her flowers and wrote her poems. One night he climbed the old water tower down by the depot and wrote her name in letters eight feet tall. She didn't stand a chance. By the time September came, your mama was in love."

Opal pictures the old tower. Anything written there had been painted over a long time before she was born.

"Of course Henry James headed back up north. Your mama, she just about set up camp out by our mailbox. About two weeks after he'd gone, she learned she was pregnant."

"Mama?" Opal feels peculiar, like she is hearing a story about someone she both knows and doesn't know at all.

"A week or two later, when she couldn't figure out what to do, she told me. Course, she couldn't tell our mama."

Opal remembers when she got pregnant how her mama went on and on about how she'd shamed the family. She thinks of the times her mama put down May. "May's no better than a revolving bed," she'd warn. "You're not careful you'll end up just like her." The hypocrite.

"One night after dinner, we went to the phone booth down at Calley's Drug Store and called up Henry James. Told him the story. He surely didn't send flowers or poetry then. No. All that boy sent was money. To take care of it, he said." May stops to take a breath. "There wasn't even a note in the envelope. That about broke Melva's heart. She kept saying that if she learned anything it was about the trouble that comes from believing every promise you hear."

What? Is she supposed to feel sorry for her mama now? Is she supposed to understand? Well she doesn't. More than ever she doesn't understand how her mama could want to take Zack away from her.

"Don't you see, Opal? Your mama couldn't keep her baby, and you got to keep Zack. She's always been bitter about losing her child, but now she's jealous too. You're stronger than she is, child. You fought to keep your son. She can't forgive you for that."

SARAH ROGERS GETS RIGHT DOWN TO BUSINESS. "AS THE judge explained, I'm Zackery's advocate. My job is to see that he is properly and fully represented."

Like Zack needs anyone to represent him. Opal scratches her hip. She doesn't like the first thing about this woman.

"I'll organize and present all relevant information to the judge so that he can make an informed decision. This includes our office's recommendations." She gives Opal a wide, fakey smile. "We all want what's best for Zackery."

Right, she thinks. As if I want what's worst for him.

"After I talk with you, I'll be talking with his teachers. Your neighbors. And of course, I'll want to talk with Zackery. I'll probably be recommending that he have a psychiatric evaluation."

"Zack. I call him Zack." One of Sarah Rogers' eyes is the tiniest bit smaller than the other.

Sarah takes a seat and digs out a notebook. "Zack goes to school. Is that right?"

Opal nods. "Half a day."

"What about out of school? Who are his friends? Does he have a special playmate?"

"Not really. Just the kids in school."

"Does he ever stay overnight anywhere else?"

"He's kind of young for sleepovers." Opal picks at her chipped nail polish. What does any of this have to do with Billy suing for custody?

Sarah Rogers makes a notation. "When was the last time he had a checkup?"

"Checkup?"

"Seen a doctor? Had a physical?"

Opal deflects the question. "Are you going to be asking Billy questions, too? He doesn't know the first thing about raising a child. Instead of talking to me, you should be checking up on him."

"Of course, we'll be talking to Zack's father," Sarah says smoothly. "But right now, I am interested in you. Let's see, where were we? Oh, yes. When did Zack have his last checkup? Who is his pediatrician?"

Could she lie? How closely do they investigate?

"He hasn't needed one," Opal finally says. "He hasn't been sick since we moved here."

Sarah checks her notes. "I see here that he had a broken arm last fall."

Opal shivers, draws her arms tight. Who has she been talking with? "That wasn't an illness. An accident."

"There was a notation about bruises on the hospital records. I gather there was some concern expressed by the covering physician. Have there been any other accidents?"

"No." Forget what Aunt May said. This was not just another woman trying to do her job. This was a bitch who was going to make her look bad. She struggles to keep her temper from flipping on.

"How do you discipline your son, Miss Gates?"

I beat him with big sticks, she thinks, but says, "Time out. If he's really naughty."

"How would you characterize Zack's relationship with his father?"

Easy answer. "He doesn't have one."

"And before you left New Zion?"

"He hardly ever saw him. Billy didn't have the least interest in seeing Zack. I don't know why the hell he wants him now."

"And your parents? How was their relationship with Billy?"

"All right, I guess."

"How is it now?"

"Better than mine."

CHAPTER 32

~ R O S E

"JUST RELAX, MRS. NELSON," THE NURSE SAYS.

Rose is prone on the examining table, stripped to her panties, although thank God the nurse has draped a sheet over her legs.

The doctor is a bantam of a man. White as an uncooked perch, probably from taking his own advice. The waiting room is filled with literature advising patients to avoid the sun. Rose remembers when people used to tan without worrying. She spent whole summers spread out on a beach blanket like a sacrifice, her skin slathered with a mixture of baby oil and iodine. Her father spent every day of his life working outside on the farm. By the end of haying season, the skin on his arms was so thick and dark it reminded her of a turtle, yet he never gave the least thought to cancer. You didn't used to hear as much about it. Not like now. At least three people she and Ned know have had skin cancer. She supposes, if you believe everything you hear, it has something to do with the thinning of the ozone layer. She is suspicious of these proclamations of scientists. Who's to know that they're not just making these things up?

"Good morning." The doctor gives her a quick nod and immediately begins to recite. "Patient female. Fifty-four. Complains of itch and redness around a mole on her abdomen."

It takes Rose a moment to realize he is speaking into a microphone clipped onto the lapel of his lab coat.

He wheels a stool over next to the table and sits. "Let's take a look." He presses a finger against the mole. "Hurt?"

"No. Just itches."

He turns to the nurse, who hands him a small instrument. "Questionable," he says to the mike. "Zero point eight centimeter, asymmetrical, variable pigmented macula on right periumbilical."

Macula. Periumbilical. His hands move over her stomach.

"I think it's a good thing to check it out," he says to her. "We'll take a biopsy. Then go from there."

Rose—never a fainter—feels dizzy. "Now?" she says.

"It's a simple procedure," he explains. "I'm going to give you a local. You'll just feel a pinch." He wipes her abdomen with a swab. She smells the alcohol. Wait, she wants to say. Let me think about it.

"Five cc's of lidocaine," he says to the nurse.

Rose grits her teeth against the anticipated pain, which, when it comes, is less than she expects. A pinch, like he said.

He pats her arm. "I'm going to let that take hold. Shouldn't be more than a minute or two."

He wheels away, drops the hypodermic on a tray, and leaves the cubicle.

A few minutes later he is back. "All set?" he says. He washes up in the basin, pulls on a mask. She hears the slap and snap as he pulls on latex gloves.

She stares at the ceiling, feels a sensation of distant pressure on her belly. A tickle. He talks into the Dictaphone, but she blocks out the words.

"All done," he says sometime later. He puts a block of gauze on her stomach and secures it with tape. Strips off his gloves.

"Any questions?"

"Well—"

"The nurse will give you instructions. We've put a dry sterile dressing on it. You'll need to change it every day for ten days and apply an antibacterial medication. Of course call us if you have any concerns."

"When will you know if it's—"

"We'll have the results in a week. I'll have the office give you a call."

"And then you might have to remove it?"

He looks at her and then laughs. "I just did."

"You did?" She had expected a big procedure. Hospital. Pain.

"Try not to worry," he says. "From the look of it right now, every-thing will be fine."

OUTSIDE THE SUN IS SO BRIGHT, IT BITES HER EYES. EVERY-thing is sharp, as if he has operated on her vision. She is surprised to find she is hungry. There is food at home, but she takes herself out for a sandwich at Friendly's, like a celebration although Lord knows she doesn't yet know if there is the least thing to celebrate.

After lunch, she stops at a nursery and buys two small pots of red geranium. Ivy trails over the edge of the planters. All the way on the bus ride back to Normal, she cradles the bag on her lap.

THE CEMETERY IS DOTTED WITH SMALL SQUARES OF RED AND white. Every Memorial Day for as long as she can remember, the American Legion has set flags out on veterans' graves.

As she approaches Todd's grave, she sees a spot of blue. Closer she sees that someone has left a tiny bouquet of lilacs by his headstone. Her mouth tightens with displeasure. Occasionally she still finds things here. Flowers for the most part. Right after the funeral girls in his class used to leave all manner of things there. Letters. Plastic flow-ers. Stuffed toys. She threw them in the trash. She has no interest in knowing the girls—it is, of course, girls—who leave these things, the same ones who made spectacles of themselves at his funeral, as if by the noise of their grief they were staking claim on her son. She removes the bouquet, already wilted, and walks to the edge of the cemetery, where she tosses it.

Four years ago, she planted a willow at the foot of Todd's grave, and the grass is thick and green beneath its shade. Newly mowed. Ned makes out a check each year to the cemetery commission to ensure that the grave is taken care of. Not far from this plot is a grave of a twelve-year-old boy. It's a patch of weeds. How anyone could let it go like that is beyond her. Rose gentles her thoughts toward forgive-ness. A grave is, after all, just ground. Maybe their way of grieving is to turn away. Maybe they've died, too. Or moved. How could they move? Perhaps a person could. The real grave, she thinks, is a place inside you.

She takes a Kleenex out of her handbag and wipes a bird dropping from the face of the headstone; then she slides the geraniums out from the shopping bag and places the pots by the stone. They won't bring him back. Nothing will bring him back, but the flowers make her feel connected to him. Grieving is about not forgetting.

She flattens the bag and sets it on the ground, then sits. The lidocaine is wearing off, and she feels a sensation—not quite pain—where the mole was removed. In the distance, she sees a man walking a retriever. He should not be here—the cemetery is posted—but she isn't up to a confrontation.

She still has not given her answer to the editor, a man named Bruce Constantine. "We have to know soon," he told her last week. "We're closing in on our deadline for the issue." He has a nice voice, calm and patient.

She had pretty much decided not to let them publish her piece. Grief is private, regardless of all the nice things Mr. Constantine said. But now she is having second thoughts. She allows herself to be consoled by the idea that no one she knows would read it. Probably not one living soul in Normal has even heard of the *Sun*. And he said what she wrote would help others. She doesn't know if this is true. She doesn't think anything she read could have helped her after Todd died. But the editor's compliments stay in her head. She wants more and feels guilty for wanting it.

"I don't know," she says to Todd's headstone. "I don't know what to do."

WHEN SHE GETS HOME, THERE IS A CAR PARKED IN THE driveway. As she nears, a woman steps out of the car.

"Mrs. Nelson?"

"Yes."

"I'm Sarah Rogers. I called you earlier."

Lord, she has completely forgotten about the appointment.

"Yes," she says. She'll be damned if she's going to apologize for being late.

The woman holds out her hand. "This won't take long. Just a few questions about your neighbor."

Rose shakes hands but doesn't invite her inside.

"As you know, I have been appointed by the court to evaluate and make a recommendation."

Evaluate. Sticking her nose in where it doesn't belong. The woman follows her inside.

"You're friends with Miss Gates. With Opal?" Sarah Rogers begins.

Rose hesitates. A land mine here. "Hmmmm," she says, noncommittally. She doesn't want to get involved, but she doesn't want to say anything to hurt Opal either. The girl may not be the best mother in the world, but the truth is, Opal loves her boy. More than a father who has shown up only once.

Sarah Rogers opens her briefcase and takes out some papers.

"What can you tell me about Zack? I'd like to know what you've observed about his relationship with his mother."

"I don't really know them that well," she says.

Sarah checks her notes. "According to Opal, you baby-sit for Zack."

"Once," Rose says. "New Year's Eve."

"Did she happen to talk to you about how she came to Normal?"

This is a safer subject. She tells her about how Opal threw a die and drove that many tanks of gas. She tells her that Opal believes in signs.

"And she said you were there when Zack broke his arm. Can you tell me about that?"

Rose hesitates. "I need a glass of water. I'm parched. Can I get you one?" Caught between a rock and a hard place. She doesn't want to lie. Buy time, she thinks. If she tells the truth, what will happen to Zack? She knows what Ned would tell her to do. But what does her heart tell her? How did she get in this deep?

"Mrs. Nelson?" Sarah prompts.

CHAPTER 33

꙳OPAL

O PAL STRETCHES AWAKE, GLANCES OVER AT THE
clock. It's after ten.

It's been years since she has had the luxury of sleeping
late. Except this doesn't feel like a luxury. It feels like a bunk in hell.

Zack has been in New Zion for one week now, with one more week
stretching ahead. It was a mistake to have agreed to the two weeks. She
should have fought for one week now and then another later, safely in
the future. Maybe Billy would be satisfied with one week. Maybe he
would give up altogether. She listens to the too-quiet house. The loss
feels physical, hollowness she can actually feel in her stomach, her
chest, her throat. Her heart.

She'd feel better if she could hear Zack's voice, but she hesitates to
phone again. Last night's conversation dissolved into tears on both
sides. "Satisfied?" she said to Billy when he'd taken the receiver. "He
was fine until you called," he shot back.

Was he? How would she know? How can she believe anything Billy
says? She doesn't trust him a quarter of a country mile. She should
have fought the visitation. What had Vivian told her? It was to her
advantage to appear reasonable? She doesn't want to be reasonable.
She wants to have Zack.

Did Billy listen when she told him that Zack likes to have orange
juice on his cereal instead of milk? Or that he can't sleep without Tig-

ger? She knows Billy thinks she's too soft on Zack. Billy's philosophy is that he's a boy, he should be tough.

Thinking of him at Melva's is worse. Her mama's rules are rigid as a flagpole: Finish everything on your plate. (Even if it's cabbage. Or lima beans, which absolutely make you puke.) Bedtime at seven-thirty. (Even if you're wide awake and just lying in bed makes your skin itch.) No night-lights. (Even if werewolves wait in dark corners.) Her mama's rules are endless, without heart. Who will protect Zack from Melva?

Fuck it. She reaches for the phone and dials Billy's number. On the other end, the line rings. Once. Twice. Four times. Seven. No answer. No machine. Where the hell are they? She is powerless here. She has no hands to touch her baby.

She feels the rumble of panic. She wants Zack.

CHAPTER 34

❧ N E D

T HEY HAVE FINISHED THEIR COFFEE AND THE LAST OF A lemon meringue pie. While Trudy clears the dishes, Ned switches off the television and opens the register. He counts the bills, notes the amount on a slip, pulls an elastic band around the money, and shoves it into the canvas night deposit bag. He has taken to helping Trudy close up. There is something about the routine that settles his nerves.

By the time he's done, she returns from the kitchen. "Can you give me a ride home?" she asks. "Phyllis needed the car."

Her daughter is shopping for an apartment, the first step to leaving her husband, although Trudy has seen this scene played out enough not to get her hopes up.

"Sure."

She waits while he makes room on the passenger side of the pickup.

"Sorry," he says, stuffing greasy rags and a parts manual behind the seat.

"I wasn't expecting a stretch limo."

In the confines of the cab, he is aware of her smell, a surprisingly pleasing mix that contains traces of cooking grease and the warm scent of a woman's body.

She lights a cigarette. "Mind?"

"No," he says, although he does. Rose will smell it on him. Although he has done nothing wrong, he feels guilty. Oh, sure, he's had *thoughts* about Trudy. What man wouldn't? She's an attractive woman. But thoughts aren't action. As far as Rose is concerned, he's been true to his vows. Never been a question of cheating.

Trudy exhales a lungful of smoke. It swirls around the cab. Ned adjusts the vent window so air is directed at him.

"You sure this isn't bothering you?"

"No. I used to smoke. Gave it up ten years ago."

"I tried. Didn't last a day."

"You should get yourself one of those patches."

"Why bother? No one lives forever. Might as well get what enjoyment you can while you're here, that's my philosophy. What's that commercial? 'Go for the gusto.' "

As far as he can see, there isn't much gusto in her life. He wonders if she sleeps with anyone. There have been rumors over the years—inevitable, a woman like Trudy alone—but never specific names. In Normal, a secret doesn't stay buried long.

"You're quiet," she says.

"Just tired." And this is true. He's glad the weekend is one day away. More and more lately, exhaustion takes him by surprise. He could use a vacation. A real one. Different scenery. Lazy days. Hammock days. Listening to ball games on the transistor. He exhales a long, tired sigh. He'd have as much chance of getting Rose to agree as winning Indy on four flat tires. He pulls up to Trudy's house. The screen door needs repair. The whole place could use a fresh coat of paint.

"Come on in."

"I should be getting along."

"Oh, come on in for a minute. I don't bite."

"Didn't think you did."

"I'll give you a beer before you head home."

She's lonely, he thinks. Living alone like that. Of course a person doesn't have to live alone to feel lonely. What the hell. Grab the gusto. Or at least a beer. One beer never killed anyone. He steps out of the truck and follows her up the walk, wondering how the hell he's going to explain beer on his breath to Rose.

The house smells stale, but it's neat. There is a woven blanket hanging on the living room wall like some kind of painting. The colors are so bold they give him a headache.

"Miller do?" she calls from the kitchen.

"Fine," he says, hoping it's not Lite. Might as well be drinking cow piss as that stuff they pass off as beer. He looks around. A row of framed snapshots line the mantel. He crosses for a better look. One of Phyllis, another of Phyllis and her little girl, Trudy's only grandchild. The third is of a dark-haired Indian child. The Lakota girl Trudy sponsors, he guesses. He picks up the photo. Bright-looking child. Brown eyes that stare straight at you asking to be liked. It's a good thing Trudy does, sponsoring this child. He wonders if Rose would be interested in doing something like that. Maybe he should bring it up.

He is setting the frame back on the mantel when the first pain hits. Out in the kitchen, Trudy is calling out something, but he can't respond. The pain isn't sharp, more like a weight, a weight so crushing he can barely breath. It radiates down his arm, up into his jaw. Christ, it's like the worst toothache he's ever had.

"Can or glass?" Trudy asks from the door.

He sinks into an armchair, struggles to get his breath. Christ, his jaw is killing him.

"Ned? You all right? What's wrong?"

"Nothing," he says, relieved he can speak. Already it's abating, leaving only the memory. But, Jesus.

"You're sweating. You sure you're all right?"

"Fine. Just a spasm of some kind. Gas." He attempts a grin. "Too many donuts and pie." He puts his hand to his chest, over the fluttery feeling.

"What happened?"

"Nothing."

She crosses to him, lifts his arm, searches for a pulse with her fingers.

"Whatta you, suddenly a nurse?" he says, managing a smile.

"I'm calling the rescue."

"No. It's nothing. Like I said. Gas."

"Listen. I watched my father go from a heart attack. I'm not watching you. Better safe than sorry."

What is she talking, heart attack? The worst of it had been in his jaw. Who has a heart attack in his jaw? He corrals enough strength to argue. "I'm telling you, I'm fine. It's already gone. If you want to do anything, get me some Maalox."

But she is already off. He listens to her make the call, embarrassed. The whole thing is a big fuss over nothing.

He loses track of time. The next thing, Bud Flynn is walking in the door. He's carrying a green duffel bag.

"Ned, what's happening?"

There is a young kid with him, the new paramedic. Jesus, the kid looks like he should be in high school. He tries to make a joke, but doesn't have the energy.

"Nothing. Indigestion. Too many donuts." The effort of speech exhausts him.

Bud takes his pulse. Peers into his eyes. "Maybe so," he says, "but let me examine you anyway." He opens the bag, takes out a cylinder of oxygen. Over Ned's protests, he places the mask over his mouth.

The kid sets up another machine. A computer of some kind.

"What the hell is that?" Ned pushes the question out.

"EKG monitor."

"I tell you I'm fine," Ned says through the mask. He is embarrassed by the fuss, embarrassed to be found here at Trudy's house. Christ, it was innocent, him being here, but he wonders what Bud is thinking. That's all he needs. Rumors about him and Trudy flying around town.

"Let me check your blood pressure," Bud says.

Ned is done trying to protest. All he wants is to go home. He hopes Rose never hears about this. He's feeling better.

"Let's hook you up to the EKG," Bud says. "Get a picture and see what's going on."

"This is a big fuss over nothing."

"Just let them do their job," Trudy says.

"We're here," Bud says. "Give us a chance to earn our pay."

"Will it take long?"

"Only a minute."

The kid wraps the blood pressure cuff around his arm and attaches the machine.

Bud checks the printout. "You're showing some arrhythmia," he says.

"What the hell does that mean?"

"It means you get to take a ride with us."

"Where?"

"Mercy Memorial."

"No," he says. "No way I'm going to the hospital." He can't remember the last time he was sick. Hasn't even had a cold in years. It's indigestion. A toothache. That's all.

"Listen, Ned. It's in your best interest," Bud says. "We'd feel better if you go in. Get you checked out. You'll feel better too. You don't want to be worried all night. Set your mind at ease."

Finally he agrees.

They make him lie on a stretcher. They keep him attached to the oxygen.

The kid—Dave—drives the rescue truck. Bud gets in back. As soon as they are underway, he inserts an IV.

"What the hell is that?"

"Saline solution."

When the IV is secured, Bud calls the hospital. "Late middle-aged man. Chest pain, arrhythmia. High BP. We've administered oxygen and have him hooked to IV."

Late middle-aged man. Christ, they went to school together. Ned repairs Bud's car.

"Any pain?" a voice says over the speaker.

"Abating."

"How about I give Rose a call?" Bud says. "Let her know what's going on?"

"No," Ned says. He can't see any sense in worrying Rose. He'll just get checked out and then head home before she even realizes he's late. Everyone is overreacting. A man can't even have indigestion in peace. He wonders if Bud will give him a ride back to Trudy's to pick up the truck.

"You sure? You'll be late showing up for dinner, and if she calls the station no one will answer. If she's like Judy she'll be imagining the worst. Why not let me call her? I won't alarm her." Neither of them mentions the fact that he had been at Trudy's house. He can just imagine how it looks.

Jesus, he's got to get on his feet, pick up the truck, and get home. Otherwise, how in hell is he going to explain this to Rose?

CHAPTER 35

⌦ R O S E

OPAL IS OUT WORKING IN THE GARDEN AGAIN. SHE'S been at it all day, weeding and watering, fussing over every tomato plant. That girl is hurting, taking badly the separation from Zack. Plus there's that woman from the court asking questions all over town. And there are plenty can't wait to give her an earful. The way the courts are allowed to meddle in a person's life is nothing short of criminal.

For once, the girl hasn't brought that tape machine out with her. She should have. Maybe it would help fill the silence created by her boy's absence. But then Rose knows better than anyone that there is no noise in creation that will fill that kind of void. She considers offering her a glass of iced tea, but before she can do anything, the phone rings.

It has been more than a week since the biopsy. The doctor's nurse said they would be calling her in a week with the results, and today is the ninth day.

If it's bad news, will they tell her straight out or ask her to come in to the office? Surely they don't just blurt things like "you have cancer" on the phone. She has tried to ready herself for this, but there is no way to prepare. She picks up the phone.

"Mrs. Nelson?"

"Yes."

"This is Dr. Murphy's office calling."

"Yes."

"The doctor asked me to give you a call."

Her fingers tighten their grip on the receiver. "Yes."

"We've gotten the results of your lab test."

So tell me, she wants to shout. Just tell me. She is forgetting to breathe.

"They're negative."

"Negative?"

"Yes. Absolutely. This is one problem you can forget, okay?"

She exhales one long sigh, thanks the nurse, hangs up. Beneath her breastbone, she feels the hard, black fist open its fingers and flex. People say things like a cloud lifted when they get good news, a weight off their shoulders, a new lease on life. Rose feels the surprising truth of these old saws. Does she want a new lease on life? She does. The fact, the *amazing* fact—the *startling* fact—is that she does.

She climbs the stairs to Todd's room. A shaft of late sun streams through the window, bathing the dresser top, the ceramic tiger he made at summer camp. She strokes the figure. She fingers his watch. Blood is still encrusted in the links of the band, after all this time. She picks up one of the photos. For years she has been unable to allow herself to remember fully the day it was taken, as if memories held the power to . . . To what? Flatten? Crush? Destroy?

She sinks down on the mattress and traces Todd's face with her fingertip. They had been having a cookout in the backyard that day. She had just come from the house with a bowl of potato salad. Ned was grilling chicken. Todd was goofing around, juggling tennis balls in the air with an air of both intense concentration and grace. He was fifteen. Taller than she was and gaining on Ned. Growing tall; growing away from them. Lately, girls had been calling, giggling when they asked for him. She doesn't remember what impulse led her to return to the house for her camera. She never was much of a picture taker.

"Aw, Ma," Todd said when she aimed the lens at him. But he smiled, and she caught him at that moment, lit with the late summer sun, hands palm up, tennis balls suspended in midair, as if hung by strings from heaven. One second of one minute of one hour in his life. Time enough to take a picture. Time, under glass.

She rises, places the frame back on the dresser top. She wishes she could talk to Ned. She would like to ask him if he remembers that cookout. If he recalls how Todd kept five tennis balls in the air, flipping them from left hand to right, from right hand into the air, around and around until it made you dizzy just watching. Where had he learned to do that? What does Ned remember of that day?

Why can't they ever talk about what matters? Has she tried? Has she tried hard enough?

The trouble with secrets is how they keep you separate. She has kept from Ned all the things that have happened to her in the past months. How she lied for Opal at the hospital. How in that class she wrote all the things she felt about Todd's death. How a magazine wanted to publish her piece in a special edition. How a mole on her stomach had been itching since last Fall and she had gone by bus to Springfield to a doctor to have it biopsied. How afterward, she had gone to Todd's grave and then decided to let the magazine publish the article. And now the phone call with the news that the biopsy proved negative. All these secrets built on the biggest one of all: She refused to let Todd take her car the day of the accident, and if she hadn't he would probably be alive today. Some mistakes are both simple and huge.

Now she wishes she had told him about the biopsy so she could share the news that the mole was benign. But it's too late to tell him. He would be angry that she hadn't told him earlier. She has missed the chance to do him good. Still, she'll make a special dinner. Swiss steak with mashed potatoes. There's time to get to the market and pick up a nice piece of meat. Lately he's not had much of an appetite when he comes home from the station.

When the phone rings again, she answers at once, sure it is Ned, he is so in her mind. Opal's rubbing off on her.

"Mrs. Nelson?" an unfamiliar voice says.

"Yes," she says, guardedly. There should be a law against these telephone solicitors.

"Mrs. Nelson, this is Helen Blake. I work in Admissions over at Mercy Memorial. Your husband Edward has been brought into emergency. We're in the process of admitting him now."

An accident, Rose thinks. *The lift.* She has never trusted that thing. Never. She pictures Ned crushed beneath it.

"Is he badly hurt?"

"I don't know, Mrs. Nelson. I just want to tell you he's being admitted. The doctors are with him. You can see him when you arrive. Get a friend to drive you, okay?"

Rose grabs her purse and heads over to get Opal. As she crosses the lawn, she begins negotiations with God. She wonders if He minds that she no longer believes in Him. She wonders if God will believe her if she says she repents of her lies.

Opal doesn't even take time to wash her hands.

"I've never trusted that lift," Rose tells her over and over all the way to Mercy. "Never."

"MRS. ROSE NELSON," SHE TELLS THE WOMAN AT ADMISsions. "Someone phoned me. My husband has been admitted."

"His name?"

"Nelson. Ned Nelson."

"We have an Edward Nelson."

"That's him." No one has called him Edward since his mother died.

"He's in North Three. Coronary Care Unit."

She is so unprepared for this information the woman might as well have been speaking Swahili. Coronary Care Unit? For an accident?

"There's some mistake."

"How do we get there?" Opal says.

"Take the elevator to the third floor and follow the green arrows." She hands them a printed card with directions. "Someone at the nurse's station there will be able to help you."

"What did she say?" she says to Opal.

Opal repeats the directions, then takes her arm, leads her to the elevators.

"He's just been brought in," a nurse tells her when they get there, shutting off Rose's questions. "Give us five minutes to get him stabilized." She points to a room at the end of the corridor. "Have a seat in the visitors' lounge, and a doctor will be with you shortly."

The lounge is empty except for a hollow-eyed woman staring at a television set. The volume is on mute. She does not look up when Rose and Opal enter.

Rose is grateful for Opal, for the soil-stained fingers that are now interlaced with her own. "It's a mistake," she says. Of course it's a mistake. A huge mistake. If you don't count an occasional cold, Ned has never been sick a day in his bed. Has never been in the hospital. Has never had his tonsils out, for heaven's sake. Or appendicitis. He's only fifty-seven.

Another nurse approaches.

"Can I see him now? What's wrong? Why is he here in Coronary Care?"

"Your husband has had a coronary episode. Right now he's stable. The doctor will explain everything."

"When can I see him?" Episode. That doesn't sound too bad. Like an interjection in a story.

"Soon. In the meantime, I have a few questions." She holds her pen over the clipboard.

"How old is Edward?"

"Ned," she says. "He's called Ned."

"How old is Ned?"

"Fifty-seven."

"You're his wife?"

Of course she's his wife. Don't these people listen? She's already said that. "Yes."

"Do you have children?"

She falls silent. Opal takes over.

"One. A son."

"And where does he live?"

Rose stares at the television. A newscast. A man staring out at her, mouth moving, no words.

"In her heart," Opal says. "He lives in her heart."

The nurse, for the moment, is silenced.

In her heart. Rose tightens her fingers around Opal's.

"When can she see her husband?" Opal says. "They told us five minutes, and it's been fifteen. What's going on?"

"And you are?"

"Her niece," Opal says, the lie rolling off her tongue without hesitation.

"Mrs. Nelson?"

This doctor looks too young to have finished college, let alone medical school.

"Yes."

"I'm Dr. Richards." He holds out a hand that Rose ignores.

"What's wrong with my husband?"

"He's had a myocardiac arrest, but he's stabilized now."

Myocardiac arrest. "You mean a heart attack?" Dear God. An episode, the nurse had said. Myocardiac arrest is no episode. "Will he be all right?"

"It looks good. We're waiting for the enzyme test results. Would you like to see him?"

"Yes."

"Five minutes. You can see him for five minutes."

Suddenly she is scared.

"It'll be all right," Opal whispers.

Rose follows the doctor to Ned's room.

He is sitting up in bed, plastic tubes running from his nose. He is hitched up to a monitor. An intravenous tube drips a colorless fluid into the vein in his right arm. "Hi, Rose," he says.

"Oh, Ned." She starts to cry. She wants to kiss him but is afraid she will disturb the tubes in his nose. She squeezes his hand.

"Hey," he says. "Hey, Rosie. Don't cry."

"I can't help it."

"I'm fine," he says. "Look." He lifts his left arm and flexes it, making a muscle with his biceps and pointing his finger out, mimicking a body builder. "Which way to the beach?" he says. It's an old joke from their courtship.

The monitor emits sharp fast beeps.

"Dear God." Rose looks around for help.

A nurse bustles in. Ned lowers his arm, looks sheepish.

"You better go," she tells Rose.

Fifteen minutes pass before she is again permitted to see him. She tiptoes in, as if even her footsteps will alert that monitor, set it off again. She has promised herself she won't cry, but the tears seep out.

"Rosie, Rosie," he whispers.

She pulls her chair close to his bed, rests her head in the crook of his shoulder. He winces, and she draws away. He pulls her head back. "That's nice," he says.

She stays there, quiet, listening to his heart, his lovely steady heartbeat. With her other ear she hears the sound of the monitor. Stereophonic sound. She giggles, tells him what's funny when he asks.

"I love you," she says.

"I love you too, Rosie. I always have."

When she returns to the lounge, Opal has ordered a sandwich for her. Coffee. She is surprised to find she is hungry, amazed to find it is after eight.

The shifts change. A new nurse tends to Ned. Another one sits at the desk watching the monitors. Rose takes an immediate, illogical dislike to this one.

"Go home," the nurse says. "We'll call you if there is any change."

"Do what the hell you want to do," Opal says. "Don't let them boss you around."

She decides to stay. Why would she want to be anywhere else? Opal stays with her.

Around eleven, she finally believes it will be safe to leave Ned for the night.

"Is he asleep right now?"

The nurse checks a monitor. "He just woke up."

"Can I go in to say good-bye?"

"Five minutes. Sleep is the best thing for him now."

"Ned? Honey? It's Rose."

"Jesus, Rosie, I know that. I had a heart attack, not amnesia."

She kisses his cheek, rough with a day's growth of whiskers. She makes a mental note to bring him a razor.

"I'm going home now. I'll be back in the morning."

"Okay. That's good."

"Oh, Ned," she says. "Are you scared?"

"No."

"Honest?" She can't believe this. "I am."

"Rosie," he says, "there's nothing to be scared of."

She forces herself to say the word. "Death. I'm afraid you're going to die."

"Death is just the next big adventure."

"Don't you say that," Rose says. "Don't you say that. It's not." Don't you leave me, she wants to say.

She is shouting and the nurse comes, makes her leave.

Outside in the corridor, she apologizes. "Let me go back. I won't get upset."

"You're tired. Go home. Get some sleep. He'll need you to be rested. Come back in the morning. He'll be here. I promise."

As if anyone can ever promise anything like that.

AS THEY CROSS THE LOBBY, A WOMAN RISES FROM A CHAIR SET in the shadows. "Rose?" she says.

It takes her a moment to recognize Trudy.

"Yes." What the hell is she doing here?

"How is Ned? They wouldn't let me come up. Only family."

"He's sleeping. He's had a heart attack."

"I know."

"You know?"

"He was at my house. He gave me a ride home."

A ride home? Ned gave Trudy a ride home?

"It all happened so quick. At first he thought it was indigestion from the pie. You know how he stops by every afternoon after work for a cup of coffee and piece of pie."

No. She doesn't know. Every day. At Trudy's. Without her knowing.

"His truck is at my place. I've taken the keys. I can drive it over to the station in the morning."

Ned was with Trudy?

"No need for that," Rose says. "I'll get it tonight. Opal can drop me off."

The truck is pulled halfway up Trudy's drive. Rose hoists herself into the cab. The steering wheel is gritty beneath her fingers. The cab smells faintly of smoke. She jams the keys into the ignition, turns the engine. She has forgotten to depress the clutch, and the pickup lurches forward and stalls. She lowers her head to the wheel, fighting tears. Trudy is watching from the stoop. Rose tightens her jaw, stomps on the clutch, and tries again. Slowly she edges down the drive. It is the first time in five years she has driven.

Beneath the tires she feels the shift of the earth. A tectonic shifting.

CHAPTER 36

ᢞ OPAL

THE PHONE WAKES OPAL, AND EVEN HALF CAUGHT IN
slumber she thinks, *Zack*. She rolls over and grabs the receiver.
"Opal?"

It's Ty. Before her mind can fully waken, her body softens, opens to desire.

"Hi." She sits up, tents the sheet around her nude body.

"How are you? How's Zack?"

"I'm fine. We're fine." She doesn't tell him that Zack is visiting Billy. That she misses her son so much she can barely eat, that she has lost five pounds, that she can count her ribs just looking in the mirror. If she loses Zack, really loses him—impossible, her mind shrieks—she will shrink and die.

"I've been thinking of you."

She catches her breath, releases it in a long exhale.

"Hardly a day goes by when I don't," he says.

No sense following that line of conversation. It's a dead end. Over. Done. Her mind knows this. Her body just hasn't gotten the news yet. "How did the taping go in Cambridge?"

"Not bad." He inhales, pauses. "Opal, I want to see you. Can I? Can I see you?"

She closes her eyes. Just once—*once*—she wishes something wonderful could happen to her without cost. Something perfect that she doesn't have to pay for. "Not possible."

"Why? Because I was arrested years ago? Because I made a mistake? Christ, Opal, even the judge didn't take that seriously. I mean, he denied the restraining order, right? *He* wasn't the one who said I can't see you. Ask Ned—he'll tell you I'm dependable."

Shit. Ned. The hospital. "Have you heard about Ned?"

"Ned? No. What about him?"

"He's in the hospital. Heart attack."

"Christ, is he all right?"

"He's in the coronary unit. He's—" What do they call it? Stable? "He's stable."

"How's Rose?"

"Rose is okay." As okay as anyone could be, Opal supposes.

"Is anyone with her?"

"I'm going over as soon as we hang up."

"And Ned's in the hospital? Can he have visitors?"

"I don't think so. Just family."

"Tell Rose I asked, okay? Tell her to call me if there's anything I can do. Tell her not to worry about the garage. I'll go down and open up, finish up the jobs. Have her tell Ned not to worry about that stuff."

"I'll tell her."

"Opal?"

"Yeah?"

"Will you call me sometimes? Let me know how things are going?"

"What's the point?"

"The point is I care. The point is after everything is settled, maybe there'll still be a chance for us. So will you? Call me?"

Will she? Can she? "I don't know. Maybe."

ROSE ISN'T DRESSED. HER GLASSES ARE SMUDGED. SHE LOOKS awful, like she didn't get much sleep.

"Am I too early?"

"No. Come on in." Rose looks down at her bathrobe, starts to say something and stops. "Coffee?" she asks.

"I'll get it," Opal says. She fills a cup, holds the pot up toward Rose in question.

"Thanks. Milk's in the fridge."

"Ty called." Opal pulls up a chair. There are only two at the table.

She must be sitting in Ned's. "He said not to worry, he'll take care of things at the station. He said to be sure and tell Ned that, so he won't worry." Rose has the dazed look of someone who's been in an accident. Opal is not certain she's listening. "Have you heard anything this morning?"

"I called the hospital about an hour ago. They said he was resting comfortably. Visiting hours start at ten."

"I'll take you," Opal says.

"You don't have to. I've got Ned's truck."

"I want to."

"You've got work."

"I don't go in until one. Please, let me."

"I don't want to be a bother."

"No bother. It will help take my mind off Zack."

Rose looks up, eyes alive. "How is he?"

"Who the hell knows?" Opal feels anger rise. "Half the time I phone there's no answer. It's driving me crazy. I don't know how I'm going to get through another week of it. I keep wondering, does Billy know he likes macaroni for breakfast? Or that he can't sleep without Tigger? Or that you have to read him a story every night before he goes to bed? Or that he worries about things like where birds go when they die? Shit, I'm sorry. You've got enough on your mind without hearing about my problems."

A thunk sounds on the porch. "The paper," Rose says. She crosses to the door and retrieves the *Daily News*. "Ned loves the sports pages. He has to read them every morning. It's like a religion with him." She stops short. "Do you think they'll let me bring it in to him?"

"Sure," Opal says. The coffee is making her have to pee. "Can I use the bathroom?"

"Upstairs. Second door on the left." Rose opens to the sports page. "The Red Sox won," she reports. "That will make Ned happy."

From the small window in the upstairs bath, Opal looks down on her house. There's a good view from here. You can see everything. Suddenly she remembers that day she and Ty had been making out on the lawn. Him on top, straddling her. Rose sure must have gotten an eyeful that day. She turns from the window, wishing it were that easy to excise memories of Ty from her mind.

She pees, washes up, then retraces her steps down the hall. As she passes a doorway, she peers in. Todd's, she guesses. It looks like he still lives here. A shell of a room, waiting for a ghost.

This is what it would be like if she lost Zack. An empty room waiting. A space there's no way to fill.

There must be a sign she has missed. Or misread. How else could Billy be laying claim on her son? How else could something so catastrophic have happened to her? She hadn't been prepared.

"Want some toast? An egg or something?" Rose asks when she returns to the kitchen.

"Nothing. I'll just finish my coffee; then I'll go and change. Visiting hours are at ten?"

"Ten. You sure you don't mind driving?"

"I *want* to," Opal says.

As she is leaving, she hesitates, then grabs Rose's hand and gives it a quick squeeze. You could knock her over with a whisper when Rose slips an arm around her and tightens it in a hug, holds on.

SHE IS STEPPING OUT OF THE SHOWER WHEN SHE HEARS THE phone. This time it's Zack.

"How you doing, sugah?" Her stomach aches. She cups the receiver close to her head so his voice won't escape, so she can hold as much of him as possible.

"Guess what?" he says.

"What?"

"Daddy's taking me to Disney World."

Daddy. "What?"

"We're going to Disney World. Tomorrow. And Melvama, too."

"Well, that's a big surprise," she says. So why is she not surprised? "Listen, bud, is Billy right there? Let me talk to him, okay?"

"Hi, Raylee." He's using his cocky, *I won* tone of voice which just sets her off.

"What the hell's going on? What the hell do you think you're doing?"

"Like Zack told you. We're taking a trip."

"You can't do that."

"Yes, I can, Raylee. Check with that lawyer of yours. It's perfectly within my rights to take a vacation with my son."

"We'll see about that." She knows Billy. The first time Zack throws a tantrum he'll be looking for a way to ship him back. Billy doesn't have staying power. "I'm calling my lawyer as soon as we hang up."

"You do that. You go ahead and do that. I know my rights, Raylee, and I'm on solid ground here."

"It's Opal, you stupid fuck. My name is Opal." She slams down the phone and turns to see Rose at the screen door.

"What's wrong?" Rose asks.

What's wrong? What isn't? Opal stands in her towel, dripping water on the kitchen floor, and wonders how everything got so mixed up. "It's Billy," she says. "He's taking Zack to Disney World. For five years he's a for-shit, no-show daddy and now he's trying out for Father of the Year."

What happens next absolutely amazes Opal. Rose crosses to her and takes hold of both her hands.

"Don't worry," she says. "He won't get Zack. We won't let him take Zack away from you."

CHAPTER 37

⮞ R O S E

"I CAN STAY," OPAL SAYS AS SHE DROPS ROSE AT THE
hospital. "If you'd like, I'll come in with you."

"No. You go ahead. There's no use in both of us sitting."

"You sure?"

"Thanks anyway."

"You'll call me later? Let me know how he is? Let me know if there
is anything I can do?"

"I'll call," Rose promises. What can anyone do? Least of all Opal.

Once on the unit, she stops and checks in with one of the nurses on
the morning shift. "How is he?"

The nurse, a plump, pleasant-faced woman about her own age,
checks the chart. "He had a good night." She smiles. "He's been giving us a hard time this morning, trying to talk us into letting him have
a cup of coffee. That's a good sign."

Rose looks down the corridor. Except for an orderly dumping trash
in the bin by the visitors' lounge, it is empty. She has hardly been able
to sleep. She has to talk to someone, someone with experience in this
kind of thing. "Last night," she begins, "when I saw him, he said he
wasn't afraid of dying. He said something about death being 'the next
big adventure.' " She pauses, searching for the words that will convey
her fears. "Is that normal? Does it . . . Does it mean he thinks he's
going to die?" She has read somewhere that a person's will to live is a

decisive factor in recovery. She needs for Ned to have this will. To not give up.

"Mrs. Nelson." The nurse smiles; her voice is reassuring. "You'd be surprised at the things we hear. When your husband came in yesterday, he was very calm, very matter-of-fact, in spite of the fact that he had had a heart attack. That's not unusual. That's denial. We often see it when a patient isn't ready to accept the significance of what has happened. When they don't get it that they've had a heart attack. The truth of it is that when someone says he's ready to accept death, it's usually because he doesn't really believe he's going to die."

Denial. Denial she can handle. It's losing Ned that she can't bear to think of. "So he's going to be all right?"

"His signs are good. The enzyme test results were what we like to see. I'd say this episode was a warning. Dr. Cassidy is the cardiologist. He'll be talking to you about diet, exercise, lifestyle changes your husband can make to reduce the chances of this happening again." She reaches over and pats Rose's hand. "Why don't you go on in and see him now? He's been asking if you're here yet."

"Hey, Rosie," he says when she enters his room. He looks good, not at all as if he's had a heart attack.

"Hi, Ned." He's wearing one of those dreadful gowns that tie in back. She makes a note to bring him pajamas. Unaccountably shy, she looks around for a place to put her purse and the things she has brought for him. There are no chairs. They discourage visitors staying.

She leans over to kiss his cheek, brushing her lips against his whiskers. "You need a shave," she says. She looks around. There is no bathroom in the room, just a bedside commode. She averts her eyes, embarrassed, and occupies herself by smoothing the sheet. Already she is growing accustomed to the sound of the monitor, reassured by its steady beat.

"The Sox won last night," she says. "I brought you the paper."

"Did ya get the score?"

She concentrates on getting it right. "Five to four. Eleven innings." She flutters around the room, looking for something to occupy her hands.

"Who pitched?"

"Clements," she says, pleased with herself that she remembers.

She straightens out the blanket, reaches behind his head, adjusts the pillow.

"For God's sake, Rosie. Stop fussing."

She pulls her hand back, hurt. She's helpless here. It frightens her, him lying there hitched up to machines.

"Rosie," he says. He averts his eyes, and she wonders what's coming. She doesn't think she can stand it if he starts up again with that foolishness about "the next great adventure." She thought when Todd died she had lost everything, but now she knows there is always something more to lose.

"The pickup. It's over at Trudy's."

She cuts in before he can continue. She doesn't need to hear about Trudy. "I know. I picked it up last night."

"You did?"

"Yes. Opal dropped me off there."

"You drove it home?"

"Yes."

"By yourself?"

"Of course, by myself," she says, irritated.

He grins. "If I'd known this it what is would take to get you driving again, I'd have had a heart attack years ago."

"Don't you even joke about such a thing." *Once* is not "driving again." *Once* was necessity. *Once* was removing his truck from in front of Trudy's house.

"Mrs. Nelson?" The nurse beckons to her. "We like to keep the visits under fifteen minutes the first day. Why don't you go down to the cafeteria, get yourself some coffee. Have you had breakfast?"

Who can eat? She shakes her head.

"The food's not bad."

"I'm not hungry."

"Mrs. Nelson," the nurse says, guiding her down the corridor. "The best way you can take care of your husband is to take care of yourself. Get rest. Eat well. You'd be surprised at the number of caregivers who get sick because they neglect themselves. Ned will need you to be strong."

Caregiver. The woman makes it sound like Ned is going to be spending the rest of his life in a wheelchair.

In the cafeteria she takes a tray and slides it along the counter. A short-order cook stands ready to take her order. "A bagel," she finally decides.

"Toasted or grilled."

"Toasted." Less fat. Already she is beginning to think this way.

When she returns to the unit, Dr. Cassidy is waiting for her. He's dressed in a plaid shirt and a pair of chinos. You wouldn't take him to be a doctor at all. She wishes he wore a white coat, something that would inspire confidence.

"Your husband is recovering nicely," he tells her. "He's filled in some history, but I have a few questions I'd like to ask."

"All right."

"How has his health been in general?"

"Good. He's hardly ever sick. I can't remember the last time he's seen a doctor."

"What about annual checkups? Has he had one recently?"

She thinks a moment. "Five years ago. When we changed insurance companies."

Insurance. Lord knows what this is going to cost. Are they covered? In the past, Ned tried to go over this kind of thing, but her ears were deaf. After Todd died he wanted to have their wills drawn up, but she refused. She has no idea about their finances or what kind of coverage they have. She hopes it is enough and then is ashamed to be thinking about money.

The doctor is asking her something.

"I'm sorry. Could you repeat that?"

"Has Ned had any complaints lately?"

"Sometimes he has indigestion. A few headaches. Nothing else. He'd take a few Tums. Some Tylenol. Or Extra Strength Excedrin."

"How about his emotional health? Would you say your husband was worried? Is he an angry person?"

"No." *Anger.* If anger caused a heart attack, she would be the one lying on that bed with tubes stuck in her arms and taped up her nostrils, not Ned.

Back when they were first married, Ned's anger used to worry her. She believed he had a real capacity for violence and that if anyone harmed her or Todd, he would seek retribution. After the accident, she found this thought comforting. Any day she expected to hear that Jimmy Sommers had been beaten up, both legs broken, ribs caved in, face bloodied, and she took deep satisfaction in imagining this. Sometimes she feared—hoped?—that Ned would do worse than break bones. Now she wonders how she could have so misread him. Or, more likely, how he could have so changed. She knows for sure that she is the one, not Ned, who holds the truest capacity for retribution.

Last year, she was driving by the garage and saw Ned with his torso half hidden beneath the hood of Jimmy's new pickup. Jimmy was standing there laughing about something, and his wife sat perched in the front seat. Ned was actually *helping* his son's killer while the man's wife looked on and drank a Coke. The sight sucked her lungs dry. How could Ned allow the boy anywhere near the station, never mind work on his truck? How could he? Later they had had a terrible fight about it.

You have to learn to forgive and move on, he told her. As if such a thing were possible. As if some things *can* be forgiven.

"No," she tells the doctor. "Ned isn't an angry man."

He finishes up with his questions.

"When can he come home?" Rose asks.

"We'd like to keep him here for another day or two. As soon as possible we'll be get him out of CCU, move him over to the West Wing."

"What about when he gets home? Can he go back to work?"

"That will depend, of course, on him. On how he progresses. My best guess right now is that he'll be able to start back part-time in four or five weeks. No heavy lifting. Nothing stressful."

"What's to prevent him from having another attack?"

"Prevention is the best way to prevent," the doctor says, smiling at his joke. "Low-fat, low-sodium diet, lots of fruits and vegetables. No smoking."

"Ned doesn't smoke."

He went right on, ignoring the interruption. "Avoid alcohol. Get regular exercise. He can start by walking a block a day. Not into the wind or uphill. Eventually work up to forty minutes a day."

"I should write this down," Rose says.

"We'll go over this before he's discharged. You'll be meeting with the team—myself, the therapist, a nutritionist—to go over everything. What I want you to keep in mind is that it's important you don't treat him like an invalid. He can live a full life. In every way," he adds, giving her a meaningful look.

She stares at him blankly.

"A lot of people worry about sex after an attack. There's absolutely no reason that he can't return to a normal sex life."

That is the farthest thing from her mind. What would he think if he knew she and Ned haven't had sex in five years?

She doesn't care about sex. All she wants is Ned back. Whole. She wants to be given a second chance.

CHAPTER 38

❧ N E D

Visiting hours are over, and Ned is relieved. Rose's constant fussing drives him crazy. It's his third day in CCU, and in point of fact, everything about the place is driving him crazy. He's amazed at how noisy the unit is. You'd think they would try and keep a place like this quiet. His room is near the nurses' station, and sound carries, especially at night. Periodically he hears the equipment cart roll down the corridor. And then there's the rhythmic banging he has finally figured out is someone stamping charts. Earlier a man from housekeeping was buffing the floor.

He wants to get back to his life, back to his own bed. He can't wait to get a good night's sleep. Here in the unit they keep the corridor lights on night and day, 24-7, as Tyrone would say. And even if you do manage to fall asleep, someone is always waking you for something. He's had enough blood drawn in the past three days to meet a Red Cross quota.

The first thing he's going to do when he gets home is drink a real cup of coffee. None of that decaf shit. Regular is forbidden here, and Rose won't sneak some in no matter how much he pleads.

Most of all, he can't wait to be able to use a bathroom. The commode is damned near impossible. They've given him something to soften his bowels, but he hasn't taken a good crap since he arrived.

This is his last day in the unit; tomorrow he's being transferred to Medical West, which will be an improvement. He'll get rid of this damn IV, the monitor wires. Be able to get up and go sit on the can where a man can have some privacy. According to Cassidy, the cardiologist, he can expect to be discharged after a day or two in the West Wing.

They've told him not to worry, and no one seems to believe him when he says he isn't worried. He's heard that he's the youngest man on the floor and finds consolation in this fact.

In the morning, he and Rose are meeting with a dietitian and another member of the cardiology team, a "lifestyle counselor." He wishes they would not make such a big deal of everything and just let him go home. If he *has* to talk to these people, he wishes he could do it alone, without Rose. Her questions go on and on: What will he be able to do when he gets home? Will he be able to go back to work? If so, when? Should they do more tests? How can they prevent this from happening again?

The team plans to evaluate his diet, identify the kind of changes he needs to make, get his cholesterol levels down. He isn't looking forward to any of it. Donuts won't be on any diet he'll be seeing.

He hasn't been particularly hungry, a good thing since the food here would make a T-shirt taste good. No salt. Reduced fat. Tonight's dinner—if you could call it that—was baked chicken without the skin. White rice. Green beans steamed to death. Jello. Decaf coffee. Skim milk. Trudy would go out of business if she served food like this.

He hasn't talked to Trudy. He wants to thank her for taking care of him, for calling the rescue squad, but he doesn't have a phone here. He wonders if she has tried to get in to see him. They only let family members on this floor. Of course he can't ask Rose to call her. He's tried to tell Rose that he was only giving Trudy a ride home, but she hasn't let him talk about it. He wonders what she thinks. She can't think he was cheating, can she? Why can't they just talk? Get things straight.

He switches on the bedside lamp. Instantly a nurse—Nancy, the older one with the faded red hair—pokes her head in. She's the best of the lot, although all the nurses are great.

"Everything all right?"

"Can't sleep."

"Do you want a sedative? The doctor's okayed it."

"No." He doesn't want to get started on that stuff. He just needs to get in his own bed. Once he's home, he'll be able to sleep fine.

She scans his chart, checks the monitor. "Any discomfort?"

"No. Just can't sleep. I'm going to read a little bit." He picks up the Sports section Rose brought in, stares at it until she leaves, then lets it drop on the blanket. He focuses on the monitor and listens to the beeps, the beating of his heart pulsing on the screen. He concentrates on his heartbeat, counting out the beats. He inhales deeply, waiting for any sign of trouble. *All is calm. All is well.* A Christmas carol floats through his head. He presses his thumb on the hydraulic button until his head is slightly raised. He lifts both arms above his head, pumps his fists in the air. A sort of early detection system. No alarming increase on the monitor. He concentrates on his chest and waits for any indication of pressure. That's what he remembers now about the episode. First inkling: a dull, *vague* ache—not a pain exactly—followed by the heavy, clammy sweat. And then the sudden, intense pressure on his chest. Like a concrete block. God-awful pressure. Then the pain in his jaw. And a fluttering beneath his breastbone, like a trapped bird beating its wings against a cage. Thinking about it now, in some ways that fluttering had been the most alarming. The misfiring of his own heart. Not exactly something a man can reach in and adjust with a wrench.

He wonders how long before he will be able to forget. How long before he won't wake from a daydream to find himself automatically checking his pulse. How long before he'll be able to take the ordinary workings of his heart for granted.

He hasn't mentioned it to Rose, but he wonders about the garage. Even if they tell him it's all right, he's not so sure he wants to go back to work. He allows himself to imagine it. No more blistered skin from red-hot manifolds. No more replacing broken bolts on rear axles.

Retirement isn't impossible. Although Rose doesn't know it, he has been approached by one of the big chains. A buy-out. It could happen. Mostly they are interested in the location, and they'll pay big for it. Now Ned wants to grab what's left of life, taste it and roll in it. Maybe now Rose would agree to a move to Florida. He feels funny thinking this—like his heart attack is a weapon he can use to bend her. But it has changed things. Like Rose driving again after all these years.

He'll start with small changes before he springs Florida on her. Maybe in the fall, he'll take a couple of weeks and go fishing. He used to rent a cabin up north where he would spend whole days standing hip-deep in a cold running stream casting for trout. It was a memorable feeling, like being outside inside, wearing those waders. Paradise on earth. Could he talk Rose into coming along? Just the two of them? It would be good for her to get away from the house. Maybe it will be the first step. There are so many things he wants to tell her. That he will tell her.

This morning the hospital chaplain, a smug stick of a man, stopped by for a visit and had the gall to tell him his heart attack had been a gift. *A gift.* "A wake-up call," he said. "We all need reminding that we are not immortal."

Jesus Chr-rist, Ned had thought.

"Each day we need to clear up unfinished business," he said. "Have you told your loved ones that you love them?"

The banality of the man's speech infuriated him. The presumption of it, the gall of it, enraged him. "Don't let that son of a bitch in here again," he told a nurse.

Now, lying here listening to his heartbeat, thinking of Rose, the chaplain's words echo. What does he wish he could say to Rose? What would he regret leaving unsaid?

For one thing he would like to tell her he read what she wrote in that writing class. He would tell her how he opened the letter that professor had mailed her and read the whole thing. He wants her to know Todd's death wasn't her fault. He doesn't blame her for it. Accidents happen.

He would like to tell her he loves her and that he has always been faithful. He would tell her that he thinks he's a lucky man to have had her love. There are a million things he has never done. He knows his life has a huge blistering wound at its heart, but it hasn't been defined only by Todd's death. His life has been filled with ordinary joys.

He listens to his heartbeat, marvels at the steady, unremarkable pace of it. Even now, he can rely on his heart.

He has been lying like that for some time—musing about his life, about how lucky he has been to have found Rose, about how he has nothing to regret and what a good thing that is for a man to be able to think—when he is suddenly seized with dread. Like a premonition. Beneath his ribs, his heart quickens.

The nurse, Nancy, reappears. "How we doing?"

It's the nurses he has come to trust. Not the doctors. The nurses touch him, listen to him, take time, meet his eyes with theirs. "If anything happens to me, will you tell my wife that I love her?"

She takes his pronouncement calmly. She picks the newspaper up and sets it on his bedside table, checks the IV. Then she slides her hand in his, leaves it there for a moment. He finds this incredibly comforting.

The second day he overheard one of the nurses tell Rose he was in denial. He isn't. He knows he had a heart attack—he's not brainless for God's sake—but he isn't afraid of death.

"Here's a funny story," he tells the nurse. "Coming here, in the rescue truck, I saw a long tunnel." He attempts a laugh. "You know those people who say they have those experiences—you know—where they die and come back?"

"Near-death experiences?"

"Right. Near-death experiences. You know how they say they see a long tunnel? Well, I saw one." He chuckles. "Turns out it was a real tunnel, the one the ambulance goes through to reach the emergency entrance."

The nurse smiles. "They should warn people about that."

"Do you believe in that stuff? Life after death? Tunnels? People coming back from clinical death?"

"Yes," she says. "I do."

"I wasn't frightened." Just like he told Rose. Another adventure is ahead. Not that he's in any way near ready yet to leave this one.

"I want Rose to know it wasn't her fault."

She smiles, misunderstanding, and pats his arm. She is used to these midnight conversations on the unit.

"My son never had a chance to say anything," Ned tells her. "He died. Accident. When he was sixteen."

"That's got to be the worst."

"He was a good kid. Kind. Everyone liked him. He could make a stone laugh."

"You sure you don't want something to help you drop off?"

"No. I'm fine now."

She lowers the bed, adjusts his pillow, not in a fussy way like Rose, but in an efficient way that makes him feel cared for.

He dozes off, wakes, dozes again.

When he wakes, he sees someone sitting in the shadows. A doctor? He squints. The form rises and comes closer. Trick of the light and the damned medication, no doubt. The boy needs a haircut—as usual—but he is whole, unharmed. And not the little boy Ned always remembers, but big, lean, almost a man. Ned struggles against the tubes and cables to sit up. Tears are smarting at the corners of his eyes, and he is aware of a loud, bright tone to his left somewhere. He opens his mouth to greet his son. "Todd," he says, and laughs aloud. Todd's shy smile widens. God, what a handsome kid; he'll give the girls some sleepless nights.

He's a sight for sore eyes. Whole, unharmed, strong. It's all right, after all. Ned can't wait to tell Rose.

CHAPTER 39

↝ROSE

ROSE HAD DONE THE STRANGEST THING. SHE'D WORN A pair of Ned's pajamas to bed. They were oddly comforting; still she spent a restless night. Even when she managed to drop off, she woke on edge, breathless with the knowledge that something was wrong, then the full awakening: *Oh, yes, Ned's had a heart attack.*

She has been up since before dawn, getting the house ready for his return, which, according to Dr. Cassidy, should be within the next two days. She has already tackled their bedroom, aired it out, vacuumed the mattress, changed the linens, waxed the furniture, set up a card table by the bed so there will be plenty of space for all the things he'll need: medicines, water carafe and glass, newspapers. She's considering a radio for the ball games if it won't get him too riled up.

As much as she wants Ned back home where she can take care of him, she thinks his release is premature. They should keep him for another week, just in case.

Don't treat him like an invalid. Fine for the doctor to say. She wonders if he would be so casual if it were his wife lying in the unit.

They push patients out of the hospital today. Just *shove* them out. One day you're hitched up to monitors and IVs and the next you're back home in your bed. A person's lucky if he's fully conscious before he's wheeled to the parking lot. Gloria Smart's daughter was released the day after she gave birth. The day after. Rose was in for five days when she had Todd and was glad of it. No. Nowadays they just roll you right out. What's the hurry? Why the rush? Can it be safe to leave so soon after a heart attack? She blames it on the insurance companies. Which reminds her, she still hasn't asked Ned about their coverage.

She goes upstairs to gather a few things he's requested. She packs his shaving kit and finds a pair of pajamas. They're not new, but anything is an improvement over those ridiculous tie-up gowns they put a person in. She would like to bring him something to eat—some little treat—but she isn't sure what's allowed. This morning he's being moved to Medical West, but even there his diet will be restricted. Well, she'll bring him the Sports section again. He'll like that.

Yesterday, during the late visiting hours, he asked her to sneak him in some coffee. Coffee. Is he crazy? After she finished getting mad, she saw it as an indication he was getting well. Still, Dr. Cassidy is cautious.

The cardiologist answered all her questions patiently—even telling her Ned will be able to have sex, as if she cares about such things—but he couldn't promise the biggest questions: Will Ned recover fully? Will he be all right?

Late last night when Rose phoned in, the nurse said Ned was sleeping. His signs are good, she reported, then added something about having him back on meds until he's stabilized. Stabilized? They had told her he *was* stabilized. The nurse had explained that around midnight the monitor had picked up some irregular beats—ventricular fibrillation, she said. *Ventricular fibrillation.* This sounds like a problem Ned would find in someone's engine. Leaky carburetor. Blown manifold.

Ventricular fibrillation. Meds. They speak a foreign language— speech that puts them in control, in charge. Well, soon enough she'll be the one in charge, and he'll be back here in his own bed.

Suddenly she considers the stairs. Will he be able to manage them? Should he even be trying it? *Don't treat him like an invalid.* But surely they can't expect him to be climbing stairs his first day home. Maybe she'll have to rent one of those hospital beds and set it up in the living room. Of course, that will create another problem. The house was built back before people had to have as many baths as they did bedrooms, and there is only the half-bath on the first floor. For years now Ned has been talking about taking that little room off the kitchen, the one they use for storage, and enlarging the bath, adding a shower. Great for resale, he'd say, as if she planned to ever sell the place.

This could get complicated. She wonders if she'll have to hire home-care people to help out. Another expense. Will insurance take care of it? Some of these questions can't be left until he is well enough to take over.

Ned keeps the desk in order. Their checkbook and savings passbook are in the top drawer on top of a manila folder. She picks up the folder, opens the flap, and withdraws several envelopes. The first one holds a life insurance policy. Suddenly superstitious, she pushes it back into the folder, as if even looking at it will bring bad luck. She flips through the other envelopes. Appliance warranties. No health insurance.

In the next drawer she finds the recorded deed for their house. At least if he is unable to return to the garage they won't have to worry about losing their home. She remembers the day he made the final mortgage payment and they owned the house free and clear. They went out to dinner at that Italian place where they always went when there were things to celebrate. Back in a time when they still had a life that held cause for celebration. Ned had ordered wine in one of those bottles encased in straw. Neither of them was crazy about the taste, but they drank every drop, toasting each other, the house, their parents who would be so proud if they were still alive. They even raised a glass to the bank.

She folds the deed and slips it back in the drawer. All the things Ned had worked so hard for. All the things they thought were so important.

She is about to close the drawer when a long white envelope catches her eye. It's tucked in back, half covered by a stack of utility receipts. She pulls it out, startled to see her name on the front. In the upper left corner she reads Anderson Jeffrey's name and address. So he *had* sent her a copy of the piece she had written in his class. When had it arrived? And Ned had opened it. Her stomach clutches at the thought of him reading it.

She pictures him unsealing it, imagines him reading all the things she spilled onto that page, all the things she could never tell him. All her bitterness and rage about Todd. All her grief. All her anger at him. All the "hot writing." And he never said a word. She checks the cancellation date. Last February, after she'd met Anderson Jeffrey over in

Pellington. Too upset to continue her search for their HMO papers, she shuts the drawer and escapes to the back porch.

So Ned knows everything. Oh, God, he even knows how she refused to let Todd take the car that day. He knows it's her fault their son is dead. How will she ever face him?

He's known since February and has never let on, never confronted her or blamed her. All those months and weeks and days he kept on with ordinary life, sitting across the table, making conversation, going to work. She feels like he is someone she doesn't know at all.

Doesn't know at all. Like after the attack, all his talk about "the next great adventure," making death sound like a trip to Disney World. Where did that come from? Before this she would have sworn Ned didn't hold much with spiritual matters. He isn't even religious. Even back when she was going to church regularly, it was a struggle to get him to go along. He only went to appease her. Once he told her he thought religion was for the weak. They had had sharp words over that, although now she thinks it's true. Religion is nothing but empty words.

The thick trill of the phone interrupts her thoughts. Ever since word of Ned's attack spread, the phone's been been ringing off the hook with calls from customers, friends, people she hasn't talked to in years. Sometimes it's people whose names she doesn't even recognize. Now, here it is barely daybreak and they've already started up again. She lets it ring on. She can't talk to one more person, can't answer one more question, can't say, "No, there's nothing anyone can do, thank you, anyway," one more time. There *is* nothing anyone can do, and that's the hard and inescapable truth.

She stares out at the sun rising on the horizon. It's going to be another hot day. The humidity is already making her skin damp. The weatherman has been forecasting a spell of record-breaking heat. She'll have to get a fan for Ned's room. Maybe even one of those air conditioners that sit in the window.

She rocks back and resumes her musing about Ned.

Does he really believe there is something beyond this life? Is that why it was so easy—so simple—for him to go on after Todd's death? Is it possible he really believes that Todd's soul—his spirit—goes on? She wants to ask him this. She feels a flash of jealously. *The next great adventure.* She remembers how he looked when he said that. Denial, the nurse told her. But Ned's face was calm, as if he knew something, had already seen a place she hasn't.

Why had they never talked about these things? What was it he had said about Opal and the custody battle? "The girl deserves a second chance." Is that what life is? A series of missed opportunities? A series of second chances because we keep getting it wrong?

At that moment, bathed by the dawning sun, she feels a stirring in her chest. Ned survived his attack. She doesn't have cancer. They are being given a new chance. This is the thought she tucks in her mind's pocket as she calls for the taxi to come pick her up.

SHE HAS BARELY STEPPED THROUGH THE SWINGING DOORS into the CCU when she sees the day nurse startle, rise, and head for her at top speed.

"Mrs. Nelson?"

She knows immediately. Even as she keeps walking—her feet on automatic—she knows. *No!* her mind, her heart cries out. *No.*

The nurse reaches out a hand out, takes hers. "Mrs. Nelson," she says again.

She allows herself to be led to the visitors' lounge. "I'm sorry," the nurse says.

"He's gone?" Rose says, as calm as if she is inquiring about the price of beef.

"I'm sorry." The nurse spills out the details, taking Rose's silence as a sign she wants to know: A massive attack. He had a good evening. A little restless. No pain.

As if these details would help.

"Was he alone?"

"Yes. Apparently he tried to get out of bed by himself, maybe to use the commode."

"Where is he now?"

"In his room. Would you like to see him?"

The nurse's words ring hollow, as if she is speaking from a distance. She reaches a hand out to steady herself.

"Here," the nurse says. "Sit. Let me get you some water."

THEY HAVE CLEANED HIM UP. ALL THE TUBES ARE GONE. THE IV feeds. The monitor hookups. He could be sleeping. If you didn't know better, you would think he is sleeping. A slight smile on his lips. Like a child having a good dream. Yes, he could be asleep, waiting for her to rouse him. Except it is too quiet. No snoring. No breath.

She thinks, shocking herself, How dare you? How dare you smile, as if you're happy to leave me alone, with no one? Later she will track down the night nurses, seek details. Listen to everything they tell her about his last night, every word he said to them, even ask to see the monitor printout. But now, at this instant, her first thoughts are for herself.

How could Ned leave her like this? How could he leave her alone?

CHAPTER 40

❧ R O S E

F UNNY THING, SHE CAN REMEMBER EVERY DETAIL OF
Todd's funeral. Even now, nearly six years later, she can recall
who gave to the scholarship fund in his name and who sent
flowers, and how rain threatened but cleared just in time for the service. She remembers exactly what they wore to church—her navy
dress, Ned's charcoal suit, even the purple pantsuit that Ethel had
on—can remember how Louisa Henderson stood in the choir loft and
sang "On the Wings of Love" in her thin soprano voice while the pall-
bearers guided the casket up the aisle, each detail as clear and sharp as
if all had occurred just this morning. She can close her eyes and recre-
ate Todd's funeral in—what's that movie word?—*Technicolor*, but she
can't even summon a black-and-white snapshot of Ned's, barely two
weeks past.

The last thing she really remembers, as she understands memory,
is being at the hospital. The nurse telling her "his heart exploded."

"That's a hard but true way of describing it," the nurse said. What
are people thinking, saying something like that? Words that will just
haunt you. That's the last she can recall. *His heart exploded.* What
image is she to hold? An engine expiring in a concussive cloud of
smoke and sparks? A valentine sputtering into shreds of lace and red
glitter?

The following days are one gray haze, a long walk down an endless
corridor of gray concrete. She must have met with Ralph Evans down

at Evans Funeral Home, must have held up her end of some discussion about the casket, the service and obituary and burial, must have made all the necessary choices one is called upon to make, choices she and Ned—mainly Ned—had to make after Todd died, but she can't remember a single thing about any of it. Like her mind shut down, a tape erased.

There is one thing: She recalls their return to the house after the service at the cemetery. Ethel was in the living room, one arm around her oldest boy, the other holding a glass of red wine, repeating to anyone who would listen, "He was a saint. My brother was a saint." Meaning, all he endured. Meaning, putting up with Rose.

"No," Rose said, shutting her sister-in-law up and shocking everyone in the room. "Ned wasn't a saint." An awkward silence fell. People avoided her eyes. They were probably thinking about where he'd been when he had the attack, even though Trudy insists he had been there only because he had given her a ride home.

Odd how she should remember that one thing: the shocked silence that greeted her proclamation that Ned wasn't a saint. Well, he wasn't. And it had nothing to do with him being at Trudy's. The truth is that Ned was a *good* man—a kind man, kinder than she'd imagined as it turned out—but no saint. Why not remember him just as he was? Isn't being as good as you were good enough? Why do people want to elevate him? Is this meant to be compensation, a payoff for having died?

She is determined not to become one of those women who speak of their dead husbands that way, turning them into perfection, recasting them into new and ideal images: Men who don't snore or pass wind or speak a harsh word. Men you'd think were a cross between Gandhi and Jim Rockford, to hear their widows talk.

"Widow." There's a word she hates. "Widow. Wife." The two words that start the same but are worlds apart. One belongs; she has a place. The other is alone.

She finds herself reading the sports pages, turning on ball games, listening to them, memorizing final scores, as if to report to Ned. It fools her mind, keeps her feeling tied to him. She still expects him to come in the back door. Nights are hard. She can't face sleeping in their bed. Instead, she stretches out on the sofa and waits for morning.

If it weren't for Opal, she wouldn't eat.

The girl has taken over, managing everything, practically moving in. Who would have thought that Opal of all people would prove so competent? Who would have thought Rose could feel such gratitude? Honestly, she doesn't think she would have made it through the past weeks otherwise. She has needed to submit, to be led. With all the troubles that child has on her plate—the custody battle and all—she's just pushed it all aside. She refuses to be denied. Opal has a heart the size of three hundred Ethels.

From where she is sitting on the couch, Rose can see a paper with Opal's handwriting sitting on the desk: a list of those who sent floral arrangements. When Rose feels up to it, Opal says they will write notes together. Or Opal will write, and Rose dictate, whatever Rose can manage.

"Who does she think she is?" Ethel sputtered one day, watching Opal answer the phone, make the coffee, put away the food an endless caravan of people insisted on bringing to the house. "She isn't even family."

"She's just trying to help out," Rose replied.

Ethel snorted. "I know the type. She wants something. You mark my words."

She does want something, and Rose knows what it is. She wants to be needed, to know the healing balm of being needed, as Rose has known.

If there's anyone who is looking for a piece of the action, it's Ethel, who is already asking questions about what will become of the station. "It was our father's, you know," she has had the nerve to say. Rose has never forgiven her for taking Todd's clothes for her sons. As far as Rose is concerned, Ethel can have anything she wants. There's nothing here Rose cares about. Let her take the lot. All the things she thought she could never part with, things like the house, mean nothing. Why hadn't she agreed to sell the house and move to Florida when Ned suggested it? Why couldn't she have given in on that? It would have meant so much to him.

What was a house? A house can't keep people alive. It can't even keep them alive in your memory. People live in your heart. Too late, she has learned that. A good lesson wasted.

She thinks of all the things they have never done: trips never taken, words never spoken. Now Ned is gone. Life isn't a thing, a—what's the word?—a noun. It's an act. A verb. It's something you do. Or don't.

"Can I get you anything?" Opal stands at the door. She looks tired. The boy is hanging on her legs. Ever since he returned from North Carolina, they haven't left each other's side.

"No, thanks," Rose says. "You don't have to stay here, you know."

"I know." She comes in, the boy with her. "I just thought I'd stick around for the afternoon. Keep you company. I brought over some work."

Rose is used to spending time alone in the house, whole days when Ned was at the garage, but with him gone—truly gone—the emptiness extends and echoes. Sometime soon, she will have to get used to this, to being alone. But not yet.

She watches as Opal threads a needle. Zack has brought in a coloring book and crayons. He stretches out on the floor and starts coloring.

"Shall I put the TV on?"

"If you want."

Rose clicks the remote until she finds a show that she thinks will be all right for Zack.

Opal lifts a doll from the protective tissue.

"What's this one?" Rose asks.

"A pioneer. A pioneer woman."

Opal's dolls are amazing. Such attention to detail. The girl has explained how she makes them. Simplicity is the secret, she's told Rose, showing her how she uses a thin, wooden dowel in the neck to keep the head from tipping, how she paints the faces with a fine-pointed sable brush. And all the sewing—painstaking stitches she has to do by hand. Right then Rose gets the idea. She will give Opal her Singer. She should have given it to her months ago.

Pleased, she lets her head fall back on the sofa cushion and closes her eyes. She lets the sound of the television wash over her, hears the boy humming lightly, hears Opal shush him. It's okay, she thinks, let him sing, it doesn't bother me, but she is too tired to manage the effort of speech. At last, sleep overtakes her.

When she wakes, it is nearly dark. She must have slept for hours. For an instant—one heart-swelling instant—she thinks Ned is there. But it's Zack. The boy is nestled next to her on the couch, his warm body curved to fit hers.

"You had a nap," he says.

"I did," she says. "I had a lovely nap."

He pats her cheek with a damp hand. "That's good."

She hugs him to her.

She has to hug *someone*, has to touch someone. She has to, or her heart will dry up and blow away.

CHAPTER 41

❧ O P A L

O PAL UNCOILS THE HOSE AND SNAKES IT TO THE GAR-
den. She adjusts the spigot so water will trickle into the soil
beneath the tomatoes. A slow, steady stream is best according to Rose, who has also shown her how to spread powdered lime
around the base of each plant, how to stake them in cages so the
fruit—tomatoes are a fruit, Rose has also instructed her, so why is
tomato juice the base of vegetable soup?—will not fall. Now the plants
reach her shoulders. As she moves among them, leaves brush her
skin, releasing their pungent scent. The tomatoes are beginning to
edge from green to red. Keep them watered, Rose tells her, and
they'll thrive. Tomatoes don't need a lot of fussing, and they give back
so much.

It hasn't rained in weeks, not even a quick thunderstorm to relieve
the suffocating heat. Everyone is complaining, but it doesn't bother
Opal in the least. No different than any summer back in New Zion.
She welcomes the heat. Heat slows things down. She likes that. It
slows her down, too.

"It doesn't wear you down?" Rose asked the other day. They were
sitting out under the maple tree, sipping iced tea from condensation-
slippery glasses. Rose was stirring the air with a folded newspaper. "It
does me. Saps the life out of me."

"What I *mind* is the cold. I about froze this winter. I like the heat.
It's one of the things I miss about home."

"What else do you miss?"

"About New Zion? Let's see." She took a minute to consider. "Porches," she finally said.

"Porches?" Rose looked at her as if she'd turned loony. "We have porches up here."

"These aren't *porches*." Opal gestured around to take in the street's prim stoops. "At home we have real proper porches." She tried to explain about Southern porches: wide, with pillars and grooved wooden ceilings and plenty of room for a table and a rocking chair or three for sitting after dinner. A porch with space to string a hammock for kids to fight over. Where adults could laze. Where grandmas could sew and doze. A place you could sleep on hot nights. Where lovers could neck. "Northern people don't use their porches, don't live on them."

"That's what you miss?" Rose said. "The weather and porches?"

"And Aunt May. I miss my Aunt May. You'd like my aunt." This is true. As different as May and Rose are, they would get along. She hadn't thought about it until then, but the two women have a lot in common. For starters they are both as different from her mama as stars from fake jewels.

"And that's all?" Rose said.

"That's the lot." Warmth, porches, and Aunt May. Mostly Aunt May. What she definitely doesn't miss is being under her mama's thumb. During the time she's been in Normal, Opal has changed. It's nothing you'd notice looking in a mirror, but something has altered, inside. If she had to choose words, she'd say she has grown up. She has begun to feel like a *real* mother, not just someone playing house with a doll that breathes. So much has happened in these months. The job at the toy shop, the success of her dolls, Ty—something in her belly still stirs at the thought of him—Ned's death, the way Rose has given her the respect of depending on her. All these things have changed her.

If she went back to New Zion, her mama would take right over, turn her into a child again. Watch her every move. Boss her around. Criticize her. Complain about her *attitude*.

That's always been the problem as far as Melva is concerned: Opal's bad attitude. But what her mama calls defiance, she sees as determination. It is the right kind of will, not like Billy's; it's the sort of determination that leads to independence, the kind that is fed by the possibility of dreams. Why can't her mama see that? Why ask why? Melva is Melva, like chicken is Sunday dinner.

She adjusts the hose. Her feet sink in the wet earth, and the water cools her down. Through a haze of wavy heat, she looks across the lawn to where Rose sits with Zack. Rose is wearing the green macaroni necklace Zack made in nursery school. She hasn't taken it off since he gave it to her. She acts as if it's made of jade.

Zack has proclaimed that Rose is his new best friend. First thing every morning he asks, "Can I go over to RoseNelson's?" He always says it that way—her whole name, RoseNelson—like it is one word.

Although Opal worries that Zack may tire Rose—from the moment he wakes, he's a steady stream of questions—she also thinks her son is good company. Since Ned's death, her neighbor has spent most days sitting out under the maple staring into space, shaking awake only when Opal or Zack is with her.

"You send him home if he's a bother," Opal tells Rose every day.

"He's no bother," Rose always replies. "And he's more fun than a soap opera."

The other day, Opal overheard a snatch of conversation between Rose and Zack. "You're a smart boy," Rose said. "I get smarter every day," Zack replied. "That's what my mama says." And then hadn't Rose leaned over and pressed her cheek to the top of his head.

Rose, too, has changed. When they first moved in, she mostly ignored them, acting like they carried some disease, like she could barely tolerate the sight of them, but now, she is . . . Well, *kind* is the word that comes to mind. *Tender.* Like when she gave her the sewing machine, right out of the blue.

"Poor Rose," that horrid Ethel gushed after the funeral. "I worry so about her. First Todd and now Ned. Her heart must be broken in half."

That woman is dumb as a sack full of hair.

Shit. Rose's heart *is* hurting, no question there. But it's like all the pain has broken her heart not *in half*, but *wide open*.

She repositions the hose and looks up just as Rose and Zack, hand in hand, head toward Rose's house. Lemonade time. Rose walks with a measured pace, steps not just matched to Zack's small stride, but slowed by heat and grief.

Opal is on slo-mo herself these days. She inches toward the custody hearing, fluctuating between dread of it and eagerness to have it settled. To have Billy out of her hair.

To date, there have been two sessions with a mediator. The meetings were Sarah Rogers' idea, proposed by the guardian in hopes of avoiding a hearing altogether. Although it nearly killed her, Opal had caved in on almost every point the mediator raised. Compromise makes you look good, Vivian had said.

During the second meeting she had agreed to a proposal allowing Billy visitation rights for *every* school vacation, as well as for six weeks in the summer and alternating holidays. Billy didn't give an inch. What more does he want? she had asked Vivian. As it turns out, he wants a lot more. He wants *everything*. He wants full custody of Zack. Well, now she knows plain. Billy's out for blood. His blood. Hasn't that been what he's called Zack?

How could she have forgotten his junkyard-dog determination, all those mornings he talked the janitor into letting him in before school so he could practice free throws and layups. No sitting during games for Billy Steele. Billy Steele got what he wanted no matter what it took to get it. When he had turned that determination to winning her, she had made the giant miscalculation of mistaking it for love.

So far, in spite of her vigilant eye, in spite of keeping alert to the possibility, she has received no sign, nothing to relieve her fears, nothing to show her the way. All she has to count on is Vivian's advice.

Their last meeting didn't go well.

"Just tell me there's no way I'll lose Zack," she demanded.

"I can't tell you that."

"Fuck. There are women in jail who have custody of their children. In jail. What makes me such a bad risk?" What she wanted here was a guarantee. She didn't get it.

We can't be complacent, Vivian said. The political climate has changed, she said, ranting on about the Green case, that mother who killed her two kids and how the sacredness of motherhood took a body blow with that one, then going on about the growing backlash fueled by the fathers' rights groups. Blah. Blah. Blah.

Vivian was still pissed.

She had confronted Opal as soon as she walked in the office. "No lies," she'd said. "That was my ground rule from the beginning."

"What are you talking about?" Opal'd hedged "I didn't."

"Can it." Vivian had picked up a pile of documents. "Sarah Rogers' report. It's all here. Everything."

"What does it say?"

"It says you're in deep shit." She'd waited for Opal to say something, then prompted, "Zack's broken arm?"

"I told you about that." She hadn't been able to meet Vivian's gaze.

"What you told me was that you had a witness to the accident. You didn't tell me the witness was lying."

"I was afraid of what it would look like. You know, 'cause I left Zack alone." How had the guardian found out? Rose, Opal'd guessed. Rose must have changed her story and told Sarah Rogers the truth.

"You think a lie looks better? Trust me, it doesn't. It makes you look guilty."

"One lie? You think I'll lose Zack because of one little lie?"

"It's no one thing. It's a pile of a lot of things. They could add up to trouble. We don't know how Judge Bowles will rule. I want you to know the truth of what we're facing."

Opal had felt the blood drain from her face. "You think Billy could win?"

Vivian had relented then. "I'll tell you what." She stubbed out her cigarette, crushing it so hard the filter split. "You've made mistakes, but Billy Steele will get full custody of your son over my bloody body."

Over my bloody body. Opal clings to the words. They are the closest thing to a guarantee she is going to get. In the absence of a true sign, they will have to do.

CHAPTER 42

↜OPAL

OPAL CAN'T SIT STILL. IF SHE BITES ANY MORE OF HER nails, she'll be chewing flesh. What she needs here is a sign.

It's raining for the first time in weeks. But if that's a sign, how should she interpret it? Are the drops tears? Meaning what? Sorrow? Loss? Or does it mean a cleansing? Washing Billy out of her life. Or does it simply mean a change in the weather pattern? Her head aches from thinking about it. She needs something big, something she can't misread or fail to understand. Something huge, like skywriting. She's keeping her eyes open.

She's waiting for Vivian. Her mama and daddy, Billy, and their lawyers have already gone into the courtroom, Billy striding by her like she wasn't even sitting there, like she was a person he'd never seen, like he'd never chased her, held her, begged her to open her legs for him, given her a child. Before he went in, her daddy stopped to hug her and tell her he loved her, nearly breaking her heart. And her mama? Well, Melva looked straight at her with that look that said, *I'm done cleaning up your messes, girl*, then walked through the double doors to the courtroom where the future will be decided. It's hard to remember all the things Aunt May told her about her mama's past. As far as her mama is concerned, it's hard for Opal to hold the least little bit of softness in her heart.

"I blame him," a fat woman off to her left is saying. "I was doing everything. Everything. I was working and bringing in money while he sat around, watching Jerry Springer." More soap opera.

Finally Vivian appears. "Sorry I'm late," she says, pushing Opal through the double doors.

Their case is first on the docket.

Numbly, Opal follows as their case number is called; they move to the table and take their seats.

Over at Billy's table the blond lawyer, Carla Olsen, takes a bottle of imported water out of her briefcase and sets it on the table.

Opal wishes she'd thought to bring water. Her mouth is dry, her palms clammy. She should have brought something along for luck. Something to hold. Her amethyst crystal, or something of Zack's. She sneaks a look over at Billy. He looks cool, confident. She straightens up in her chair. She can pretend anyway.

The clerk hands a sheaf of papers to Judge Bowles. While he reads, Opal studies him, searching for kindness, understanding. She can't read a thing. She looks over at Sarah Rogers, the woman who is here to represent Zack's best interests. As if anyone on earth but his mama could represent his best interests. Opal doesn't trust the judge or the guardian. She certainly doesn't trust anyone sitting at the other table. Not even her daddy. Who can she trust? Vivian? Vivian with her shabby office and nicotine habit and cheap clothes? She gives a sideways glance at her lawyer. *Over my bloody body.* Vivian for sure.

While Judge Bowles reads, the room is silent except for the hum of the air conditioner. Several times he raises his gaze from the documents, once to look at Opal, once to where Billy sits. At last he sets the papers down. He takes off his glasses and rubs his temples, then readjusts his glasses. He takes a deep breath and looks out at them. Opal can't read a thing in his expression.

"The last thing this court wants to do is decide the fate of Zackery until you both have tried reaching a compromise. Do I understand that both parties have exhausted all attempts at arriving at an agreement?"

"They have, Your Honor," Vivian says.

"That's right, Your Honor." Again it is Carla Olsen who speaks for that side. Opal tries to imagine her fighting for Billy until her body is bloodied, but can't picture it. Not this woman. Surface scratches, a broken fingernail or two perhaps, but not bloodied. She feels immeasurably better.

"It's perfectly clear," Carla Olsen begins, "because of the geographic separation caused by Miss Gates' relocation to this state, Mr. Steele is being denied his rights as a father. While Miss Gates has agreed to grant brief visitation rights to Mr. Steele, having Zackery for a few weeks a year is not acceptable."

A few weeks? She had agreed to every school vacation, six weeks in the summer, holidays. That's a few weeks? She nudges Vivian, but the attorney motions her to be still.

"As long as Miss Gates insists on living out of state," Carla Olsen continues, "Mr. Steele has no alternative but to seek full custody. He wants his son returned to North Carolina where the child can have daily contact with not only Mr. Steele but his extended family as well. Both sets of grandparents."

"Am I to take it that if Miss Gates agrees to relocate, to return to North Carolina, Mr. Steele would be flexible on the issue of custody?"

Relocate? Return to New Zion? No way. Fuck, she'd rather eat sand, rather eat bat shit, than return to New Zion.

"Not necessarily, Your Honor. My client has other concerns, serious concerns, that lead him to believe his son's best interests are not served by his remaining in his mother's care. In fact, it is not putting it too strongly to say that Mr. Steele has grave concerns about Zackery's welfare."

"That's bullshit." Opal hops up, shaking off Vivian's hand. "Billy didn't even want him. Don't you get it? He wanted me to have an abortion." Why can't these people understand?

"Miss Gates, please sit down. This is very inappropriate. And it is not in your best interests. Miss Cummings, please remind your client of the rules of the courtroom."

"I'm sorry, Your Honor," Opal says. "But how can he say he wants him when he didn't, not from the get-go?"

The judge rubs his fingers along his jaw, as if checking for five o'clock shadow, and peers down at her. "Miss Gates, that fact is not pertinent to this hearing. Mr. Steele has demonstrated to the court's satisfaction that however he may have felt in the past about having a son, he is currently most definitely interested in playing a primary role in his son's life. That is, in fact, why we are here."

"Your Honor, may I continue?" Carla Olsen lifts a sheaf of papers. "Miss Gates likes to depict herself as a loving mother, but we have a list of serious concerns. Our documentation, backed up by depositions—"

She shakes the papers. "—paints a far different portrait." She ticks off her accusations, flicking a fingernail against the papers with each charge. "A good mother is not repeatedly late picking her child up from school. A good mother sees that her child gets routine medical and dental care. A good mother has a solid plan of child care in place. A good mother is not a run away, lacking any kind of financial security." She pauses, takes a sip of water.

It's no one thing. It's a pile of a lot of things. Opal is afraid to look at the judge.

"Excuse me, Your Honor." Vivian rises. "It is an unfortunate but true commentary that what my colleague is describing is not unrepresentational of seventy percent of single mothers in the Commonwealth, mothers coping with the stress of single parenthood. It isn't grounds for the child's removal."

"I will be happy to address that issue in a minute, Your Honor," Carla Olsen says, resuming her litany.

"A good mother attends to the nutritional needs of her son." She lowers her voice theatrically. "Judge Bowles, we have depositions here showing that not a half hour after her son's broken arm was set, at ten o'clock in the morning, Miss Gates took Zackery out for ice cream, causing him to vomit and indicating, at the very least, a remarkable lack of common sense. And on the subject of ordinary good sense, what kind of mother becomes involved with a drug dealer, spends the night with the dealer while her son sleeps in a room not twelve feet away? What kind of mother leaves her five-year-old son alone? We believe Miss Gates is a negligent mother. At best."

Vivian leaps up before Opal can move. "Your Honor—"

Judge Bowles waves her down. "You'll have your opportunity."

"We agree with Miss Cummings that Miss Gates is operating under stress," Carla Olsen continues. Opal hates her. *Hates* her. She would like to see *her* bloody. She would like to see her dead.

"Clearly the financial and physical, not to mention emotional stress, is too much for her. If Mr. Steele is awarded custody of his son, he has a support system in place. He has a job. He's financially secure." She pauses to place a hand on Billy's shoulder. "My client has the full support of not only his own parents, but the boy's maternal grandparents as well, Miss Gates' own parents. In effect four other people will help in raising the boy and seeing to his daily care. Mr. Steele will provide a stable and safe home environment, something Miss Gates clearly cannot do." She pauses. What? Waiting for applause? Then she sits. Death would be too good for her.

Opal's clenches her hands into fists. She will not cry. She absolutely will not give them the satisfaction.

"Mr. Steele? Do you have anything you would like to say to the court?"

Billy rises, like he's getting a prize or something. "No, Your Honor." Asshole.

"Well, then. Miss Cummings?"

"Your Honor, before I say anything, my client would like to address the court." She nods at Opal. "You're on," she whispers.

Opal swallows, stands, locks her knees, which helps but doesn't totally stop the trembling.

"Sir." She could really use a glass of water, something to relieve the dryness in her throat. Vivian whispers for her to go on. "Sir, I love Zack. He's my life. I may not be a perfect mother. Fu— Heck, I'm definitely not a perfect mother. I don't know if there is such a thing. Maybe some days I'm only passably good. But I love Zack. I love him so much, I didn't think it was possible to love something like I love him." She swallows. There is no one else in the room. Just her and the judge. She *has* to make him understand. "Zack and me, we're a team. Since he was born it's only been him and me. Really, since he was born. No one else was there. Not my mama or my daddy. Not Billy." She stops herself from bringing up the abortion thing. "Since that day, I've been the only one caring for him. I know I've made some mistakes, but Zack's happy with me. We're happy together. I read to him. He's smart. It would kill Zack to be taken from me. And it would kill me, Your Honor. It surely would kill me."

Judge Bowles stares at her, unblinking. Opal sits. One of the court officers coughs. The judge flips through the pile of documents, slips out a page, studies it.

"I'm trying to understand," he says. "Now according to Mrs. Rogers' report you told her that you moved to Normal because you rolled a three on a die?" His voice is incredulous. "Is that right? You left your home and drove to Massachusetts because of a three-spot on a die?"

"It was a sign, Your Honor."

"A sign?"

From the other table, Opal hears a snort. Her mama.

"Your Honor." Vivian stands. "Sometimes a well-intentioned person does the right things for the wrong reasons. Three tankfuls of gas may be the wrong reason for Opal to move from North Carolina to Massachusetts, but searching for independence from an overprotective—some might even say overbearing—family was a positive move, a step toward independence. If you check with the deposition taken from Dr. Emily Jackman, you will see that it is her opinion that Opal's move was a healthy choice. She was looking for a new start—a place where no one knew her history. Her family and friends all live in her hometown, and Miss Gates had no connection to any other place. In that context, rolling dice might be seen as a creative, if unusual, solution."

Opal could just hug Vivian.

The judge shuffles through the papers, chooses another. "According to the admitting doctor, Miss Gates brought her son to the emergency room with a broken arm and suspicious bruises."

"Bruise," Opal says. "There was only one." Jesus, they make it sound like Zack was covered with belt marks.

"Your Honor, Zackery Gates is an active, lively child. I would bet that you could walk into his nursery school and choose any of fifteen children and find a bruise or Band-Aid or two. In Zack's case the admitting doctor was satisfied there was absolutely no abuse involved. Children's services was not even contacted."

"According to Mrs. Rogers' report, Miss Gates lied at the hospital."

"Your Honor, if I may. Miss Gates was traumatized by her son's injury. When the boy got hurt—he fell in his bedroom—Miss Gates had left him alone, just long enough for her to run to the store. The boy was sound asleep when she left. Naturally, she knew what this would sound like if she admitted it to the doctor. She was being accused of abuse. She was terrified."

"With the court's permission, at this time we would like to call a witness, someone who was with Opal at the hospital."

"Go ahead."

One of the bailiffs opens the side door.

"Rose?" Opal whispers.

Rose moves slowly toward the front of the room. Her face is calm, stong. Opal is suddenly reminded of the first time she saw Rose, the day Dorothy Barnes told her about Todd's death and then she'd seen

Rose pinning clothes on the line. She had reminded her of a figure-head. A square-shouldered pioneer woman. Someone solid. Someone who could help her.

"Please state your name?"

"Rose Nelson." Rose's face is red. She is wearing the macaroni necklace. A sweat-smudged line of green stains her neck.

"Your relationship to Miss Gates?"

"I'm Opal's neighbor." Her face turns ever brighter, a flush that creeps from her collar to her hairline. "I want to tell the court something. It wasn't Opal who lied at the hospital. It was me. It was me who told the doctor I was there when Zack broke his arm."

"Well, Mrs. Nelson, I'm curious. Why would you lie for Miss Gates?"

"I had to."

"You *had* to? You've lost me, Mrs. Nelson."

"I could see what he was thinking. Anyone could see it. It was in his voice, the way he was talking to her. I'm not blaming him. He probably sees more than his share. But he was mistaken about Opal. She would never hurt that boy."

"Thank you, Mrs. Nelson, for clearing that up."

Rose is not done. "Your Honor, I know what it's like to lose your son. My Todd was killed. I lost him. I know what it's like. It isn't right that Opal should lose her boy. She loves Zack. You've got half a brain, you can see that. And that boy loves her. Opal may not have much money, but she can give that boy love. And that's something no money in the world can buy."

The judge stares at Rose.

"And she isn't alone, like they say." Rose glares over at Billy, at Melva. "She has me."

DURING THE RECESS, OPAL DOESN'T TRUST HER LEGS TO hold her weight. She remains at the table clutching Rose's hands. "Where's Zack?" she asks as soon as the Judge goes to his chambers.

"He's with Maida, at the shop. She'll watch him until you get back. She sends her love."

"Maida?"

"A lot of people are pulling for you, Opal."

Opal swallows, tightens her grip on Rose's hand. They sit like that until the judge returns.

"Making a decision in cases like these calls for a compromise," he begins. "Perhaps one neither of you would agree with. What the court seeks is a solution that serves the interest of your son: care, nurturing, love. Who best can provide that?

"Miss Gates, you have been careless, and you have made mistakes. You have lied. When you left your son alone you exposed him to risk, and you were therefore negligent.

"In arriving at my decision, I have to take into consideration that not only does the boy's father want him back in North Carolina, but he is joined by both sets of grandparents."

She is going to be sick right there. She shrinks back, afraid to hear more, afraid to breathe. Rose's arm encircles her waist.

"According to Mrs. Rogers' report, Zack is a well-adjusted child. Remarkably well adjusted."

Opal allows the tiniest speck of hope.

"Mrs. Rogers, in her role as guardian ad litem, believes that it would be an erroneous wrenching of a nurturing bond—a wrenching of long-lasting relationship between mother and son—to grant Mr. Steele full custody." He pauses to smile down at Rose Nelson. "And I would like it noted that I do have at least half a brain. I can see that Miss Gates has a deep and unwavering love for her son, a love that outweighs lesser considerations. I concur with Mrs. Rogers. Miss Gates retains physical custody of Zackery."

"Yes," Vivian mutters.

Opal looks at her lawyer, confused. Is that it? It's over? She's won?

"However, this court—and Mrs. Rogers emphatically agrees on this point—cannot condone your removing the boy from his father. By doing so, you have deprived not only Mr. Steele of his rights, but have deprived your son of a relationship with his father, a relationship Mr. Steele is eager to pursue.

"Mr. Steele, I am going to deny your petition for full custody."

"Your Honor." Carla Olsen is on her feet.

The judge raises a hand, motions for her to sit down.

"Physical custody of the boy will remain with Miss Gates, but Mr. Steele will have full and unlimited visitation rights." He peers over his glasses at Opal. "Full and unlimited visitation rights. Miss Gates, I cannot adjudicate, in other words I cannot order, that you return to North Carolina. That is not within my powers. What I can do is strongly encourage you to return, keeping in mind that it is in the best interests of your son. As far as I can determine, you have no pressing need to remain in Massachusetts.

"While it is certainly true that you have built a life here, made friends—" Here he stops and glances over at Rose. "—I believe that those considerations are overshadowed by other factors that are in the best interest of Zack, by which I mean the need for a boy to have access to his father, a father who has clearly and forcefully established that—in spite of his past history—he now wants to be a part of his son's daily life. I must warn you that should you decide to stay here in primary concern for your own independence rather than in consideration of Zackery's needs, I would be inclined to rule differently if in the future Mr. Steele should reappear before me and reenter a petition for custody."

He raps his gavel. "Next case," he says to the clerk.

"You've won," Vivian says.

She's won. She has Zack.

And she's lost.

She has to leave Normal. And Rose.

CHAPTER 43

❧ R O S E

ROSE CHECKS THE WINDOW AGAIN. TYRONE IS GONE. A few minutes earlier she heard his pickup drive up—Ned's truck, actually, which she has given to Ty. What earthly use is it to her? She refused his offer of payment. The very last thing she needs is money. Between the sale of the garage and the astonishing amount of Ned's life insurance, money is the least of her worries. She could fly to the Grand Canyon every day for the rest of her life and still not go through the money she now has.

When she looked out, she saw Tyrone hoisting Zack up in the air. Next he hugged Opal, holding the embrace longer than was decent to watch. Let them have their privacy, Rose told herself, turning away, although she wanted to stay glued to the window until the Buick pulled out and they were truly gone. The last thing she saw was Tyrone kissing Opal. They're not done yet, she thinks. Opal hasn't seen the last of that man. This is like those TV shows in May. A cliff-hanger. To be continued.

The pile of boxes and bags stacked on the driveway since daybreak is nearly all loaded. Rose would have liked to help, but Opal refused. She won't even let Rose come out to say good-bye.

"I don't like good-byes, Rose," Opal said last night when they met for dinner. Zack's choice: pizza and Coke. "Please, don't come over tomorrow. Okay? Promise?"

Rose turned away so Opal wouldn't see the way her face collapsed.

Why should she be surprised? Opal leaves things behind: Her name. Her family. The father of her son. She makes and breaks ties. It's what she does, and Rose won't judge her for that.

Left to say good-bye from a distance, Rose stands at the window, wishing she could hold them here. Opal will be all right, she tells herself. She's not totally alone. She has her Aunt May. She wishes she could believe this.

The boy keeps looking over. When he sees her, his face splits into a grin, and he lifts a hand and waves. Rose's throat closes up. He turns to his mother, says something, pointing over toward Rose.

Opal nods, and the boy runs toward her.

She meets him at the door, hugs him hard.

"You're squishing me," he says.

She instructs her arms to release him. "Here," she says, handing him a brown bag. "These are for the trip. I made them last night." Last night when sleep was impossible, she went to the kitchen and baked and baked and baked.

"Thank you, RoseNelson," he says.

"You be good for your mama, you hear me? She's a big lady, but she needs looking after, too. And tell her I said to drive carefully." She'll have to let him go. He's not hers to keep.

Outside she hears Opal yelling for the boy.

"Your mama's calling," she says. "You better get going."

"Okay," he says.

"I love you, Zack," she says, too softly for him to hear.

But he has. "I love you, too, RoseNelson."

She can't bear to return to the window. It will be easier after they've really gone. The doll Opal gave her last night—the pioneer girl—is on the counter. Even that hurts to look at. What had the girl said? *It reminds me of you.* Rose looks away. She pours herself coffee, picks up the newspaper, turns to the Sports section. For Ned. She'll go on. After all, that's what one does. Keeps going on. Regardless.

She settles herself at the table. Have the Red Sox won again? She checks the sports and then—then she can't believe her eyes. She reads the headline twice. A third time. What? Is Opal wearing off on her? But she laughs right out loud. Out in the drive, the Buick starts up.

She dashes for the door, paper still in hand. "Opal!" she yells. "Opal, wait."

The car heads down the drive.

"Wait, Opal." She runs behind the car so Opal has no choice but to stop. "Wait."

Opal brakes, rolls down the window. "Rose," she says. "I told you, no good-byes." She is crying, tears just streaming down her cheeks. "I can't. I just can't. It's way too hard."

"Well, I have something else to tell you."

"What else?"

"Turn off that engine. I have to tell you something. Listen."

"I'm listening." She tries to stop the tears.

"You want company?"

"Company? Where?"

"In that car." Rose stops, hit by another *wonderful* idea. "Or, actually, in a new car—a proper car that will make the trip."

"Huh?"

"You want me to come with you?"

"Come with me?"

"With you. And Zack."

"What?"

"To New Zion."

"Fuck, Rose, what are you talking about?"

"Go with you. I'll help out. I'll baby-sit for Zack while you make your dolls."

Opal's so surprised she stops crying.

"I mean it," Rose says.

"But how? Why?"

"I don't know why. I just know it's best."

"Best?"

"For you. And for me."

"Rose, no one has ever said anything so wonderful before. It makes me feel . . . all different."

This girl is overdue for wonderful things.

"Thanks, Rose. Thanks for even thinking of it. But I can't let you. I can't let you do that for me."

"It's not for you I'm doing it. It's for me."

Opal looks at her. "You're serious," she says.

"That I am. I most certainly am serious."

"But you can't leave here."

"Why not? What have I got to keep me here?"

"What about your house? Ned's here. And so is Todd."

"No. No, Opal, they're not." And that is God's honest truth. "They're not here. A house can't hold a person, or even keep a memory alive. And the cemetery? It's just a piece of earth. Ned and Todd aren't really there." Someday she'll explain to Opal. For Ned and Todd to stay alive, she has to let them go. It isn't memories that keep us going. Being loved and needed is what keeps us from dying inside.

"Oh, Rose. Thanks, but I can't let you."

"You have to." Rose beams at her. "You have to, Opal, 'cause I got a sign."

"A sign?"

"A sign too big to ignore." She opens the paper and holds the headline up for Opal.

"Read it out loud," she says.

" 'LOVE LEADS THE WAY: Davis Love III points the way home for his American teammates in the final day of the Ryder Cup play.' "

"See? *Love leads the way.* It leads the way home, Opal. Sure as I'm standing here it's a sign I'm supposed to go with you."

"A sign?" Zack pipes up from the rear seat. "That's exactly, exactly what my mama says. She always says she sees signs."

"Are you sure, Rose?" Opal asks.

"*And,*" Zack breaks in, "my mama's going to help me read my letters on the road signs going home."

"I know," Rose says. "We're all going to read the signs, Zack. All the way home."